Richard Henry Stoddard

Anecdote Biography of Percy Bysshe Shelley

Ed. by Richard Henry Stoddard

Richard Henry Stoddard

Anecdote Biography of Percy Bysshe Shelley
Ed. by Richard Henry Stoddard

ISBN/EAN: 9783337010690

Printed in Europe, USA, Canada, Australia, Japan

Cover: Foto ©Raphael Reischuk / pixelio.de

More available books at **www.hansebooks.com**

Sans-Souci Series

ANECDOTE BIOGRAPHY

OF

PERCY BYSSHE SHELLEY

EDITED BY

RICHARD HENRY STODDARD

NEW YORK

SCRIBNER, ARMSTRONG AND COMPANY

1877

JOHN F. TROW & SON,
PRINTERS,
205-213 East 12th Street,
NEW YORK.

CONTENTS.

CONTENTS.

ix

ILLUSTRATIONS.

"*Laon and Cythna*," Canto ix.

PREFACE.

O F all the poets who have illustrated the Literature of England, there is no one whose life presents so many difficulties to the biographer as Percy Bysshe Shelley. Every poet, even the humblest, differs in some respects from the majority of mankind,—at any rate, he is more impressionable than his prosaic brethren, and more easily influenced by the spirit which possesses him. The outward facts of his life are easily ascertained, and their arrangement in an orderly manner requires no great skill. What requires the greatest skill is the detection and interpretation of the spiritual facts of his life, the motives which actuated him, which guided him to goodness, and which drove him to evil ; the angelic impulses by which he soared, the demoniac impulses by which he sank,—in a word, the thorough understanding of his heart, his mind, his genius. The ideal poetic biographer, when he comes, will be a poet who is more than a poet. He does not exist at present. What does exist is the average biographer, whose self-imposed mission is to convince his readers that his hero was either the best or worst of men. Yesterday he was Dr. Griswold, to-day he is Mr. Ingram, to-morrow he will be —who ? It is difficult to say who in the case of Shelley, whose life, which has been written many times, still remains to be written. He was one of the most extraordinary men that ever walked the earth, so extraordinary, I think, that Shakespeare alone could have plucked out the heart of his mystery. He led at all times a dual life, and at most times a life of contradictions. To say that he was eccentric is to say nothing. He was as much out of place in this world as a being of another world would be, and he moved among its men and women like some strange creature of the elements. He neither understood himself, nor was understood by others, or at most by very few. The saintly Byron was warned against him by the clique in Murray's back parlor; but Byron defended him—after he was dead. He had a passion for reforming the world, and the world never wants to be reformed. Of course, it was too strong for him—the many are always too strong for the one. He learned the lesson which he states so tersely :

> " Most wretched men
> Are cradled into poetry by wrong :
> They learn in suffering what they teach in song."

If the history of the Shelleys could be written in full, we might know what ancestor was repeated by this immortal member of the family. He seems to have inherited elopement from his grandfather, Sir Bysshe, who eloped with two of his wives, and who is said to have been born in Newark, New Jersey, and to have practised there as a quack doctor. There is a story of an American wife, the authority for which is Shelley himself, who said that his grandfather behaved badly to *three* wives. An early Shelley figures in the Star Chamber Reports about two hundred and fifty years ago. There was a woman in his case, and she appeared to have entrapped him. At any rate, somebody was thought to have entrapped him, and several somebodies were punished for it. They were all sent to the Fleet, and one Ridley, the parson who married him in the night time, without license or banns, was fined five hundred pounds, and left to the High Commission Court. Mrs. Ridley was let off with a fine of ten pounds. Barton, who gave the woman away, was fined one hundred pounds, and Godfrey and his wife, who kept an ale-house, where some of the party were drinking a great part of the service-time on Sunday, were debarred from ever keeping an inn or ale-house. Who was she ? asked the old alcalde. Two shes are mentioned in this story, both named Margaret, one a daughter of Sir Sigismund Zinzen, alias Alexander, the other a daughter of one Lineham, whose son Henry made Master Shelley drunk, and after supper persuaded him to marry his sister Margaret, at the house of the above-mentioned Godfrey, on Palm Sunday. Parson Ridley, according to this version of the story, was fined three hundred pounds ; but as he showed that he married young Shelley, who was not seventeen, at his own request, it is to be presumed that he was let off with a reprimand. This little episode of William and Margaret was repeated nearly two hundred years later by Percy and Harriet, without the excuse of drunkenness on the part of Percy. Mr. Galton might make something out of this in a new edition of his work on hereditary transmission ; *I* humbly add it to the ever-increasing cairn of Shelleyana.

There are abundant materials for a Life of Shelley, but they are so contradictory on some points, and so perplexing on others, that it is difficult to know what to accept and what to reject. Every biography that I have read appears to have been written under a bias, and that of Lady Shelley under the strongest of all. Her " Shelley Memorials," which was originally published in 1859, omitted an important fact in the life of Shelley,—a fact which was brought to light by one of his early friends within a few months after the publication of her volume,—a fact which cannot have escaped her notice, but which she has kept her readers ignorant of for more than sixteen years. This fact, which was disinterred from a Church Register by Mr. Thomas Love Peacock, is Shelley's second marriage to his first wife about four months before his elopement with Mary Godwin. Lady Shelley suppressed this damaging fact, and by so doing laid herself open to—is it too much to say—the charge of literary dishonesty? It has been known to the world since January, 1860, when it was published by Mr. Peacock in *Fraser's Magazine*, but it is not known to-day to the little world of Lady Shelley's readers. Mr. Richard Garnett, who published in 1862 a little book entitled "Shelley Relics," and who writes with the Shelley bias, calls it a formal re-marriage, and says practically that it is devoid of importance. I cannot agree with him. It was certainly of importance to Harriet Shelley, who was obliged to return to her father's roof, where she soon became a mother for the second time. Mr. Garnett refers to certain mysterious documents in the possession of Shelley's family, and Lady Shelley, in the Preface to the third edition of her volume, published in 1875, harps on the same string. The time has not yet arrived, she thinks, when facts should be disclosed ; she feels confident that the more there is really known, the more all mists of false aspersion and misconception will clear away from Shelley's memory ; that the wishes of the dead are obeyed in keeping silence on all beyond what she has told, and so on. This is womanly writing, but it is not biographical writing. Lady Shelley's first great mistake, according to her point of view, was in placing Shelley documents in the hands of Mr. Thomas Jefferson Hogg, whose " Life " of Shelley was published a year before her "Memorials."   It was a mistake, but no reader of Shelley can wish that it had not been committed.   We know him through Hogg's curious volumes, as we could not have known him in any other biography, and as Lady Shelley would not have us know him at all.   She could not imagine how they could have been produced from the materials furnished by Shelley's family.   They were shocked, astonished, dismayed, at Hogg's fantastic caricature, and they withdrew the documents they had entrusted to him, and which he had so strangely misused.   Their feeling was natural, but the mischief was done, and could not be undone.   I, for one, do not wish it undone, for I believe that Hogg's portrait of Shelley is the *vera effigies* of the erratic young gentleman whom he knew in his own erratic youth. There was another Shelley, but it was only dimly perceived at the time by his porcine friend, who, I think, really admired him in his grim, caustic way.   I see nothing in his Memoir of the Divine Poet which should have shocked his family, but many things which should have amused them, as they did the world.   We cannot judge for others, however, especially when they claim that they alone have the greatest right to form an opinion on so puzzling a subject as the character of Shelley.   With all its defects, Hogg's truncated book, as Mr. Rossetti calls it, is an invaluable record of Shelley's early career, and is a masterly example of eccentric biography.

The portrait of another Shelley,—the Shelley whom his admirers believe to be the only true one,—was sketched in the same year as the alleged caricature of Hogg's, 1858, by the skilful and loving pencil of Captain E. J. Trelawny, in his " Recollections of the Last Days of Shelley and Byron." Trelawny's Shelley is to me Hogg's Shelley, ripened by eight years of thought, and sorrow, and happiness, into the

most gentle and the most courageous of human beings.   He
was a complete foil to Byron, whose Christianity, what
was left of it, was not to be named on the same day with
his supposed Atheism, and whose conduct of life was as bad
as his was good.   He was much wiser than the Pilgrim
of Eternity, whose genius he stimulated to its most daring
flights, and whom he sought to better, as he did the world,
though neither would be bettered, in his way:

These two portraits, *alter et idem*, are transferred to this
volume, somewhat corrected, if I may be allowed the expression, by the side-lights of other memoirs.   The most
important, to the students of Shelley, is "Shelley's Early
Life from Original Sources," by Mr. Denis Florence Mac-
Carthy; Peacock's papers in *Fraser's Magazine* (1858-60),
which are reprinted in the third volume of his "Works"
(London, 1875); the Rev. C. Kegan Paul's "William Godwin, his Friends and Contemporaries" (London, 1876), and
the Memoir prefixed to his edition of Shelley's "Poetical
Works" (London, 1870), by Mr. William Michael Rossetti.
Besides these, I should mention Thomas Medwin's "Life
of Shelley" (London, 1847), which is a mass of inaccura-
cies, and Charles S. Middleton's "Shelley and His Writings" (London, 1858), which is merely a compilation from
earlier biographies.   What I have drawn from these sources
will generally be found in foot-notes, though I have occasionally introduced passages into what I have written,
which is distinguished from the rest of the text by its inclosure of brackets.   To characterize these writings and their
writers, I should say that Mr. Rossetti was the most thorough, Mr. Mac-Carthy the most acute, and Mr. Peacock the
most satisfactory.   The Irish episode in Shelley's early
career was never thoroughly told until Mr. Mac-Carthy told
it; and the cause of one long separation between Hogg

and Shelley was never understood until he obtained the clue to it. It was—but the curious reader must go to his volume, for I am not going to spread any scandal about Queen Elizabeth at this late day. Mr. Mac-Carthy clears up one point which I had often mooted, viz., Shelley's acquaintance with Leigh Hunt. It did not begin so early as Hunt would have us believe,—certainly not while he was imprisoned for calling the Prince Regent "a fat Adonis of fifty," or words to that effect; and its utmost duration was about six years, only two of which were passed by Shelley in England. He was a princely friend to Hunt, as he acknowledges in his "Autobiography," and once made him a present of fourteen hundred pounds, to extricate him from a debt. "I was not extricated, for I had not yet learned to be careful," Hunt naïvely adds, "but the shame of not being so. after such generosity, and the pain which my friend afterward underwent, when I was in trouble and he was helpless, were the first causes of my thinking of money matters to any purpose." Which is precisely what Leontius never did. It was happy go lucky with him all his life, and down to the day of his death he was a Shelley pensioner.

Shelley was the most subjective of poets, but he rose at times to high objective art, as in "The Cenci," and in portions of "Adonais." His portrait of himself is a beautiful example of poetic characterization :

> " A pard-like Spirit, beautiful and swift—
> A love in desolation masked ;—a Power
> Girt round with weakness ; it can scarce uplift
> The weight of the superincumbent hour ;
> It is a dying lamp, a falling shower,
> A breaking billow ;—even while we speak
> Is it not broken ? On the withering flower
> The killing sun smiles brightly ; on a cheek
> The life can burn in blood, even while the heart may break.

> " His head was bound with pansies, over-blown,
> And faded violets, white, and pied, and blue ;
> And a light spear topped with a cypress cone,
> Round whose rude sheft dark ivy-tresses grew
> Yet dripping with the forest's noon-day dew,
> Vibrated, as the ever-beating heart
> Shook the weak hand that grasped it ; of that crew
> He came the last, neglected and apart,
> A herd-abandoned deer, struck by the hunter's dart.

> " All stood aloof, and at his partial moan
> Smiled through their tears; well knew that gentle band
> Who in another's fate now wept his own ;
> As in the accents of an unknown land
> He sang new sorrow ; sad Urania scanned
> The Stranger's mien, and murmured, ' Who art thou?'
> He answered not, but with a sudden hand
> Made bare his branded and ensanguined brow,
> Which was like Cain's or Christ's.   Oh, that I should be so!"

Fifty-four years have passed since his death, and the verdict of his contemporaries concerning his poetry has been reversed.   His name, execrated in his lifetime, stands now among the great names of English Literature.   Precisely what place he will finally fill will be settled by a more distant posterity than this. In his own day he seemed to write for antiquity, as Lamb quaintly said of himself.   Lamb, by the way, did not understand Shelley, whose poetry, he wrote Bernard Barton, was thin-sown with profit or delight.   " For his theories and nostrums, they are oracular enough, but I either comprehend 'em not, or there is ' minching mallecho,' and mischief in 'em, but, for the most part, ringing with their own emptiness.   Hazlitt said well of 'em, ' Many are the wiser or better for reading Shakespeare, but nobody was ever wiser or better for reading Shelley.' "   Hazlitt's opinions of his contemporaries were as worthless as his strong prejudices could make them. Macaulay, I think, sums up Shelley fairly : " We doubt whether any modern poet has possessed in an equal degree the highest qualities of the great ancient masters. The words bard and inspiration, which seem so cold and affected when applied to other modern writers, have a perfect propriety when applied to him. He was not an author, but a bard. His poetry seems not to have been an art, but an inspiration. Had he lived to the full age of man, he might not improbably have given to the world some great work of the very highest rank in design and execution."

There is but one portrait of Shelley, and that was painted by Miss Curran, a daughter of the Irish statesman, who was rather an amateur than an artist. It was taken in Rome in 1819, when he was about twenty-seven, and is now in the possession of his son, Sir Percy Shelley at Boscombe. Mr. Rossetti has jotted down the impression it made upon him when he saw it in 1868, in the Exhibition of National Portraits at South Kensington. " Small life-size ; age about nineteen ; plain green background ; waved hair, dark or darkening brown ; complexion fair, but as if a good deal exposed to air, giving a rather coppery-red hue ; eyes quite a dark-blue ; mouth *entrouvert*, with a kind of curl of aspiration and apprehending ; open shirt ; blue coat ; quill in hand ; left not seen. Gives a decided impression of a poet, and the bad qualities of the picture are not of an offensive kind ; flat, broad painting, very slight, but not thin." Mulready, the painter, who knew Shelley well, he adds, declared that it was simply impossible to paint his portrait—he was " too beautiful."

From the many portraits of Byron, I have selected for this volume the one which was painted by T. Holmes. Byron sat for it in 1815, when he was about Shelley's age, twenty-seven. He was at the height of his fame and happiness; for had he not published two cantos of " Childe Harold," and the " Bride of Abydos," and " The Corsair " ? And had he not lately won the hand of that rich heiress, and very superior woman, Miss Milbanke ? He was very. beautiful at the time, if we may trust this portrait as a faithful likeness. Byron pinned his own faith to it in the following letter to the artist :

"GENOA, *May 19th*, 1823.

" MY DEAR SIR : I will thank you very much to present to or obtain for the bearer a *print* from the miniature you drew of me in 1815. I prefer that likeness to any which has been done of me by any artist whatever. My sister, Mrs. Leigh, or the Honorable Douglas Kinnaird, will pay you the price of the engraving. Ever yours,

" NOEL BYRON."

The only copy of the print that I have ever seen was published on September 1, 1835, by F. G. Moon, printseller to the King, 20 Threadneedle Street, from the original in the possession of the Honorable Mrs. Leigh.

R. H. S.

PERCY BYSSHE SHELLEY.

SHELLEY'S CHILDHOOD.

PERCY BYSSHE SHELLEY was born at Field Place, near Horsham, in the county of Sussex, on Saturday, the 4th of August, 1792.

His father was Timothy Shelley ; his mother, a lady of rare beauty, Elizabeth, the daughter of Charles Pilfold, Esquire. They were married in the year 1791, and of this union their eldest son, Percy Bysshe, was the first child. The poet had four sisters ; Elizabeth, Mary, Hellen, and Margaret, all of whom lived to be distinguished for remarkable beauty, so that it was frequently observed, " very few families indeed can boast four such handsome girls ! " He had only one brother, John, the youngest child.

Of the earliest infancy, the babyhood, of the wonderful child we know nothing. As a boy he was gentle, affectionate, intelligent, amiable ; ever loving, and universally beloved.

His relatives have supplied interesting details. To give these just as they were received, will be a better illustration of the truth of things than a re-arrangement and classification of facts would afford.

MY DEAREST J., [Nov., 1856.]

At this distant period I can scarcely remember my *first* impressions of Bysshe, but he would frequently come to the nursery and was full of a peculiar kind of pranks. One piece of mischief, for which he was rebuked, was running a stick through the ceiling of a low passage to find some new chamber, which could be made effective for some flights of his vivid imagination. The tales, to which we have sat and listened, evening after evening, seated on his knee, when we came to the dining-room for dessert, were anticipated with that pleasing dread, which so excites the minds of children, and fastens so strongly and indelibly on the memory. There was a spacious garret under the roof of Field Place, and a room, which had been closed for years, excepting an entrance made by the removal of a board in the garret floor. This unknown land was made the fancied habitation of an Alchemist, old and grey, with a long beard. Books and a lamp, with all the attributes of a picturesque fancy, were poured into our listening ears. We were to go and see him "some day;" but we were content to wait, and a cave was to be dug in the orchard for the better accommodation of this Cornelius Agrippa. Another favorite theme was the "Great Tortoise,"* that lived in Warnham Pond; and any unwonted noise was accounted for by the presence of this great beast, which was made into the fanciful proportions most adapted to excite awe and wonder.

Bysshe was certainly fond of eccentric amusements, but they delighted us, as children, quite as much as if our minds had been naturally attuned to the same tastes; for we dressed ourselves in strange costumes to personate spirits, or fiends, and Bysshe would take a fire-stove and fill it with some inflammable liquid and carry it flaming into the kitchen and to the back-door; but discovery of this dangerous amusement soon put a stop to many repetitions. When my brother commenced

* [I never heard Shelley mention the "Great Tortoise," but he spoke often of the "Great Old Snake." It was a snake of unusual magnitude, which had inhabited the garden at Field Place for several generations, and which, according to tradition, had been known, as the "Old Snake," three hundred years ago. It was killed, accidentally, through the carelessness of the gardener, in mowing the grass: killed by the same fatal instrument with which the universal destroyer, Time, kills every thing besides,—by that two-handed engine, the scythe. There is so strong an affinity between serpents and all imaginative and demoniacal characters, that I cannot but regret to have entirely forgotten the legends of the "Old Snake;" narratives perfectly true, no doubt,—not with the common-place truth of ordinary matters of fact, but with the far higher truth of poetical verity and mythological necessity.—H.]

his studies in chemistry, and practised electricity upon us, I confess my pleasure in it was entirely negatived by terror at its effects. Whenever he came to me with his piece of folded brown packing-paper under his arm, and a bit of wire and a bottle (if I remember right) my heart would sink with fear at his approach; but shame kept me silent, and, with as many others as he could collect, we were placed hand-in-hand round the nursery table to be electrified; but when a suggestion was made that chilblains were to be cured by this means, my terror overwhelmed all other feelings, and the expression of it released me from all future annoyance. I have heard that Bysshe's memory was singularly retentive. Even as a little child, Gray's lines on the Cat and the Gold Fish were repeated, word for word, after once reading; a fact I have frequently heard from my mother. He used, at my father's bidding, to repeat long Latin quotations, probably from some drama; for he would act, and the expression of his face and movement of his arms are distinct recollections, though the subject of his declamations was a sealed book to his infant hearers. Poor fellow! Why did he not live fifty years later: when he would have been assisted by the wonderful improvements of the age in directing his gifted and inquisitive mind?

My dearest Jane,

The tranquillity of our house must have frequently been rudely invaded by experiments, for, on one occasion, on the morning our Poet and experimentalist left home (for Eton, probably), the washing-room was discovered to have been filled with smoke, by a fire in the grate with the valve closed; the absence of draught had probably prevented mischief, but much was made of this accident, probably to deter any admiring imitators; and there might have been circumstances connected with it relating to chemical preparations, which did not reach us. My younger brother, John, was a child in petticoats, when I remember Bysshe playing with him under the fir-trees on the lawn, pushing him gently down to let him rise and beg for a succession of such falls, rolling with laughing glee on the grass; then, as a sequel to this game, the little carriage was drawn through the garden walks at the rate a big boy could draw a little one, and in an unfortunate turn the carriage was upset, and the occupant tossed into the cabbages, or strawberry bed. Screams, of course, brought sympathetic aid, and, though the child was unhurt, the boy was rebuked; and when the former was brought down after dinner, in the nurse's arms, " Bit," (Bysshe) was apostrophised as a culprit. His great delight was to teach his infant brother schoolboy words, and his first attempt at his knowledge of the devil, was an innocent " Debbee ! "

My dearest Jane,

I feel more confidence in writing when I commence a page, as I have now done ; and after having talked over the small things we remember of our brother, I place them on paper without chronological order ; for you will readily believe that to me it would be impossible, as I do not remember even seeing him after I was eleven years of age. I went to school before Margaret, so that she recollects how Bysshe came home in the midst of the half-year to be nursed ; and when he was allowed to leave the house, he came to the dining-room window, and kissed her through the pane of glass. She remembers his face there, with nose and lips pressed against the window, and at that time she must have been about five years old. In the holidays he would walk with us, if he could steal away with us; and on one occasion he walked with us through the fields to Strood ; where, in those days, there was a park stile, to encourage good neighborhood : there was a sunk fence to divide the lawn from the meadows, and gates were despised, where difficulty would augment the pleasure ; and we were assisted up this perpendicular wall. I was big enough to be pulled over, but Margaret was gently thrown across on the grass. Our shoes were sadly soiled, and the little one of the party was tired, and required carrying ; but she was to be careful to hold her feet so that the trousers might not be damaged. This trait does not seem characteristic, but it is nevertheless true ; and subsequently, Bysshe ordered clothes according to his own fancy at Eton, and the beautifully fitting silk pantaloons, as he stood, as almost all men and boys do, with their coat tails near the fire, excited my silent, though excessive admiration.

MY DEAREST JANE,

I meant in my last letter to have given you an illustration of Bysshe's boyish traits of imagination, but flew off to a later period. On one occasion he gave the most minute details of a visit he had paid to some ladies, with whom he was acquainted at our village : he described their reception of him, their occupations, and the wandering in their pretty garden, where there was a well-remembered filbert-walk and an undulating turf-bank, the delight of our morning visit. There must have been something peculiar in this little event, for I have often heard it mentioned as a singular fact, and it was ascertained almost immediately, that the boy had never been to the house. It was not considered as a falsehood to be punished ; but, I imagine, his conduct altogether must have been so little understood, and unlike that of the generality of children, that these tales were left unnoticed. He was, at a later period, in the habit of walking out at night, and the prosaic minds of ordinary mortals could not understand the pleasure to be derived from contemplating the stars, when he probably was repeating to himself lines, which were so soon to astonish those, who looked on him as a boy. The old servant of the family would follow him, and say, that " Master Bysshe only took a walk, and came back again." He was full of cheerful fun, and had all the comic vein so agreeable in a household : details of this kind would be trifling in many instances : but, as a child at school, I remember some verses, that were sent by him to one of my elder sisters, illustrating something unfavorable to a French teacher, who was accused of being fond of those pupils, who could supply her with fruit and cakes. I believe it was clever, for the sisters were proud enough of it to be imprudent, and by some means it became known to *Madame,* and I can

just remember the commotion it made and the " very bold
boy our *broder* must be."   I have somewhere in my possession
a very early effusion of Bysshe's, with a cat painted on the top
of the sheet.· I will try and find it ; but there is no promise of
future excellence in the lines, the versification is defective.
At one time, he, with my eldest sister, wrote a play secretly,
and sent it to Matthews, the comedian ; who, after a time,
returned it, with the opinion, that it would not do for acting.
I wonder, whether Matthews knew the age of the boy and girl,
who ventured upon writing a play. The subject was never
known to me ; and most likely, the youthful authors made a
good blaze with the MS.

MY DEAREST JANE,

   Every one has heard of Mrs. Hemans, if they have not
read her poetry. She published a large volume, when quite a
girl and Miss Browne. Early talent attracted Bysshe's admiration and sympathy : he wrote to Miss Felicia Dorothea
Browne, and he received an answer, but it was to an effect
which gave no encouragement to farther correspondence : and
he was probably disappointed, as all young, ardent, and
admiring spirits would be in such a case. He fancied that I
might, with encouragement, write verses, and his first lesson
to me, I perfectly remember. Monk Lewis's Poems had a
great attraction for him, and any tale of spirits, fiends, etc.,
seemed congenial to his taste at an early age. I was so young,
that I really can remember nothing of the verses I made,
farther than to give you as a sample of them :—

> "There was an old woman, as I have heard say,
> Who worked metamorphoses every day."

—and these two lines are probably left in my memory, because
Bysshe expressed so much astonishment at my knowledge of
the word *metamorphoses*. There were several short poems, I
think, of which he gave me the subject ; and one line about
" an old woman in her bony gown," (even the rhyme to which
line I forget), elicited the praise for which I wrote. Subse-

quently he had them printed, and a mistake I made about sending one of my heroes, or heroines, out by night and day in the same stanza, he would not alter, but excused it by quoting something from Shakespeare. When I saw my name on the title-page " H—ll—n Sh—ll—y," I felt much more frightened than pleased, and as soon as the publication was seen by my superiors, it was bought up and destroyed. I should not think there could have been anything in it worth either keeping or destroying, but it will tend to show, that my brother was full of pleasant attention to children, though his mind was so far above theirs. He had a wish to educate some child, and often talked seriously of purchasing a little girl for that purpose; a tumbler, who came to the back door to display her wonderful feats, attracted him, and he thought she would be a good subject for the purpose, but all these wild fancies came to naught. He would take his pony and ride about the beautiful lanes and fields surrounding the house, and would *talk* of his intention, but he did not consider that board and lodging would be indispensable, and this difficulty, probably, was quite sufficient to prevent the talk from becoming reality.

MY DEAREST JANE,

I think you have heard me mention a few things concerning Bysshe, which may only be interesting to you, and me, and two or three others ; for when I write about him, whose poems and writings, and attainments, which were never known to the world in all their wonderful profusion, I feel that *my* anecdotes are scarcely indicative of his character ; but you remember that my knowledge of Bysshe ended at ten years of age, and probably the last time I saw him was at Clapham, where we were at school, and he came occasionally to see us, and ask questions about our comfort. One day his ire was greatly excited at a black mark hung round one of our throats, as a penalty for some small misdemeanor. He expressed great disapprobation, more of the system than that one of his sisters should be so punished. Another time he found me, I think, in an iron collar, which certainly was a dreadful instrument of torture in my opinion. It was not worn as a punishment, but because I *poked ;* but Bysshe declared it would make me grow crooked, and ought to be discontinued immediately. The old lady who kept the school, would not, I believe, have hurt one of her pupils for any amount of approbation, so that she was not likely to continue an objectionable practice, if boldly disapproved of, and I was released forthwith. He came once with the elders of the family, and Harriet Grove, his early love, was of the party : how fresh and pretty she was ! Her assistance was invoked to keep the wild boy quiet, for he was full of pranks, and upset the port wine on the tray cloth, for our schoolmistress was hospitable, and had offered refreshments ; then we all walked in the garden, and there was much ado to calm the spirits of the wild boy. His disappointment a few years afterwards, in losing the lady of his love, had a great effect upon him ; and my eldest sister has frequently told me how narrowly she used to watch him and accompany him in his walks with his dog and gun. I believe this matter has been discussed amongst others, probably with little knowledge of the truth. It was not put an end to by *mutual* consent ; but both parties were very young, and her father did not think the marriage would be for his daughter's happiness. He, however, with truly honorable feeling, would not have persisted in his objection, if his daughter had considered herself bound by a promise to my brother, but this was not the case, and time healed the wound, by means of another Harriet, whose name and similar complexion, perhaps, attracted the attention of my brother. I do not consider any details of a later date would be in my province, for I only know his history as I have been told it.

MY DEAREST JANE,

I began my last letter intending to tell you of a morning's event. As we were sitting in the little breakfast room our eyes were attracted by a countryman passing the window with a truss of hay on a prong over his shoulders ; the intruder was wondered at and called after, when it was discovered that

Bysshe had put himself in costume to take some hay to a young lady at Horsham, who was advised to use hay-tea for chilblains. When visitors were announced during his visit to the vicar's daughter, he concealed himself under the table, but the concealment did not probably last long. We have lately been on a visit to Cuckfield Park, and it was singular enough that our host, without having heard this story, mentioned his single recollection of having once, when quite a little boy, seen Bysshe, who came to his uncle, Colonel Sergison, whilst on a visit to his lawyer in Horsham, and asked, in Sussex language, to be hired as gamekeeper's boy. My informant thought his suit was successful, and then, of course, there was an explosion of laughter. I remember *incidents*, but nothing that either preceded or followed them, connectedly. My reminiscences must necessarily be limited to a few early years, for the tales of others, with regard to my brother, do not appear to me truthful. I read of his discordant voice and stooping figure, and I think excitement, in one case, and deep thinking in another, might have made this true in a measure; but, as I remember Bysshe, his figure was slight and beautiful, his hands were models, and his feet are treading the earth again in one of his race; his eyes, too, have descended in their wild, fixed beauty to the same person. As a child, I have heard that his skin was like snow, and bright ringlets covered his head. He was, I have heard, a beautiful boy. His old nurse lived, within the last two or three years, at Horsham. One of the curates there—a Mr. Du Barry—was a great admirer of my brother's poetry, and we were able, through him, to remind her of those years, when she used to come regularly every Christmas to Field Place, to receive a substantial proof that she was not to be forgotten, though her nurse-child was gone from earth, forever.

MY DEAREST JANE,

I have just found the lines which I mentioned; a child's effusion about some cat, which evidently *had* a story, but it must have been before I can remember. It is in Elizabeth's

1*

hand-writing, copied probably later than the composition of the lines, though the hand-writing is unformed. It seems to be a tabby cat, for it has an indistinct, brownish-gray coat.

I have not painted it for you :—

> A cat in distress,
> Nothing more, nor less :
> Good folks, I must faithfully tell ye,
> As I am a sinner,
> It waits for some dinner
> To stuff out its own little belly.
>
> You would not easily guess
> All the modes of distress
> Which torture the tenants of earth :
> And the various evils,
> Which like so many devils,
> Attend the poor souls from their birth.
>
> Some a living require,
> And others desire
> An old fellow out of the way ;
> And which is the best
> I leave to be guessed,
> For I cannot pretend to say.
>
> One wants society,
> Another variety,
> Others a tranquil life ;
> Some want food,
> Others. as good,
> Only want a wife.
>
> But this poor little cat
> Only wanted a rat,
> To stuff out its own little maw ;
> And it were as good
> *Some* people had such food,
> To make them *hold their jaw* !

That last expression is, I imagine, still *classical* at boys' schools, and it was a favorite one of Bysshe's, which I remember from a painful fact, that one of my sisters ventured to make use of it, and was punished in some old-fashioned way, which impressed the sentence on my memory.

HELLEN.

At ten years of age Shelley was sent to Sion House, Brentford. In walking with him to Bishopsgate from London, he pointed out to me, more than once, a gloomy brick-house, as being this school. He spoke of the master, Dr. Greenlaw, not without respect, saying, "he was a hard-headed Scotchman, and a man of rather liberal opinions." Of this period of his life he never gave me an account; nor have I heard or read any details, which appeared to bear the impress of truth. How long he remained at Sion House I know not; nor at what age he was removed to Eton.

My dearest Jane,

I remember well how he used to sing to us; he could not bear any turns or twists in music, but liked a tune played quite simply.

About Miss Westbrook; I recollect hearing Bysshe married her, because her name was Harriet. She was not a person likely to attach him permanently; I remember her well; a very handsome girl, with a complexion quite unknown in these days—brilliant in pink and white—with hair quite like a poet's dream, and Bysshe's peculiar admiration.

I should not remember many of her contemporaries, but the governess and teachers used to remark upon her beauty; and once I heard them talking together of a possible Fête Champêtre, and Harriet Westbrook might enact Venus.

The engraved portraits of Bysshe, which have hitherto been published, are frightful pictures for a spiritual-looking being, like the poet. Yet I do not expect that my ideal will ever be created, because he must have altered from boy to man. His forehead was white, the eyes deep blue,—darker than John's. He had an eccentric quantity of hair, in those days, when he came by stealth to Field Place; and Elizabeth, on one occasion, made him sit down to have it cut, and be made to look like a Christian. His good temper was a pleasant memory always, and I do not recollect an instance of the reverse towards any of us. I tell you little things as they pass in my mind, and you had better tear them off and paste them in the

book, for I find a difficulty in recalling far-off memories, when
I set about it as a task, however palatable the task may be.
There is no life which could bear the test of a detective, and
Bysshe's faults and feelings were all laid bare by a too great
moral courage, which made him witness against himself, when
the rest of his fellow-men conceal their failings, and set their
virtues only upon high ; for we are all erring mortals.

HELLEN.

SHELLEY AT ETON.

While at Eton he formed several sincere friendships ;
although disliked by the masters, and hated by his superiors
in age, he was adored by his equals. He was all passion,—
passionate in his resistance to injury, passionate in his love.
Kindness could win his whole soul, and the idea of self never
for a moment tarnished the purity of his sentiments.

He became intimate, also, at Eton, with a man whom he
never mentioned, except in terms of the tenderest respect.
This was Dr. Lind, a name well known among the professors
of medical science. " This man," he has often said, " is exactly what an old man ought to be. Free, calm-spirited, full
of benevolence, and even of youthful ardor ; his eye seemed
to burn with supernatural spirit beneath his brow, shaded by
his venerable white locks ; he was tall, vigorous, and healthy
in his body : tempered, as it had ever been, by his amiable
mind. I owe to that man far, ah ! far more than I owe to my
father ; he loved me, and I shall never forget our long talks,
where he breathed the spirit of the kindest tolerance and the
purest wisdom. Once, when I was very ill during the holidays,
as I was recovering from a fever which had attacked my brain,
a servant overheard my father consult about sending me to a
private madhouse. I was a favorite among all our servants, so
this fellow came and told me as I lay sick in bed. My horror
was beyond words, and I might soon have been mad indeed,
if they had proceeded in their iniquitous plan. I had one
hope. I was master of three pounds in money, and, with the

servant's help, I contrived to send an express to Dr. Lind. He came, and I shall never forget his manner on that occasion. His profession gave him authority; his love for me ardor. He dared my father to execute his purpose, and his menaces had the desired effect."

I relate this in my Shelley's words, for I well remember them. I well remember where they were spoken; it was that night that decided my destiny; when he opened at first with the confidence of friendship, and then with the ardor of love, his whole heart to me.

Amongst his other self-sought studies, he was passionately attached to the study of what used to be called the occult sciences, conjointly with that of the new wonders, which chemistry and natural philosophy have displayed to us. His pocket money was spent in the purchase of books relative to these darling pursuits,—of chemical apparatus and materials. The books consisted of treatises on magic and witchcraft, as well as those more modern ones detailing the miracles of electricity and galvanism. Sometimes he watched the livelong nights for ghosts. At his father's house, where his influence was, of course, great among the dependants, he even planned how he might get admission to the vault, or charnel-house, at Warnham Church, and might sit there all night, harrowed by fear, yet trembling with expectation, to see one of the spirit-ualized owners of the bones piled around him. He consulted his books, how to raise a ghost; and once, at midnight,— he was then at Eton,—he stole from his dame's house, and, quitting the town, crossed the fields towards a running stream. As he walked along the pathway amidst the long grass, he heard it rustle behind him; he dared not look back; he felt convinced that the devil followed him; he walked fast, and held tight the skull, the prescribed assistant of his incan-tations.

When he had crossed the field he felt less fearful, for the grass no longer rustled, so the devil no longer followed him. He came to some of the many beautiful clear streams near Eton, and sought for one which he could bestride Colossuslike ; * then, standing thus, he repeated his charm, and drank thrice from the skull. No ghost appeared, but for the credit of glamor-books, he did not doubt that the incantation failed from some mistake of his own. It was useless to repeat it that night. Very probably the human skull was wanting, a tumbler, or mug supplying its place, but inadequately, and therefore the youthful enchanter was baffled.

Shelley had several attached friends at Eton ; I will insert the kind testimonial of one of them, because it is equally creditable to both the friends :

My dear Madam,   Glenthorne, *February 27th,* 1857.

Your letter has taken me back to the sunny time of boyhood, " when thought is speech, and speech is truth ; " when I was the friend and companion of Shelley at Eton. What brought us together in that small world was, I suppose, kindred feelings, and the predominance of fancy and imagination. Many a long and happy walk have I had with him in the beautiful neighborhood of dear old Eton. We used to wander for hours about Clewer, Frogmore, the Park at Windsor, the Terrace ; and I was a delighted and willing listener to his marvellous stories of fairy-land, and apparitions, and spirits, and haunted ground ; and his speculations were then (for his mind was far more developed than mine) of the world beyond the grave. Another of his favorite rambles was Stoke Park, and the picturesque churchyard, where Gray is said to have written his Elegy, of which he was very fond. I was myself far too young to form any estimate of character, but I loved Shelley for his kindliness and affectionate ways: he was not made to endure the rough and boisterous pastime at Eton, and his shy and gentle nature was glad to escape far away to muse over strange fancies, for his mind was reflective and teeming with deep thought. His lessons were child's play to him, and his power of Latin versification marvellous. I think I remem-

---

* No devil, ghost, or spirit, can cross running water (this superstition may have some reference to the rite of baptism) ; it is prudent, therefore, in all dealings with demons, to have a running stream at hand.

ber some long work he had even then commenced, but I never saw it. His love of nature was intense, and the sparkling poetry of his mind shone out of his speaking eye, when he was dwelling on anything good or great. He certainly was not happy at Eton, for his was a disposition that needed especial personal superintendence, to watch, and cherish, and direct all his noble aspirations, and the remarkable tenderness of his heart. He had great moral courage, and feared nothing, but what was base, and false, and low. He never joined in the usual sports of the boys, and, what is remarkable, never went out in a boat on the river. What I have here set down will be of little use to you, but will please you as a sincere, and truthful, and humble tribute to one whose good name was sadly whispered away. Shelley said to me, when leaving Oxford under a cloud : " Halliday, I am come to say good-bye to you, if you are not afraid to be seen with me!" I saw him once again in the autumn of 1814, in London, when he was glad to introduce me to his wife. I think he said, he was just come from Ireland. You have done quite right in applying to me direct, and I am only sorry that I have no anecdotes, or letters, of that period, to furnish.

I am yours truly,
WALTER S. HALLIDAY.

Dr. Keate, the head-master of Eton school, was a short, short-necked, short-legged man ; thick-set, powerful, and very active. His countenance resembled that of a bull-dog; the expression was not less sweet and bewitching ; his eyes, his nose, and especially his mouth were exactly like that comely and engaging animal ; and so were his short, crooked legs. It was said in the school that old Keate could pin and hold a bull with his teeth. His iron sway was the more unpleasant and shocking, after the long, mild, Saturnian reign of Dr. Goodall, whose temper, character, and conduct corresponded precisely with his name, and under whom Keate had been master of the lower school. Discipline, wholesome and necessary in moderation, was carried by him to an excess; it is reported, that on one morning he flogged eighty boys. Although he was rigid, coarse, and despotical, some affirm that, on the whole, he was not unjust, nor altogether devoid of kindness. His behavior was accounted vulgar and ungentlemanlike, and therefore he was peculiarly odious to the gentlemen of the school, especially to the refined and aristocratical Shelley. Being universally unpopular, to torment him was excusable, legitimate, and even commendable. In school the head-master sate enthroned in a spacious elevated desk, enclosed on all sides, like a pew, with two doors, one on each side. These the boys one morning screwed fast. The Doctor entered the school at eleven o'clock, advanced to his desk, tried to open one door, and found it was fastened. He went round, grinning, growling, and snarling, to the other side; the door there had been secured also. Then, turning furiously to the boys, he said :

" You think to keep me out, eh! You think I cannot get in here, eh! But I will soon show you the difference, eh!"

The desk was as high as the breast of an ordinary man, and as high as the little Doctor's head, but laying his hand on it, he lightly vaulted in. The season was summer ; in school old Keate wore a long gown and cassock, and in warm weather, it seemed, nothing under them ; for, in his leap, the learned and reverend Doctor displayed not only his agility, but his naked stern, all lower integuments being wanting. The unwonted spectacle was saluted with loud cheers, and a hearty laugh. The mutinous explosion inflamed his wrath to the utmost.

" You shall pay for this, eh! I will make some of you suffer for it, eh!"

However, nothing came of it ; the enraged and insulted pedagogue could not discover the offenders. The screws had been bought by two boys, a tall boy and a short one. That was all the detectives could find out.

SHELLEY AT OXFORD.

At the commencement of Michaelmas term, that is, at the end of October, in the year 1810, I happened one day to sit next to a freshman at dinner : it was his first appearance in hall. His figure was slight, and his aspect remarkably youthful, even at our table, where all were very young. He seemed thoughtful and absent. He ate little, and had no acquaintance with any one. I know not how it was that we fell into conversation, for such familiarity was unusual, and, strange to say, much reserve prevailed in a society where there could not possibly be occasion for any. We have often endeavored in vain to recollect in what manner our discourse began, and especially by what transition it passed to a subject sufficiently remote from all the associations we were able to trace. The stranger had expressed an enthusiastic admiration for poetical and imaginative works of the German school. I dissented from his criticisms. He upheld the originality of the German writings. I asserted their want of nature.

" What modern literature," said he, " will you compare to theirs ? "

I named the Italian. This roused all his impetuosity; and few, as I soon discovered, were more impetuous in argumentative conversation. So eager was our dispute, that when the servants came to clear the tables, we were not aware that we had been left alone. I remarked that it was time to quit the hall, and I invited the stranger to finish the discussion at my rooms. He eagerly assented. He lost the thread of his discourse in the transit, and the whole of his enthusiasm in the cause of Germany ; for as soon as he arrived at my rooms, and whilst I was lighting the candles, he said calmly, and to my great surprise, that he was not qualified to maintain such a discussion, for he was alike ignorant of Italian and German, and had only read the works of the Germans in translations, and but little of Italian poetry, even at second hand. For my part, I confessed, with an equal ingenuousness, that I knew nothing of German, and but little of Italian ; that I had spoken only through others, and like him, had hitherto seen by the glimmering light of translations.

I inquired of the vivacious stranger, as we sat over our wine and dessert, how long he had been at Oxford, how he liked it ?

He answered my questions with a certain impatience, and, resuming the subject of our discussion, he remarked that, " Whether the literature of Germany, or of Italy, be the more original, or in a purer and more accurate taste, is of little importance, for polite letters are but vain trifling ; the study of languages, not only of the modern tongues, but of Latin and Greek also, is merely the study of words and phrases, of the names of things ; it matters not how they are called ; it is surely far better to investigate things themselves." I inquired, a little bewildered, how this was to be effected ? He answered, " through the physical sciences, and especially through chemistry ; " and raising his voice, his face flushing as he spoke, he discoursed with a degree of animation, that far outshone his zeal in defence of the Germans, of chemistry and chemical analysis. Concerning that science, then so popular, I had merely a scanty and vulgar knowledge, gathered from elementary books, and the ordinary experiments of popular lecturers. I listened, therefore, in silence to his eloquent disquisition, interposing a few brief questions only, and at long intervals, as to the extent of his own studies and manipulations. As I felt, in truth, but a slight interest in the subject of his conversation, I had leisure to examine, and I may add, to admire, the appearance of my very extraordinary guest. It was a sum of many contradictions. His figure was slight and fragile, and yet his bones and joints were large and strong. He was tall, but he stooped so much, that he seemed of a low stature. His clothes were expensive, and made according to the most approved mode of the day ; but they were tumbled, rumpled, unbrushed. His gestures were abrupt, and sometimes violent, occasionally even awkward, yet more frequently gentle and graceful. His complexion was delicate, and almost feminine, of the purest red and white ; yet he was tanned and freckled by exposure to the sun, having passed the autumn, as he said, in shooting. His features, his whole face, and particularly his head, were, in fact, unusually small ; yet the last *appeared* of a remarkable bulk, for his hair was long and bushy, and in fits of absence, and in the agonies (if I may use the word) of anxious thought, he often rubbed it fiercely with his hands, or passed his fingers quickly through his locks unconsciously, so that it was singularly wild and rough. In times when it was the mode to imitate stage-coachmen as closely a possible in costume, and when the hair was invariably cropped, like that of our soldiers, this eccentricity was very striking. His features were not symmetrical (the mouth, perhaps, excepted), yet was the effect of the whole extremely powerful. They breathed an animation, a fire, an enthusiasm, a vivid and pre-ternatural intelligence, that I never met with in any other countenance. Nor was the moral expression less beautiful than the intellectual; for there was a softness, a delicacy, a gentle-ness, and especially (though this will surprise many) that air of profound religious veneration, that characterizes the best works, and chiefly the frescoes (and into these they infused their whole souls), of the great masters of Florence and of Rome. I recognized the very peculiar expression in these wonderful productions long afterwards, and with a satisfaction mingled with much sorrow, for it was after the decease of him in whose countenance I had first observed it. I admired the enthusiasm of my new acquaintance, his ardor in the cause of science, and his thirst for knowledge. I seemed to have found in him all those intellectual qualities which I had vainly expected to meet with in an University. But there was one physical blemish that threatened to neutralize all his excellence. " This is a fine, clever fellow! " I said to myself, " but I can never bear his society; I shall never be able to endure his voice; it would kill me. What a pity it is! " I am very sensible of imperfections, and especially of painful sounds,— and the voice of the stranger was excruciating; it was intoler-ably shrill, harsh, and discordant; of the most cruel intension, —it was perpetual, and without any remission,—it excoriated the ears. He continued to discourse of chemistry, sometimes sitting, sometimes standing before the fire, and sometimes pacing about the room; and when one of the innumerable clocks that speak in various notes during the day and the night at Oxford, proclaimed a quarter to seven, he said suddenly that he must go to a lecture on mineralogy, and declared enthusiastically that he expected to derive much pleasure and instruction from it.   I am ashamed to own that the cruel voice made me hesitate for a moment ; but it was impossible to omit so indispensable a civility—I invited him to return to tea ; he gladly assented, promised that he would not be absent long, snatched his cap, hurried out of the room, and I heard his footsteps, as he ran through the silent quadrangle, and afterwards along High-street.

An hour soon elapsed, whilst the table was cleared, and the tea was made, and I again heard the footsteps of one running quickly.   My guest suddenly burst into the room, threw down his cap, and as he stood shivering and chafing his hands over the fire, he declared how much he had been disappointed in the lecture.   Few persons attended ; it was dull and languid, and he was resolved never to go to another.

" I went away, indeed," he added, with an arch look, and in a shrill whisper, coming close to me as he spoke,—" I went away, indeed, before the lecture was finished.   I stole away ; for it was so stupid, and I was so cold, that my teeth chattered. The Professor saw me, and appeared to be displeased.   I thought I could have got out without being observed ; but I struck my knee against a bench, and made a noise, and he looked at me.   I am determined that he shall never see me again."

" What did the man talk about ? "

" About stones ! about stones ! " he answered, with a downcast look and in a melancholy tone, as if about to say something excessively profound.   " About stones !—stones, stones, stones !—nothing but stones !—and so dryly.   It was wonderfully tiresome—and stones are not interesting things in themselves ! "

We took tea, and soon afterwards had supper, as was usual. He discoursed after supper with as much warmth as before of the wonders of chemistry ; of the encouragement that Napoleon afforded to that most important science ; of the French chemists and their glorious discoveries ; and of the happiness of visiting Paris, and sharing in their fame and their experiments. The voice, however, seemed to me more cruel than ever. He spoke likewise of his own labors and of his apparatus, and starting up suddenly after supper, he proposed that I should go instantly with him to see the galvanic trough. I looked at my watch, and observed that it was too late ; that the fire would be out, and the night was cold. He resumed his seat, saying that I might come on the morrow, early, to breakfast, immediately after chapel. He continued to declaim in his rapturous strain, asserting that chemistry was, in truth, the only science that deserved to be studied. I suggested doubts. I ventured to question the pre-eminence of the science, and even to hesitate in admitting its utility. He described in glowing language some discoveries that had lately been made ; but the enthusiastic chemist candidly allowed that they were rather brilliant than useful, asserting, however, that they would be soon applied to purposes of solid advantage.

With fervor did the slender, beardless stranger speculate concerning the march of physical science ; his speculations were as wild as the experience of twenty-one years has shown them to be ; but the zealous earnestness for the augmentation of knowledge, and the glowing philanthropy and boundless benevolence that marked them, and beamed forth in the whole deportment of that extraordinary boy, are not less astonishing than they would have been if the whole of his glorious anticipations had been prophetic ; for these high qualities, at least, I have never found a parallel. When he had ceased to predict the coming honors of chemistry, and to promise the rich harvest of benefits it was soon to yield, I suggested that, although its results were splendid, yet for those who could not hope to make discoveries themselves, it did not afford so valuable a course of mental discipline as the moral sciences ; moreover, that if chemists asserted that their science alone deserved to be cultivated, the mathematicians made the same assertion, and with equal confidence, respecting their studies ; but that I was not sufficiently advanced myself in mathematics to be able to judge how far it was well founded. He declared that he knew nothing of mathematics, and treated the notion of their paramount importance with contempt.

" What do you say of metaphysics ? " I continued; " is that science, too, the study of words only ? "

" Ay, metaphysics," he said, in a solemn tone, and with a mysterious air, " that is a noble study indeed! If it were possible to make any discoveries there, they would be more valuable than anything the chemists have done, or could do; they would disclose the analysis of mind, and not of mere matter!" Then rising from his chair, he paced slowly about the room, with prodigious strides, and discoursed of souls with still greater animation and vehemence than he had displayed in treating of gases—of a future state—and especially of a former state—of pre-existence, obscured for a time through the suspension of consciousness—of personal identity, and also of ethical philosophy, in a deep and earnest tone of elevated morality, until he suddenly remarked that the fire was nearly out, and the candles were glimmering in their sockets, when he hastily apologized for remaining so long. I promised to visit the chemist in his laboratory, the alchemist in his study, the wizard in his cave, not at breakfast on that day, for it was already one, but in twelve hours—one hour after noon—and to hear some of the secrets of nature; and for that purpose, he told me his name, and described the situation of his rooms. I lighted him down stairs as well as I could with the stump of a candle which had dissolved itself into a lamp, and I soon heard him running through the quiet quadrangle in the still night. That sound became afterwards so familiar to my ear, that I still seem to hear Shelley's hasty steps.

I trust, or I should perhaps rather say, I hope, that I was as much struck by the conversation, the aspect, and the deportment of my new acquaintance, as entirely convinced of the value of the acquisition I had just made, and as deeply impressed with surprise and admiration, as became a young student not insensible of excellence, to whom a character so extraordinary, and indeed almost preternatural, had been

suddenly unfolded.　During his animated and eloquent discourses I felt a due reverence for his zeal and talent, but the
human mind is capable of a certain amount of attention only.
I had listened and discussed for seven or eight hours, and my
spirits were totally exhausted ; I went to bed as soon as Shelley
had quitted my rooms, and fell instantly into a profound sleep ;
and I shook off with a painful effort, at the accustomed signal,
the complete oblivion which then appeared to have been
but momentary.　Many of the wholesome usages of antiquity
had ceased at Oxford ; that of early rising, however, still lingered.

As soon as I got up, I applied myself sedulously to my academical duties and my accustomed studies.　The power of
habitual occupation is great and engrossing, and it is possible
that my mind had not yet fully recovered from the agreeable
fatigue of the preceding evening, for I had entirely forgotten
my engagement, nor did the thought of my young guest once
cross my fancy.　It was strange that a person so remarkable
and attractive should have thus disappeared for several hours
from my memory; but such in truth was the fact, although I
am unable to account for it in a satisfactory manner.

At one o'clock I put away my books and papers, and prepared myself for my daily walk ; the weather was frosty, with
fog, and whilst I lingered over the fire with that reluctance to
venture forth into the cold air, common to those who have
chilled themselves by protracted sedentary pursuits, the recollection of the scenes of yesterday flashed suddenly and vividly
across my mind, and I quickly repaired to a spot that I may perhaps venture to predict many of our posterity will hereafter
reverently visit, to the rooms in the corner next the hall of the
principal quadrangle of University College ; they are on the
first floor, and on the right of the entrance, but by reason of
the turn in the stairs, when you reach them, they will be upon
your left hand.　I remember the directions given at parting,
and I soon found the door ; it stood ajar.　I tapped gently, and
the discordant voice cried shrilly,—

" Come in ! "

It was now nearly two. I began to apologize for my delay, but I was interrupted by a loud exclamation of surprise—

"What! is it one? I had no notion it was so late; I thought it was about ten or eleven."

"It is on the stroke of two, sir," said the scout, who was engaged in the vain attempt of setting the apartment in order.

"Of two!" Shelley cried, with increased wonder, and presently the clock struck, and the servant noticed it, retired, and shut the door.

I perceived at once that the young chemist took no note of time. He measured duration, not by minutes and hours, like watchmakers and their customers, but by the successive trains of ideas and sensations; consequently, if there was a virtue of which he was utterly incapable, it was that homely, but pleasing and useful one, punctuality. He could not tear himself from his incessant abstraction to observe at intervals the growth and decline of the day; nor was he ever able to set apart even a small portion of his mental powers for a duty so simple as that of watching the course of the pointers on the dial.

I found him cowering over the fire, his chair planted in the middle of the rug, and his feet resting upon the fender; his whole appearance was dejected. His astonishment at the unexpected lapse of time roused him; as soon as the hour of the day was ascertained, he welcomed me, and seizing one of my arms with both his hands, he shook it with some force, and very cordially expressed his satisfaction at my visit. Then resuming his seat and his former posture, he gazed fixedly at the fire, and his limbs trembled and his teeth chattered with cold. I cleared the fire-place with the poker and stirred the fire, and when it blazed up, he drew back, and looking askance towards the door, he exclaimed with a deep sigh,—

"Thank God, that fellow is gone at last!"

The assiduity of the scout had annoyed him, and he presently added—

"If you had not come, he would have stayed until he had

put everything in my room into some place where I should
never have found it again ! "

He then complained of his health, and said that he was very
unwell; but he did not appear to be affected by any disorder
more serious than a slight aguish cold. I remarked the same
contradiction in his rooms which I had already observed in his
person and dress; they had just been papered and painted;
the carpet, curtains, and furniture were quite new, and had
not passed through several academical generations, after the
established custom of transferring the whole of the movables
to the successor on payments of thirds, that is, of two-thirds
of the price last given. The general air of freshness was
greatly obscured, however, by the indescribable confusion in
which the various objects were mixed; notwithstanding the
unwelcome exertions of the officious scout, scarcely a single
article was in its proper position.

Books, boots, papers, shoes, philosophical instruments,
clothes, pistols, linen, crockery, ammunition, and phials innumerable, with money, stockings, prints, crucibles, bags, and
boxes, were scattered on the floor and in every place; as if
the young chemist, in order to analyze the mystery of creation,
had endeavored first to reconstruct the primeval chaos. The
tables, and especially the carpet, were already stained with
large spots of various hues, which frequently proclaimed the
agency of fire. An electrical machine, an air-pump, the galvanic trough, a solar microscope, and large glass jars and
receivers, were conspicuous amidst the mass of matter. Upon
the table by his side were some books lying open, several
letters, a bundle of new pens, and a bottle of japan ink, that
served as an inkstand; a piece of deal, lately part of the lid
of a box, with many chips, and a handsome razor that had
been used as a knife. There were bottles of soda water, sugar,
pieces of lemon, and the traces of an effervescent beverage.
Two piles of books supported the tongs, and these upheld a
small glass retort above an argand lamp. I had not been seated
many minutes before the liquor in the vessel boiled over,
adding fresh stains to the table, and rising in fumes with a

2

most disagreeable odor. Shelley snatched the glass quickly, and dashing it in pieces among the ashes under the grate, increased the unpleasant and penetrating effluvium.*

He then proceeded, with much eagerness and enthusiasm, to show me the various instruments, especially the electrical apparatus ; turning round the handle very rapidly, so that the fierce, crackling sparks flew forth ; and presently standing upon the stool with glass feet, he begged me to work the machine until he was filled with the fluid, so that his long, wild locks bristled and stood on end. Afterwards he charged a powerful battery of several large jars ; laboring with vast energy, and discoursing with increasing vehemence of the marvellous powers of electricity, of thunder and lightning ; describing an electrical kite that he had made at home, and projecting another and an enormous one, or rather a combination of many kites, that would draw down from the sky an immense volume of electricity, the whole ammunition of a mighty thunderstorm ; and this being directed to some point would there produce the most stupendous results.

In these exhibitions and in such conversation the time passed away rapidly, and the hour of dinner approached. Having pricked *æger* that day, or, in other words, having caused his name to be entered as an invalid, he was not required, or permitted, to dine in hall, or to appear in public within the college, or without the walls, until a night's rest should have restored the sick man to health.

He requested me to spend the evening at his rooms ; I consented, nor did I fail to attend immediately after dinner. We

* "In this story there may be one or two of the circumstances which we can rely upon as having actually occurred ; as to the rest of the description, it is evidently as complete a *study* as a chapter in *The Old Curiosity Shop*. Mr. Hogg had forgotten that a few pages before that Shelley had but just entered the University, that he had dined the preceding evening for the first time in hall, and that as far as Mr. Hogg's information goes, this might have been only the third day of Shelley's residence at Oxford, and yet there was time in this short interval to burn the carpets and the tables, and create the chaos which Mr. Hogg depicts with the hand of a master. The 'bundle of newspapers,' the 'bottle of Japan ink,' and the 'traces of an effervescent mixture,' recorded after twenty years, are wonderful results of the imagination, if not of the memory of the writer."—*Dennis Florence MacCarthy.*

conversed until a late hour on miscellaneous topics. I remember that he spoke frequently of poetry, and that there was the same animation, the same glowing zeal, which had characterised his former discourses, and was so opposite to the listless languor, the monstrous indifference, if not the absolute antipathy, to learning, that so strangely darkened the collegiate atmosphere. It would seem, indeed, to one who rightly considered the final cause of the institution of an University, that all the rewards, all the honors, the most opulent foundation could accumulate, would be inadequate to remunerate an individual, whose thirst for knowledge was so intense, and his activity in the pursuit of it so wonderful and so unwearied. I participated in his enthusiasm, and soon forgot the shrill and unmusical voice that had at first seemed intolerable to my ear.

He was, indeed, a whole University in himself to me, in respect of the stimulus and incitement which his example afforded to my love of study, and he amply atoned for the disappointment I had felt on my arrival at Oxford. In one respect alone could I pretend to resemble him, in an ardent desire to gain knowledge ; and as our tastes were the same in many particulars, we immediately became, through sympathy, most intimate and altogether inseparable companions. We almost invariably passed the afternoon and evening together ; at first alternately at our respective rooms, through a certain punctiliousness, but afterwards, when we became more familiar, most frequently by far at his ; sometimes one or two good and harmless men of our acquaintance were present, but we were usually alone. His rooms were preferred to mine, because there his philosophical apparatus was at hand; and at that period he was not perfectly satisfied with the condition and circumstances of his existence, unless he was able to start from his seat at any moment, and seizing the air-pump, some magnets, the electrical machine, or the bottles containing those noxious and nauseous fluids, wherewith he incessantly besmeared and disfigured himself and his goods, to ascertain by actual experiment the value of some new idea that rushed into his brain. He spent much time in working by fits and starts and in an irregular manner with his instruments, and especially consumed his hours and his money in the assiduous cultivation of chemistry.

We have heard that one of the most distinguished of modern discoverers was abrupt, hasty, and to appearance disorderly in the conduct of his manipulations; the variety of the habits of great men is indeed infinite; it is impossible, therefore, to decide peremptorily as to the capabilities of individuals from their course of proceeding, yet it certainly seemed highly improbable that Shelley was qualified to succeed in a science wherein a scrupulous minuteness and a mechanical accuracy are indispensable. His chemical operations seemed to an unskilful observer to promise nothing but disasters. His hands, his clothes, his books, and his furniture were stained and corroded by mineral acids. More than one hole in the carpet could elucidate the ultimate phenomenon of combustion; especially a formidable aperture in the middle of the room, where the floor also had been burnt by the spontaneous ignition caused by mixing ether with some other fluid in a crucible; and the honorable wound was speedily enlarged by rents, for the philosopher, as he hastily crossed the room in pursuit of truth, was frequently caught in it by the foot. Many times a day, but always in vain, would the sedulous scout say, pointing to the scorched boards with a significant look—

"Would it not be better, sir, for us to get this place mended?"

It seemed but too probable that in the rash ardor of experiment he would some day set the college on fire, or that he would blind, maim, or kill himself by the explosion of combustibles. It was still more likely indeed that he would poison himself, for plates and glasses, and every part of his tea equipage were used indiscriminately with crucibles, retorts, and recipients, to contain the most deleterious ingredients. To his infinite diversion I used always to examine every drinking-vessel narrowly, and often to rinse it carefully, after that evening when we were taking tea by firelight, and my attention being attracted by the sound of something in the cup into which

I was about to pour tea, I was induced to look into it. I found a seven-shilling piece partly dissolved by the *aqua regia* in which it was immersed. Although he laughed at my caution, he used to speak with horror of the consequences of having inadvertently swallowed, through a similar accident, some mineral poison, I think arsenic, at Eton, which he declared had not only seriously injured his health, but that he feared he should never entirely recover from the shock it had inflicted on his constitution. It seemed probable, notwithstanding his positive assertions, that his lively fancy exaggerated the recollection of the unpleasant and permanent taste, or the sickness and disorder of the stomach, which might arise from taking a minute portion of some poisonous substance by the like chance, for there was no vestige of a more serious and lasting injury in his youthful and healthy, although somewhat delicate aspect.

I knew little of the physical sciences, and I felt therefore but a slight degree of interest in them; I looked upon his philosophical apparatus merely as toys and playthings, like a chess-board or a billiard-table. Through lack of sympathy, his zeal, which was at first so ardent, gradually cooled; and he applied himself to these pursuits, after a short time, less frequently and with less earnestness. The true value of them was often the subject of animated discussion; and I remember one evening at my own rooms, when we had sought refuge against the intense cold in the little inner apartment, or study, I referred, in the course of our debate, to a passage in Xenophon's " Memorabilia," where Socrates speaks in disparagement of Physics. He read it several times very attentively, and more than once aloud, slowly and with emphasis, and it appeared to make a strong impression on him.

Notwithstanding our difference of opinion as to the importance of chemistry, and on some other questions, our intimacy rapidly increased, and we soon formed the habit of passing the greater part of our time together; nor did this constant intercourse interfere with my usual studies. I never visited his rooms until one o'clock, by which hour, as I rose very early, I had not only attended the college lectures, but had read in pri-

vate for several hours. I was enabled, moreover, to continue
my studies afterwards in the evening, in consequence of a
very remarkable peculiarity. My young and energetic friend
was then overcome by extreme drowsiness, which speedily and
completely vanquished him ; he would sleep from two to four
hours, often so soundly that his slumbers resembled a deep
lethargy ; he lay occasionally upon the sofa, but more commonly stretched upon the rug before a large fire, like a cat ;
and his little round head was exposed to such a fierce heat,
that I used to wonder how he was able to bear it. Sometimes
I have interposed some shelter, but rarely with any permanent
effect ; for the sleeper usually contrived to turn himself, and
to roll again into the spot where the fire glowed the brightest.
His torpor was generally profound, but he would sometimes
discourse incoherently for a long while in his sleep. At six he
would suddenly compose himself, even in the midst of a most
animated narrative or of earnest discussion ; and he would lie
buried in entire forgetfulness, in a sweet and mighty oblivion,
until ten, when he would suddenly start up, and rubbing his eyes
with great violence, and passing his fingers swiftly through his
long hair, would enter at once into a vehement argument, or
begin to recite verses, either of his own composition or from
the works of others, with a rapidity and an energy that were
often quite painful. During the period of his occultation I
took tea, and read or wrote without interruption. He would
sometimes sleep for a shorter time, for about two hours ; post-
poning for the like period the commencement of his retreat to
the rug, and rising with tolerable punctuality at ten ; and sometimes, although rarely, he was able entirely to forego the
accustomed refreshment.

We did not consume the whole of our time, when he was
awake, in conversation ; we often read apart, and more frequently together ; our joint studies were occasionally interrupted by long discussions—nevertheless I could enumerate
many works, and several of them are extensive and important,
which we perused completely and very carefully in this manner.
At ten, when he awoke, he was always ready for his supper,

which he took with a peculiar relish ; after that social meal his mind was clear and penetrating, and his discourses eminently brilliant. He was unwilling to separate ; but when the college clock struck two, I used to rise and retire to my room. Our conversations were sometimes considerably prolonged, but they seldom terminated before that chilly hour of the early morning ; nor did I feel any inconvenience from thus reducing the period of rest to scarcely five hours.

A disquisition on some difficult question in the open air was not less agreeable to him than by the fireside ; if the weather was fine, or rather not altogether intolerable, we used to sally forth, when we met at one.

I have already pointed out several contradictions in his appearance and character ; his ordinary preparation for a rural walk formed a very remarkable contrast with his mild aspect and pacific habits. He furnished himself with a pair of duelling pistols, and a good store of powder and ball ; and when he came to a solitary spot, he pinned a card, or fixed some other mark upon a tree or a bank, and amused himself by firing at it ; he was a pretty good shot, and was much delighted at his success. He often urged me to try my hand and eye, assuring me that I was not aware of the pleasure of a good hit. One day when he was peculiarly pressing, I took up a pistol and asked him what I should aim at ? And observing a slab of wood, about as big as a hearth-rug, standing against a wall, I named it as being a proper object. He said that it was much too far off, it was better to wait until we came nearer ; but I answered—" I may as well fire here as anywhere," and instantly discharged my pistol. To my infinite surprise, the ball struck the elm target most accurately in the very centre. Shelley was delighted ; he ran to the board, placed his chin close to it—gazed at the hole where the bullet was lodged—examined it attentively on all sides many times, and more than once measured the distance to the spot where I had stood.

I never knew any one so prone to admire as he was, in whom the principle of veneration was so strong ; he extolled my skill, urged me repeatedly to display it again, and begged that I would give him instructions in an art in which I so much excelled. I suffered him to enjoy his wonder for a few days, and then I told him, and with difficulty persuaded him, that my success was purely accidental; for I had seldom fired a pistol before, and never with ball, but with shot only, as a schoolboy, in clandestine and bloodless expeditions against blackbirds and yellowhammers.

The duelling pistols were a most discordant interruption of the repose of a quiet country walk: besides, he handled them with such inconceivable carelessness, that I had perpetually reason to apprehend that, as a trifling episode in the grand and heroic work of drilling a hole through the back of a card, or the front of one of his father's franks, he would shoot himself, or me, or both of us. How often have I lamented that Nature, which so rarely bestows upon the world a creature endowed with such marvellous talents, ungraciously rendered the gift less precious by implanting a fatal taste for perilous recreations, and a thoughtlessness in the pursuit of them, that often caused his existence from one day to another to seem in itself miraculous. I opposed the practice of walking armed, and I at last succeeded in inducing him to leave the pistols at home, and to forbear the use of them. I prevailed, I believe, not so much by argument or persuasion, as by secretly abstracting, when he equipped himself for the field, and it was not difficult with him, the powder-flask, the flints, or some other indispensable article. One day, I remember, he was grievously discomposed, and seriously offended, to find, on producing his pistols, after descending rapidly into a quarry, where he proposed to take a few shots, that not only had the flints been removed, but the screws and the bits of steel at the tops of the cocks, which hold the flints, were also wanting. He determined to return to college for them,—I accompanied him. I tempted him, however, by the way, to try to define anger, and to discuss the nature of that affection of the mind, to which, as the discussion waxed warm, he grew exceedingly hostile in theory, and could not be brought to admit that it could possibly be excusable in any case.   In the course of conversation, moreover, he suffered himself to be insensibly turned away from his original path and purpose.   I have heard, that some years after he left Oxford he resumed the practice of pistol-shooting, and attained to a very unusual degree of skill in an accomplishment so entirely incongruous with his nature.

Of rural excursions he was at all times fond; he loved to walk in the woods, to stroll on the banks of the Thames, but especially to wander about Shotover Hill.   There was a pond at the foot of the hill before ascending it, and on the left of the road ; it was formed by the water which had filled an old quarry : whenever he was permitted to shape his course as he would, he proceeded to the edge of this pool, although the scene had no other attraction than a certain wildness and barrenness.   Here he would linger until dusk, gazing in silence on the water, repeating verses aloud, or earnestly discussing themes that had no connection with surrounding objects. Sometimes he would raise a stone as large as he could lift, deliberately throw it into the water as far as his strength enabled him ; then he would loudly exult at the splash, and would quietly watch the decreasing agitation, until the last faint ring and almost imperceptible ripple disappeared on the still surface.   "Such are the effects of an impulse on the air," he would say ; and he complained of our ignorance of the theory of sound,—that the subject was obscure and mysterious, and many of the phenomena were contradictory and inexplicable. He asserted that the science of acoustics ought to be cultivated, and that by well-devised experiments valuable discoveries would undoubtedly be made ; and he related many remarkable stories connected with the subject, that he had heard or read.   Sometimes, he would busy himself in splitting the slaty stones, in selecting thin and flat pieces, and in giving them a round form ; and when he had collected a sufficient number, he would gravely make ducks and drakes with them, counting, with the utmost glee, the number of bounds, as they flew along skimming the surface of the pond.   He was a devoted worshipper of the water-nymphs ; for whenever he

2*

found a pool, or even a small puddle, he would loiter near it, and it was no easy task to get him to quit it. He had not yet learned that art, from which he afterwards derived so much pleasure—the construction of paper boats. He twisted a morsel of paper into a form that a lively fancy might consider a likeness of a boat, and committing it to the water, he anxiously watched the fortunes of the frail bark, which, if it was not soon swamped by the faint winds and miniature waves, gradually imbibed water through its porous sides, and sank. Sometimes, however, the fairy vessel performed its little voyage, and reached the opposite shore of the puny ocean in safety. It is astonishing with what keen delight he engaged in this singular pursuit. It was not easy for an uninitiated spectator to bear with tolerable patience the vast delay, on the brink of à wretched pond upon a bleak common, and in the face of a cutting north-east wind, on returning to dinner from a long walk at sunset on a cold winter's day; nor was it easy to be so harsh as to interfere with a harmless gratification, that was evidently exquisite. It was not easy, at least, to induce the ship-builder to desist from launching his tiny fleets, so long as any timber remained in the dockyard. I prevailed once, and once only; it was one of those bitter Sundays that commonly receive the new year; the sun had set, and it had almost begun to snow. I had exhorted him long in vain, with the eloquence of a frozen and famished man, to proceed; at last, I said in despair—alluding to his never-ending creations, for a paper-navy that was to be set afloat simultaneously lay at his feet, and he was busily constructing more, with blue and swollen hands,—" Shelley, there is no use in talking to you; you are the Demiurgus of Plato!" He instantly caught up the whole flotilla, and bounding homeward with mighty strides, laughed aloud—laughed like a giant, as he used to say. So long as his paper lasted, he remained riveted to the spot, fascinated by this peculiar amusement; all waste paper was rapidly consumed, then the covers of letters, next letters of little value; the most precious contributions of the most esteemed correspondence, although eyed wistfully many times, and often returned to the pocket, were sure to be sent at last in pursuit of the former squadrons.   Of the portable volumes which were the companions of his rambles, and he seldom went out without a book, the fly-leaves were commonly wanting,—he had applied them as our ancestor Noah applied Gopher wood ; but learning was so sacred in his eyes, that he never trespassed farther upon the integrity of the copy ; the work itself was always respected.   It has been said, that he once found himself on the north bank of the Serpentine river without the materials for indulging those inclinations, which the sight of water invariably inspired, for he had exhausted his supplies on the round pond in Kensington Gardens.   Not a single scrap of paper could be found, save only a bank-post bill for fifty pounds ; he hesitated long, but yielded at last ; he twisted it into a boat with the extreme refinement of his skill, and committed it with the utmost dexterity to fortune, watching its progress, if possible, with a still more intense anxiety than usual.   Fortune often favors those who frankly and fully trust her ; the north-east wind gently wafted the costly skiff to the south bank, where, during the latter part of the voyage, the venturous owner had awaited its arrival with patient solicitude. The story, of course, is a Mythic fable, but it aptly portrays the dominion of a singular and most unaccountable passion over the mind of an enthusiast.

But to return to Oxford.   Shelley disliked exceedingly all college-meetings, and especially one which was the most popular with others—the public dinner in the hall ; he used often to absent himself, and he was greatly delighted whenever I agreed to partake with him in a slight luncheon at one, to take a long walk into the country, and to return after dark to tea and supper in his rooms.   On one of these expeditions we wandered farther than usual, without regarding the distance or the lapse of time ; but we had no difficulty in finding our way home, for the night was clear and frosty, and the moon at the full ; and most glorious was the spectacle as we approached the City of Colleges, and passed through the silent streets.   It was near ten when we entered our college ; not only was it too late for tea, but supper was ready, the cloth laid, and the table spread. A large dish of scalloped oysters had been set within the fender, to be kept hot for the famished wanderers.

Among the innumerable contradictions in the character and deportment of the youthful poet was a strange mixture of a singular grace, which manifested itself in his actions and gestures, with an occasional awkwardness almost as remarkable. As soon as we entered the room, he placed his chair as usual directly in front of the fire, and eagerly pressed forward to warm himself, for the frost was severe, and he was very sensible of cold. Whilst cowering over the fire and rubbing his hands, he abruptly set both his feet at once upon the edge of the fender; it immediately flew up, threw under the grate the dish, which was broken into two pieces, and the whole of the delicious mess was mingled with the cinders and ashes, that had accumulated for several hours. It was impossible that a hungry and frozen pedestrian should restrain a strong expression of indignation, or that he should forbear, notwithstanding the exasperation of cold and hunger, from smiling and forgiving the accident at seeing the whimsical air and aspect of the offender, as he held up with the shovel the long-anticipated food, deformed by ashes, coals, and cinders, with a ludicrous expression of exaggerated surprise, disappointment, and contrition.

Our supper had disappeared under the grate, but we were able to silence the importunity of hunger. As the supply of cheese was scanty, Shelley pretended, in order to atone for his carelessness, that he never ate it; but I refused to take more than my share, and notwithstanding his reiterated declarations, that it was offensive to his palate and hurtful to his stomach, as I was inexorable, he devoured the remainder, greedily swallowing not merely the cheese, but the rind also, after scraping it cursorily, and with a curious tenderness. A tankard of the stout brown ale of our college aided us greatly in removing the sense of cold, and in supplying the deficiency of food, so that we turned our chairs towards the fire, and began to brew our negus as cheerfully as if the bounty of the hospitable gods had not been intercepted.

We reposed ourselves after the fatigue of an unusually long walk, and silence was broken. by short remarks only, and at considerable intervals, respecting the beauty of moonlight scenes, and especially of that we had just enjoyed ; the serenity and clearness of the night exceeded any we had before witnessed ; the light was so strong it would have been easy to read or write. " How strange it was, that light proceeding from the sun, which was at such a prodigious distance, and at that time entirely out of sight, should be reflected from the moon, and that was no trifling journey, and sent back to the earth in such abundance, and with so great force ! "

Languid expressions of admiration dropped from our lips, as we stretched our stiff and wearied limbs towards the genial warmth of a blazing fire. On a sudden, Shelley started from his seat, seized one of the candles, and began to walk about the room on tiptoe in profound silence, often stooping low, and evidently engaged in some mysterious search. I asked him what he wanted, but he returned no answer, and continued his whimsical and secret inquisition, which he prosecuted in the same extraordinary manner in the bed-room and the little study. It had occurred to him that a dessert had possibly been sent to his rooms whilst we were absent, and had been put away. He found the object of his pursuit at last, and pro-, duced some small dishes from the study; apples, oranges, almonds and raisins, and a little cake. These he set close together at my side of the table, without speaking, but with a triumphant look, yet with the air of a penitent making restitution and reparation, and then resumed his seat. The unexpected succor was very seasonable ; this light fare, a few glasses of negus, warmth, and especially rest, restored our lost vigor, and our spirits.

Adventure with an Ass.

We were walking one afternoon in Bagley Wood ; on turning a corner, we suddenly came upon a boy who was driving an ass. It was very young, and very weak, and was staggering beneath a most disproportionate load of fagots, and he was belaboring its lean ribs angrily and violently with a short, thick, heavy cudgel.

At the sight of cruelty Shelley was instantly transported far beyond the usual measure of excitement : he sprang forward, and was about to interpose with energetic and indignant vehemence.   I caught him by the arm, and to his present annoyance held him back, and with much difficulty persuaded him to allow me to be the advocate of the dumb animal.   His cheeks glowed with displeasure, and his lips murmured his impatience during my brief dialogue with the young tyrant.

" That is a sorry little ass, boy," I said ; " it seems to have scarcely any strength."

" None at all ; it is good for nothing."

" It cannot get on ; it can hardly stand ; if anybody could make it go, you would ; you have taken great pains with it."

" Yes, I have ; but it is to no purpose ! "

" It is of little use striking it, I think."

" It is not worth beating ; the stupid beast has got more wood now than it can carry ; it can hardly stand, you see ! "

" I suppose it put it upon its back itself ? "

The boy was silent : I repeated the question.

" No ; it has not sense enough for that," he replied, with an incredulous leer.

By dint of repeated blows he had split one end of his cudgel, and the sound caused by the divided portion had alarmed Shelley's humanity ; I pointed to it and said, " You have split your stick ; it is not good for much now."

He turned it, and held the divided end in his hand.

" The other end is whole, I see ; but I suppose you could split that too on the ass's back, if you chose ; it is not so thick."

" It is not so thick, but it is full of knots ; it would take a great deal of trouble to split it, and the beast is not worth that ; it would do no good ! "

" It would do no good, certainly ; and if anybody saw you, he might say that you were a savage young ruffian, and that you ought to be served in the same manner yourself."

The fellow looked at me with some surprise, and sank into sullen silence.

He presently threw his cudgel into the wood as far as he was able, and began to amuse himself by pelting the birds with pebbles, leaving my long-eared client to proceed at its own pace, having made up his mind, perhaps, to be beaten himself, when he reached home, by a tyrant still more unreasonable than himself, on account of the inevitable default of his ass.

Shelley was satisfied with the result of our conversation, and I repeated to him the history of the injudicious and unfortunate interference of Don Quixote between the peasant, John Haldudo, and his servant, Andrew. Although he reluctantly admitted that the acrimony of humanity might often aggravate the sufferings of the oppressed by provoking the oppressor, I always observed, that the impulse of generous indignation, on witnessing the infliction of pain, was too vivid to allow him to pause and consider the probable consequences of the abrupt interposition of the knight errantry, which would at once redress all grievances. Such exquisite sensibility and a sympathy with suffering so acute and so uncontrolled may possibly be inconsistent with the calmness and forethought of the philosopher, but they accord well with the high temperature of a poet's blood.

SHELLEY AS A READER.

No student ever read more assiduously. He was to be found, book in hand, at all hours; reading in season and out of season; at table, in bed, and especially during a walk; not only in the quiet country, and in retired paths; not only at Oxford, in the public walks, and High Street, but in the most crowded thoroughfares of London. Nor was he less absorbed by the volume that was open before him, in Cheapside, in Cranbourne Alley, or in Bond Street, than in a lonely lane, or a secluded library.

Sometimes a vulgar fellow would attempt to insult or annoy the eccentric student in passing. Shelley always avoided the malignant interruption by stepping aside with his vast and quiet agility.

Sometimes I have observed, as an agreeable contrast to these wretched men, that persons of the humblest station have paused and gazed with respectful wonder as he advanced, almost unconscious of the throng, stooping low, with bent knees and outstretched neck, poring earnestly over the volume, which he extended before him : for they knew this, although the simple people knew but little, that an ardent scholar is worthy of deference, and that the man of learning is necessarily the friend of humanity, and especially of the many. I never beheld eyes that devoured the pages more voraciously than his : I am convinced that two-thirds of the period of day and night were often employed in reading. It is no exaggeration to affirm, that out of the twenty-four hours, he frequently read sixteen. At Oxford, his diligence in this respect was exemplary, but it greatly increased afterwards, and I sometimes thought that he carried it to a pernicious excess : I am sure, at least, that I was unable to keep pace with him.

On the evening of a wet day, when we had read with scarcely any intermission from an early hour in the morning, I have urged him to lay aside his book. It required some extravagance to rouse him to join heartily in conversation ; to tempt him to avoid the chimney-piece, on which commonly he had laid the open volume.

"If I were to read as long as you read, Shelley, my hair and my teeth would be strewed about on the floor, and my eyes would slip down my cheeks into my waistcoat pockets ; or at least I should become so weary and nervous that I should not know whether it were so or not."

He began to scrape the carpet with his feet, as if teeth were actually lying upon it, and he looked fixedly at my face, and his lively fancy represented the empty sockets ; his imagination was excited, and the spell that bound him to his books was broken, and, creeping close to the fire, and, as it were, under the fire-place, he commenced a most animated discourse. Few were aware of the extent, and still fewer, I apprehend, of the profundity of his reading ; in his short life, and without ostentation, he had, in truth, read more Greek than many an aged pedant, who, with pompous parade, prides himself upon this study alone. Although he had not entered critically into the minute niceties of the noblest of languages, he was thoroughly conversant with the valuable matter it contains. A pocket edition of Plato, of Plutarch, of Euripides, without interpretation or notes, or of the Septuagint, was his ordinary companion; and he read the text straightforward for hours, if not as readily as an English author, at least with as much facility as French, Italian, or Spanish.

"Upon my soul, Shelley, your style of going through a Greek book is something quite beautiful!" was the wondering exclamation of one who was himself no mean student.

SHELLEY'S DIETETICS.

Bread became his chief sustenance, when his regimen attained to that austerity which afterwards distinguished it. He could have lived on bread alone without repining. When he was walking in London with an acquaintance, he would suddenly run into a baker's shop, purchase a supply, and breaking a loaf, he would offer half of it to his companion.

"Do you know," he said to me one day, with much surprise, "that such an one does not like bread? Did you ever know a person who disliked bread?" and he told me that a friend had refused such an offer.

I explained to him, that the individual in question probably had no objection to bread in a moderate quantity, at a proper time and with the usual adjuncts, and was only unwilling to devour two or three pounds of dry bread in the streets, and at an early hour.

Shelley had no such scruple; his pockets were generally well-stored with bread. A circle upon the carpet, clearly defined by an ample verge of crumbs, often marked the place where he had long sat at his studies, his face nearly in contact with his book, greedily devouring bread at intervals amidst his profound abstractions. For the most part he took no condiment; sometimes, however, he ate with his bread the common raisins which are used in making puddings, and these he would buy at little mean shops.

He was walking one day in London with a respectable solicitor, who occasionally transacted business for him; with his accustomed precipitation he suddenly vanished, and as suddenly reappeared; he had entered the shop of a little grocer in an obscure quarter, and had returned with some plums, which he held close under the attorney's nose, and the man of fact was as much astonished at the offer, as his client, the man of fancy, at the refusal.

The common fruit of stalls, and oranges and apples, were always welcome to Shelley; he would crunch the latter as heartily as a schoolboy. Vegetables, and especially salads, and pies and puddings, were acceptable: his beverage consisted of copious and frequent draughts of cold water, but tea was ever grateful, cup after cup, and coffee. Wine was taken with singular moderation, commonly diluted largely with water, and for a long period he would abstain from it altogether; he avoided the use of spirits almost invariably, and even in the most minute portions.

Like all persons of simple tastes, he retained his sweet tooth; he would greedily eat cakes, ginger-bread, and sugar; honey, preserved or stewed fruit, with bread, were his favorite delicacies, these he thankfully and joyfully received from others, but he rarely sought for them, or provided them for himself. The restraint and protracted duration of a convivial meal were intolerable; he was seldom able to keep his seat during the brief period assigned to an ordinary family dinner.

Shelley the Atheist.

One morning, a few days after I made Shelley's acquaintance, I was at his rooms, and we were reading together, two Etonians called on him, as they were wont to do; they remained a short time conversing with him.

"Do you mean to be an Atheist here, too, Shelley?" one of them inquired.

"No!" he answered, "certainly not. There is no motive

for it; there would be no use in it; they are very civil to us here; they never interfere with us; it is not like Eton."

To this they both assented. When his visitors were gone, I asked him what they meant. He told me that at Eton he had been called Shelley the Atheist; and he explained to me the true signification of the epithet. This is the substance of his explanation :—

All persons who are familiar with public schools, are well aware that there is a set of nicknames, many of them denoting offices, as the Pope, the Bishop, the Major, the General, the Governor, and the like, and these are commonly filled by successive generations. At Eton, but at no other school, that I ever heard of, they had the name and office of Atheist; but this usually was not full, it demanded extraordinary daring to attain to it; it was commonly in commission, as it were, and the youths of the greatest hardihood might be considered as boys commissioners for executing the office of Lord High Atheist.

Shelley's predecessor had filled the office some years before his time; he also was called Blank the Atheist, we must say, for I have forgotten his name. The act of Atheism, in virtue of which he obtained the title, was gross, flagrant, and down-right.

A huge bunch of grapes, richly gilded, hung in front of " The Christopher," as the sign, or in aid of the sign, of the inn. This the profane young wretch took down one dark winter's night, and suspended at the door of the head-master of his day. In the morning, when he rushed out in the twilight to go to chapel, being habitually too late, and always in a hurry, he ran full butt against the bunch of grapes, which was at least as big as himself, a little man. From this it is evident that the word Atheist was used by the learned at Eton, not in a modern, but in an ancient and classical sense, meaning an Antitheist, rather than an Atheist; for an opposer and con-temner of the gods, not one who denies their existence.

Two or three Eton boys called another day, and begged their former schoolfellow to curse his father and the king, as

he used occasionally to do at school. Shelley refused, and for
some time persisted in his refusal, saying that he had left it off;
but as they continued to urge him, by reason of their importunity
he suddenly broke out, and delivered, with vehemence and animation, a string of execrations, greatly resembling in its absurdity a papal anathema; the fulmination soon terminated in a
hearty laugh in which we all joined. When we were alone, I
said :

" Why, you young reprobate, who in the world taught you to
curse your father—your own father ? "

" My grandfather, Sir Bysshe, partly; but principally my
friend, Dr. Lind, at Eton. When anything goes wrong at
Field Place, my father does nothing but swear all day long
afterwards. Whenever I have gone with my father to visit Sir
Bysshe, he always received him with a tremendous oath, and
continued to heap curses upon his head so long as he remained
in the room."

Sir Bysshe being Ogygian, gouty, and bed-ridden, the poor
old baronet had become excessively testy and irritable; and a
request for money instantly aggravated and inflamed every
symptom, moved his choler, and stirred up his bile, impelling
him irresistibly to alleviate his sufferings by the roundest
oaths.

SHELLEY'S EARLY WRITINGS.

[The exact order of publication of Shelley's earliest attempts
at authorship has not been ascertained. Three were issued in
1810, *ie.*, *Zastrozzi*, *Victor and Cazire*, and *Posthumous
Fragments of Margaret Nicholson*. *Zastrozzi* was written
while he was at Eton, if the memory of one of his schoolfellows
is to be trusted : " Among my latest recollections of Shelley's
life at Eton is the publication of *Zastrozzi*, for which I think he
received 40*l*. With part of the proceeds he gave a most magnificent banquet to eight of his friends, among whom I was included. I cannot now call to mind the names of the other
guests, excepting those of two or three who are not now living."
Shelley gave a banquet at Eton no doubt, but that any

publisher gave him 40*l.* for the copyright of *Zastrozzi*, is incredible; it would have been dear at 40 shillings.

No copy of *Victor and Cazire* is known to exist, but we are not without knowledge concerning it, as well as Shelley's second romance, *St. Irvyne; or, the Rosicrucian.* Both were published by J. J. Stockdale, a London bookseller of no note, who published his reminiscences of Shelley in a weekly *Budget*, edited by him in 1826–27. They are given below.]

STOCKDALE'S RECOLLECTIONS OF SHELLEY.

The unfortunate subject of these very slight recollections introduced himself to me early in the autumn of 1810. He was extremely young; I should think he did not look more than eighteen. With anxiety in his countenance, he requested me to extricate him from a pecuniary difficulty, in which he was involved with a printer, whose name I cannot call to mind, but who resided at Horsham, near to which Timothy Shelley, Esq., M.P., afterwards I believe made a baronet, the father of our poet, had a seat called Field Place. I am not quite certain how the difference between the poet and the printer was arranged ; but, after I had looked over the account, I know that it was paid : though, whether I assisted in the payment by money or acceptance, I cannot remember. Be that as it may, on the 17th September, 1810, I received fourteen hundred and eighty copies of a thin royal 8vo volume, in sheets, and not gathered. It was entitled " Original Poetry, by Alonzo and Cazire,"* or two names, something like them. The author told me that the poems were the joint production of himself and a friend, whose name was forgotten by me as soon as I heard it. I advertised the work, which was to be retailed at 3s. 6d., in nearly all the London papers of the

---

* In *The Morning Post* of September 19th, 1810, is the following advertisement;

"*This day is Published, in royal 8vo., price 4s., in boards,*
ORIGINAL POETRY,
BY VICTOR AND CAZIRE,
Sold by Stockdale, Junior, No. 41, Pall Mall."

day, seventeen in number; but I was told that, though paid
for, it did not appear in the *Times.* * In many papers, however, I saw it.   I am only particular on this point, because few,
if any, were sold in consequence, as I intimated was not un-
likely to be the case ; though, even from these boyish trifles,
assisted by my personal intercourse with the author, I at once
formed the opinion that he was not an every-day character.

In the various wrecks, to which my property has been subjected, I have recovered none of Mr. Shelley's letters, previous
to September, 1810 ; though I attach little interest to them,
beyond their having emanated from such a pen.

"FIELD PLACE, *September 6th,* 1810.

"SIR,—I have to return you my thankful acknowledgment

---

* "This omission, of which Stockdale had no doubt, was, he considers, done designedly. In this supposition the publisher must have had a consciousness that at
some period of his career a certain watchfulness and caution were occasionally exercised in the offices of respectable journals before advertisements from the house of
'Stockdale Junior' were given to the public. This, however, refers to a later stage
of his business. In 1810 he had not commenced that downward course that ended in
his ruin. For more than half a century the house of Stockdale had been an eminent
one. The elder Stockdale and his sons had carried on a respectable and extensive
business in Piccadilly before and after John Joseph had set up for himself in Pall
Mall. Theology, history, and fiction issued continually under their name. They
were in great request among amateur poets and poetesses, who, if they could 'write,'
could also pay 'with ease.' The lady song-birds flocked to them by hundreds. I
have seen a large collection of poetical works written exclusively by women, the
greater part of which was published by the Stockdales. Among these was Mary
Stockdale's *Effusions of the Heart*, a volume published in 1790, by her father,
John Stockdale.

The house being thus established for the production of this not very dangerous class
of literature, the statement that an advertisement of a harmless book of juvenile
poetry like *Victor and Cazire* was deliberately suppressed by *The Times* seemed
very improbable. An examination of the file of *The Times* for 1810 removed all
doubt upon the point. Mr. Garnett had found in *The Morning Chronicle* of September 18th an advertisement of the volume, but twenty-four days later—that is, on
Friday, October 12th—*The Times* contains the following :—

"In royal 8vo, price 4s. boards, ORIGINAL POETRY. By VICTOR and CAZIRE.
Sold by Stockdale Jun., 41, Pall Mall."

This is important as showing that the volume was on sale for more than a fortnight
longer than Stockdale remembered it to have been. In that time some additional
copies were doubtless sent out for review, or presented by the author and publisher to
their friends, thus increasing the probabilities that this very interesting volume may yet
be found."—*MacCarthy.*

for the receipt of the books, which arrived as soon as I had
any reason to expect. The superfluity shall be balanced as
soon as I pay for some books which I shall trouble you to bind
for me.

"I enclose you the title-page of the Poems, which, as you
see, you have mistaken on account of the illegibility of my
handwriting. I have had the last proof impression from my
printer this morning, and I suppose the execution of the work
will not be long delayed. As soon as it possibly can, it shall
reach you, and believe me, sir, grateful for the interest you
take in it.

"I am, sir,
"Your obedient humble servant,
"PERCY B. SHELLEY."

Some short time after the announcement of his poems I happened to be perusing them with more attention than I had, till
then, had leisure to bestow upon them, when I recognized in
the collection one which I knew to have been written by
Mr. M. G. Lewis, the author of "The Monk," and I fully
anticipated the probable vexation of the juvenile-maiden-
author, when I communicated my discovery to Mr. P. B.
Shelley.

With all the ardor incidental to his character, which em-
braced youthful honor in all its brilliancy, he expressed the
warmest resentment at the imposition practised upon him by
his coadjutor, and entreated me to destroy all the copies,
of which I may say that, through the author and me, about
one hundred, in the whole, have been put into circulation.
Notwithstanding their comparative demerits, this information may give them value in the eyes of their possessors,
and must have the charm of novelty, perhaps, to all my
readers.

In due course I received the following epistle, including one,
which is subjoined, from Messrs. Ballantyne and Co. The
letters, I should premise, are transcribed literally, in every
particular.

"FIELD PLACE, *September 28th*, 1810.

"SIR,—I sent, before I had the pleasure of knowing you, the MSS. of a poem to Messrs. Ballantyne and Co. Edinburgh ; they have declined publishing it, with the enclosed letter. I now offer it to you, and depend upon your honour as a gentleman for a fair price for the copyright. It will be sent to you from Edinburgh. The subject is, ' The Wandering Jew.' As to its containing atheistical principles, I assure you I was wholly unaware of the fact hinted at. Your good sense will point out to you the impossibility of inculcating pernicious doctrines in a poem which, as you will see, is so totally abstract from any circumstances which occur under the possible view of mankind.

" I am, sir,
" Your obliged and humble servant,

" PERCY B. SHELLEY.

" Mr. Stockdale, Bookseller, 41, Pall Mall, London."

[Enclosed in the above was the following letter from Messrs. Ballantyne to Shelley :—]

"EDINBURGH, *September 24th*, 1810.

" SIR,—The delay which has occurred in our reply to you respecting the poem you have obligingly offered us for publication, has arisen from our literary friends and advisers (at least such as we have confidence in) being in the country at this season, as is usual, and the time they have bestowed in its perusal.

" We are extremely sorry, at length, after the most mature deliberation, to be under the necessity of declining the honour of being the publishers of the present poem ;—not that we doubt its success; but that it is, perhaps, better suited to the character and liberal feeling of the English, than the bigoted spirit which yet pervades many cultivated minds in this country. Even Walter Scott is assailed on all hands at present, by our Scotch spiritual and evangelical magazines and instructors, for having promulgated atheistical doctrines in the ' Lady of the Lake.'

" We beg you will have the goodness to advise us how it

should be returned, and we think its being consigned to the care of some person in London would be more likely to ensure its safety than addressing it to Horsham.

"We are, sir,

"Your most obedient humble servants,

"JOHN BALLANTYNE & CO."

It should be observed that Mr. Shelley, having found from my conversation that I was not likely to publish any work against religion, disavowed that imputation on his poem, which, though long expected, did not arrive. On the 13th November, 1810, as I find by my own endorsement, I received a letter which, with his desire to have other books of a similar tendency (Godwin's Political Justice, &c.) satisfied me that he was in a situation of impending danger, from which the most friendly and cautious prudence alone could withdraw him. The letter was as follows :

"OXFORD, *Sunday, November 11th,* 1810.

"SIR,—I wish you to obtain for me a book which answers to the following description. It is an Hebrew essay, demonstrating that the Christian religion is false, and is mentioned in one of the numbers of the *Christian Observer* of last spring, by a clergyman, as an unanswerable, yet sophistical argument. If it is translated in Greek, Latin, or any of the European languages, I would thank you to send it to me.

"I am, sir, your humble servant,

"PERCY B. SHELLEY."

I was at this time not a little confirmed in my apprehensions by perusing his manuscript of *St. Irvyne, the Rosicrucian,* which I promised to revise and print for him. His ardent mind, and somewhat natural haughtiness of disposition, rendered him very impatient of control. He also knew, as his father told me, that he would inherit from his grandfather an estate of £5000 a-year, which would be wholly at his own disposal. His

3

father did not appear to me, in the few conversations I had
with him in my shop, to be particularly bright, though he did
seem, as I thought, inclined to exercise the parental authority
with most injudicious despotism. I was not long in discover-
ing that be kept his son very short of money, and that he was
especially desirous of wielding the power of a father, while his
son was too little inclined to submit his own superior talents,
natural and acquired, to the harsh orders of a mind utterly inadequate to such an office. The consequence was that a
mutual disposition to irritation and obstinacy produced mutual
resistance and distrust, if not dislike and alienation. These
details I give wholly from memory. I must continue Mr.
Shelley's letters.

"UNIVERSITY COLLEGE, *November 14th,* 1810.

"DEAR SIR,—I return you the romance by this day's coach.
I am much obligated by the trouble you have taken to fit it for
the press.   I am myself by no means a good hand at correction,
but I think I have obviated the principal objections which you
allege.

"Ginotti, as you will see, did *not* die by Wolfstein's hand,
but by the influence of that natural magic which, when the
secret was imparted to the latter, destroyed him. Mountfort
being a character of inferior import, I did not think it necessary to state the catastrophe of *him*, as at best it could be
but uninteresting. Eloise and Fitzeustace are married, and
happy, I suppose, and Megalena dies by the same means
as Wolfstein. I do not myself see any other explanation that
is required. As to the method of publishing it, I think, as
it is a thing which almost *mechanically* sells to circulating
libraries, &c., I would wish it to be published on my *own*
account.

"I am surprised that you have not received the 'Wandering
Jew,' and in consequence write to Mr. Ballantyne to mention
it; you will doubtlessly, therefore, receive it soon.—Should
you still perceive in the romance any error of flagrant incoher-

ency, &c., it must be altered, but I should conceive it will (being wholly so abrupt) not require it.

> "I am,
> "Your sincere humble servant,
> "PERCY B. SHELLEY.

"Shall you make this in one or two volumes? Mr. Robinson, of Paternoster Row, published 'Zastrozzi.'"

"UNI. COLL., *Monday* [*19th Nov.*, 1810].

"MY DEAR SIR,—I did not think it possible that the romance would make but one small volume. It will at all events be larger than 'Zastrozzi.' What I mean as 'Rosicrucian' is, the elixir of eternal life which Ginotti had obtained. Mr. Godwin's romance of 'St. Leon' turns upon that superstition. I enveloped it in mystery for the greater excitement of interest, and, on a re-examination, you will perceive that Mountfort physically did kill Ginotti, which must appear from the latter's paleness.

"Will you have the goodness to send me Mr. Godwin's 'Political Justice?'

"When do you suppose 'St. Irvyne' will be out? If you have not yet got the 'Wandering Jew' from Mr. B., I will send you a MSS. copy which I possess.

> "Yours sincerely,
> "P. B. SHELLEY.

"Mr. Stockdale, Bookseller, 41, Pall Mall, London."

"OXFORD, *Dec. 2d*, 1810.

"DEAR SIR,—Will you, if you have got two copies of the 'Wandering Jew,' send one of them to me, as I have thought of some corrections which I wish to make? Your opinion on it will likewise much oblige me.

"When do you suppose that Southey's 'Curse of Kehama' will come out? I am curious to see it, and when *does* 'St. Irvyne' come out?

" I shall be in London the middle of this month, when I will do myself the pleasure of calling on you.

" Yours sincerely,

" P. B. SHELLEY.

" Mr. Stockdale, Bookseller, 41, Pall Mall, London."

"FIELD PLACE, *Dec.* 18th, 1810.

" MY DEAR SIR,—I saw your advertisement of the Romance, and approve of it highly; it is likely to excite curiosity. I would thank you to send copies directed as follows :—

Miss Marshall, Horsham, Sussex.

T. Medwin, Esq., Horsham, Sussex.

T. J. Hogg, Esq., Rev.—Dayrell's, Lynnington Dayrell, Buckingham,

and six copies to myself. In case the ' *Curse of Kehama* ' has yet appeared, I would thank you for that likewise. I have in preparation a novel; it is principally constructed to convey metaphysical and political opinions by way of conversation. It shall be sent to you as soon as completed, but it shall receive more correction than I trouble myself to give to wild romance and poetry.

" Mr. Munday, of Oxford,* will take some romances; I do not know whether he sends directly to you, or through the medium of some other bookseller. I will enclose the printer's account for your inspection in a future letter.

Dear sir,

Yours sincerely,

" Mr. Stockdale.   P. B. SHELLEY."

" FIELD PLACE, 23rd *Dec.* 1810.

" SIR,—I take the earliest opportunity of expressing to you my best thanks for the very liberal and handsome manner in which you imparted to me the sentiments you held towards my son, and the open and friendly communication.

" I shall ever esteem it, and hold it in remembrance. I will

---

* The publisher of *Margaret Nicholson.*

take an opportunity of calling on you again, when the call at St. Stephen's Chapel enforces my attendance by a call of the House.

" My son begs to make his compliments to you.

" I have the honor to be, sir,
" Your very obedient humble servant,

" Mr. Stockdale.   T. SHELLEY."

" *January* 11*th*, 1811.

" DEAR SIR,—I would thank you to send a copy of ' St. Irvyne' to Miss Harriet Westbrook, 10, Chapel Street, Grosvenor Square. In the course of a fortnight I shall do myself the pleasure of calling on you. With respect to the printer's bill, I made him explain the distinctions of the costs, which I hope are intelligible.

" Do you find that the public are captivated by the title-page of ' St. Irvyne ? '

" Your sincere

" Mr. Stockdale.   P. B. SHELLEY."

About this time not merely slight hints, but constant allusions, personally and by letters, which are mislaid, lost, or destroyed, rendered me extremely uneasy respecting Mr. Shelley's religious or indeed irreligious sentiments, towards which all his conversation, reading, and pursuits clearly tended. I felt certain that *The Wandering Jew* had disclosed such sentiments as had excited Ballantyne's alarm, which I much regretted having been expressed in a way far from discouraging to their promulgation. It is singular that, after all, the poem of *The Wandering Jew* never reached my hands, nor have I either seen or heard of it, from that time.

I was more decided than ever that Shelley had some companions, who pandered to his unhappy predisposition against revealed religion. I had already given some delicate hints on that subject to his father, who was not the quickest in the world at comprehending anything less conspicuous than a pike-staff. I had told him what my own mode of action would have been towards a son so wretchedly deluded. But I could make very little way. Notwithstanding his father had expressed such delight and obligation for the interest I had given proofs of feeling for his son, when, by the appearance of St. Irvyne, he found that his son had probably incurred some expense, for which he knew that he must stand indebted to me, he told me that he was not of age, and that he, his father, would never pay a farthing of it. I repeated my expressions (and they really emanated from my heart) of the fullest assurance of his son's honor and rectitude, and my conviction that he would vegetate, rather than live, to effect the discharge of every honest claim upon him. I will now repeat that such opinion has not been shaken, although I have never received, directly or indirectly, one farthing of my just claim, which, principal and interest together, cannot be less than £300.

Young Mr. Shelley's readiness in conceding his opinion to me, even on his most enthusiastic topics, convinced me, as I strove to explain to his father, that a sound, steady friend, who would enter into his son's feelings with correspondent warmth might (&c). I was too fatally convinced that all my efforts had been vain ; and that the work of the destroyer was in active operation by the very means which I had, in such good time, suggested for, shall I not say his salvation.

Mr. Jefferson Hogg had called upon me occasionally, as Mr. Bysshe Shelley's friend, at his request ; but I really did not credit that, with, as I thought, a mind so infinitely beneath that of his friend, he could be the master spirit to lead him astray ; but seeing, by Mr. Hogg's address, that he was connected, in some way, with the worthy Rev. John Dayrell, of Lynnington Dayrell, not far from my wife's native place, and that Shelley was unquestionably in a most devious path, I inquired of Mrs. Stockdale's possible knowledge of him.

Mrs. Stockdale's recollection and inquiry left no doubt on my mind that if I did not rush forward, and, however rudely, pull my young candidate for the bays from the precipice, over which he was suspended by a hair, his fate must be inevitable.

Shelley had informed me, either verbally, or by letter, or,

not improbably, by both, of his having completed a metaphysical essay, in support of Atheism, and which he intended to promulgate throughout the university. I represented that his expulsion would be the inevitable consequence of so flagrant an insult to such a body. He however, was unmoved, and I instantly wrote to his father explicitly enough for any other person than himself.

"OXFORD, *28th of January*, 1811.

"SIR,—On my arrival at Oxford, my friend Mr. Hogg communicated to me the letters which passed in consequence of your misrepresentations of his character, the abuse of that confidence which he invariably reposed in you. I now, sir, desire to know whether you mean the evasions in your first letter to Mr. Hogg, your insulting *attempt* at coolness in your second, as a means of escaping *safely* from the opprobrium naturally attached to so ungentlemanlike an abuse of confidence (to say nothing of misrepresentations) as that which my father communicated to me, or as a *denial* of the fact of having acted in this unprecedented, this *scandalous* manner. If the former be your intention, I will compassionate your cowardice, and my friend, pitying your *weakness*, will take no further notice of your contemptible *attempts* at calumny. If the latter is your intention, I feel it my duty to declare, as my veracity and that of my father is thereby called in question, that I will never be satisfied, despicable as I may consider the author of that affront, until my friend has ample apology for the injury you have *attempted* to do him. I expect an immediate, and *demand* a satisfactory letter.

"Sir, I am,
"Your obedient and humble servant,
"PERCY B. SHELLEY.
"Mr. J. J. Stockdale, Bookseller, 41 Pall Mall, London."

"FIFLD PLACE, *30th of January*, 1811.

"SIR,—I am so surprised on the receipt of your letter of this morning, that I cannot comprehend the meaning of the language you use. I shall be in London next week, and will then call on you.

" I am, sir,
" Your obedient humble servant,
" T. SHELLEY.

" Mr. Stockdale, Bookseller, Pall Mall, London."

On Mr. Shelley's arrival in London, he called, agreeably to his promise, and I gave him such particulars as the urgency of the case required. The consequence was, as but too often happens, that all concerned became inimical to me. I had satisfied my own feelings at the expense of my purse ; and how much those feelings were aggravated by the arrival of news of the catastrophe which I had too truly predicted, I shall not attempt to describe. On Mr. Bysshe Shelley's arrival in London, he, on the 11th of April, wrote me the following brief letter, for we had already met for the last time.

" 15 POLAND STREET, OXFORD STREET.

" SIR,—Will you have the goodness to inform me of the number of copies which you have sold of ' St. Irvyne ' ? Circumstances may occur which will oblige me, in case of their event, to wish for my accounts suddenly ; perhaps you had better make them out.

" Sir,
" Your obedient humble servant,
" P. B. SHELLEY.

" Mr. Stockdale, 41 Pall Mall."

" SIR,—Your letter has at length reached me ; the remoteness of my present situation must apologize for my apparent neglect. I am sorry to say, in answer to your requisition, that the state of my finances render immediate payment perfectly impossible. It is my intention, at the earliest period of my power to do so, to discharge your account. I am aware of the imprudence of publishing a book so ill-digested as ' St. Irvyne ; ' but are there no expectations on the profits of its sale ?

My studies have, since my writing it, been of a more serious nature. I am at present engaged in completing a series of moral and metaphysical essays—perhaps their copyright would be accepted in lieu of part of my debt?

> " Sir, I have the honor to be,
> "Your very humble servant,
> " PERCY B. SHELLEY.

"CWMELAN, RHAYADER, RADNORSHIRE, *August 1st, 1811.*"

SHELLEY READING PLATO.

We are told in the editor's preface to the " Poetical Works of Shelley," that it was not until he resided in Italy that he made Plato his study. If it be meant, as no doubt it is, that he did not study Plato in the original, the assertion is correct. It would be absurd to affirm that a profound, accurate, critical knowledge of the author may be acquired through the medium of traslations, and at second-hand by abstracts and abridgments. But enough of the philosopher's doctrines and principles may be, and were, in fact, imbibed at Oxford, and at an early age, without consulting the Greek text to convince him of the incorrectness and inconclusiveness, of the dangers indeed, of the reasonings and conclusions of the school of Locke and his disciples. Many of the tenets of Plato, of Socrates their common master, are exhibited by Xenophon, whose writings we had already read in the original. The English version of the French translation by Dacier of the " Phædo," and several other dialogues of Plato, was the first book we had, and this we read together several times very attentively at Oxford. We had a French translation of the " Republic ; " and we perused with infinite pleasure the elegant translation of Floyer Sydenham. We had several of the publications of the learned and eccentric Platonist, Thomas Taylor. In truth, it would be tedious to specify and describe all the reflected lights borrowed from the great luminary, the sun of the Academy, that illumined the path of two young students. That Shelley had not read any portion of Plato in the original before he went to Italy, is not strictly true. He had a very legible

3*

edition of the Works of Plato in several volumes; a charming
edition, the Bipont, I think, and I have read passages out of it
with him. I remember going up to London with him from
Marlow one morning; he took a volume of Plato with him,
and we read a good deal of it together, sitting side by side on
the top of the coach. Phædrus, I am pretty sure, was the
dialogue—on beauty.

THE WANDERING JEW.

Before Shelley came to Oxford, he composed a tale, or a
fragment of a tale, on the subject of the Wandering Jew, giving
to him, however, the name of a Persian, not of a Jew—
Ahasuerus, Artaxerxes. This no learned, accurate German
would have done. That he found the composition in the streets
of London is an integral portion of the fiction. " This fragment is the translation of part of some German work, the title
of which I have vainly endeavored to discover. I picked it up,
dirty and torn, some years ago, in Lincoln's Inn Fields."

It is a common device to add to the interest of a romance by
asserting that the MS. was discovered in a cavern, in a casket;
that it had lain long hidden in an old chest, or a tomb. From
the preface of Dictys the Cretan, whose history of the Trojan
war was discovered, we are told, in Crete, the author's tomb
having been opened by an earthquake, down to the most modern fictions, this embellishment has been in constant use. Respecting the finding of this fragment, some have affirmed one
thing, and some another. It has been said that it was part of
a printed book in the German language. If it had been in
German, Shelley could not have translated it at that time, for
he did not know a word of German. The study of that tongue
—being both equally ignorant of it—we commenced together
in 1815. Of this our joint study hereafter. Somebody or other,
determined not to be left behind in the race, declares that he
found it himself, if I mistake not, and presented it to Shelley.
Was not this worthy gentleman also present at Gnossus when
the tablets of Dictys were brought to light by the earthquake?

A portion of the fragment has been printed in the notes to

"Queen Mab." I have amongst Shelley's papers a fragment of the fragment, in his handwriting. It is one leaf only, and it appears to be the last, the conclusion of the story. The last sentence has never been printed; it presents the narrative of the sufferings of Ahasuerus in a totally different point of view with reference to moral and religious considerations, and is therefore not undeserving attention.

Fragment of The Wandering Jew.

——did the elephant trample on me, in vain the iron hoof of the wrathful steed. The mine, big with destructive power, burst upon me and hurled me high in the air. I fell down upon a heap of smoking limbs, but was only singed. The giant's steel club rebounded from my body. The executioner's hand could not strangle me ; nor would the hungry lion in the circus devour me ; I cohabited with poisonous snakes ; I pinched the red crest of the dragon ; the serpent stung, but could not kill me ; the dragon tormented, but could not devour me. I now provoked the fury of tyrants. I said to Nero, " Thou art a bloodhound ; " said to Christern, " Thou art a bloodhound ; " said to Muley Ismail, " Thou art a bloodhound." The tyrants invented cruel torments, but could not kill me. Ha ! Not to be able to die ; *not to be permitted to rest after the toils of life ;* to be doomed for ever to be imprisoned in this *clay-formed* dungeon ; to be for ever clogged with this worthless body, its load of diseases and infirmities ; to be condemned to hold for millenniums that yawning monster, Time, that hungry hyena, ever bearing children, ever devouring again her offspring.

Ha ! Not to be permitted to die ! Awful Avenger in Heaven, hast Thou in Thine armoury of wrath a punishment more dreadful ? Then let it thunder upon me. Command a hurricane to sweep me down to the foot of Carmel, that I there may lie extended, may pant, and writhe, and die !

And Ahasuerus dropped down. Night covered his bristly eyelid. The Angel bore me back to the cavern. " Sleep here," said the Angel, " sleep in peace ; the wrath of thy Judge is appeased ; when thou shalt awake, He will be arrived, He whose blood thou sawest flow upon Golgotha. Whose mercy is extended even to thee!"

ROUGH DRAFT OF A POEM.

MY DEAR SIR,   LONDON, *May* 30, 1834.

I did not inquire, but, as you did not show it to me, I presume you do not possess in your inestimable collection the autograph of poor Shelley. I now send you a poem, or rather a rough draft of part of a poem, by his hand, and from his head and heart. The papers amongst which it was found, and other circumstances, lead me to believe that it was written in 1810, when the young poet was but seventeen or eighteen years old. It is doubtless unpublished, and of a more early date than any of his published poems; on all accounts, therefore, it is most interesting. I selected it for you soon after my return, but I mislaid it, and when I wrote to you the other day I could not find it. With kind regards to Mrs. Turner,

I am, &c.,
T. J. HOGG.

Dawson Turner, Esq.,
    Yarmouth.

DEATH.

> For my dagger is bathed in the blood of the brave,
> I come, care-worn tenant of life, from the grave,
> Where Innocence sleeps 'neath the peace-giving sod,
> And the good cease to tremble at Tyranny's nod;
> I offer a calm habitation to thee,
> Say, victim of grief, wilt thou slumber with me?
> My mansion is damp, cold silence is there,
> But it lulls in oblivion the fiends of despair,
> Not a groan of regret, not a sigh, not a breath,
> Dares dispute with grim silence the empire of Death.
> I offer a calm habitation to thee,
> Say, victim of grief, wilt thou slumber with me?

MORTAL.

> Mine eyelids are heavy: my soul seeks repose,
> It longs in thy cells to embosom its woes,
> It longs in thy cells to deposit its load,
> Where no longer the scorpions of Perfidy goad;

Where the phantoms of Prejudice vanish away,
And Bigotry's bloodhounds lose scent of their prey ;
Yet tell me, dark Death, when thine empire is o'er,
What awaits on Futurity's mist-covered shore?

DEATH.

Cease, cease, wayward Mortal ! I dare not unveil
The shadows that float on Eternity's vale ;
Nought waits for the good, but a spirit of Love,
That will hail their blest advent to regions above.
For Love, Mortal, gleams thro' the gloom of my sway,
And the shades which surround me fly fast at its ray.
Hast thou loved ?—Then depart from these regions of hate,
And in slumber with me blunt the arrows of fate.
I offer a calm habitation to thee,
Say, victim of grief, wilt thou slumber with me ?

MORTAL.

Oh ! sweet is thy slumber ! oh ! sweet is the ray
Which after thy night introduces the day ;
How concealed, how persuasive, self-interest's breath,
Tho' it floats to mine ear from the bosom of Death.
I hoped that I quite was forgotten by all,
Yet a lingering friend might be grieved at my fall,
And duty forbids, tho' I languish to die,
When departure might heave virtue's breast with a sigh.
Oh, Death ! oh, my friend ! snatch this form to thy shrine,
And I fear, dear destroyer, I shall not repine.

The following unfinished verses were written at Oxford ; they
have never been published.

Death ! where is thy victory ?
To triumph whilst I die,
To triumph whilst thine ebon wing
Infolds my shuddering soul.
Oh, Death ! where is thy sting ?
Not when the tides of murder roll,
When nations groan, that kings may bask in bliss.
Death ! canst thou boast a victory such as this ?
When in his hour of pomp and power
His blow the mightiest murders gave,
'Mid nature's cries the sacrifice
Of millions to glut the grave ;
When sunk the tyrant desolation's slave ;
Or Freedom's life-blood streamed upon thy shrine ;
Stern tyrant, couldst thou boast a victory such as mine ?

To know in dissolution's void,
  That mortals baubles sunk decay,
That everything, but Love, destroyed
  Must perish with its kindred clay.
    Perish Ambition's crown,
    Perish her sceptered sway;
From Death's pale front fades Pride's fastidious frown.
In Death's damp vault the lurid fires decay,
That Envy lights at heaven-born Virtue's beam—

    That all the cares subside,
    Which lurk beneath the tide
    Of life's unquiet stream.
    Yes! this is victory!
And on yon rock, whose dark form glooms the sky,
  To stretch these pale limbs, when the soul is fled;
To baffle the lean passions of their prey,
  To sleep within the palace of the dead!
Oh! not the King, around whose dazzling throne
His countless courtiers mock the words they say,
Triumphs amid the bud of glory blown,
As I in this cold bed, and faint expiring groan!

Tremble, ye proud, whose grandeur mocks the woe,
  Which props the column of unnatural state,
    You the plainings faint and low,
    From misery's tortured soul that flow,
      Shall usher to your fate.

Tremble, ye conquerors, at whose fell command
The war-fiend riots o'er a peaceful land.
    You desolation's gory throng
    Shall bear from Victory along
      To that mysterious strand.

A Poem by Shelley's Sister.

Cold, cold is the blast when December is howling,
  Cold are the damps on a dying man's brow.
Stern are the seas, when the wild waves are rolling,
  And sad the grave where a loved one lies low.
But colder is scorn from the being who loved thee,
  More stern is the sneer from the friend who has proved thee,
More sad are the tears when these sorrows have moved thee,
  Which mixed with groans, anguish, and wild madness flow.

And, ah! poor Louisa has felt all this horror;
  Full long the fallen victim contended with fate,
Till a destitute outcast, abandoned to sorrow,
  She sought her babe's food at her ruiner's gate.

Another had charmed the remorseless betrayer,
  He turned callous aside from her moan and her prayer,—
She said nothing, but wringing the wet from her hair,
  Crossed the dark mountain's side, tho' the hour it was late.

'Twas on the dark summit of huge Penmanmauer
  That the form of the wasted Louisa reclined;
She shrieked to the ravens that croaked from afar,
  And she sighed to the gusts of the wild-sweeping wind.
" I call not yon clouds, where the thunder-peals rattle,
I call not yon rocks, where the elements battle,
  But thee, perjured Henry, I call thee unkind ! "

Then she wreathed in her hair the wild flowers of the mountain,
  And, deliriously laughing, a garland entwined,
She bedewed it with tears, then she hung o'er the fountain,
  And, laving it, cast it a prey to the wind.
" Ah, go ! " she exclaimed, " where the tempest is yelling ;
  'Tis unkind to be cast on the sea that is swelling ;
But I left, a pitiless outcast, my dwelling ;
  My garments are torn—so, they say, is my mind."

Not long lived Louisa—but over her grave
  Waved the desolate form of a storm-blasted yew,
Around it no demons or ghosts dare to rave,
  But spirits of Peace steep her slumbers in dew.
Then stay thy swift steps 'mid the dark mountain heather
  Tho' chill blow the wind and severe be the weather,
For Perfidy, traveller, cannot bereave her
  Of the tears to the tombs of the innocent due !

Oh ! sweet is the moonbeam that sleeps on yon fountain,
  And sweet the mild rush of the soft-sighing breeze,
And sweet is the glimpse of yon dimly-seen mountain
  'Neath the verdant arcades of yon shadowy trees ;
But sweeter than all——

And ah ! she may envy the heart-shocked quarry,
  Who bids to the scenery of childhood farewell,
She may envy the bosom all bleeding and gory,
  She may envy the sound of the drear passing knell.
Not so deep are his woes on his death-couch reposing
  When on the last vision his dim eyes are closing,
As the outcast——

Those notes were so sad and so soft, that, ah ! never
  May the sound cease to vibrate on memory's ear !

Bysshe wrote down these verses for me at Oxford from
memory. I was to have a complete and more correct copy of

them some day. They were the composition of his sister Elizabeth, and he valued them highly as well as their author, with whom, except an occasional tiff, when she preferred less dry and abstruse matters to his ethical and metaphysical speculations, he agreed most affectionately, cordially, and perfectly. I was to undertake to fall in love with her ; if I did not I had no business to go to Field Place, and he would never forgive me. I promised to do my best ; and, probably, it would not have been difficult to have kept my promise, at least, in a poetical sense. For any one whose age, fortune, and inclinations disposed him to settle in life, it might have been very easy to fall in love in a more earnest and practical manner, for she was one of those young ladies who win golden opinions from all their acquaintance.

I often found Shelley reading " Gebir." There was something in that poem which caught his fancy. He would read it aloud, or to himself sometimes, with a tiresome pertinacity. One morning, I went to his rooms to tell him something of importance, but he would attend to nothing but " Gebir." With a young impatience, I snatched the book out of the obstinate fellow's hand, and threw it through the open window into the quadrangle. It fell upon the grass-plat, and was brought back presently by the servant. I related this incident, some years afterwards, and after the death of my poor friend, at Florence to the highly gifted author. He heard it with his hearty, cordial, genial laugh. " Well, you must allow it is something to have produced what could please one fellow creature and offend another so much."

SHELLEY AS A LATINIST.

He composed Latin verses with singular facility. On visiting him soon after his arrival at the accustomed hour of one, he was writing the usual exercise which we presented, I believe, once a week—a Latin translation of a paper in the Spectator. He soon finished it, and as he held it before the fire to dry, I offered to take it from him ; he said it was not worth looking at ; but as I persisted, through a certain scholastic curiosity to examine the Latinity of my new acquaintance, he gave it to me. The Latin was sufficiently correct, but the version was paraphrastic, which I observed ; he assented, and said that it would pass muster, and he felt no interest in such efforts, and no desire to excel in them. I also noticed many portions of heroic verses, and even several entire verses, and these I pointed out as defects in a prose composition. He smiled archly, and asked, in his piercing whisper—"Do you think they will observe them ? I inserted them intentionally to try their ears ! I once showed up a theme at Eton to old Keate, in which there were a great many verses ; but he observed them, scanned them, and asked why I had introduced them ? I answered, that I did not know they were there ; this was partly true and partly false ; but he believed me, and immediately applied to me the line, in which Ovid says of himself—

'Et quod tentabam dicere, versus erat.' "

Shelley then spoke of the facility with which he could compose Latin verses ; and, taking the paper ont of my hand, he began to put the entire translation into verse. He would sometimes open at hazard a prose writer, as Livy, or Sallust, and by changing the position of the words, and occasionally substituting others, he would transmute several sentences from prose to verse—to heroic, or more commonly elegiac, verse, for he was peculiarly charmed with the graceful and easy flow of the latter—with surprising rapidity and readiness. He was fond of displaying this accomplishment during his residence at Oxford, but he forgot to bring it away with him when he quitted the University ; or perhaps he left it behind him designedly, as being suitable to academic groves only and to the banks of the Isis.

SHELLEY AND HIS NEW SUIT.

I was surprised at the contrast between the general indifference of Shelley for the mechanical arts, and his intense admiration of a particular application of one of them the first time I noticed the latter peculiarity. During our residence at Oxford,

I repaired to his rooms one morning at the accustomed hour, and I found a tailor with him. He had expected to receive a new coat on the preceding evening; it was not sent home, and he was mortified, I know not why, for he was commonly altogether indifferent about dress, and scarcely appeared to distinguish one coat from another. He was now standing erect in the middle of the room in his new blue coat, with all its glittering buttons, and to atone for the delay, the tailor was loudly extolling the beauty of the cloth and the felicity of the fit; his eloquence had not been thrown away upon his customer, for never was man more easily persuaded than the master of persuasion. The man of thimbles applied to me to vouch his eulogies; I briefly assented to them. He withdrew, after some bows, and Shelley, snatching his hat, cried with shrill impatience :

"Let us go!"

"Do you mean to walk in the fields in your new coat?" I asked.

"Yes, certainly," he answered, and we sallied forth.

We sauntered for a moderate space through lanes and byeways, until we reached a spot near to a farm-house, where the frequent trampling of much cattle had rendered the road almost impassable, and deep with black mud; but by crossing the corner of a stack-yard, from one gate to another, we could tread upon clean straw, and could wholly avoid the impure and impracticable slough. ·

We had nearly effected the brief and commodious transit, I was stretching forth my hand to open the gate that led us back into the lane, when a lean, brindled, and most ill-favoured mastiff, that had stolen upon us softly over the straw unheard, and without barking, seized Shelley suddenly by the skirts. I instantly kicked the animal in the ribs with so much force, that I felt for some days after the influence of his gaunt bones on my toe. The blow caused him to flinch towards the left, and Shelley, turning round quickly, planted a kick in his throat, which sent him away sprawling, and made him retire hastily among the stacks, and we then entered the lane. The fury of the mastiff, and the rapid turn, had torn the skirts of the new blue coat across the back, just about that part of the human loins which our tailors, for some wise, but inscrutable purpose, are wont to adorn with two buttons. They were entirely severed from the body, except a narrow strip of cloth on the left side, and this Shelley presently rent asunder.

I never saw him so angry either before or since ; he vowed that he would bring his pistols and shoot the dog, and that he would proceed at law against the owner. The fidelity of the dog towards his master is very beautiful in theory, and there is much to admire and to revere in this ancient and venerable alliance ; but, in practice, the most unexceptionable dog is a nuisance to all mankind, except his master, at all times, and very often to him also, and a fierce surly dog is the enemy of the whole human race. The farm-yards, in many parts of England, are happily free from a pest that is formidable to everybody but thieves by profession ; in other districts savage dogs abound, and in none so much, according to my experience, as in the vicinity of Oxford. The neighborhood of a still more famous city, of Rome, is likewise infested by dogs, more lowering, more ferocious, and incomparably more powerful.

Shelley was proceeding home with rapid strides, bearing the skirts of his new coat on his left arm, to procure his pistols, that he might wreak his vengeance upon the offending dog. I disliked the race, but I did not desire to take an ignoble revenge upon the miserable individual.

"Let us try to fancy, Shelley," I said to him, as he was posting away in indignant silence, " that we have been at Oxford, and have come back again, and that you have just laid the beast low—and what then ? "

He was silent for some time, but I soon perceived, from the relaxation of his pace, that his anger had relaxed also.

At last he stopped short, and taking the skirts from his arm, spread them upon the hedge, stood gazing at them with a mournful aspect, sighed deeply, and after a few moments continued his march.

"Would it not be better to take the skirts with us?" I inquired.

"No," he answered, despondingly, "let them remain as a spectacle for men and gods!"

We returned to Oxford, and made our way by back streets to our College. As we entered the gates, the officious scout remarked with astonishment Shelley's strange spenser, and asked for the skirts, that he might instantly carry the wreck to the tailor. Shelley answered, with his peculiarly pensive air, "They are upon the hedge."

The scout looked up at the clock, at Shelley, and through the gate into the street as it were at the same moment and with one eager glance, and would have run blindly in quest of them, but I drew the skirts from my pocket, and unfolded them, and he followed us to Shelley's rooms.

We were sitting there in the evening, at tea, when the tailor who had praised the coat so warmly in the morning, brought it back as fresh as ever, and apparently uninjured. It had been fine-drawn; he showed how skilfully the wound had been healed, and he commended, at some length, the artist who had effected the cure. Shelley was astonished and delighted : had the tailor consumed the new blue coat in one of his crucibles, and suddenly raised it, by magical incantation, a fresh and purple Phœnix from the ashes, his admiration could hardly have been more vivid. It might be, in this instance, that his joy at the unexpected restoration of a coat, for which, although he was utterly indifferent to dress, he had, through some unaccountable caprice, conceived a fondness, gave force to his sympathy with art; but I have remarked in innumerable cases, where no personal motive could exist, that he was animated by all the ardor of a maker in witnessing the display of the creative energies.

"Konx Ompax."

I was walking one afternoon, in the summer, on the western side of that short street leading from Long Acre to Covent Garden, wherein the passenger is earnestly invited, as a personal favor to the demandant, to proceed straightway to High-gate or to Kentish Town, and which is called, I think, James Street; I was about to enter Covent Garden, when an Irish laborer, whom I met, bearing an empty hod, accosted me somewhat roughly, and asked why I had run against him; I told him briefly that he was mistaken. Whether somebody had actually pushed the man, or he sought only to quarrel, and although he doubtless attended a weekly row regularly, and the week was already drawing to a close, he was unable to wait until Sunday for a broken head, I know not, but he discoursed for some time with the vehemence of a man who considers him-self injured or insulted, and he concluded, being emboldened by my long silence, with a cordial invitation just to push him again. Several persons not very unlike in costume had gath-ered round him, and appeared to regard him with sympathy. When he paused, I addressed to him slowly and quietly, and it should seem with great gravity, these words, as nearly as I can recollect them :—

"I have put my hand into the hamper; I have looked upon the sacred barley; I have eaten out of the drum! I have drunk and was well pleased: I have said, $\kappa \grave{o}\gamma\xi\ \mathring{o}\mu\pi\alpha\xi$, and it is fin-ished!"

"Have you, Sir?" inquired the astonished Irishman, and his ragged friends instantly pressed round him with "Where is the hamper, Paddy?"—"What barley?" and the like. And ladies from his own country, that is to say, the basket-women, suddenly began to interrogate him, "Now, I say, Pat, where have you been drinking? What have you had?"

I turned therefore to the right, leaving the astounded neophyte, whom I had thus planted, to expound the mystic words of initiation, as he could, to his inquisitive companions.

As I walked slowly under the piazzas, and through the streets and courts, towards the west, I marvelled at the ingenuity of Orpheus—if he were indeed the inventor of the Eleusinian mys-teries—that he was able to devise words that, imperfectly as I had repeated them, and in the tattered fragment that has reached us, were able to soothe people so savage and barbarous as those to whom I had addressed them, and which, as the apologists for those venerable rites affirm, were manifestly well adapted to incite persons, who hear them for the first time, however rude they may be, to ask questions. Words, that can awaken curiosity, even in the sluggish intellect of a wild man, and can thus open the inlet of knowledge!

"*Konx ompax*, and it is finished!" exclaimed Shelley, crowing with enthusiastic delight at my whimsical adventure. A thousand times as he strode about the house, and in his rambles out of doors, would he stop and repeat aloud the mystic words of initiation, but always with an energy of manner, and a vehemence of tone and of gesture, that would have prevented the ready acceptance which a calm, passionless delivery had once procured for them. How often would he throw down his book, clasp his hands, and starting from his seat, cry suddenly, with a thrilling voice, "I have said *Konx ompax*, and it is finished!"

BABIES AND PRE-EXISTENCE.

One Sunday we had been reading Plato together so diligently that the usual hour of exercise passed away unperceived; we sallied forth hastily to take the air for half an hour before dinner. In the middle of Magdalen Bridge we met a woman with a child in her arms. Shelley was more attentive at that instant to our conduct in a life that was past, or to come, than to a decorous regulation of the present, according to the established usages of society, in that fleeting moment of eternal duration, styled the nineteenth century. With abrupt dexterity he caught hold of the child. The mother, who might well fear that it was about to be thrown over the parapet of the bridge into the sedgy waters below, held it fast by its long train.

"Will your baby tell us anything about pre-existence, Madam?" he asked, in a piercing voice, and with a wistful look.

The mother made no answer, but perceiving that Shelley's object was not murderous, but altogether harmless, she dismissed her apprehension, and relaxed her hold.

"Will your baby tell us anything about pre-existence, Madam?" he repeated, with unabated earnestness.

"He cannot speak, sir," said the mother seriously.

"Worse and worse," cried Shelley, with an air of deep disappointment, shaking his long hair most pathetically about his young face; "but surely the babe can speak if he will, for he is only a few weeks old. He may fancy perhaps that he cannot, but it is only a silly whim; he cannot have forgotten entirely the use of speech in so short a time; the thing is absolutely impossible."

"It is not for me to dispute with you, gentlemen," the woman meekly replied, her eye glancing at our academical garb; "but I can safely declare that I never heard him speak, nor any child, indeed, of his age."

It was a fine placid boy; so far from being disturbed by the interruption, he looked up and smiled. Shelley pressed his fat cheeks with his fingers, we commended his healthy appearance and his equanimity, and the mother was permitted to proceed, probably to her satisfaction, for she would doubtless prefer a less speculative nurse. Shelley sighed deeply as we walked on.

"How provokingly close are those new-born babes!" he ejaculated; "but it is not the less certain, notwithstanding the cunning attempts to conceal the truth, that all knowledge is reminiscence; the doctrine is far more ancient than the times of Plato, and as old as the venerable allegory that the Muses are the daughters of Memory; not one of the nine was ever said to be the child of Invention!"

PATRONIZES THE PAWNBROKERS.

Whenever Shelley was imprisoned in London—for to a poet a close and crowded city must be a dreary jail—his steps would take the direction of Kentish Town unless his residence was too remote, or he was accompanied by one who chose to guide his walk. On this occasion I was led thither, as indeed I had anticipated; the weather was fine, but the autumn was already advanced; we had not sauntered long in these fields when the dusky evening closed in, and the darkness gradually thickened.

" How black those trees are," said Shelley, stopping short, and pointing to a row of elms ; " it is so dark the trees might well be houses, and the turf, pavement,—the eye would sustain no loss ; it is useless therefore to remain here, let us return." He proposed tea at his hotel ; I assented ; and hastily buttoning his coat, he seized my arm, and set off at his great pace, striding with bent knees over the fields and through the narrow streets.   We were crossing the New Road, when he said shortly, " I must call for a moment, but it will not be out of the way at all," and then dragged me suddenly towards the left.   I inquired whither we were bound, and, I believe, I suggested the postponement of the intended call till the morrow. He answered, it was not at all out of our way.

I was hurried along rapidly towards the left ; we soon fell into an animated discussion respecting the nature of the virtue of the Romans, which in some measure beguiled the weary way.   Whilst he was talking with much vehemence and a total disregard of the people who thronged the streets, he suddenly wheeled about and pushed me through a narrow door ; to my infinite surprise I found myself in a pawnbroker's shop !   It was in the neighborhood of Newgate Street ; for he had no idea whatever in practice either of time or space, nor did he in any degree regard method in the conduct of business.

There were several women in the shop in brown and gray cloaks with squalling children ; some of them were attempting to persuade the children to be quiet, or at least to scream with moderation ; the others were enlarging upon and pointing out the beauties of certain coarse and dirty sheets that lay before them to a man on the other side of the counter.

I bore this substitute for our proposed tea some minutes with tolerable patience, but as the call did not promise to terminate speedily, I said to Shelley, in a whisper, " Is not this almost as bad as the Roman virtue ? "   Upon this he approached the pawnbroker ; it was long before he could obtain a hearing, and he did not find civility.   The man was unwilling to part with a valuable pledge so soon, or perhaps he hoped to retain it eventually; or it might be, that the obliquity of his nature disqualified him for respectful behavior.

A pawnbroker is frequently an important witness in criminal proceedings; it has happened to me, therefore, afterwards to see many specimens of this kind of banker; they sometimes appeared not less respectable than other tradesmen, and sometimes I have been forcibly reminded of the first I ever met with, by an equally ill-conditioned fellow. I was so little pleased with the introduction, that I stood aloof in the shop, and did not hear what passed between him and Shelley.

On our way to Covent-Garden, I expressed my surprise and dissatisfaction at our strange visit, and I learned that when he came to London before, in the course of the summer, some old man had related to him a tale of distress,—of a calamity which could only be alleviated by the timely application of ten pounds; five of them he drew at once from his pocket, and to raise the other five he had pawned his beautiful solar microscope! He related this act of beneficence simply and briefly, as if it were a matter of course, and such indeed it was to him. I was ashamed of my impatience, and we strode along in silence.

It was past ten when we reached the hotel; some excellent tea and a liberal supply of hot muffins in the coffee-room, now quiet and solitary, were the more grateful after the wearisome delay and vast deviation. Shelley often turned his head, and cast eager glances towards the door; and whenever the waiter replenished our teapot, or approached our box, he was interrogated whether any one had yet called.

At last the desired summons was brought; Shelley drew forth some bank notes, hurried to the bar, and returned as hastily, bearing in triumph under his arm a mahogany box, followed by the officious waiter, with whose assistance he placed it upon the bench by his side. He viewed it often with evident satisfaction, and sometimes patted it affectionately in the course of calm conversation. The solar microscope was always a favorite plaything or instrument of scientific inquiry; whenever he entered a house his first care was to choose some

4

window of a southern aspect, and, if permission could be obtained by prayer or by purchase, straightway to cut a hole through the shutter to receive it.

His regard for his solar microscope was as lasting as it was strong ; for he retained it several years after this adventure, and long after he had parted with all the rest of his philosophical apparatus.

MARGARET NICHOLSON.

Shelley was was quick to conceive, and not less quick to execute. When I called one morning at one, I found him busily occupied with some proofs, which he continued to correct and re-correct with anxious care. As he was wholly absorbed in this occupation, I selected a book from the floor, where there was always a good store, and read in silence, for at least an hour.

My thoughts being as completely abstracted as those of my companion, he startled me by suddenly throwing a paper with some force on the middle of the table, and saying, in a penetrating whisper, as he sprung eagerly from his chair, " I am going to publish some poems."

In answer to my inquiries, he put the proofs into my hands. I read them twice attentively, for the poems were very short ; and I told him there were some good lines, some bright thoughts, but there were likewise many irregularities and incongruities. I added, that correctness was important in all compositions, but it constituted the essence of short ones ; and that it surely would be imprudent to bring his little book out so hastily ; and I then pointed out the errors and defects.

He listened in silence with much attention, and did not dispute what I said, except that he remarked faintly that it would not be known that he was the author, and therefore the publication could not do him any harm.

I answered, that although it might not be disadvantageous to be the unknown author of an unread work, it certainly could not be beneficial.

He made no reply; and we immediately went out, and strolled about the public walks.

We dined, and returned to his rooms, where we conversed on indifferent subjects. He did not mention his poems, but they occupied his thoughts; for he did not fall asleep as usual. Whilst we were at tea, he said abruptly, " I think you disparage my poems. Tell me what you dislike in them, for I have forgotten."

I took the proofs from the place where I had left them, and looking over them, repeated the former objections, and suggested others. He acquiesced; and, after a pause, asked, might they be altered ? I assented.

" I will alter them."

" It will be better to rewrite them; a short poem should be of the first impression."

Some time afterwards he anxiously inquired—" But in their present form you do not think they ought to be published ? "

I had been looking over the proofs again, and I answered : " Only as burlesque poetry; " and I read a part, changing it a little here and there.

He laughed at the parody, and begged I would repeat it.

I took a pen and altered it; and he then read it aloud several times in a ridiculous tone, and was amused by it. His mirth consoled him for the condemnation of his verses, and the intention of publishing them was abandoned.

The proofs lay in his rooms for some days, and we occasionally amused ourselves during an idle moment by making them more and more ridiculous; by striking out the more sober passages; by inserting whimsical conceits; and especially by giving them what we called a dithyrambic character, which was effected by cutting some lines in two, and joining the different parts together that would agree in construction, but were the most discordant in sense.*

---

* " It is necessary here to interrupt Mr. Hogg for a moment. The *Posthumous Fragments of Margaret Nicholson*, though a rare volume, is not inaccessible. A copy of the original edition is in the British Museum, and a *fac-simile* reprint, of which a limited number of copies were issued some time ago, may be seen without much diffi-

When we had conferred a competent absurdity upon the proofs, we amused ourselves by proposing, but without the intention of executing our project, divers ludicrous titles for the work. Sometimes we thought of publishing it in the name of some one of the chief living poets, or possibly of one of the graver authorities of the day; and we regaled ourselves by describing his wrathful renunciations, and his astonishment at finding himself immortalized, without his knowledge and against his will : the inability to die could not be more disagreeable even to Tithonus himself; but how were we to handcuff our ungrateful favorite, that he might not tear off the unfading laurel, which we were to place upon his brow? I hit upon a title at last, to which the pre-eminence was given, and we inscribed it upon the cover. A mad washerwoman, named Peg Nicholson, had attempted to stab the King, George the Third, with a carving-knife ; the story has long been forgotten, but it was then fresh in the recollection of every one ; it was proposed that we should ascribe the poems to her. The poor woman was still living, and in green vigor within the walls of Bedlam ; but since her existence must be uncomfortable, there could be no harm in putting her to death, and in creating a nephew and administrator to be the editor of his aunt's poetical works.

The idea gave an object and purpose to our burlesque ; to ridicule the strange mixture of sentimentality with the murderous fury of revolutionists, that was so prevalent in the compo-

culty. The poems, with the exception of the first, which extends to eighty-eight lines in couplets, are also given in Mr. Rossetti's edition, (vol. ii. p. 511.) They are thus within the reach of all, and it will be found that in no single respect do they bear out the description of Mr. Hogg. There is no intentional burlesque traceable in them. There is no example of this process of cutting lines in two, and then joining them, so as to agree in construction but to differ in sense. Indeed Mr. Hogg seems to have had a misgiving, after all this display of his own drollery and cleverness, that some day or the other his statements would be examined and his description put to the test. This difficulty did not put him to much inconvenience. Three pages later he introduces this saving clause, which is highly creditable to his professional skill : 'The work, however, was *altered a little,* I believe, *before the final impression;* but *I never read it afterwards*' (vol. i. p. 267)—a statement that may well be believed after his utterly erroneous description of its character and contents."—*MacCarthy.*

sitions of the day; and the proofs were altered again to adapt them to this new scheme, but still without any notion of publication. When the bookseller called to ask for the proofs, Shelley told him that he had changed his mind, and showed them to him.

The man was so much pleased with the whimsical conceit, that he asked to be permitted to publish the book on his own account; promising inviolable secrecy, and as many copies *gratis* as might be required : after some hesitation, permission was granted, upon the plighted honor of the trade.

In a few days, or rather in a few hours, a noble quarto appeared ; it consisted of a small number of pages, it is true, but they were of the largest size, of·the thickest, the whitest, and the smoothest drawing-paper ; a large, clear, and handsome type had impressed a few lines with ink of a rich glossy black, amidst ample margins. . The poor maniac laundress was gravely styled " the late Mrs. Margaret Nicholson, widow ; " and the sonorous name of Fitzvictor had been culled for her inconsolable nephew and administrator : to add to his dignity, the waggish printer had picked up some huge text types, of so unusual a form, that even an antiquary could not spell the words at the first glance. The effect was certainly striking : Shelley had torn open the large square bundle, before the printer's boy quitted the room, and holding out a copy with both his hands, he ran about in an ecstasy of delight, gazing at the superb title-page.

The first poem was a long one, condemning war in the lump ; puling trash, that might have been written by a quaker, and could only have been published in sober sadness by a society instituted for the diffusion of that kind of knowledge which they deem useful—useful for some end which they have not been pleased to reveal, and which unassisted reason is wholly unable to discover. The MS. had been confided to Shelley by some rhymester of the day, and it was put forth in this shape to astonish a weak mind ; but principally· to captivate the admirers of philosophical poetry by the manifest incongruity of disallowing all war, even the most just, and then turning

sharp round and recommending the dagger of the assassin as
the best cure for all evils, and the sure passport to a lady's
favor.

Our book of useful knowledge—the philosopher's own book
—contained sundry odes and other pieces, professing an ardent
attachment to freedom, and proposing to stab all who were less
enthusiastic than the supposed authoress. The work, however,
was altered a little, I believe, before the final impression ; but
I never read it afterwards, for when an author once sees his
book in print, his task is ended, and he may fairly leave the
perusal of it to posterity. I have one copy, if not more, somewhere or other, but not at hand. There were some verses, I
remember, with a good deal about sucking in them ; to these I
objected, as unsuitable to the gravity of an university, but
Shelley declared they would be the most impressive of all.
There was a poem concerning a young woman, one Charlotte
Somebody, who attempted to assassinate Robespierre, or some
such person ; * and there was to have been a rapturous monologue to the dagger of Brutus. The composition of such a
piece was no mean effort of the muse; it was completed at
last, but not in time—as the dagger itself has probably fallen
a prey to rust, so the more pointed and polished monologue,
it is to be feared, has also perished through a more culpable
neglect.

A few copies were sent, as a special favor, to trusty and
sagacious friends at a distance, whose gravity would not permit
them to suspect a hoax ; they read and admired, being charmed
with the wild notes of liberty ; some, indeed, presumed to cen
sure, mildly, certain passages as having been thrown off in too

* " Poor Margaret Nicholson's happily unsuccessful attempt on the life of the king
preceded by seven years the famous act of tyrannicide perpetrated by Charlotte Cor-
day in 1793, not on Robespierre, but on Marat. Careless of the anachronism, Mr.
Hogg boldly assigned the poem to the 'mad washerwoman' as a happy stroke of
humor. The supposed authoress speaks in the first poem of 'wife and children ;'
this, too, must be taken as a delicious bit of burlesque, in making Mrs. Nicholson
imagine herself to have been a man and a father. On the whole, we cannot but think
that the poems would have fared all the better had they been published by Shelley, as
they evidently were written by him, as serious compositions."—*MacCarthy.*

bold a vein.   Nor was a certain success wanting,—the remaining copies were rapidly sold in Oxford at the aristocratical price of half-a-crown for half-a-dozen pages. We used to meet gownsmen in High-street reading the goodly volume as they walked—pensive with a grave and sage delight—some of them, perhaps, more pensive, because it seemed to portend the instant overthrow of all royalty, from a king to a court-card.

What a strange delusion to admire our stuff—the concentrated essence of nonsense!   It was indeed a kind of fashion to be seen reading it in public, as a mark of a nice discernment, of a delicate and fastidious taste in poetry, and the very criterion of a choice spirit.

Nobody suspected, or could suspect, who was the author; the thing passed off as the genuine production of the would-be regicide. It is marvellous, in truth, how little talent of any kind there was in our famous university in those days; there was no great encouragement, however, to display intellectual gifts.

The Necessity of Atheism.

The operation of Peg Nicholson was bland and innoxious; the next work that Shelley printed was highly deleterious, and was destined to shed a baneful influence over his future progress ; in itself it was more harmless than the former, but it was turned to a deadly poison by the unprovoked malice of fortune.

We had read together attentively several of the metaphysical works that were most in vogue at that time, as " Locke concerning Human Understanding," and " Hume's Essays," particularly the latter, of which we had made a very careful analysis, as was customary with those who read the Ethics and the other treatises of Aristotle for their degrees. Shelley had the custody of these papers, which were chiefly in his handwriting, although they were the joint production of both in our common daily studies. From these, and from a small part of them only, he made up a little book, and had it printed, I believe, in the country, certainly not at Oxford. His motive was this. He not only read greedily all the controversial writings on subjects interesting to him, which he could procure, and disputed vehemently in conversation with his friends, but he had several correspondents with whom he kept up the ball of doubt in letters ;—of these he received many, so that the arrival of the postman was always an anxious moment with him. This practice he had learned of a physician, from whom he had taken instructions in chemistry, and of whose character and talents he often spoke with profound veneration. It was, indeed, the usual course with men of learning formerly, as their biographies and many volumes of such epistles testify. The physician was an old man, and a man of the old school; he confined his epistolary discussions to matters of science, and so did his disciple for some time; but when metaphysics usurped the place in his affections that chemistry had before held, the latter gradually fell into disceptations respecting existences still more subtle than gases and the electric fluid. The transition, however, from physics to metaphysics was gradual. Is the electric fluid material? he would ask his correspondent; is light—is the vital principle in vegetables—in brutes—is the human soul?

His individual character had proved an obstacle to his inquiries, even whilst they were strictly physical; a refuted or irritated chemist had suddenly concluded a long correspondence by telling his youthful opponent that he would write to his master, and have him well flogged. The discipline of a public school, however salutary in other respects, was not favorable to free and fair discussion; and Shelley began to address inquiries anonymously, or rather, that he might receive an answer, as Philalethes, and the like; but, even at Eton, the postmen do not ordinarily speak Greek—to prevent miscarriages, therefore, it was necessary to adopt a more familiar name, as John Short, or Thomas Long.

When he came to Oxford, he retained and extended his former practice without quitting the convenient disguise of an assumed name. His object in printing the short abstract of some of the doctrines of Hume was to facilitate his epistolary disquisitions. It was a small pill, but it worked powerfully;

the mode of operation was this :—He enclosed a copy in a letter, and sent it by the post, stating, with modesty and simplicity, that he had met accidentally with that little tract, which appeared unhappily to be quite unanswerable. Unless the fish was too sluggish to take the bait, an answer of refutation was forwarded to an appointed address in London, and then in a vigorous reply he would fall upon the unwary disputant, and break his bones. The strenuous attack sometimes provoked a rejoinder more carefully prepared, and an animated and protracted debate ensued ; the party cited, having put in his answer, was fairly in court, and he might get out of it as he could. The chief difficulty seemed to be to induce the person addressed to acknowledge the jurisdiction, and to plead ; and this, Shelley supposed, would be removed by sending, in the first instance, a printed syllabus instead of written arguments. An accident greatly facilitated his object. We had been talking some time before about geometrical demonstration ; he was repeating its praises, which he had lately read in some mathematical work, and speaking of its absolute certainty and perfect truth.

I said that this superiority partly arose from the confidence of mathematicians, who were naturally a confident race, and were seldom acquainted with any other science than their own ; that they always put a good face upon the matter, detailing their arguments dogmatically and doggedly, as if there was no room for doubt, and concluded, when weary of talking in their positive strain, with Q. E. D. : in which three letters there was so powerful a charm, that there was no instance of any one having ever disputed any argument, or proposition, to which they were subscribed. He was diverted by this remark and often repeated it, saying, if you ask a friend to dinner, and only put Q. E. D. at the end of the invitation, he cannot refuse to come ; and he sometimes wrote these letters at the end of a common note, in order, as he said, to attain to a mathematical certainty. The potent characters were not forgotten when he printed his little syllabus ; and their efficacy in rousing his antagonists was quite astonishing.

It is certain that the three obnoxious letters had a fertilizing

4*

effect, and raised rich crops of controversy; but it would be unjust to deny, that an honest zeal stimulated divers worthy men to assert the truth against an unknown assailant. The praise of good intention must be conceded; but it is impossible to accord that of powerful execution also to his antagonists; this curious correspondence fully testified the deplorable condition of education at that time. A youth of eighteen, was able to confute men who had· numbered thrice as many years; to vanquish them on their own ground, although he gallantly fought at a disadvantage by taking the wrong side.

His little pamphlet was never offered for sale; * it was not addressed to an ordinary reader, but to the metaphysician alone; and it was so short, that it was only designed to point out the line of argument. It was in truth a general issue; a compendious denial of every allegation, in order to put the whole case in proof; it was a formal mode of saying, you affirm so and so, then prove it; and thus was it understood by his more candid and intelligent correspondents. As it was shorter,

---

* "That it 'was never offered for sale' was certainly not the fault or the intention of the author, as proved by the following advertisement, now for the first time given in connection with Shelley's life. It was this bold and open announcement on the part of the author that the work would be published and sold in the ordinary way, that probably compelled the authorities to take notice of a tract, the existence of which they might not otherwise have known. Had it been announced in the London papers that a work entitled *The Necessity of Atheism* was about to be published, even ' by a gentleman of the University,' it would have provoked little attention at Oxford, whither the waifs and strays of blasphemy, ever floating in the metropolis, seldom found their way. Far different was it when in a journal circulating largely in the University, and calling itself ' The Oxford *University* and City Herald,' the following portentous announcement appeared :—

Speedily will be published,
To be had of the booksellers of London and Oxford,

THE
NECESSITY OF ATHEISM.

' Quod clara et perspicua demonstratione caveat pro vero habere, mens omnino nequit humanæ.'—*Bacon, de Augment. Scient.*

"This advertisement appears in *The Oxford University and City Herald* of Saturday, Feb. 9th, 1811. It has hitherto been unknown. Should the authorities of Oxford require any defence for the manner in which they acted towards the author, this advertisement will, I think, show that it was scarcely possible for them to overlook the carrying out of an intention so audaciously announced."—*MacCarthy.*

so was it plainer, and perhaps, in order to provoke discussion, a little bolder, than Hume's Essays,—a book which occupies a conspicuous place in the library of every student. The doctrine, if it deserves the name, was precisely similar; the necessary and inevitable consequence of Locke's philosophy, and of the theory that all knowledge is from without. I will not admit your conclusions, his opponent might answer; then you must deny those of Hume : I deny them; but you must deny those of Locke also; and we will go back together to Plato. Such was the usual course of argument; sometimes, however, he rested on mere denial, holding his adversary to strict proof, and deriving strength from his weakness.

The young Platonist argued thus negatively through the love of argument, and because he found a noble joy in the fierce shocks of contending minds ; he loved truth, and sought it everywhere, and at all hazards, frankly and boldly, like a man who deserved to find it ; but he also loved dearly victory in debate, and warm debate for its own sake. Never was there a more unexceptionable disputant; he was eager beyond the most ardent, but never angry and never personal; he was the only arguer I ever knew who drew every argument from the nature of the thing, and who could never be provoked to descend to personal contention. He was fully inspired indeed, with the whole spirit of the true logician; the more obvious and indisputable the proposition which his opponent undertook to maintain, the more complete was the triumph of his art if he could refute and prevent him.

To one who was acquainted with the history of our University, with its ancient reputation as the most famous school of logic, it seemed that the genius of the place, after an absence of several generations, had deigned to return at last; the visit, however, as it soon appeared, was ill-timed.

The schoolman of old, who occasionally labored with technical subtleties to prevent the admission of the first principles of belief, could not have been justly charged with the intention of promoting scepticism ; his was the age of minute and astute disceptation, it is true, but it was also the epoch of the most firm, resolute, and extensive faith. I have seen a dexterous fencing-master, after warning his pupil to hold his weapon fast, by a few turns of his wrist throw it suddenly on the ground and under his feet ; but it cannot be pretended that he neglected to teach the art of self-defence, because he apparently deprived his scholar of that which is essential to the end proposed. To be disarmed is a step in the science of arms, and whoever has undergone it has already put his foot within the threshold ; so is it likewise with refutation.

In describing briefly the nature of Shelley's epistolary contentions, the recollections of his youth, his zeal, his activity, and particularly of many individual peculiarities, may have tempted me to speak sometimes with a certain levity, notwithstanding the solemn importance of the topics respecting which they were frequently maintained. The impression that they were conducted on his part, or considered by him, with frivolity, or any unseemly lightness, would, however, be most erroneous ; his whole frame of mind was grave, earnest, and anxious, and his deportment was reverential, with an edification reaching beyond the age—an age wanting in reverence; an unlearned age ; a young age, for the young lack learning. Hume permits no object of respect to remain ; Locke approaches the most awful speculations with the same indifference as if he were about to handle the properties of triangles ; the small deference rendered to the most holy things by the able theologian, Paley, is not the least remarkable of his characteristics.

Wiser and better men displayed anciently, together with a more profound erudition, a superior and touching solemnity ; the meek seriousness of Shelley was redolent of those good old times before mankind had been despoiled of a main ingredient in the composition of happiness, a well-directed veneration.

Whether such disputations were decorous or profitable may be perhaps doubtful ; there can be no doubt, however, since the sweet gentleness of Shelley was easily and instantly swayed by the mild influences of friendly admonition, that, had even the least dignified of his elders suggested the propriety of pursuing his metaphysical inquiries with less ardor, his obedience would have been prompt and perfect.

Not only had all salutary studies been long neglected in Oxford at that time, and all wholesome discipline was decayed, but the splendid endowments of the University were grossly abused; the resident authorities of the college were too often men of the lowest origin, of mean and sordid souls, destitute of every literary attainment, except that brief and narrow course of reading by which the first degree was attained; the vulgar sons of vulgar fathers, without liberality, and wanting the manners and the sympathies of gentlemen.

A total neglect of all learning, an unseemly turbulence, the most monstrous irregularities, open and habitual drunkenness, vice, and violence, were tolerated or encouraged, with the basest sycophancy, that the prospect of perpetual licentiousness might fill the colleges with young men of fortune; whenever the rarely exercised power of coercion was exerted, it demonstrated the utter incapacity of our unworthy rulers by coarseness, ignorance, and injustice.

If a few gentlemen were admitted to fellowships, they were always absent; they were not persons of literary pretensions, or distinguished by scholarship; and they had no more share in the government of the college than the overgrown guardsmen, who, in long white gaiters, bravely protect the precious life of the sovereign against such assailants as the tenth Muse, our good friend, Mrs. Nicholson.

As the term was drawing to a close, and a great part of the books we were reading together still remained unfinished, we had agreed to increase our exertions and to meet at an early hour.

·EXPULSION FROM OXFORD.

It was a fine spring morning on Lady-day, in the year 1811, when I went to Shelley's rooms; he was absent; but before I had collected our books he rushed in. He was terribly agitated. I anxiously inquired what had happened.

" I am expelled," he said, as soon as he had recovered himself a little, "I am expelled! I was sent for suddenly a few minutes ago ; I went to the common room, where I found our master, and two or three of the fellows. The master produced a copy of the little syllabus, and asked me if I were the author of it. He spoke in a rude, abrupt, and insolent tone. I begged to be informed for what purpose he put the question. No answer was given : but the master loudly and angrily repeated, ' Are you the author of this book ? ' If I can judge from your manner, I said, you are resolved to punish me, if I should acknowledge that it is my work. If you can prove that it is, produce your evidence ; it is neither just nor lawful to interrogate me in such a case and for such a purpose. Such proceedings would become a court of inquisitors, but not free men in a free country. ' Do you choose to deny that this is your composition ? ' the master reiterated in the same rude and angry voice." Shelley complained much of his violent and ungentlemanlike deportment, saying, "I have experienced tyranny and injustice before, and I well know what vulgar violence is ; but I never met with such unworthy treatment. I told him calmly, but firmly, that I was determined not to answer any questions respecting the publication on the table. He immediately repeated his demand ; I persisted in my refusal ; and he said furiously, ' Then you are expelled ; and I desire you will quit the college early to-morrow morning at the latest.' One of the fellows took up two papers, and handed one of them to me ; here it is." He produced a regular sentence of expulsion, drawn up in due form, under the seal of the college.*

* "I accept Mr. Hogg's account of this transaction as substantially correct. In Shelley's account to me, there were material differences ; and making all allowance for the degree in which, as already noticed, his imagination colored the past, there is one matter of fact which remains inexplicable. According to him, his expulsion was a matter of great form and solemnity ; there was a sort of public assembly, before which he pleaded his own cause, in a long oration, in the course of which he called on the illustrious spirits who had shed glory on those walls to look down on their degenerate successors. Now, the inexplicable matter to which I have alluded is this : he showed me an Oxford newspaper, containing a full report of the proceedings, with his own oration at great length. I suppose the pages of that diurnal were not deathless, and that it would now be in vain to search for it ; but that he had it, and showed it to me,

Shelley was full of spirit and courage, frank and fearless ; but he was likewise shy, unpresuming, and eminently sensitive. I have been with him in many trying situations of his after-life, but I never saw him so deeply shocked and so cruelly agitated as on this occasion. A nice sense of honor shrinks from the most distant touch of disgrace—even from the insults of those men whose contumely can bring no shame. He sat on the sofa, repeating, with convulsive vehemence, the words, " Expelled, expelled ! " his head shaking with emotion, and his whole frame quivering. The atrocious injustice and its cruel consequences roused the indignation, and moved the compassion of a friend, who then stood by Shelley. He has given the following account of his interference :

" So monstrous and so illegal did the outrage seem, that I held it to be impossible that any man, or any body of men, would dare to adhere to it ; but, whatever the issue might be, it was a duty to endeavor to the utmost to assist him. I at once stepped forward, therefore, as the advocate of Shelley ; such an advocate, perhaps, with respect to judgment, as might be expected at the age of eighteen, but certainly not inferior to the most practised defenders in good will and devotion. I wrote a short note to the masters and fellows, in which, as far as I can remember a very hasty composition after a long inter-val, I briefly expressed my sorrow at the treatment my friend had experienced, and my hope that they would reconsider their sentence ; since, by the same course of proceeding, my-self, or any other person, might be subjected to the same penalty, and to the imputation of equal guilt. The note was despatched ; the conclave was still sitting ; and in an instant the porter came to summon me to attend, bearing in his coun-tenance a promise of the reception which I was about to find. The angry and troubled air of men, assembled to commit in-justice according to established forms, was then new to me ;

is absolutely certain. His oration may have been, as some of Cicero's published orations were, a speech in the potential mood ; one which might, could, should, or would, have been spoken ; but how in that case it got into the Oxford newspaper passes conjecture."
—*Peacock.*

but a native instinct told me, as soon as I entered the room, that it was an affair of party ; that whatever could conciliate the favor of patrons was to be done without scruple ; and whatever could tend to impede preferment was to be brushed away without remorse. The glowing master produced my poor note. I acknowledged it ; and he forthwith put into my hand, not less abruptly, the little syllabus. ' Did you write this? ' he asked, as fiercely as if I alone stood between him and the rich see of Durham. I attempted, submissively, to point out to him the extreme unfairness of the question ; the injustice of punishing Shelley for refusing to answer it ; that if it were urged upon me I must offer the like refusal, as I had no doubt every man in college would—every gentleman, indeed, in the University ; which, if such a course were adopted with all,— and there could not be any reason why it should be used with one and not with the rest,—would thus be stripped of every member. I soon perceived that arguments were thrown away upon a man possessing no more intellect or erudition, and far less renown, than that famous ram, since translated to the stars, through grasping whose tail less firmly than was expedient, the sister of Phryxus formerly found a watery grave, and gave her name to the broad Hellespont.

" The other persons present took no part in the conversation ; they presumed not to speak, scarcely to breathe, but looked mute subserviency. The few resident fellows, indeed, were but so many incarnations of the spirit of the master, whatever that spirit might be. When I was silent, the master told me to retire, and to consider whether I was resolved to persist in my refusal. The proposal was fair enough. The next day, or the next week, I might have given my final answer—a deliberate answer ; having in the mean time consulted with older and more experienced persons, as to what course was best for myself and for others. I had scarcely passed the door, however, when I was recalled. The master again showed me the book, and hastily demanded whether I admitted, or denied, that I was the author of it. I answered that I was fully sensible of the many and great inconveniences of being dismissed with disgrace from the University, and I specified some of them, and expressed an humble hope that they would not impose such a mark of discredit upon me without any cause. I lamented that it was impossible either to admit, or to deny, the publication,—no man of spirit could submit to do so ;—and that a sense of duty compelled me respectfully to refuse to answer the question which had been proposed. ' Then you are expelled,' said the master angrily, in a loud, great voice. A formal sentence, duly signed and sealed, was instantly put into my hand ; in what interval the instrument had been drawn up I cannot imagine. The alleged offence was a contumacious refusal to disavow the imputed publication. My eye glanced over it, and observing the word *contumaciously*, I said calmly that I did not think that term was justified by my behavior. Before I had concluded the remark, the master, lifting up the little syllabus, and then dashing it on the table, and looking sternly at me, said, ' Am I to understand, sir, that you adopt the principles contained in this work ? ' or some such words ; for, like one red with the suffusion of college port and college ale, the intense heat of anger seemed to deprive him of the power of articulation ; by reason of a rude provincial dialect and thickness of utterance, his speech being at all times indistinct. ' The last question is still more improper than the former,' I replied,—for I felt that the imputation was an insult ; ' and since, by your own act, you have renounced all authority over me, our communication is at an end.' ' I command you to quit my college to-morrow at an early hour.' I bowed and withdrew. I thank God I have never seen that man since ; he is gone to his bed, and there let him sleep. Whilst he lived, he ate freely of the scholar's bread, and drank from his cup ; and he was sustained, throughout the whole term of his existence, wholly and most nobly, by those sacred funds that were consecrated by our pious forefathers to the advancement of learning. If the vengeance of the all-patient and long-contemned gods can ever be roused, it will surely be by some such sacrilege ! The favor which he showed to scholars, and his gratitude, have been made manifest. If he were still alive, he would doubtless be as little desirous that his zeal should now be remembered as those bigots who had been most active in burning Archbishop Cranmer could have been to publish their officiousness, during the reign of Elizabeth." *

Thus not only were we driven rudely and lawlessly from a common table, spread for us by the provident bounty of our pious and prudent forefathers, where we had an undoubted right to be fed and nurtured ; but my incomparable friend and myself were hunted hastily out of Oxford. The precipitate violence and indecent outrage was the act of our college, not of the University ; the evil-doers seemed to fear that, if we remained among them but a little while, the wrong might be redressed. It is true that I was told, but as it were at the moment of departure, that if it was inconvenient to us to quit the place so suddenly, we might remain for a time ; and that, if Shelley would ask permission of the master to stay for a short period, it would most probably be granted. I immediately informed him of this proposal, but he was far too indignant at the insult which he had received, and at the brutal indignity with which he had been treated, to apply for any favor whatever, even if his life had depended on the concession. The delicacy of a young high-bred gentleman makes him ever most

* " His expulsion from Oxford brought to a summary conclusion his boyish passion for Miss Harriet Grove. She would have no more to say to him : but I cannot see from his own letters, and those of Miss Hellen Shelley, that there had ever been much love on her side ; neither can I find any reason to believe that it continued long on his. Mr. Middleton follows Captain Medwin, who was determined that on Shelley's part it should be an enduring passion, and pressed into its service as testimonies some matters which had nothing to do with it. He says *Queen Mab* was dedicated to Harriet Grove, whereas it was certainly dedicated to Harriet Shelley ; he even prints the dedication with the title, ' To Harriet G.,' whereas in the original the name of Harriet is only followed by asterisks ; and of another little poem, he says, ' that Shelley's disappointment in love affected him acutely, may be seen by some lines inscribed erroneously ' On F. G.,' instead of ' H. G.,' and doubtless of a much earlier date than the one assigned by Mrs. Shelley to the fragment. Now I know the circumstances to which the fragment refers. The initials of the lady's name were F. G., and the date assigned to the fragment, 1817, was strictly correct. The intrinsic evidence of both poems will show their utter inapplicability to Miss Harriet Grove."—*Peacock.*
[I hazard the conjecture that F. G. was Mary Godwin's half-sister, Fanny Godwin, as she was called, the daughter of Gilbert Imlay and Mary Wollstoncroft, who committed suicide at Swansea, *not* in 1817, but on the night of Oct. 9th, 1816. R. H. S.]

unwilling to intrude, and more especially to remain in any society, where his presence is not acceptable. Nevertheless, I have sometimes regretted, and more particularly for the sake of my gifted friend, to whom the residence at Oxford was exceedingly delightful, and, on all accounts, most beneficial, that we yielded so readily to these modest, retiring feelings. For if license to remain for some days would have been formally given upon a specific application, no doubt it would have been tacitly allowed; although no request had been made, permission would have been implied. At any rate it is perfectly certain that force—brute force—would not have been resorted to; that the police of the University would never have been directed to turn us out of our rooms, and to drive us beyond the gates of our college, roughly casting the poor students' books into the street. The young martyr had never been told—he never received any admonition, not even the slightest hint, that his speculations were improper, or unpleasing to any one; those persons alone had taken notice of, or a part in, them to whom they were agreeable; persons, who, like himself, relish them, and had a taste for abstruse and, perhaps, unprofitable discussions.

IN LODGINGS IN LONDON.

We had determined to quit Oxford immediately (this probably was a mistake), being under the ban of an absurd and illegal sentence. Having breakfasted together, the next morning, March 26, 1811, we took our places on the outside of a coach, and proceeded to London.

We put up for the night at some coffee-house near Piccadilly, and dined; and then we went to take tea in Lincoln's Inn Fields with Shelley's cousins. Here we passed a very silent evening; the cousins were taciturn people—the maxim of the family appeared to be, that a man should hold his tongue and save his money. I was a stranger; Bysshe (I heard him called by that name then for the first time; he was always called so by his family, probably to propitiate the old baronet)—Bysshe attempted to talk, but the cousins held their peace, and so conversation remained cousin-bound. At a coffee-house one can read nothing but a newspaper ; this did not suit us ; we went out after breakfast to look for lodgings.

We found several sets which seemed to me sufficiently comfortable, but in this matter Bysshe was rather fanciful. We entered a pleasant parlor,—a man in the street vociferated, "Mackarel, fresh mackarel!" or "Muscles! lilywhite muscles!" Shelley was convulsed with horror, and, clapping his hands on his ears, rushed wildly out of doors. At the next house we were introduced to a cheerful little first floor, the window was open, a cart was grinding leisurely along, the driver suddenly cracked his whip, and Shelley started ; so that would not do. At one place he fell in dudgeon with the maid's nose ; at another he took umbrage at the voice of the mistress. Never was a young beauty so hard to please, so capricious! I began to grow tired of the vain pursuit. However, we came to Poland Street ; it reminded him of Thaddeus of Warsaw and of freedom. We must lodge there, should we sleep even on the step of a door. A paper in a window announced lodgings ; Shelley took some objection to the exterior of the house, but we went in, and this time auspiciously.

There was a back sitting-room on the first-floor, somewhat dark, but quiet ; yet quietness was not the principal attraction. The walls of the room had lately been covered with trellised paper ; in those days it was not common. There were trellises, vine-leaves with their tendrils, and huge clusters of grapes, green and purple, all represented in lively colors. This was delightful ; he went close up to the wall, and touched it : "We must stay here ; stay for ever!" There was some debate about a second bed-room, and the authorities were consulted below ; he was quite uneasy, and eyed the cheerful paper wistfully during the consultation. We might have another bed-room ; it was upstairs. That room, of course, was to be mine. Shelley had the bed-room opening out of the sitting-room ; this also was overspread with the trellised paper. He touched the wall and admired it.

"Do grapes really grow in that manner anywhere?"

" Yes, I believe they do ! "

" We will go and see them then, soon ; we will go together ! "

" Then we shall not stay here for ever ! "

When could we have the lodgings ?   Now, immediately. We brought our luggage in a hackney-coach.   I had ordered a fire ; to this he rather objected in a plaintive voice, staring piteously at the ripe clusters, and seeming actually to feel the genial warmth of the sweet South ; but we were still in March, and had the grapes been real grapes, a cheerful fire was indispensable.   The weather was fine ; we took long walks together, as before, and we dined at some coffee-house, wherever we might chance to find ourselves at dinner-time, and returned to the trellised room to tea.

We walked one day to Wandsworth,* where some of his younger sisters were at school.   At that time Bysshe had a warm affection for his mother, and was passionately fond of his sisters.   I remained outside, whilst he went into the house for a little while.   When we stopped at the gate, a little girl, eight or ten years old, with long, light locks streaming over her shoulders, was scampering about.   " Oh ! there is little Hellen ! " the young poet screamed out with rapturous delight. On our return he informed me, that the pretty child was his third sister, and he then first told me the object of our walk ; for he took a pocketful of cakes to a school-girl with as much mystery as Pierre and Jaffier plotted against the government of Venice.   We read much together, and often read aloud to each other, leading a quiet, happy life.   But Shelley was not so comfortable as he had been at Oxford ; a college-life, with its manifold conveniences and all its appliances and aptitudes for study, exactly suited him.

At that time " English Bards and Scotch Reviewers " attracted much attention.   We had not yet seen it.   Shelley bought the poem one morning—a pretty little volume—at a bookseller's shop in Oxford Street.   He put it under his arm, and we walked into the country ; when we were sufficiently re-

* [Mr. Hogg's memory was at fault.   It was not at Wandsworth, but at Clapham, that Shelley's sisters were at school, and it was here that he met Harriet Westbrook.—S.]

moved from observation, he began to read it aloud. He read the whole poem aloud to me with fervid and exulting energy, and all the notes. He was greatly delighted with the bitter, wrathful satire. There are good things in it—some strong and striking passages—but it did not much please me ; it is full of pride, 'of hot, weak, impatient indignation. I never read it myself, I only heard it read once during this country walk, and I never saw the volume again. When he had finished it, he put it into his pocket hastily, or perhaps rather intended to do so, and missed his pocket, or—and it was no uncommon case with him—his pocket had been torn out, or there was a hole at the bottom, for, when he got home, the book had disappeared. The poem afterwards became exceedingly scarce, so that a large price was often given for a copy, and some curious persons even took the trouble to transcribe it. I have met with such MSS. Such was his first introduction to Byron ; such his first acquaintance with his brother poet, for he had never read those early attempts which were the moving cause of the furious onslaught.

Notwithstanding his admiration of the poem, he did not express, as was his course, whenever he was pleased with any work, a desire or determination to become personally acquainted with the author. He did not foresee that their lives would be blended and bound up together, as they were subsequently ; still less did he anticipate that the irate satirist would be his executor, and as such, at the expiration of a few short years, would preside at obsequies, so strange, so mournful! To us, blind mortals, ignorant of the future, this present life is hardly to be borne. If we knew what is to come, it would be absolutely intolerable !

We occasionally visited the cousins in Lincoln's Inn Fields again, to tea, or to dinner. They were mute, as before, and we met other cousins, not less reserved and retiring.

John G—— took us one Sunday morning into Kensington Gardens. We had never been there before. Bysshe was charmed with the sylvan—and in those days somewhat neglected—aspect of the place. It soon became, and always continued to be, a favorite resort. In the more retired parts of the gardens he especially delighted, and particularly in one dark nook where there were many old yew-trees.

One day we were invited to dine in Garden Court. Shelley, J. G., and myself, repaired thither. On our way I stopped to look at an object, which, so to say, I have seen every day of my life since, that is, for some fifty years, but which was then new to me. I had seen fountains represented in books, in views of old-fashioned mansions, but, I think, I had never actually set my eyes on one before.

"How many dukes shall we have to-day, Bysshe?" John G—— asked.

"Several, no doubt."

I quitted the fountain, and considered much within myself what this question could mean. Having ascended pretty high, we arrived at the chambers of our host, and were welcomed. Two or three persons were there already. We were introduced to them, but of these none were dukes,—not one. We had a comfortable dinner

> Of steaks, and other Temple messes,
> Which some neat-handed Phillis dresses.

We heard them hissing in a small kitchen adjoining our dining-room, and Phillis brought them in, hot and hot. I still thought about the dukes, but I soon discovered what John G—— meant. No dukes were mentioned, but several marchionesses, countesses, and baronesses were named, at whose parties Tom had figured lately, and who were excessively flattered and gratified when they were assured of the satisfaction with their arrangements which he had condescendingly expressed. After dinner there was some port wine, and much conversation ; it rolled chiefly on the superiority of women. Bysshe spoke with great animation of their purity, disinterestedness, generosity, kindness, and the like. I supported him humbly and feebly, by affirming, that girls, as far as my observation went, learned more readily than boys, especially the mathematical sciences ; that they had not the same repugnance to receive instruction—

not the same antipathy to learning, but were happy to be taught.

John G——, a surgeon, said, the female sex had been unfairly treated ; they had an undue share of pain, and sickness, and suffering, which they bore with an amount of patience and fortitude, of which men were incapable.

Most of these assertions met with warm opposition ; one fierce little man in particular got wonderfully angry. "When I take to myself a wife, do you suppose I shall allow her to set herself up, as being cleverer than myself? No, indeed, I will just get a horsewhip, and I will soon beat her conceit out of her! You may take my word for it!"

His word was taken, but his arguments, if such they might be called, did not go for much.

Bysshe was disgusted with him, and in walking home, remarked : "Since mild expostulations were unavailing, the fellow" (so he termed the choleric little gentleman) "ought to have been thrown out of the window. What do you think, John?"

"I think, if that had been done, we should probably have had some very pretty cases of compound fractures!"

TIMOTHY SHELLEY, M.P.

Shelley took me one Sunday to dine with his father, by invitation, at Miller's hotel, over Westminster Bridge. We breakfasted early, and sallied forth, taking, as usual, a long walk. He told me that his father would behave strangely, and that I must be prepared for him ; and he described his ordinary behavior on such occasions. I thought the portrait was exaggerated, and I told him so ; he assured me that it was not.

Shelley had, generally, one volume at least in his pocket, whenever he went out to walk. He produced a little book, and read various passages from it aloud. It was an unfavorable and unfair criticism on the Old Testament, some work of Voltaire's if I mistake not, which he had lately picked up on a stall. He found it amusing, and read many pages aloud to me, laughing heartily at the excessive and extravagant ridicule of the Jewish nation, their theocracy, laws, and peculiar usages.

We arrived at the appointed hour of five at the hotel, but dinner had been postponed until six.　Mr. Graham, whom I had seen before, was there.　Mr. Timothy Shelley received me kindly; but he presently began to talk in an odd, unconnected manner; scolding, crying, swearing, and then weeping again; no doubt, he went on strangely.

" What do you think of my father? " Shelley whispered to me.

I had my head filled with the book which I had heard read aloud all the morning, and I whispered in answer : " Oh, he is not your father.　It is the God of the Jews; the Jehovah you have been reading about ! "

Shelley was sitting at the moment, as he often used to sit, quite on the edge of his chair.　Not only did he laugh aloud, with a wild, demoniacal burst of laughter, but he slipped from his seat, and fell on his back at full length on the floor.

" What is the matter, Bysshe?　Are you ill? are you dead? are you mad?　Why do you laugh? "

It was not easy to return a satisfactory answer to his father, or to Mr. Graham, who came to raise him from the ground; but the announcement of dinner put an end to the confusion.

We dined comfortably.　Some time after dinner, Bysshe had gone out on an errand for his father,—I think, to order post-horses for the next morning.　The father addressed me thus :

" You are a very different person, sir, from what I expected to find ; you are a nice, moderate, reasonable, pleasant gentleman.　Tell me what you think I ought to do with my poor boy? He is rather wild, is he not? "

" Yes, rather."

" Then, what am I to do? "

" If he had married his cousin, he would perhaps have been less so.　He would have been steadier."

" It is very probable that he would."

" He wants somebody to take care of him ; a good wife. What if he were married? "

5

" But how can I do that ?   It is impossible ; if I were to tell Bysshe to marry a girl, he would refuse directly.   I am sure he would ; I know him so well."

" I have no doubt that he would refuse, if you were to order him to marry ; and I should not blame him.   But if you were to bring him in contact with some young lady, who, you believed, would make him a suitable wife, without saying anything about marriage, perhaps he would take a fancy to her ; and if he did not like her, you could try another."

Mr. Graham then interposed, and said that was an excellent plan, and Mr. Shelley conversed with him for some time in a low voice.   They went over a list of young women of their acquaintance.   I did not know these ladies even by name, so I paid little attention to their conversation, which terminated suddenly when Bysshe returned.

Another bottle of port was proposed, for the honorable member, whatever his merits or defects might be, was jolly and hospitable.

" They have older wine in this house, than any they have brought us yet ; let us have a bottle of that ! "

Nobody was inclined to drink more wine, and therefore we had tea.   Mr. Graham made tea ; he was Mr. Shelley's factotum, and he was always civil and attentive.

After tea our jovial host became characteristic again ; he discoursed of himself and his own affairs ; he cried, laughed, scolded, swore, and praised himself, at great length.   He was so highly respected in the House of Commons : he was respected by the whole House, and by the Speaker in particular, who told him that they could not get on without him.   He assured us that he was greatly beloved in Sussex.   Mr. Graham assented to all this.   He was such an excellent magistrate. He told a very long story, how he had lately committed two poachers : " You know the fellows, Graham, you know who they are."

Mr. Graham assented.

" And when they got out of prison, one of them came and thanked me."

Why the poacher was so grateful the worthy magistrate did not inform us.

" There is certainly a God," he then said ; " there can be no doubt of the existence of a Deity ; none whatever."

Nobody present expressed any doubt.

" You have no doubt on the subject, sir, have you ? " he inquired, addressing himself particularly to me.

" None whatever."

" If you have, I can prove it to you in a moment."

" I have no doubt."

" But perhaps you would like to hear my argument ? "

" Very much."

" I will read it to you, then."

He felt in several pockets, and at last drew out a sheet of letter-paper, and began to read.

Bysshe, leaning forward, listened with profound attention. " I have heard this argument before," he said : and, by-and-by, turning to me, he said again, " I have heard this argument before."

" They are Paley's arguments," I said.

" Yes ! " the reader observed, with much complacency, turning towards me, " you are right, sir," and he folded up the paper, and put it into his pocket; " they are Palley's arguments ; I copied them out of Palley's book this morning myself : but Palley had them originally from me ; almost everything in Palley's book he had from me."

When we parted, Mr. Shelley shook hands with me in a very friendly manner. " I am sorry you would not have any more wine. I should have liked much to have drunk a bottle of the old wine with you. Tell me the truth, I am not such a bad fellow after all, am I ? "

" By no means."

" Well, when you come to see me at Field Place, you will find that I am not."

We parted thus ; he lived just thirty-three years longer, but we never met again. I have sometimes thought that if he had been taken the right way, things might have gone better ; but this his son, Bysshe, could never do, for his course, like that of true love, was not to run smooth.

"Palley's arguments! Palley's books!" I said to my friend, as we walked home.

"Yes; my father always will call him Palley; why does he call him so?"

"I do not know, unless it be to rhyme to Sally."

After a deep, long-drawn sigh, he exclaimed: "Oh, how I wish you would come to Field Place! How I wish my father would invite you again, and you would come! You would set us all to rights, for you know how to put everybody in good humor."

The real author of the meagre and inconclusive treatises, which had been published under the name of Paley, and had been erroneously received, as being the compositions of the Archdeacon of Carlisle, was manifestly fond of making a fuss, of attracting attention to himself and his concerns, and of filling a space in the eyes of so much of the public as could be induced to attend to his manifestations.

As a senator, an integral portion of the collective wisdom, he loved, if not in the honorable house, at least out of doors, to move standing orders, to carry resolutions, by which nothing was resolved, to give notices, to record protests, and, in one word, to give full play to the whole machinery of pompous folly. To draw up protocols, like an accomplished statesman, as he was, to pen diplomatic notes, to sketch the outline of treaties, and to submit propositions and articles of capitulation provisionally; all these devices and many more, he tried on with my family. But his success was small; for, although Mr. Speaker, as he said, could not get through the business of the Session without his powerful aid, he appeared to us all to be a bore of the first magnitude, and a serious impediment to the carrying into effect any ordinary arrangements.

HARRIET WESTBROOK.

[Whether the life of Shelley would have been other than it was, if he had married his cousin Harriet Grove, is a matter for speculation. She was his first love, as Mary Chaworth was the first love of Byron, and Mary Campbell was the first love of Burns. He appears to have been more attached to her than she was to him, and to have surrounded her with a poetic halo. His sister pleaded for him, but without success. "Even supposing I take your representation of your brother's qualities and sentiments, which, as you coincide in and admire, I may fairly imagine to be exaggerated, although you may not be aware of the exaggeration, what right have I, admitting that he is so superior, to enter into an intimacy which must end in delusive disappointment, when he finds how really inferior I am to the being his heated imagination has pictured?" Two weeks later, on January 3d, 1811, Shelley writes: "She is no longer mine. She abhors me as a sceptic, as what she was before." On the 11th of January he writes again : "She is gone. She is lost to me for ever. She married—married to a clod of earth. She will become as insensible herself; all those fine capabilities will moulder." It is to be hoped that Harriet Grove was happy with her clod, and that her fine capabilities did not moulder, as her cousinly lover anticipated. Another Harriet soon appeared upon the scene, and he shifted his allegiance to her. Harriet Westbrook was a school companion of his sister Hellen, at Clapham, and when, after his expulsion from Oxford, he was in London, without money, his father having refused him assistance, this sister had requested her fair schoolfellow to be the medium of conveying to him such small sums as she and her sisters could afford to send, and other little presents which they thought would be acceptable. Under these circumstances, says Shelley's friend Peacock, the ministry of the young and beautiful girl presented itself like that of a guardian angel, and there was a charm about their intercourse which he readily persuaded himself could not be exhausted in the duration of life. Miss Westbrook was not a free-thinker when Shelley first met her, whatever she may have become afterwards; for, in a letter of hers, which MacCarthy was the first to publish, she wrote : "Being brought up in the Christian religion, you may conceive with what horror I first heard that

Percy was an Atheist—at least so it was given out at Clapham. At first I did not comprehend the meaning of the word, therefore when it was explained ⁂ was truly petrified. I wondered how he could live a moment professing such principles, and solemnly declared he should never change mine." Shelley's letters to Hogg at this period, contain several references to his guardian angel. " Miss Westbrook has this moment called on me with her sister," he writes, April 18th, 1811, from the trellised room in Poland Street. " It was certainly very kind of her." Six days later he wrote, "My little friend Harriet W. is gone to her prison house. She is quite well in health : at least so she says, though she looks very much otherwise. I saw her yesterday. I went with her sister to Miss H.'s, and walked about Clapham Common with them for two hours. The youngest is a most amiable girl, the eldest is really conceited, but very condescending. I took the sacrament with her on Sunday." The author of *The Necessity for Atheism* taking the sacrament with a school-girl ! What would the expelling Dons of Oxford have said to that ? " You say I talk philosophically of her kindness in calling on me," this curious sceptic continued. " She is very charitable and good. I shall always think of it with gratitude, because I certainly did not deserve it, and she exposed herself to much possible odium. It is perhaps scarcely doing her a kindness—it is perhaps inducing positive unhappiness, to point out to her a road which leads to perfection, the attainment of which, perhaps, does not repay the difficulties of the progress." If Shelley had pondered more deeply on this last suggestion, or if Hogg had been a wiser friend than he seems to have been, the fate of Harriet might have been different from what it was. Some days later he wrote again, this time from Lincoln's Inn Fields, " at Grove's," meaning probably the chambers of Harriet Grove's brother. " My poor little friend has been ill, her sister sent for me the other night. I found her on a couch, pale ; her father is civil to me, very strangely : the sister is too civil by half. She began talking about *l'Amour*. I philosophized, and the youngest said she had such a headache that she could not bear conversation. Her sister then went away, and I stayed till half-past twelve. Her father had a large party below, he invited me ; I refused." After a Voltairish paragraph which need not be quoted, he continues : " They are both very clever, and the youngest (my friend) is amiable. Yesterday she was better, and to-day her father compelled her to go to Clapham, whither I have conducted her ; and am but now returned." A few days later we found the guardian angel reading Voltaire's Dictionnaire Philosophique. " I spend most of my time at Miss Westbrook's. I was a great deal too hasty in criticising her character. How often have we to alter the impressions which first sight, or first anything produces. I really now consider her as amiable, not perhaps in a high degree, but perhaps she is." Allusions to Miss Westbrook, and the Miss Westbrooks, enliven Shelley's correspondence with Hogg. He discusses both, but declares that if he knows anything about love, he is *not* in love. It was a pity, for he was about to take an important step in life. " My dear friend," he writes from Rhayader, about the middle of May, 1811, " you will perhaps see me before you can answer this ; perhaps not ; Heaven knows ! I shall certainly come to York, but *Harriet Westbrook* will decide whether now or in three weeks. Her father has persecuted her in a most horrible way, by endeavoring to compel her to go to school. She asked my advice : resistance was the answer, at the same time that I essayed to mollify Mr. W. in vain ! And in consequence of my advice *she* has thrown herself upon *my* protection.

" I set off for London on Monday. How flattering a distinction !—I am thinking of ten million things at once.

" What have I said ? I declare, quite *ludicrous*. I advised her to resist. She wrote to say that resistance was useless, but that she would fly with me, and threw herself upon my protection. We shall have £200 a year : when we find it run short, we must live, I suppose, upon love ! Gratitude and admiration, all demand, that I should love her *for ever*. We shall see you at York. I will hear your arguments for matrimonialism, by which I am now almost convinced. I can get lodgings at

York, I suppose. Direct to me at Graham's, 18, Sackville Street, Piccadilly.

" Your inclosure of £10 has arrived ; I am now indebted to you £30.   In spite of philosophy, I am rather ashamed of this unceremonious exsiccation of your financial river. But indeed, my dear friend, the gratitude which I owe you for your society and attachment ought so far to over-balance this consideration as to leave me nothing but that. I must, however, pay you when I can."

The history of Shelley's courtship of Harriet Westbrook, or Harriet Westbrook's courtship of Shelley, has never been written, and perhaps never will be. It seems to have been promoted by others quite as much as by themselves. That her father was not averse to her marriage with the oldest son of a baronet, may be taken for granted. The marriage, as Hogg remarks, was not so hasty an affair as it is commonly represented to have been. " The wooing continued for half a year at least, and this is a long time in the life, in the life of love, of such young persons. Harriet Westbrook appears to have been dissatisfied with her school, but without any adequate cause, for she was kindly treated and well educated there. It is not impossible that this discontent was prompted and suggested to her, and that she was put up to it, and to much besides, by somebody, who conducted the whole affair—who had assumed and steadily persisted in keeping the complete direction of her.

When a young man finds a young woman discontented with her school, or convent, and with her own family and friends, without much reason, a pretty face and soft manners too often make him forget that she is very probably a girl of a discontented disposition, and is likely to be dissatisfied wherever she may afterwards be placed.

The advocates of divorce, legal or illegal, formal or informal, would do well to remember, that a wife who quarrels with her present husband is perhaps a person of a nature very apt to disagree with her next also, and with all future husbands. Thus, a man who cannot make himself comfortable in the dwelling which he now inhabits, is commonly of a restless, roving disposition, a rolling stone, and he will never find a house that will suit him long. ' A man ought to be able to live with any woman ; ' Shelley told me his friend Robert Southey once said to him, ' You see that I can, and so ought you. It comes to pretty much the same thing, I apprehend. There is no great choice, or difference ! ' " Shelley was summoned from Rhayader by the pressing appeals of Miss Westbrook, Lady Shelley tells us, and hastily returning to London he eloped with Harriet. This was in September, 1811. He had attained the mature age of nineteen, and was her elder by three years. They proceeded to Edinburgh, where they were married. " They had absorbed their stock of money," Peacock says. " They took a lodging, and Shelley immediately told the landlord who they were, what they had come for, and the exhaustion of their finances, and asked him if he would take them in, and advance them money to get married and to carry them on till they could get a remittance. This the man agreed to do, on condition that Shelley would treat himself and his friends to a supper in honor of the occasion. It was arranged accordingly ; but the man was more obtrusive and officious than Shelley was disposed to tolerate. The marriage was concluded, and in the evening Shelley and his bride were alone together, when the man tapped at their door. Shelley opened it, and the man said to him : ' It is customary here at weddings for the guests to come in, in the middle of the night, and wash the bride with whiskey.' ' I immediately,' said Shelley, ' caught up my brace of pistols, and pointing them both at him, said to him, " I have had enough of your impertinence ; if you give me any more of it I will blow your brains out ; " on which he ran or rather tumbled downstairs, and I bolted the doors.' The custom of washing the bride with whiskey is more likely to have been so made known to him than to have been imagined by him."]

SHELLEY IN EDINBURGH.

I soon set foot in George Street, a spacious, noble, wellbuilt street ; but a deserted street, or rather a street which people had not yet come fully to inhabit. I soon found the number indicated at the post-office; I have forgotten it, but it was on the left side—the side next to Princes Street. I knocked at the door of a handsome house; it was all right; and in a handsome front parlor I was presently received rapturously by my friend. He looked just as he used to look at Oxford, and as he looked when I saw him last in April, in our trellised apartment; but now joyous at meeting again, not as then sad at parting. I also saw—and for the first time—his lovely young bride, bright as the morning,—as the morning of that bright day on which we first met; bright, blooming, radiant with youth, health, and beauty. I was hailed triumphantly by the new-married pair; my arrival was more than welcome; they had got my letter and expected to rejoice at my coming every moment. "We have met at last once more!" Shelley exclaimed, "and we will never part again! You must have a bed in the house!" It was deemed necessary, indispensable. At that time of life a bed a mile or two off, as far as I was concerned, would have done as well; but I must have a bed in the house. The landlord was summoned, he came instantly; a bed in the house; the necessity was so urgent that they did not give him time to speak. When the poor man was permitted to answer, he said, "I have a spare bed-room, but it is at the top of the house. It may not be quite so pleasant." He conducted me up a handsome stone staircase of easiest ascent; the way was not difficult, but very long. It appeared well-nigh interminable. We came at length to an airy, spacious bed-room. "This will do very well." A stone staircase is handsome and commodious, and, in case of fire, it must be a valuable security; but whenever a door was shut it thundered; the thunder rolled pealing for some seconds. I was to lodge with Jupiter Tonans at the top of Olympus. Of all the houses in London, with which I am acquainted, those in Fitzroy Square alone remind me, by their sonorous powers, of Edinburgh, and of the happy days I passed in that beautiful city. On returning to my friends, our mutual greetings were repeated; each had a thousand things to tell and to ask of the rest. Our joy being a little calmed, we agreed to walk. "We are in the capital of the unfortunate Queen Mary," said Harriet; "we must see her palace first of all." We soon found Holyrood House; a beggarly palace, in truth. We saw the long line of Scottish monarchs, from Fergus the First downwards, disposed in two rows, being evidently the productions of some very inferior artist, who could not get employment as a sign-painter. We saw Mary's bed-room, the stains of Rizzio's blood, and all the other relics. These objects, intrinsically mean and paltry, greatly interested my companions, especially Harriet, who was well-read in the sorrowful history of the unhappy queen. Bysshe must go home and write letters, I was to ascend Arthur's Seat with the lady. We marched up the steep hill boldly, and reached the summit. The view may be easily seen, it is impossible to describe it. It was a thousand pities Bysshe was not with us, and then we might remain there; one ought never to quit so lovely a scene.

"Let us sit down; probably when he has finished writing he will come to us."

We sat a long time, at first gazing around, afterwards we looked out for the young bridegroom, but he did not appear. It was fine while we ascended; it was fine, sunny, clear, and still, whilst we remained on the top; but when we began to descend, the wind commenced blowing. Harriet refused to proceed; she sat down again on the rock, and declared that we would remain there for ever! For ever is rather a long time; to sit until the wind abated would have been to sit there quite long enough. Entreaties were in vain. I was hungry, for I had not dined on either of the two preceding days. The sentence—never to dine again—was a severe one, and although it was pronounced by the lips of beauty, I ventured to appeal against it; so I left her and proceeded slowly down the hill, the wind blowing fresh. She sat for some time longer, but finding that I was in earnest, she came running down after me. Harriet was always most unwilling to show her ankles, or even her feet, hence her reluctance to move in the presence of a rude, indelicate wind, which did not respect her modest scrupulousness.　If there was not much to admire about these carefully-concealed ankles, certainly there was nothing to blame.

The accommodations at our lodgings in George Street were good, and the charges reasonable; the food was abundant and excellent; everything was good, the wine included; in one particular only was there a deficiency, the attendance was insufficient, except at meals, when our landlord officiated in person.　One dirty little nymph, by name Christie, was the servant of the house—the domestic, she was termed; she spoke a dialect which we could not comprehend, and she was, for the most part, unable to understand what we southerns said to her, or indeed anything else, save only perchance political economy and metaphysics.　After ringing the well-hung bells many times in vain, she would suddenly open the door, and exclaiming, "Oh! The kittle!" darted off to be brought back again, after a long delay, by the like exertions and with the like result.　Her sagacity had discovered that we drank much tea, and therefore often required the services of the tea-kettle.　However, if she was of no great use to us, the poor little girl at least afforded us some amusement.

Shelley was of an extreme sensibility—of a morbid sensibility—and strange, discordant sounds he could not bear to hear; he shrank from the unmusical voice of the Caledonian maiden.　Whenever she entered the room, or even came to the door, he rushed wildly into a corner and covered his ears with his hands.　We had, to our shame be it spoken, a childish, mischievous delight in tormenting him; in catching the shy virgin and making her speak in his presence.　The favorite interrogatory so often administered was, "Have you had your dinner to-day, Christie?'　"Yes."　"And what did you get?"　"Sengit heed and bonnocks," was the unvarying answer, and its efficacy was instantaneous and sovereign.　Our poor sensitive poet assumed the air of the Distracted Musician, became nearly frantic, and, had we been on the promontory, he would certainly have taken the Leucadian leap for Christie's sake, and to escape for ever from the rare music of her voice.

"Oh! Bysshe, how can you be so absurd? What harm does the poor girl do you?"

"Send her away, Harriet! Oh! send her away; for God's sake, send her away!"

Shelley went every morning himself, before breakfast, to the post-office for his letters, of which he received a prodigious number; and he used to bring back with him splendid plates of virgin honey. I never saw such fine honeycombs before or since, and it was delicious. Shelley was for the most part indifferent to food, to all meats and drinks, but he relished this honey surprisingly; so much did he enjoy it, that he was almost offended when I said, exquisite though it was, it was a shame to eat it; wantonly to destroy, merely to flatter the palate, so beautiful and so wonderful a structure, was as barbarous as it would be to devour roses and lilies. It was far too great a marvel to be eaten; it should only be looked at, kept entire, to be admired. It approaches cannibalism to feed on it; indeed, it is too like eating Harriet! I think you would eat Harriet herself!

"So I would, if she were as good to eat, and I could replace her as easily!"

"Oh! fie, Bysshe!" the young lady exclaimed, who inclined somewhat to my heresy, feasting her eyes with the honeycomb, and declaring it was quite a pity to eat it; this the greedy poet said was tiresome.

A Sunday in Edinburgh.

After breakfast on Sunday, a verbal announcement was made to us by our landlord himself: "They are drawing nigh unto the kirk!"

On looking from the windows, we saw the grave Presbyterians, with downcast looks, like conscience-stricken sinners, slowly crawling towards their place of gathering. We were admonished—for Shelley said, one Sunday, "Let us go and take a walk,"—that it was not lawful to go forth to walk purposely and avowedly on the Sabbath, a day of rest and worship; but if a man happen to find himself in the streets casually, he may walk a little with perfect innocence, only it is altogether unlawful to go out from his door with the mind of taking a walk of pure pleasure.

After this serious and edifying warning we sometimes casually found ourselves without the house on a Sunday, and walked about a little, as we believed, innocently.

We were taking such a harmless stroll, by mere accident, in Princes Street : Bysshe laughed aloud, with a fiendish laugh, at some remark of mine.

" You must not laugh openly, in that fashion, young man," an ill-looking, ill-conditioned fellow said to him. " If you do, you will most certainly be convened ! "

" What is that ? " asked Shelley, rather displeased, at the rude interpellation.

" Why, if you laugh aloud in the public streets and ways on the Christian Sabbath, you will be cast into prison, and eventually banished from Scotland."

The observance of the Sabbath in North Britain, as I have been credibly informed, has been, since the year of the comet, like the manufacture of hats in England, decidedly improved, both articles being now much lighter, and less oppressive.

I once asked the way to some place in Edinburgh of a staid old gentlewoman : " I am going the same road in part, and I will attend you."

We proceeded leisurely along together ; she conversed gravely, but affably : How do you like this ; how that ; " How do you like our public worship ? "

" I have not assisted at it yet."

" Oh ! but you must ; you must go and hear Dr. Mac Quis-quis ; he is a fine preacher ; an accomplished divine ; he wrestles most powerfully with Satan, every Sabbath morn ! "

I promised my obliging conductress to go and witness these spiritual struggles with a ghostly enemy ; but I could not redeem a pledge somewhat rashly given, for I did not know in what arena this powerful gymnast fought. I did not even catch the name of the accomplished divine. One Sabbath morn,

however, when we were again advised that they were drawing
nigh unto the Kirk, Shelley and myself boldly resolved to draw
nigh also ; the lovely Harriet would not accompany us, alleg-
ing, and with some probability, that the wearisome perform-
ances would give her a headache. We joined the scattered
bands, which increased in number as we advanced, creeping
with them for a considerable distance. We reached a place
of worship, and entered it with the rest ; it was plain, spacious,
and gloomy. We suffered ourselves rather incautiously to be
planted side by side, on a bench in the middle of the devout
assembly, so that escape was impossible. There was singing,
in which all, or almost all, the congregation joined ; it was
loud, and discordant, and protracted. There was praying,
there was preaching,—both extemporaneous. We prayed for
all sorts and conditions of men, more particularly for our ene-
mies. The preacher discoursed at a prodigious length, repeating many times things that were not worthy to be said once,
and threatening us much with the everlasting punishments,
which, solemnly and confidently, he declared were in store for
us. I never saw Shelley so dejected, so desponding, so despairing ; he looked like the picture of perfect wretchedness ;
the poor fellow sighed piteously, as if his heart would break.
If they thought that he was conscience-stricken, and that his
vast sorrow was for his sins, all, who observed him, must
have been delighted with him, as with one filled with the comfortable assurance of eternal perdition. No one present could
possibly have comprehended the real nature of his acute sufferings,—could have sympathized in the anguish and agony of a
creature of the most poetic temperament that ever was bestowed, for his weal or his woe, upon any human being, at feeling
himself in the most unpoetic position in which he could possibly be placed. At last, after expectations many times disappointed of an approaching deliverance, and having been repeatedly deceived by glimpses of an impending discharge, and
having long endured that sickness of heart caused by hopes
deferred, the tedious worship actually terminated.

We were eagerly pressing forward to get out of our prison,

and out of the devout crowd, but a man in authority pushed us aside :

" Make way for the Lord Provost and the Bellies ! "

We stood on one side for a while, that the civic dignitaries might pass. My friend asked, in a whisper, what in the world the man meant? I informed him that a Provost is a Mayor, and that a Belly (Baillie) is Scotch for an Alderman.

It was a consolation to the poor sufferer to laugh once more. It had seemed to him in his captivity that his healthful function had ceased for ever.

We made the best of our way homewards, and at a brisker pace than the rude apostle of the north, John Knox, would have approved of, discussing the wonderful advantages of a ritual, and their comfortless, inhuman church music.

Acknowledging the superiority of our chapels, churches, and cathedral in Oxford, and the vast benefits of written sermons, after having just had painful experience how tedious a thing it was to listen to an extemporaneous discourse ; and, moreover, how distressing for the hearer to have to sit and wonder what monstrous extravagance, what stupid and preposterous absurdity the heavy orator, with no succor at hand, would utter next.

The malicious Harriet laughed at our sufferings, and made herself merry with the deep dejection of her husband.

The Catechist.

Yet were we, poor Oxford scholars, predestined to undergo another trial of the same kind, but less severe, and far more brief,—sharp, though short. It was notified to us one Sunday evening, as we were sitting together after dinner, that " They are drawing nigh unto the Catechist,—children and domestics must attend."

We had discovered that little Christie was going, and as we already knew something of her temporal concerns, (" oh ! the kittle !") we were curious to learn a little about her spiritual condition. Accordingly, we followed her at a distance.

At the first notification, Bysshe, to my surprise, exclaimed, " Let us go ! "

Harriet sought to dissuade him, and earnestly, as if she thought we were going to a place where he would probably have his throat cut. But persuasioñ availed not. We followed the slow advance of children and domestics still more slowly, and entered a roomy building, gloomy and unadorned, like a Kirk. A man in rusty black apparel, of a mean and somewhat sinister aspect, was standing in the middle of the floor ; children and domestics were standing round him ; we remained in a corner.

" Wha was Adam ? " he suddenly and loudly asked.

Nobody answered. He appeared to be much displeased at their silence ; and after a while he repeated the question, in a louder voice,

" Wha was Adam ? "

Still no answer. The name is so common in these anti-episcopalian regions. Did he ask after Adam Black, Willie Adam, or Adam, late of Eden, the protoplast ; he did not limit his question, but put it in the most general terms. Nobody answered it.

The indignation of the Catechist waxing hot, in a still louder and very angry tone he broke forth with,—

" Wha's the Deel ? "

This was too much ; Shelley burst into a shrieking laugh, and rushed wildly out of doors. I slowly followed him, thinking seriously of Elders, Presbyteries, and Kirk Synods. However, nothing came of it ; we were not cast into prison.

HARRIET'S READINGS.

It has been represented by reckless or ill-informed biographers that Harriet was illiterate, and therefore she was not a fit companion for Shelley. This representation is not correct ; she had been well-educated ; and as the coffee-house people could not have taught her more than they knew themselves, which was little or nothing, she must have received her education at school; and she was unquestionably a credit to the establishment.

Drawing she had never learned, at least she gave no indications of taste or skill in that department; her proficiency in music was moderate, and she seemed to have no very decided natural talent for it ; her accomplishments were slight, but with regard to acquirements of higher importance, for her years, she was exceedingly well read. I have seldom, if ever, met with a girl who had read so much as she had, or who had so strong an inclination for reading. I never once saw a Bible, a prayer-book, or any devotional work, in her hand; I never heard her utter a syllable on the subject of religion, either to signify assent or dissent, approbation, or censure, or doubt ; Eucharis, or Egeria, or Antiope, could not have appeared more entirely uninstructed than herself in such matters. I never heard her say that she had been at church, or ever once visited any place of worship; never, in my hearing, did she criticise any sermon, as is so common with the generality of young ladies, or express admiration of, or curiosity concerning, a popular preacher. Her music was wholly secular; of the existence of sacred music she seemed to be unconscious, and never to have heard the illustrious name of Handel. Her reading was not of a frivolous description ; she did not like light, still less trifling, ephemeral productions. Morality was her favorite theme ; she found most pleasure in works of a high ethical tone. Telemachus and Belisarius were her chosen companions, and other compositions of the same leaven, but of less celebrity.

She was fond of reading aloud ; and she read remarkably well, very correctly, and with a clear, distinct, agreeable voice, and often emphatically. She was never weary of this exercise, never fatigued ; she never ceased of her own accord, and left off reading only on some interruption. She has read to me for hours and hours ; whenever we were alone together, she took up a book and began to read, or more commonly read aloud, from the work, whatever it might be, which she was reading to herself. If anybody entered the room she ceased to read aloud, but recommenced the moment he retired. I was grateful for her kindness; she has read to me grave and excellent books innumerable. If some few of these were a little wearisome, on the whole I profited greatly by her lectures. I have sometimes certainly wished for rather less of the trite moral discourses of Idomeneus and Justinian, which are so abundant in her two favorite authors, and a little more of something less in the nature of truisms; but I never showed any signs of impatience. In truth, the good girl liked a piece of resistance, a solid tome, where a hungry reader might read and come again. I have sometimes presumed to ask her to read some particular work, but never to object to anything which she herself proposed. If it was agreeable to listen to her, it was not less agreeable to look at her; she was always pretty, always bright, always blooming; smart, usually plain in her neatness; without a spot, without a wrinkle, not a hair out of its place. The ladies said of her, that she always looked as if she had just that moment stepped out of a glass-case; and so indeed she did. And they inquired, how that could be? The answer was obvious; she passed her whole life in reading aloud, and when that was not permitted, in reading to herself, and invariably works of a calm, soothing, tranquillizing, sedative tendency; and in such an existence there could be nothing to stain, to spot, to heat, to tumble, to cause any the slightest disorder of the hair or dress. Hers was the most distinct utterance I ever heard; I do not believe that I lost a single word of the thousands of pages which she read to me. Of course I never dared to yield to sleep, even when the virtuous Idomeneus was giving wise laws to Crete, and therefore I am now alive to write our simple story.

The more drowsy Bysshe would sometimes drop off: his innocent slumbers gave serious offence, and his neglect was fiercely resented; he was stigmatized as an inattentive wretch.

Eliza Westbrook.

This harbinger of all felicity was her sister; she had no brothers, and only one sister, an elder sister; old enough, indeed, to have been her mother.   She bore her sister great love, or perhaps she had entire faith in her ; she worshipped her, not so much through a feeling of veneration, but a strong sense of paramount duty, and yielded her implicit, unreasoning obedience.   Her mother was as dignified as silk and satin could make her, and was fully capable of sitting all day long with her hands before her, but utterly incapable of aught besides, good or bad, except possibly of hearing herself addressed occasionally as Mamma.   Eliza had tended, guided, and ruled Harriet from her earliest infancy ; she doubtless had married her, had made the match, had put her up to everything that was to be said, or done, as Shelley's letters plainly show ; and she was now about to come on board again, after a short absence on shore, to hoist her flag at the mast head, to take the entire command, and for ever to regulate and direct the whole course of her married life.   Eliza, I was told, was beautiful, exquisitely beautiful ; an elegant figure, full of grace ; her face was lovely,—dark bright eyes ; jet black hair, glossy ; a crop upon which she bestowed the care it merited,—almost all her time ; and she was so sensible, so amiable, so good !

Bysshe's return was ardently desired ; partly for his own sake, but principally on account of the lost treasure, which he was to restore, and whose protracted absence began to be severely felt, on account of the rich freight of beauty and virtue which the homeward-bound vessel would surely bring back.

One evening, I returned to our lodgings from a stroll after dinner, and found to my surprise that the peerless Eliza had arrived.

Harriet was seated on the sofa by the side of her good genius, her guardian angel, her familiar demon :—" Eliza has come ; was it not good of her ; so kind ? " I was presented to her.   She hardly deigned to notice me. -

Such neglect on the part of so superior a being, although a barmaid by origin, or at best a daughter of the house, appeared reasonable enough.

" I thought Bysshe was to have brought you with him."

" Oh dear, no ! "

The tea things were on the table ; the new comer was of too sublime a nature to endure the contact of a tea-pot, and poor Harriet's being was too highly sublimated by the august presence to attend, as usual, to the vulgar requisitions of the tea-table. The case was important and urgent.

" Shall I make tea ? "

This was not forbidden, and it was made. Eliza looked contemptuously at the cup of tea, which I placed before her. Harriet descended from the seventh heaven so far as to stir, and even to sip, her tea. I helped myself freely, like a good Philistine as I was, whilst the music of the spheres held its thrilling course. Poor little Harriet was wrapt in ecstasy ; she whispered inaudibly to Eliza : Eliza sighed, and returned a still lower whisper.

I had ample leisure to contemplate the acquisition to our domestic circle. She was older than I had expected, and she looked much older than she was. The lovely face was seamed with the small-pox, and of a dead white, as faces so much marked and scarred commonly are ; as white, indeed, as a mass of boiled rice, but of a dingy hue, like rice boiled in dirty water. The eyes were dark, but dull, and without meaning ; the hair was black and glossy, but coarse ; and there was the admired crop,—a long crop, much like the tail of a horse,—a switch tail. The fine figure was meagre, prim, and constrained. The beauty, the grace, and the elegance existed, no doubt, in their utmost perfection, but only in the imagination of her partial young sister. Her father, as Harriet told me, was familiarly called " Jew Westbrook," and Eliza' greatly resembled one of the dark-eyed daughters of Judah.

The arrival of Bysshe was acknowledged by Harriet, but it was plain that he had been superseded ; Eliza once or twice betrayed a faint consciousness of his presence, as if the lamp of her life had been faintly glimmering in its socket, which fortunately it was not ; that was all the notice she took of her sister's husband. His course, therefore, was plain ; his peace might have been assured ; whether his happiness would ever have been great, may well be doubted. It was absolutely necessary to declare peremptorily, " Either Eliza goes, or I go ; " and instantly to act upon the declaration. This so necessary course the poor fellow did not take ; and it is certain that the Divine Poet could not have taken it, for with super-human strength, weakness less than human was strangely blended ; accordingly, from the days of the blessed advent, our destinies were entirely changed. The house lay, as it were, under an interdict ; all our accustomed occupations were suspended ; study was forbidden ; reading was injurious—to read aloud might terminate fatally ; to go abroad was death, to stay at home the grave ! Bysshe became nothing ; I, of course, very much less than nothing—a negative quantity of a very high figure.

Harriet still existed, it was true ; but her existence was to be in future a seraphic life, a beatific vision, to be passed exclusively in the assiduous contemplation of Eliza's infinite perfections.

That all this was very well meant, very disinterested, kind, benevolent, sisterly, it would be unjust to deny, or even to doubt ; but it was all the more pernicious on that account.

Before the angelic visit, we had never heard of Harriet's nerves, we had never once suspected that such organs existed ; now we heard of little else. " Dearest Harriet, you must not do that ; think of your nerves ; only consider, dearest, the state of your nerves ; Harriet, dear, you must not eat this ; you are not going to drink that, surely ; whatever will become of your poor nerves? Gracious heaven! What would Miss Warne say ? "

Miss Warne was the highest sanction ; her name was often invoked, and her judgment appealed to. " What will Miss Warne say ? " That single, simple, but momentous question set every other question at rest.

Who was Miss Warne? I inquired of the now nervous Harriet. She informed me, that she stood in the same relation to some coffee-house or hotel in London, as the lovely Eliza ; she was a daughter of the house ; a mature virgin also, quite ripe, perhaps rather too mellow ; a prim old maid indeed, an old frump, she said ; there was nothing particular about her in any way ; but Eliza had the highest opinion of Miss Warne ; she had been long her bosom friend !

Eliza was vigilant, keeping a sharp look-out after the nerves ; yet was she frequently off duty ; her time was chiefly spent in her bed-room. What does that dear Eliza do alone in her bed-room? Does she read ? No.—Does she work? Never. —Does she write ? No.—What does she do, then ?

Harriet came quite close to me, and answered in a whisper, lest peradventure her sister should hear her, with the serious air of one who communicates some profound and weighty secret, " She brushes her hair ! " The coarse black hair was glossy, no doubt ; but to give daily sixteen hours out of four-and-twenty to it, was certainly to bestow much time on a crop. Yet it was by no means impossible, that whilst she plied her hair-brush, she was revolving in her mind dearest Harriet's best interests ; or seriously reflecting upon what Miss Warne would say.

The poor Poet was overwhelmed by the affectionate invasion ; he lay prostrated and helpless, under the insupportable pressure of our domiciliary visit ; but the good Harriet knew how, school-girl like, and contrary to her sisterly allegiance, sometimes to take advantage, by stealth, of dear Eliza's absence. " Come quite close to me, and I will read to you. I must not speak loud, lest I should disturb poor Eliza."

Sometimes she could escape for a short walk before dinner. One day, whilst the guardian angel kept on brushing, we brushed off, and wandered to the river. We stood on the high centre of the old Roman bridge ; there was a mighty flood ; father Ouse had overflowed his banks, carrying away with him timber and what not.

" Is it not an interesting, a surprising sight ? "

" Yes, it is very wonderful. But, dear Harriet, how nicely that dearest Eliza would spin down the river ! How sweetly she would turn round and round, like that log of wood ! And, gracious heaven, what would Miss Warne say ? "

She turned her pretty face away, and laughed—as a slave laughs, who is beginning to grow weary of an intolerable yoke.

Harriet talks of Suicide.

"What is your opinion of suicide?　Did you never think of destroying yourself?"　It was a puzzling question indeed, for the thought had never entered my head.

"What do you think of matricide; of high treason; of rick-burning?　Did you never think of killing any one; of murdering your mother; of setting stack-yards on fire?"　I had never contemplated the commission of any of these crimes, and I should scarcely have been more astonished if I had been interrogated concerning my dispositions and, inclinations with respect to them, than I was when, early in our acquaintance, the good Harriet asked me, "What do you think of suicide?"

She often discoursed of her purpose of killing herself some day or other, and at great length, in a calm, resolute manner. She told me that at school, where she was very unhappy, as she said, but I could never discover why she was so, for she was treated with much kindness and exceedingly well instructed, she had conceived and contrived sundry attempts and purposes of destroying herself.　It is possible that her sister had assured her that she was very unhappy, and had supported the assurance by the incontrovertible opinion of Miss Warne, and of course Harriet became firmly convinced of her utter wretchedness.　She got up in the night, she said, sometimes with a fixed intention of making away with herself—in what manner she did not unfold—and bade a long farewell to the world, looked out of the window, taking leave of the bright moon and of all sublunary things, and then, it should seem, got into bed again and went quietly to sleep, and rose in the morning and wrote neatly upon her slate, in the school-room at Clapham, the admirable ordinances of Idomeneus and Numa Pompilius as sedately as before.

She spoke of self-murder serenely before strangers; and at a dinner party I have heard her describe her feelings, opinions, and intentions with respect to suicide with prolix earnestness;

and she looked so calm, so tranquil, so blooming, and so hand-some, that the astonished guests smiled. She once, in particu-lar—I well remember the strange scene and the astonishment of the harmless company—at a Pythagorean dinner in the house of a medical philosopher, scattered dismay amongst a quiet party of vegetable-eaters, persons who would not slay a shrimp, or extinguish animal life in embro by eating an egg, by asking, whether they did not feel sometimes strongly in-clined to kill themselves.

The poor girl's monomania of self-destruction, which we long looked upon as a vain fancy, a baseless delusion, an in-consequent hallucination of the mind, amused us occasionally for some years; eventually it proved a sad reality, and drew forth many bitter tears.

SHELLEY AND SOUTHEY.

How Bysshe made the acquaintance of Southey, whether by personal or epistolary introduction, or through poetic sympa-thy, I never knew.

Concerning the intercourse of these two remarkable persons, I have heard from Shelley, and from others, several anecdotes.

"Southey had a large collection of books, very many of them old books, some rare works,—books in many languages, more particularly in Spanish. The shelves extended over the walls of every room in his large, dismal house in Keswick; they were in the bed-rooms, and even down the stairs. This I never saw elsewhere. I took out some volume one day, as I was going down stairs with him. Southey looked at me, as if he was dis-pleased, so I put it back again instantly, and I never ventured to take down one of his books another time. I used to glance my eye eagerly over the backs of the books, and read their titles, as I went up or down stairs. I could not help doing so, but I think he did not quite approve of it."

"Do you know that Southey did not like to have his books touched. Do you know why?"

"No! I do not know."

"You do not know? How I hate that there should be any

6

thing which you do not know!   For who will tell me if you will not?"

"I only know that persons who have large libraries sometimes have the same feeling."

"How strange that a man should have many thousands of books, and should have a secret in every book, which he cannot bear that anybody should know but himself. How rare and grim!   Do you believe, then, that Southey really had a secret in every one of his books?"

"No! I do not, indeed, Bysshe."

After musing for some minutes, he added : "There were not secrets in all his books, certainly, for he often took one down himself and showed me some remarkable passage ; and then he would let me keep it as long as I pleased, and turn over the leaves, if he had taken it down himself ; so there could be no secret there.   And yet," he continued, after further reflection, "perhaps there was a secret ; but he thought that I could not find it out."

"Were the passages which he showed you really remarkable?"

"They might be, sometimes ; but for the most part they were not ; at least, I did not think them so.   They usually appeared trifling.   He never discussed any subject ; he gave his own opinion, commonly, in a very absolute manner ; he used to lay down the law, to dogmatize.   What he said was seldom his own,—it seldom came from himself.   He repeated long quotations, read extracts which he had made, or took down books and read from them aloud, or pointed out something for me to read, which would settle the matter at once without appeal.   His conversation was rather interesting, and only moderately instructive ; he was not so much a man as a living common-place book, a talking album filled with long extracts from long-forgotten authors on unimportant subjects.   Still his intercourse was very agreeable.   I liked much to be with him ; besides, he was a good man and exceedingly kind."

When Southey died his books were brought to the hammer

—as the phrase is. I picked up a few of them, rather as memorials than for their intrinsic value. Several of these were bound in the Chinese fashion, as I had heard that many of his books were, that is to say, in silk, cloth, velvet, and not in leather.

Mrs. Southey had been a milliner at Bath, a certain Miss —— * a lovely creature, as I have been told, as every Bath milliner ought to be; and no doubt a very estimable person. After her marriage she used up her remnants in a truly conjugal and most beneficial manner, in binding strongly and very neatly such of her husband's books as required it. I possess one of these bound with a bit of modest gingham, and another in a pretty piece of Irish poplin; both volumes are likewise adorned by the autograph of the author of Madoc; they are therefore, on all accounts, to be cherished.

In associating with Southey, not only was it necessary to salvation to refrain from touching his books, but various rites, ceremonies, and usages must be rigidly observed. At certain appointed hours only was he open to conversation; at the seasons which had been predestined from all eternity for holding intercourse with his friends. Every hour of the day had its commission—every half-hour was assigned to its own peculiar, undeviating function. The indefatigable student gave a detailed account of his most painstaking life, every moment of which was fully employed and strictly pre-arranged, to a certain literary Quaker lady.

" I rise at five throughout the year; from six till eight I read Spanish; then French, for one hour; Portuguese, next, for half an hour,—my watch lying on the table; I give two hours to poetry; I write prose for two hours; I translate so long; I

* [Edith Fricker. Southey married her on the 14th of November. 1795, at Radcliff Church, Biistol. "Immediately after the ceremony they parted," writes his son, the Rev. Cuthbert Southey. "My mother wore her wedding ring hung round her neck, and preserved her maiden name until the report of their marriage had spread abroad." Joseph Cottle was very kind to the lovers. "The very money with which I bought my wedding ring," Southey wrote in 1808, "and paid my marriage fees was supplied by you." Coleridge married one of the Misses Fricker, for there were three of them, Sara, and Lovell I think another.—S.]

make extracts so long;" and so of the rest, until the poor fellow had fairly fagged himself into his bed again.

"And, pray, when dost thou think, friend?" she asked, drily, to the great discomfiture of the future Laureate.

From morn till night, from the cradle to the grave, the hard reading, hard writing pansophist had never once found a single spare moment for such a purpose. The fable, if it be a fable, is told of thee, too, dearest Bysshe. Shelley also was always reading; at his meals a book lay by his side, on the table, open. Tea and toast were often neglected, his author seldom; his mutton and potatoes might grow cold; his interest in a work never cooled. He invariably sallied forth, book in hand, reading to himself, if he was alone, if he had a companion reading aloud. He took a volume to bed with him, and read as long as his candle lasted; he then slept—impatiently, no doubt—until it was light, and he recommenced reading at the early dawn. One day we were walking together, arm-in-arm, under the gate of the Middle Temple, in Fleet Street; Shelley, with open book, was reading aloud; a man with an apron said to a brother operative, "See, there are two of your damnation lawyers; they are always reading!" The tolerant philosopher did not choose to be reminded that he had once been taken for a lawyer; he declared the fellow was an ignorant wretch! He was loth to leave his book to go to bed, and frequently sat up late reading; sometimes indeed he remained at his studies all night. In consequence of this great watching, and of almost incessant reading, he would often fall asleep in the day-time—dropping off in a moment—like an infant. He often quietly transferred himself from his chair to the floor, and slept soundly on the carpet, and in the winter upon the rug, basking in the warmth like a cat; and like a cat his little round head was roasted before a blazing fire. If any one humanely covered the poor head to shield it from the heat, the covering was impatiently put aside in his sleep. "You make your brains boil, Bysshe. I have seen and heard the steam rushing out violently at your nostrils and ears!"

SOUTHEY'S EPIC.

Southey was addicted to reading his terrible epics—before they were printed—to any one who seemed to be a fit subject for the cruel experiment. He soon set his eyes on the new comer, and one day having effected the caption of Shelley, he immediately lodged him securely in a little study up-stairs, carefully locking the door upon himself and his prisoner and putting the key in his waistcoat-pocket. There was a window in the room, it is true, but it was so high above the ground that Baron Trenck himself would not have attempted it. " Now you shall be delighted," Southey said ; " but sit down." Poor Bysshe sighed, and took his seat at the table. The author seated himself opposite, and placing his MS. on the table before him, began to read slowly and distinctly. The poem, if I mistake not, was " The Curse of Kehama."* Charmed with his own composition the admiring author read on, varying his voice occasionally, to point out the finer passages and invite applause. There was no commendation ; no criticism ; all was hushed. This was strange. Southey raised his eyes from the neatly-written MS. ; Shelley had disappeared. This was still more strange. Escape was impossible ; every precaution had been taken, yet he had vanished. Shelley had glided noiselessly from his chair to the floor, and the insensible young Vandal lay buried in profound sleep underneath the table. No wonder the indignant and injured bard afterwards enrolled the sleeper as a member of the Satanic school, and inscribed his name, together with that of Byron, on a gibbet ! I have been told on his own authority, that wherever Southey passed the night in travelling, he bought some book, if it were possible to pick one up on a stall, or in a shop, and wrote his own name and the name of the place at the bottom of the title-page, and the date, including the day of the week. This inscription, he found, served in some measure the purpose of a

[* It could not have been "The Curse of Kehama," for it was already in print; but it might have been "Roderick, the Last of the Goths," which was published in 1814.—S.]

journal, for when he looked at such a date it reminded him, through the association of ideas, of many particulars of his journey. I have a small volume in the German language, thus inscribed by Southey, at the foot of the title-page; the place is some town in France.

MRS. SOUTHEY'S TEA-CAKES.

Bysshe chanced to call, one afternoon, during his residence at Keswick, on his new acquaintance, a man eminent, and of rare epic fertility. It was at four o'clock; Southey and his wife were sitting together at their tea after an early dinner, for it was washing-day. A cup of tea was offered, which was accepted, and a plate piled high with tea-cakes was handed to the illustrious visitor; of these he refused to partake, with signs of strong aversion. He was always abstemious in his diet, at this period of his life peculiarly so; a thick hunch of dry bread, possibly a slice of brown bread and butter, might have been welcome to the Spartan youth; but hot tea-cakes heaped up, in scandalous profusion, well buttered, blushing with currants or sprinkled thickly with carraway-seeds, and reeking with allspice, shocked him grievously. It was a Persian apparatus, which he detested,—a display of excessive and unmanly luxury by which the most powerful empires have been overthrown,—that threatened destruction to all, social order, and would have rendered abortive even the divine Plato's scheme of a frugal and perfect republic. A poet's dinner is never a very heavy meal; on a washing-day, we may readily believe, that it is as light as his own fancy. So far in the day Southey, no doubt, had fared sparingly; he was a hale, healthy, hearty man, breathing the keen mountain air, and working hard, too hard, poor fellow; he was hungry, and did not shrink from the tea-cakes which had been furnished to make up for his scanty mid-day repast. Shelley watched his unworthy proceedings, eying him with pain and pity. Southey had not noticed his distress, but he held his way, clearing the plates of buttered currant-cakes, and buttered seed-cakes, with an equal relish.

" Why! good God, Southey ! " Bysshe suddenly exclaimed, for he could no longer contain his boiling indignation, " I am ashamed of you !   It is awful, horrible, to see such a man as you are greedily devouring this nasty stuff ! "

" Nasty stuff, indeed ! How dare you call my tea-cakes nasty stuff, sir ? "

Mrs. Southey was charming, but it is credibly reported that she was also rather sharp.

" Nasty stuff ! What right have you, pray, Mr. Shelley, to come into my house, and to tell me to my face that my tea-cakes, which I made myself, are nasty ; and to blame my husband for eating them ? How in the world can they be nasty ? I washed my hands well before I made them, and I sprinkled them with flour. The board and the rolling-pin were quite clean ; they had been well scraped and sprinkled with flour. The flour was taken out of the meal-tub, which is always kept locked ; here is the key ! There was nothing nasty in the ingredients, I am sure ; we have a very good grocer in Keswick. Do you suppose that I would put anything nasty into them ? What right have you to call them nasty ; you ought to be ashamed of yourself, and not Mr. Southey ; he surely has a right to eat what his wife puts before him ! Nasty stuff ! I like your impertinence ! "

In the course of this animated invective, Bysshe put his face close to the plate, and curiously scanned the cakes. He then took up a piece and ventured to taste it, and, finding it very good, he began to eat as greedily as Southey himself. The servant, a neat, stout, little, ruddy Cumberland girl, with a very white apron, brought in a fresh supply ; these also the brother philosophers soon despatched, eating one against the other in generous rivalry. Shelley then asked for more, but no more were to be had ; the whole batch had been consumed. The lovely Edith was pacified on seeing that her cakes were relished by the two hungry poets, and she expressed her regret that she did not know that Mr. Shelley was coming to take tea with her, or she would have made a larger provision. Harriet, who told me the tale, added : " We were to have hot tea-cakes every evening 'for ever.' I was to make them myself, and Mrs. Southey was to teach me."

" More Bacon."

The Divine Poet, like many other wiser men, used to pass very readily and suddenly from one extreme to the other. I myself witnessed, some years later, a like rapid transition. When he resided at Bishopsgate, I usually walked down from London, and spent Sunday with him. One frosty Saturday, in the middle of the winter, being overcome by hunger, I halted by the way—it was a rare occurrence—for refreshment, at a humble inn on Hounslow Heath. I had just taken my seat on a Windsor chair, at a small round beechen table in a little dark room with a well-sanded floor, when I saw Bysshe striding past the window. He was coming to meet me; I went to the door, and hailed him.

" Come along! It is dusk; tea will be ready; we shall be late!"

" No! I must have something to eat first; come in!"

He walked about the room impatiently.

" When will your dinner be ready; what have you ordered?"

" I asked for eggs and bacon, but they have no eggs; I am to have some fried bacon."

He was struck with horror, and his agony was increased at the appearance of my dinner. Bacon was proscribed by him; it was gross and abominable. It distressed him greatly at first to see me eat the bacon; but he gradually approached the dish, and, studying the bacon attentively, said, "So this is bacon!" He then ate a small piece. "It is not so bad either!" More was ordered; he devoured it voraciously.

" Bring more bacon!" It was brought, and eaten.

" Let us have another plate."

" I am very sorry, gentlemen," said the old woman, "but indeed I have no more in the house."

The Poet was angry at the disappointment, and rated her.

" What business has a woman to keep an inn, who has not

enough bacon in the house for her guests? She ought to be killed !"

" Really, gentlemen, I am very sorry to be out of bacon; but I only keep by me as much as I think will be wanted. I can easily get more from Staines; they have very good bacon always in Staines!"

" As there is nothing more to be had, come along, Bysshe; let us go home to tea!"

" No! Not yet; she is going to Staines, to get us some more bacon."

" She cannot go to-night; come along!"

He departed with reluctance, grumbling as we walked home-wards at the scanty store of bacon, lately condemned as gross and abominable. The dainty rustic food made a strong impression upon his lively fancy, for when we arrived the first words he uttered were, " We have been eating bacon together on Hounslow Heath, and do you know it was very nice. Cannot we have bacon here, Mary?"

" Yes, you can, if you please; but not to-night. Here is your tea; take that!"

" I had rather have some more bacon!" sighed the Poet.

SHELLEY IN IRELAND.

On the 12th of February, 1812, a young Englishman, with his wife and sister-in-law, arrived in the capital of Ireland, and took up his residence in the principal street of that city. The gentleman had completed his nineteenth year a few months before, but still preserved the appearance of a boy. His wife, remarkable for her fair and girlish beauty, was still younger than her husband, and her sister, the eldest of the party, was but little in advance of her companions as to age. This not very formidable-looking trio had come to Ireland on a business of no small importance, for which they had been long preparing. Their object was, "as far as in them lay"—to use the language of the chief organizer—to effect a fundamental change in the constitution of the British Empire, to restore to Ireland its native Parliament, to carry the great measure of justice

6*

called Catholic Emancipation, and to establish a philanthropic association for the amelioration of human society all over the world. The young man was perfectly unknown in Ireland, or even in England outside the circle of his own family and a few friends. He had published anonymously two or three little books, both in prose and verse, which perhaps may be considered the least promising first attempts ever made public by a man of genius.

On the 12th of February, 1812, he arrived an unknown stranger; by the 27th of the same month he had already become famous. To use his own language in an unpublished letter, he had within that short time "excited a sensation of wonder in Dublin," and "expectation was on the tiptoe." The day following the date of this letter he made his first public appearance in a great assembly, which he roused to enthusiasm by his fervid eloquence, and a week later appeared the first of the innumerable papers which year after year, and perhaps century after century, were destined to be written upon the genius and the story of that then unknown young man, under the now familiar headline of Percy Bysshe Shelley.

[Just before leaving Keswick Shelley had introduced himself to Godwin by letter. It was answered, and a correspondence ensued. It is rather dull reading in spite of the reputation of one of the writers, and the genius of the other. " I have been preparing an address to the Catholics of Ireland, which, however deficient may be its execution, I can by no means admit that it contains one sentiment which *can* harm the cause of liberty and happiness. It consists of the benevolent and tolerant deductions of philosophy reduced into the simplest language. I know it can do no harm; it cannot excite rebellion, as its main principle is to trust the success of a cause to the energy of its truth. It cannot ' widen the breach between the kingdoms,' as it attempts to convey to the vulgar mind sentiments of universal philanthropy; and whatever impressions it may produce, they can be no other but those of peace and harmony; it owns no religion but benevolence, no cause but virtue, no party but the world. I shall devote myself with unremitting zeal, as far as an uncertain state of health will permit, towards forwarding the great ends of virtue and happiness in Ireland, regarding as I do the present state of that country's affairs as an opportunity which, if I, being thus disengaged, permit to pass unoccupied, I am unworthy of the character which I have assumed." Two days after his arrival in Dublin, he wrote to a female correspondent that he had nothing to fear there but Government, which would not *dare* to be so bare-facedly oppressive as to attack his Address, which would breathe the spirit of peace, toleration, and patience. Godwin had given him a letter of introduction to the Hon. John Philpot Curran, the Master of the Rolls, but no attention was paid to it. "He seems studiously to have kept out of his way," Mr. MacCarthy observes, "and Shelley did not succeed even in seeing him until some time after the 18th of March—a period of at least five or six weeks. Godwin had some misgivings as to the reception Shelley possibly might meet with; for before the latter had made any complaint of inattention, he wrote to him in the following words :—"How did you manage with Curran? I hope you have seen him. I should not wonder, however, if your pamphlet has frightened him. You should have left my letter with your card the first time you called, and then it was his business to have sought you." But this is precisely what Shelley had done ten days before his pamphlet was printed ; and in those ten days it is plain that Curran had not thought it his business to walk over to Sackville Street to seek Shelley. *The Address to the Irish People* was first announced for publication on Tuesday, February 25th, 1812. In *The Dublin Evening Post* of that day is the following advertisement :—

This day is published, price Fivepence, to be had of all the Booksellers,
AN ADDRESS TO THE IRISH PEOPLE.
By Percy B. Shelley.

"Advertisement.—The lowest possible price is set on this publication, because it is the intention of the Author to awaken in the minds of the Irish poor a knowledge of their real state, summarily pointing out the evils of that state, and suggesting rational means of remedy.—Catholic Emancipation, and a Repeal of the Union Act (the latter the most successful engine that England ever wielded over the misery of fallen

Ireland) being treated of in the following Address, as grievances which unanimity and resolution may remove, and associations conducted with peaceable firmness, being earnestly recommended as means for embodying that unanimity and firmness which must finally be successful."

Shelley's *Address to the Irish People* came from the printer's hand on the 24th of February, 1812. On that day, as we have seen, he sent an early copy by post to Godwin. On the following day, the 25th, the pamphlet was published. The advertisement which appeared in the *Dublin Evening Post* of that date has already been given. We may be sure that one of the earliest copies presented personally by Shelley was to the Master of the Rolls. "I have not seen Mr. Curran," says Shelley, in a letter to Godwin of the 8th of March. "I have called repeatedly, left my address and my pamphlet. I *will* see him before I leave Dublin." On the day of publication he sent a copy of the *Address to the Irish People* to Hamilton Rowan, with the following letter :—

"7, Lower Sackville Street, Feb. 25th, 1812.

"SIR,—Although I have not the pleasure of being personally known to you, I consider the motives which actuated me in writing the inclosed sufficiently introductory to authorize me in sending you some copies, and waiving ceremonials in a case where public benefit is concerned. Sir, although an Englishman, I feel for Ireland ; and I have left the country in which the chance of birth placed me for the sole purpose of adding my little stock of usefulness to the fund which I hope that Ireland possesses to aid me in the unequal yet sacred combat in which she is engaged. In the course of a few days more I shall print another small pamphlet, which shall be sent to you. I have intentionally vulgarized the language of the enclosed. I have printed 1500 copies, and am now distributing them throughout Dublin.

"Sir, with respect,

"I am your obedient humble servant,

"P. B. SHELLEY."

The two days that followed the writing of the letter to Hamilton Rowan must have been busy and exciting ones for Shelley. How he was occupied, and the extraordinary steps he took to circulate his pamphlet among the people of Dublin, will be best shown by the following copious extracts from a hitherto unpublished letter of Shelley to his philosophical female friend at Hurstpierpoint in Sussex. Long as these extracts are, they form only a portion of the letter. . I have selected only those passages that refer to the public objects he had in view—such explanations as seem needful will be given at the end.

From an unpublished letter of Shelley to Miss Hitchener.

"Feb. 27 [1812], 7, Lower Sackville Street.

"I have already sent 400 of my Irish pamphlets into the world, and they have excited a sensation of wonder in Dublin. 1100 yet remain for distribution. Copies have been sent to sixty public-houses. No prosecution is yet attempted. I do not see how it can be. Congratulate me, my friend, for everything proceeds well. I could not expect more rapid success. The persons with whom I have got acquainted approve of my principles . . . . but they differ from the mode of my improving their principles." . . . . [Referring to his wish to have his friend with him in Dublin, he says that it did not arise from any private partiality], "but because you would share with me the high delight of awaking a noble nation from the lethargy of its bondage. Expectation is on the tip-toe. I send a man out every-day to distribute copies, with instructions where and how to give them. His account corresponds with the multitudes of people who possess them. I stand at the balcony of our window, and watch till I see a man *who looks likely.* I throw a book to him. On Monday my next book makes its appearance ; this is addressed to a different class, recommending and proposing associations. I have in my mind a plan for proselytizing the young men at Dublin College. Those who are not entirely given up to the grossness of dissipation are perhaps reclaimable." . . . . "Whilst you are with us in Wales I shall attempt to organize one there" [that is, a "philanthropic association "], which will co-operate with the Dublin one. Might I not extend them all over England, and *quietly* revolutionize the country?" . . . . "My *youth* is much against me here. Strange that truth should not be judged by its inherent excellence, independent of any reference to the utterer. To improve on this *advantage*, the servant gave out I was only fifteen years of age." . . . . "I have not yet seen Curran. I do not like him for accepting the office of Master" [of the Rolls]. "O'Connor, brother to the rebel Arthur, is here." [I have] "written to him. Do not fear what you say in your letters. I am resolved. Good principles are scarce here. The public papers are either Oppositionists or Ministerial. One is as contemptible and narrow as the other. I wish I could change this. I am of course hated by both of those parties. The remnant of united Irishmen whose wrongs make them hate England, I have more hope of. I have met with no determined republicans, but have found some who are democrat*ifiable*." . . . . "We shall leave this place at the end of April. I must not be idle in Wales: there you will come to us. Bring the dear little Americans, resign your school, and live with us for ever."

The postcript is by Harriet.

"Percy has given me his letter to fill up, but what I'm to say I really do not know. Oh, yesterday I received a most affectionate letter from dear Mrs. C——" [probably Calvert]. "Now don't you be jealous when I mention her name. She is afraid we shall effect no good here, and thinks our opinions will change of the Irish. We have seen very little of them as yet, but when Percy is more known, I suppose that we shall know more at the same time. My pen is very bad, according to custom. I am sure you would laugh were you to see us give the pamphlets. We throw them out of window, and give them to men that we pass in the streets. For myself I am ready to die of laughter when it is done, and Percy looks so grave. Yesterday he put one into a woman's hood of a cloak. She knew nothing of it, and we passed her and could hardly get on, my muscles (?) were so irritated."(?)

There is a second postscript by Shelley.

"I have been necessarily called away whilst Harriet has been scribbling. You may guess how much my time is taken up. Adieu—the post will go. You will soon hear again from your affectionate and unalterable PERCY."

The whole of these curious extracts will be read with interest, particularly perhaps the girlish and simple postscript of Harriet. The eleven hundred copies of the *Address to the Irish People* which remained for distribution seem to have been almost all dispersed by the 18th of March. It is to be noticed that at the moment when Shelley "could not expect more rapid success," he had fixed the time of his intended departure from Ireland. This disposes of the statement so frequently repeated that Shelley abandoned his Irish project in disgust. The man whom Shelley sent out every day to distribute the pamphlets, was in all probability "the servant" who gave out that Shelley was only fifteen years of age. This was Daniel Hill, who accompanied the Shelleys to Barnstaple, who was arrested and imprisoned there, who turned up at a critical moment at Tanyrallt, returned with the Shelleys to Dublin, and eventually went with them to London. The letter of Shelley corroborates the story told in the *North British Review*, for November, 1847, in an article on the *Life and Writings of Shelley*. The paper was written by my lamented friend the late Dr. Anster, the translator of *Faust*. He says :—" Shelley's pamphlet is before us. Medwin it seems searched in vain for a copy. Ours was obtained through an Irish friend of Shelley's, whose acquaintance with the poet originated accidentally. A poor man offered the pamphlet for a few pence— its price stated on the title-page was fivepence. On being asked how he got it, he said a parcel of them were given him by a young gentleman, who told him to get what he could for them—at all events to distribute them. Inquiry was made at

Shelley's lodgings to ascertain the truth of the vendor's story. He was not at home ; but when he heard of it he went to return the visit, and kindly acquaintanceship thus arose. The Shelleys—husband and wife—were then Pythagoreans. Shelley spoke as a man believing in the metempsychosis—and they did not eat animal food. They seem however to have tolerated it ; for on one occasion a fowl was murdered for our friend's dinner. Of the first Mrs. Shelley the recollection of our friend is faint, but it is of an amiable and unaffected person ; very young and very pleasing, and she and Shelley seem much attached."

The balcony in front of 7, Lower Sackville Street, from which Shelley and Harriet threw the pamphlets to whoever looked " likely," still remains. It runs across the whole width of the house, so that Percy and Harriet had each a window from which they could bombard the astonished town with " books." We have no doubt that he must have enjoyed this mode of diffusing useful knowledge immensely—quite as much as he did the following year at Lymouth when he substituted for it his oil-skin boats and air-tight bottles. The house then belonging to Mr. Dunne, was occupied for many years by Messrs. Köhler and Co., and is now in possession of Messrs. Stark Brothers, printsellers and artists. As long as the balcony remains it will always be an object of interest to those who regard with something like affection even the " local habitation " of an author whom they love as well as admire.

SHELLEY IN FISHAMBLE STREET.

The next important movement made by Shelley in his Dublin crusade took place three days after the publication of his *Address to the Irish People*. That pamphlet had appeared on Tuesday, the 25th of February, 1812, and on the Friday following, the 28th of the same month, the long announced Aggregate Meeting of the Catholics of Ireland took place in the historic little theatre in Fishamble Street. Shelley attended that meeting, and spoke to an important resolution for the space of an hour.

The morning of Friday the 28th of February, 1812, must have been an exciting one for the three propagandists of philanthropy—Shelley, Harriet, and Eliza Westbrook, as they met together in the drawing-room of No. 7, Lower Sackville Street, Dublin. The youthful Shelley was on that day to present himself before an immense assembly, and to put to the test his power of addressing or influencing an audience. The ladies we may be sure had determined to accompany him to the meeting, and with all her confidence in the ability of Percy, we can have little doubt that the gentle Harriet was full of anxiety as to his success.

The vigilance exercised by the Irish Government in ascertaining through their secret agents the arrangements of the Catholics for the intended meeting of February 28th, 1812, did not relax when the meeting took place. Two persons were sent to Fishamble Street Theatre to furnish special reports of the proceedings. Both reporters were connected with the police—one a chief constable, Mr. Michael Farrell, well known in the local history of the period ; the other a Mr. Manning, who held an inferior position. These reports are preserved among the State Papers in the Record Office. Unfortunately they give us little or no information on the subject of Shelley. In one he is not mentioned at all ; in the other he is barely alluded to. Of the two reports, that signed Thos. K. Manning is the longest. In this Shelley's name does not appear. Another young man, afterwards very distinguished, the late Sir Thomas Wyse, the English Ambassador in Greece, made his first appearance in public at the same meeting. He proposed the resolution to which Shelley spoke, and is thus described by Mr. Manning :—

" On this resolution, Mr. Wise, a young boy, delivered a speech of considerable length and replete with much elegant language ; the principal matter it contained of notice was, that he lamented that the Regent should abandon Mr. Fox's principles and join in a shameful coalition, or that he had been so far *womanized*—here he was interrupted by a question of order."

In 1812, Mr. Wyse was twenty-one years of age, having been born in 1791 ; the description "a young boy" could therefore be scarcely applicable to him. Shelley was nineteen years and six months old, but looked so young that his servant could give out with some appearance of truth that he was but fifteen. The full report of the elaborate speech of Mr. Wyse is now before us, and it contains no language in the slightest degree disrespectful to the Prince Regent, neither was the speaker called to order. In fact, the business of the meeting was to adopt an address to his Royal Highness, and the observations alluded to by the reporter could scarcely have been used by any one who had been selected by the managers to take an important part in its proceedings. Shelley's speech was volunteered. His strong feeling towards the Prince at this time we know from his own letters, and he may easily have strayed into the expression of them. In one of his letters, hitherto unpublished, an extract from which will presently be given, he tells us that some of his observations met with interruption. On the whole we think that Mr. Manning, in copying his notes, transferred the description from Shelley to Mr. Wyse.

The second reporter, Mr. Farrell, the peace officer, mentions Shelley but very slightly. He says :—

" Lord Glentworth said a few words—a Mr. Bennett spoke, also Mr. Shelley, who stated himself to be a native of England."

With these manuscript reports the Lord Lieutenant forwarded to the Home Secretary a copy of *The Dublin Evening Post* of Saturday, the 29th February, 1812, containing a full report of the proceedings at the meeting which took place the day before. It is from this paper that the only version of Shelley's speech hitherto published has been taken. It was originally extracted by the present writer, from whose transcript it was copied into Mr. Middleton's *Shelley and his Writings* (vol. i. p. 212).

There are two other versions of the speech which have not previously been known. One of these is indeed very short, but as it expressly mentions the kind manner in which the youthful speaker was received by the meeting, it is very valuable as part of the refutation of the calumnious statement made years after by Mr. Hogg, which has been so improperly repeated by others who reject Mr. Hogg's testimony when they dislike it, and adopt it when it is in accordance with their own prejudices. This brief report appeared on the morning after the meeting in *The Freeman's Journal*, of Saturday, Feb. 29th, 1812. It was repeated in *The Hibernian Journal, or Daily Chronicle of Liberty*, Dublin, Monday, March 2d, 1812. And again in a more accessible shape in *Walker's Hibernian Magazine* for February, 1812, p. 83. As it was the earliest report, it may be here given first :—

*Shelley's Speech at Fishamble Street Theatre, Dublin,
Feb. 28th, 1812.*

From *The Freeman's Journal*, Dublin, Feb. 29th, 1812.

" On the fifth [it should have been the *sixth*] resolution being proposed, Mr. Shelley, an English gentleman (very young), the son of a Member of Parliament, rose to address the meeting. He was received with great kindness, and declared that the greatest misery this country endured was the Union Law, the Penal Code, and the state of the representation. He drew a lively picture of the misery of the country, which he attributed to the unfortunate Act of Legislative Union."

On the evening of the same day, in the *Dublin Evening Post* of Saturday, the 29th of February, 1812, a fuller report of the speech is given. The italics are in the original.

Shelley's Speech.

From *The Dublin Evening Post*, Saturday, 29th Feb., 1812.

" Mr. Shelley requested a hearing. He was an Englishman, and when he reflected on *the crimes committed by his nation on Ireland*, he could not but blush for his countrymen, did he not know that arbitrary power never failed to corrupt the heart of man.   (Loud applause for several minutes.)

" He had come to Ireland for the sole purpose of interesting himself in her misfortunes. He was deeply impressed with a sense of the evils which Ireland endured, and he considered them to be truly ascribed to the fatal effects of the legislative union with Great Britain.

" He walked through the streets, and he saw the *fane of Liberty converted into a temple of Mammon.* (Loud applause.) He beheld beggary and famine in the country, and he could lay his hand on his heart and say that the cause of such sights was the union with Great Britain. (Hear, hear.) He was re-solved to do his utmost to promote a Repeal of the Union. Catholic Emancipation would do a great deal towards the amelioration of the condition of the people, but he was con-vinced that the Repeal of the Union was of more importance. He considered that the victims whose members were vibrating on gibbets were driven to the commission of the crimes which they expiated by their lives by the effects of the Union."

The third and longest report of Shelley's speech is as follows. It is taken from *The Patriot*, Dublin, 2d March, 1812 :—

" Mr. Shelley then addressed the Chair. He hoped he should not be accounted a transgressor on the time of the meeting. He felt inadequate to the task he had undertaken, but he hoped the feelings which urged him forward would plead his pardon. He was an Englishman ; when he reflected on the outrages that his countrymen had committed here for the last twenty years he confessed that he blushed for them. He had come to Ireland for the sole purpose of interesting himself in the misfortunes of this country, and impressed with a full conviction of the necessity of Catholic Emancipation, and of the baneful effects which the union with Great Britain had entailed upon Ireland. He had walked through the fields of the country and the streets of the city, and he had in both seen the miserable effects of that fatal step. He had seen that edifice which ought to have been the fane of their liberties converted to a temple of Mammon. Many of the crimes which are daily committed he could not avoid attributing to the effect of that measure, which had thrown numbers of people out of the employment they had in manufacture, and induced them to commit acts of the greatest desperation for the support of their existence.

" He could not imagine that the religious opinion of a man should exclude him from the rights of society. The original founder of our religion taught no such doctrine. Equality in this respect was general in the American States, and why not here ? Did a change of place change the nature of man ? He would beg those in power to recollect the French Revolution : the suddenness, the violence with which it burst forth, and the causes which gave rise to it.

" Both the measures of Emancipation and a Repeal of the Union should meet his decided support, but he hoped many years would not pass over his head when he would make himself conspicuous at least by his zeal for them."

In these versions of the speech, which are the only ones I have been able to find in the Irish papers of the period, or rather in those of them that are still extant, there is no suggestion that Shelley met with the slightest discourtesy from those he addressed. Indeed, it would be strange if he had. His youth, his enthusiasm, his eloquence, as we will find, delighted the assembly by which, as we are told in *The Freeman's Journal,* " he was received with great kindness." Some slight interruption he *did* meet with at the beginning, but that was, as he tells us himself in the unpublished letter we have referred to, when he spoke of " religion." In this letter, which is dated " 17, Grafton Street, Dublin, March 14th, 1812," he says :—

" My speech was misinterpreted. I spoke for more than an hour. The hisses with which they greeted me when I spoke of *religion,* though in terms of respect, were mixed with applause when I avowed my mission. The newspapers have only noted that which did not excite disapprobation."

Shelley as an Orator.

The following important letter, now for the first time given in connection with the life of Shelley, settles the interesting question, which has often been raised, of Shelley's probable success as an orator had he devoted himself to the cultivation of eloquence instead of poetry.

Medwin, Trelawny, and Captain Williams the partner of his fate, speak highly of the elevation of Shelley's ordinary conversation, which rose occasionally into an unstudied eloquence. But they never heard him address a public assembly. The only one hitherto recorded—except the anonymous writers subsequently to be mentioned—who had this opportunity, and made some allusion to it, was the late Chief Baron Woulfe. His description leaves the impression that Shelley was a cold, methodical, and ineffective speaker. Chief Baron Woulfe was in bad health when he is reported to have mentioned his recollection of Shelley's manner. Many years had elapsed, and Shelley could have scarcely been recalled to his memory except by an effort. Of far different value is the testimony wrung most reluctantly at the moment from an unwilling witness. That testimony is contained in the following letter, which was published in the Government organ of the day, *The Dublin Journal*, a paper originally started by George Faulkner, the publisher of Swift :—

Shelley as an orator, described by " An Englishman" in 1812.

"Saturday, March 7th, 1812.

"To the Editor of The Dublin Journal.

" Sir,—Our public meetings now-a-days, instead of exhibiting the deliberations of men of acknowledged wisdom and experience, resemble mere debating societies, where unfledged candidates for national distinction rant out a few trite and commonplace observations with as much exultation and self-applause as if they possessed the talents or eloquence of a Saurin or a Burke. This remark is particularly applicable to almost the whole of the meetings which have been assembled within the last twelve months by the Catholics ; at which young gentlemen of this description have constantly intruded themselves upon the public notice, and by the unseasonable and injudicious violence of their language, have not a little prejudiced the cause they attempted to support. Curiosity and the expected gratification of hearing a display of oratory by some of the leading members of the Catholic body led me on Friday, for the first time, to the Aggregate Meeting in Fishamble Street. Being rather late I missed the orations of Mr. Connell [*sic*] and the leading orators, and only heard a dry monotonous effusion from Counsellor ——, and, to me, a most disgusting harangue from a stripling, with whom I am unacquainted, but who, I am sorry to say, styles himself my countryman—an Englishman. This young gentleman, after stating that he had been only a fortnight in Ireland, expatiated on the miseries which this country endured in consequence of its connection with his own, and asserted (from the knowledge, I presume, which his peculiar sagacity enabled him to acquire in so short a period) that its cities were depopulated, its fields laid waste, and its inhabitants degraded and enslaved ; and all this by its union with England. If it revolted against my principles, Mr. Editor, to hear such language from one of my own countrymen, you will readily conceive that my disgust was infinitely heightened to observe with what transport the invectives of this renegade Englishman against his native country were *hailed* by the assembly he addressed. Joy beamed in every countenance and rapture glistened in every eye at the aggravated detail : the delirium of ecstasy got the better of prudential control; the veil was for a moment withdrawn. I thought I saw the *purpose*, in spite of the *pretence*, written in legible characters in each of their faces, and though emancipation *alone* flowed from the tongue, separation and ascendancy were rooted in the heart.

" As for the young gentleman alluded to, I congratulate the Catholics of Ireland on the acquisition of so *patriotic* and *enlightened* an advocate ; and England, I dare say, will spare him without regret. I must, however, remark that as the love of his country is one of the strongest principles implanted in the breast of man by his Maker, and as the affections are more ardent in youth than in maturer years, that this young gentleman should at so early an age have overcome the strongest impulses of nature, seems to me a complete refutation of the hitherto supposed infallible maxim that *Nemo fuit repente turpissimus.*

"AN ENGLISHMAN."

The same day, the 7th of March, 1812, on which *The Dublin Journal* published this sarcastic allusion to the speech of "a stripling" it does not condescend to name, is memorable in the life of Shelley as that on which he is first spoken of openly in terms of enthusiastic admiration and praise. It appeared in *The Weekly Messenger*, another Dublin journal, but differing very widely in politics from that which contains the letter of "An Englishman." Shelley seems to have been rather proud of the notice, as he sent it at once to Godwin. Writing to the philosopher on the following day, he says, "You will see the account of ME in the newspapers. I am vain, but not so foolish as not to be rather piqued than gratified at the eulogia of a journal."

The following is this very interesting article, the first public notice of Shelley. It is printed exactly as in the original :—

From *The Weekly Messenger*, Dublin, Saturday, March 7th, 1812.

"*Pierce Byshe Shelly Esq.*

" The highly interesting appearance of this young gentleman at the late Aggregate Meeting of the Catholics of Ireland, has naturally excited a spirit of enquiry, as to his objects and views, in coming forward at *such* a meeting; and the publications which he has circulated with such uncommon industry, through the Metropolis, has set curiosity on the wing to ascertain who he is, from whence he comes, and what his pretensions are to the confidence he solicits, and the character he assumes. To those who have read the productions we have alluded to, we need bring forward no evidence of the cultivation of his mind

—the benignity of his principles—or the peculiar fascination with which he seems able to recommend them.

"Of this gentleman's family we can say but little, but we can set down what we have heard from respectable authority. That his father is a member of the Imperial Parliament, and that this young gentleman, whom we have seen, is the *immediate* heir of one of the *first* fortunes in England. Of his principles and his manners we can say more, because we can collect from conversation, as well as from reading, that he seems devoted to the propagation of those divine and Christian feelings which purify the human heart, give shelter to the poor, and consolation to the unfortunate. That he is the *bold* and *intrepid* advocate of those principles which are calculated to give energy to truth, and to depose from their guilty eminence the bad and vicious passions of a corrupt community;—that a universality of charity is *his* object, and a perfectibility of human society *his* end, which cannot be attained by the *conflicting* dogmas of religious sects, *each* priding itself on the extinction of the *other*, and *all* existing by the mutual misfortunes which flow from polemical warfare. The principles of this young gentleman embrace *all* sects and all persuasions. His doctrines, *political* and *religious*, may be accommodated to *all*; every friend to true Christianity will be his religious friend, and every enemy to the liberties of Ireland will be his *political* enemy. The weapons he wields are those of reason, and the most *social benevolence*. He deprecates violence in the accomplishment of his views, and relies upon the mild and merciful spirit of toleration for the completion of all his designs, and the consummation of all his wishes. To the religious bigot such a *missionary of truth* is a formidable opponent, by the political monopolist he will be considered the child of Chimera, the creature of fancy, an imaginary legislator who presumes to make laws without reflecting upon his *materials*, and despises those considerations which have baffled the hopes of the most philanthropic and the efforts of the most wise. It is true, human nature may be too depraved for such a hand as Mr. Shelly's to form to anything that is good, or liberal, or beneficent. Let him but take down *one* of the rotten pillars by which society is *now* propped, and substitute the purity of his own principles, and Mr. Shelly shall have done a great and lasting service to human nature. To this gentleman Ireland is much indebted, for selecting *her* as the theatre of his first attempts in this holy work of human regeneration; the Catholics of Ireland should listen to him with respect, because they will find that an enlightened Englishman has interposed between the treason of their own countrymen and the almost conquered spirit of their country; that Mr. Shelly has come to Ireland to demonstrate in his person that there are hearts in his own country not rendered callous by six hundred years of injustice; and that the genius of freedom, which has communicated comfort and content to the cottage of the Englishman, has found its way to the humble roof of the Irish peasant, and promises by its presence to dissipate the sorrows of past ages, to obliterate the remembrance of persecution, and close the long and wearisome scene of centuries of human depression. We extract from Mr. Shelly's last production, which he calls "PROPOSALS FOR AN ASSOCIATION, &C."

THE SHELLEYS IN LONDON.

I had returned from the country at the end of October, 1812, and had resumed the duties of a pleader; I was sitting in my quiet lodgings with my tea and a book before me : it was one evening at the beginning of November, probably about ten o'clock. I was roused by a violent knocking at the street door, as if the watchman was giving the alarm of fire; some one ran furiously up-stairs, the door flew open, and Bysshe rushed into the middle of the room. I had not seen him for a year; not since they left me at York. I had not heard from him, nor indeed any tidings of him, for many months; not once after his departure from Keswick. I made several fruitless attempts to find out what had become of him soon after I came to reside in London the last spring.

The civil and obliging Mr Graham had unfortunately quitted his lodgings and the people could not tell me where he was;

he could have given me at once the information, which I so ardently desired. I called in Lincoln's Inn Fields, and I saw the elder of the cousins, the younger and more communicative one had gone to Edinburgh to study medicine. I had a very cold reception; of Bysshe he either knew, or chose to know, nothing.

It was evident there was a screw loose; he gave me no encouragement to call again, nothing, it was plain, was to be made of him, and I have never seen him since.

From this untoward sample it was conspicuously of no use to address myself to any other members of his family, or to their agents; the poor Poet was a prohibited book, closely sealed up and put away to be out of sight, and indeed out of mind. There was nothing to be done but to draw pleas, to keep terms, and to bide my time.

The time had now come suddenly and unexpectedly. Bysshe looked, as he always looked, wild, intellectual, unearthly; like a spirit that had just descended from the sky; like a demon risen at that moment out of the ground.

How had he found me out? I could never have discovered his hiding-place; in truth I had often tried in vain. He knew of my intention to become a law-student; he had been at the Treasury in Lincoln's Inn; they sent him to the Temple. I had dined that day in the Hall of the Middle Temple, and from thence they dispatched him to my special pleader, and he, with considerable hesitation, gave him my address.

The next morning this gentleman said to me, not without a certain trepidation :

" You had just left chambers last night, when a very wild-looking man came here, and asked for you—he must see you instantly. He was in a great hurry; he must see you. He required your address; I doubted whether I ought to give it him, for he would not tell me his name. Leave your own name and a written direction; Mr. Hogg will be here in the morning, he will see it, and if he pleases, he can call upon you; but he would not agree to this : he must see you immediately. My clerk thought, that in a frequented part of London there could not be much danger, so I permitted him, though rather unwillingly, to write down your lodgings, and at last I gave it him. Did you see him? I hope he did not do you any harm."

Bysshe did not approve of the caution of the prudent pleader; next day, when I told him of his suspicions, he exclaimed, " Like all lawyers, he is a narrow-minded fool! How can you bear the society of such a wretch? The old fellow looked at me, as if he thought I was going to cut his throat ; the clerk was rather better, but he is an ass!" He had ten thousand things to tell me, and as he told me a thousand at least of them at a time without order, and with his natural vehemence and volubility, I got only a very indistinct notion of his history during the preceding year ; I picked up a few facts afterwards, many more very recently, but even at this moment I can trace only an imperfect narrative of this portion of his life. I learned that he had been in Ireland, in Wales, and in other places ; that was nearly all which I could then make out. He eagerly asked me innumerable questions, but he seldom heard, or waited for, my answers. He was soon coming to reside in London—to stay there "for ever ;" so we should never be separated again. He stayed late, and would have remained conversing with me all night, but I took him by the arm, and led him down stairs and into the street, that the people of the house, who began to show their uneasiness, might go to bed ; for my landlord was a judge's clerk, and kept good hours. I promised at parting to dine with him the next day. I should see Harriet, who had much to tell me.

Accordingly, on the morrow at six o'clock, in some hotel very near to St. James's Palace, I found in a sitting-room high up in the house Eliza, who smiled faintly upon me in silence, and Harriet, who received me cordially and with much shaking of hands. " It really seemed as if we were never to meet more ! What a separation ! But it will never occur again, for we are coming to live in London."

" You are looking surprising well, Harriet!" And so she was, and in the full bloom of radiant health.

"Oh no, poor dear thing," said Eliza, feebly, "her nerves are in a fearful state ; most dreadfully shattered."

I took a seat, and conversed a little while with the bright and nervous beauty. Harriet then produced a large sheet of thick paper, printed on one side only, and with an engraving at the top, much like an Oxford Almanack, and handed it to me with a certain unction, as if it were something sacred and full of edification. I looked at it in a cursory way. The letterpress was a report of the trial of Robert Emmett ; the engraving represented a court of justice with the usual accompaniments. The principal figure was the unfortunate young man ; he was standing at the bar and addressing the bench, vainly endeavoring to charm two deaf adders, Baron George and Baron Daly, and to persuade them to feel commiseration for, if not sympathy with, high treason. When I had looked at the paper a short time, the good Harriet asked me, not without emotion, "Well, what do you think ? Do not you pity him ? Poor young man !"—"Not the least in the world !" "What do you think of it ?" The paper was filled for the most part with the speech of the prisoner. I had read formerly a fuller report of Emmett's trial. "I think the sooner all such rascals are hanged the better !" Eliza eyed me with calm contempt, with mute languid disgust.

"Yes, it is just like you !" Harriet ejaculated. "You are so horribly narrow-minded ! So terribly unfeeling !"

Presently Bysshe came thundering up stairs from the street, like a cannon-ball, and we had dinner. After dinner the Poet spoke of Wales with enthusiasm. I was to come and see it. He talked rapturously of the waterfalls, walking about the room gesticulating as he described them. What effect they had upon him when they were actually present before his eyes I know not ; the recollection of them absent filled him with wonder and ecstasy in St. James's Street. Soon after tea Eliza said they must go and pack up ; they were to set out for Wales early next morning, and she trembled for poor dear Harriet's nerves !

A few shabby, ill-printed books, productions of the Irish

press, were lying about the room ; they treated of the history of Ireland, and of the affairs of that country. Bysshe did not say a word about Ireland ; on the contrary, when I took up an ill-favored volume, and remarked, what a shockingly printed book, it is hardly legible ; he gently drew it out of my hands, closed it, and laid it aside. He spoke on two subjects only ; his project to come and reside in London, when we should be always with each other, and should read together every book that was ever written by man ; and about the Welsh waterfalls, which I was soon to visit in company with him ; and some day we must take a look at the falls of Niagara. The lovely Eliza in her languishing manner whispered to her sister, that a cer- Mrs. Madocks was a most delightful creature ; and she had named in the course of the evening, more than once, with faint rapture, some Mr. Madocks, as the benefactor of the human species. Bysshe also informed me in confidence, that Mr. Madocks, of Tremadoc, was the true Prince of Wales, being the lineal descendant and heir-at-law of that Prince Madoc, who had been immortalized in a never-dying epic by the immortal Robert Southey. No doubt the worthy squire by genealogical syllogisms might easily by proved to be Prince of Wales, Duke of Cornwall, and Earl of Chester, and Duke of York to boot : this would be but a modest and moderate assumption in a Welsh pedigree.

ATTEMPTED ASSASSINATION OF SHELLEY.

I had promised to visit my young friends in their wilderness during the Spring Circuit ; that is to say, at the beginning of March. It would have been a great pleasure to have met again ; to have spent a few pleasant weeks with them ; to have seen the famous embankment, and all the other wonders of nature and art, and to have examined in a course of long walks, in company with my friend, that part of the Principality, an interesting tract of country which I had never set eyes upon. This project was rudely and abruptly put an end to by a very remarkable incident, if incident it may be called. Although I had known Bysshe intimately for three or four years, I could still be surprised, and I was not a little surprised by a letter which I received one morning from Harriet.

DEAR SIR, TANYRALLT, *March* 3, 1813.

I have just escaped an atrocious assassination. O send the twenty pounds, if you have it! You will perhaps hear of me no more!

Your Friend,
PERCY SHELLEY.

Mr. Shelley is so dreadfully nervous to-day, from being up all night, that I am afraid what he has written will alarm you very much.

We intend to leave this place as soon as possible, as our lives are not safe as long as we remain. It is no common robber we dread, but a person who is actuated by revenge,— who threatens my life and my sister's as well.

If you can send us the money, it will greatly add to our comfort,

Sir, I remain,
Your sincere Friend,

To Mr. H. T., London. H. SHELLEY.

DEAR SIR, BANGOR FERRY, *March* 6, 1813.

In the first stage of our journey towards Dublin we met with your letter; the remittance rescued us from a situation of peculiar perplexity.

I am now recovered from an illness brought on by watching, fatigue, and alarm, and we are proceeding to Dublin to dissipate the unpleasing impressions associated with the scene of our alarm; we expect to be there on the 8th; you shall then hear the detail of our distresses.

The ball of the assassin's pistol (he fired at me twice) penetrated my nightgown, and pierced the wainscot. He is yet undiscovered, though not unsuspected, as you will learn from my next.

Yours faithfully,

To Mr. H. T., London. PERCY B. SHELLEY.

35 Cuff Street, Stephen's Green, Dublin,
March 12, 1813.

My Dear Sir,

We arrived here last Tuesday, after a most tedious passage of forty hours, during the whole of which time we were dreadfully ill. I'm afraid no diet will prevent us from the common lot of suffering when obliged to take a sea voyage.

Mr. Shelley promised you a recital of the horrible events that caused us to leave Wales. I have undertaken the task, as I wish to spare him, in the present nervous state of his health, everything that can recall to his mind the horrors of that night, which I will relate :

On the night of the 26th February, we retired to bed between ten and eleven o'clock. We had been in bed about half-an-hour, when Mr. S. heard a noise proceeding from one of the parlors. He immediately went down stairs with two pistols which he had loaded that night, expecting to have occasion for them. He went into the billiard-room, when he heard footsteps retreating ; he followed into another little room, which was called an office. He there saw a man in the act of quitting the room through a glass window which opened into the shrubbery ; the man fired at Mr. S., which he avoided. Bysshe then fired ; but it flashed in the pan. The man then knocked Bysshe down, and they struggled on the ground. Bysshe then fired his second pistol, which he thought wounded him in the shoulder, as he uttered a shriek and got up, when he said these words : "By God, I will be revenged. I will murder your wife, and will ravish your sister! By God, I will be revenged!" He then fled, as we hoped, for the night. Our servants were not gone to bed, but were just going, when this horrible affair happened. This was about eleven o'clock. We all assembled in the parlor, where we remained for two hours. Mr. S. then advised us to retire, thinking it was impossible he would make a second attack. We left Bysshe and our man-servant—who had only arrived that day, and who knew nothing of the house —to sit up. I had been in bed three hours when I heard a pistol go off. I immediately ran down stairs, when I perceived that Bysshe's flannel gown had been shot through, and the window curtain. Bysshe had sent Daniel to see what hour it was; when he heard a noise at the window: he went there, and a man thrust his arm through the glass, and fired at him. Thank Heaven! the ball went through his gown, and he remained unhurt. Mr. S. happened to stand sideways; had he stood fronting, the ball must have killed him. Bysshe fired his pistol, but it would not go off; he then aimed a blow at him with an old sword, which we found in the house. The assassin attempted to get the sword from him, and just as he was pulling it away, Dan rushed into the room, when he made his escape. This was at four in the morning. It had been a most dreadful night; the wind was as loud as thunder, and the rain descended in torrents. Nothing has been heard of him, and we have every reason to believe it was no stranger, as there is a man of the name of Luson, who, the next morning that it happened, went and told the shop-keepers that it was a tale of Mr. Shelley's to impose upon them, that he might leave the country without paying his bills. This they believed, and none of them attempted to do anything towards his discovery. We left Tanyrallt on Sunday, and stayed, till everything was ready for our leaving the place, at the house of the Solicitor-General of the County, who lived seven miles from us. This Mr. Luson had been heard to say, that he was determined to drive us out of the country. He once happened to get hold of a little pamphlet which Mr. S. had printed in Dublin. This he sent up to Government; in fact, he was for ever saying something against us, and that because we were determined not to admit him to our house, because we had heard his character, and from acts of his, we found that he was malignant and cruel to the greatest degree.

We experienced pleasure in reading your letter, at the time when every one seemed to be plotting against us; when those who, a few weeks back, had been offering their services, shrunk from the task, when called upon in a moment like that.

Mr. Shelley and my sister unite with me in kind regards; whilst I remain,   Yours truly,

To Mr. H. T., London.   H. SHELLEY.

7*

Dear Sir,

Harriet related to you the mysterious events which caused our departure from Tanyrallt. I was at that time so nervous and unsettled as to be wholly incapable of the task. By your kindness, we are relieved from all pecuniary difficulties. We only wanted a little breathing time, which the rapidity of our persecutions was unwilling to allow. I will readily repay the twenty pounds when I hear from my correspondent in London.

Yours faithfully,

To Mr. H. T.

PERCY B. SHELLEY.

Harriet's letter to me was written from Tanyrallt, a day or two after the catastrophe ; it bore an earlier date, but in other respects it was, to the best of my recollection, precisely similar, word for word, indeed, to her letter from Dublin of the 12th of March. I have been informed that she also sent to other persons a narrative of the nightly fears in the same terms, writing descriptive circulars, and dispatching them in different directions. Persons acquainted with the localities and with the circumstances, and who had carefully investigated the matter, were unanimous in the opinion that no such attempt was ever made. I never met with any person who believed in it. I have heard other histories, alike apocryphal, of attacks made by the good people of North Wales upon persons of whose sentiments, religious or political, they were supposed to disapprove ; but the ale-bibbers and devourers of Welsh-rabbits are too wise, or too stolid, to care how much logic any man may chop within the Principality, or how fine he may chop it. What could the quiet, sheep-tending, mutton-eating, stocking-knitting folks in a secluded corner of Carnarvonshire care about an unread and unreadable pamphlet on Catholic claims and the wrongs of Ireland, privately printed in Dublin ? Apollo, the shepherd, would not credit that a simple pastoral race could murderously assault, and basely assassinate, a brother shepherd. How could the countrymen of Talliessin and the other immortal bards persecute and expel from their land of poesy and song the special favorite and ·pet of the

Aonian maids?　Neither Bysshe nor Harriet ever spoke to me of the assassination; and the lovely Eliza observed on this subject, as on all others, her wonted silence.*

"AS LADIES WISH TO BE."

He had taken, or sent, a considerable number of books to the happy cottage on the blissful lake; many useful volumes collected in the solitude of Tanyrallt, and for which he had so earnestly written to his correspondent in London. When he started off hastily to overtake me in Dublin, or to join me in London, he had left Eliza in charge of his library. He was evidently weary of angelic guardianship, and exulted with a malicious pleasure that he had fairly planted her at last. He made no secret of his satisfaction, but often gave vent to his feelings with his accustomed frankness and energy. The good Harriet smiled in silence, and looked very sly; she did not dare to express her joy, if she really rejoiced at the absence of her affectionate and tiresome sister, by uttering treasons against her liege lady, the defender of her nerves. The de-

* " I was in North Wales in the summer of 1813, and heard the matter much talked of. Persons who had examined the premises on the following morning, had found that the grass on the lawn had been much trampled and rolled on, but there were no footmarks on the wet ground, except between the beaten spot and the window; and the impression of the ball on the wainscot showed that the pistol had been fired towards the window, and not from it. This appeared conclusive as to the whole series of operations having taken place from within."—*Peacock.*

" No trace could ever be found of the assassin. The Shelleyan theory was that a certain Mr. Leeson, a man whom they avoided as 'malignant and cruel to the greatest degree,' was at the bottom of the affair. The Leesonian and irreverent theory was at least as tenable *prima facie*, viz., ' that it was a tale of Mr. Shelley's to impose upon the neighboring shopkeepers, that he might leave the country without paying his bills.' People in general. along with Messrs. Hogg, Madocks and Peacock, and Mr. Browning among later analysts, have disbelieved the story, and attributed it to an excited imagination, or nerves unstrung by laudanum; Hogg suggests that the Irishman Daniel may possibly have had something to do with it. The night was one of rain and 'wind as loud as thunder,' which may have started in Shelley's perturbed brain the notion of pistol-snappings; it is a fact, however, that *some* pistol was really fired. One singular point (hardly fitted to dwell on) is that Shelley *expected*, on going to bed, to need his fire-arms; if the expectation was a mere fantasy, the subsequent actual need of them may have been the same. But Lady Shelley and Mr. Thornton Hunt discover no ground for scepticism. Miss Westbrook was also in the house at the time, and often, in after years, related the circumstance as a frightful fact."—*Rossetti.*

liverance was of brief duration,—surprisingly brief, for in an incredibly short space of time Eliza reappeared and resumed her sovereign functions. They remained for some time at hotels, and during this period Eliza was with them, mute, smiling, and languishing as before. Whether she lived constantly with them I was not exactly informed; it seemed rather that she went and came in a hushed, mystical manner. However, she was often present when I visited them, but retired frequently to her bed-room, probably to brush her hair assiduously as of old. Whenever she joined us, she displayed the same painful interest in Harriet's nerves; their condition was authoritatively pronounced to be shattered and deplorable; and when she deigned to wonder at anything, she wondered what Miss Warne would say. On some days she was unquestionably absent; and then, perhaps, she had gone to hold a chaste conference with her virgin friend respecting the nervous system, and actually to hear what the oracle said.

Harriet gave visible promise of being about to provide an heir for an ancient and illustrious house; and, like all little women, she looked very large upon the occasion. She was in excellent voice, and fonder than ever of reading aloud; she promptly seized every opportunity of indulging her taste; she took up the first book that came to hand as soon as I entered the room, and the reading commenced. Sir William Drummond's Academical Questions, Smith's Theory of Moral Sentiments, some of Bishop Berkeley's Works, Southey's Chronicle of the Cid, had taken the place of Telemachus, Belisarius, Volney's Ruins, and the other works which she had formerly read to me. Whenever Eliza made a descent upon us, silence was immediately proclaimed, and the book was carried away.

" Dearest Harriet, what are you about? Only consider the state of your poor nerves! Think of your condition! You are killing yourself as fast as you can; you are, indeed, dear! Gracious heaven! What would Miss Warne say ? "

I dined with my young friends one day at a hotel in Dover Street. Bysshe was to go somewhere with all haste—a common occurrence with him,—to perform, or to procure, something mysterious and prodigious. He could hardly be prevailed upon to take his dinner ; he restrained his impatience until our meal was finished, and whilst the waiter was removing the cloth, he sprang on his feet, snatched up his hat and ran away, leaving me alone with Harriet. We sat and conversed for awhile ; she probably was wishing for the moment, when with a decent and proper regard for the paramount duty of digestion, she might begin to read aloud.

Before the desired moment came, Dr. S. was announced, and a quiet Quaker physician quickly entered the room,. his hat upon his head, and a bland smile upon his countenance. I rose instantly to depart, but the doctor seized my arm, and made me sit down again. I felt uneasy, but believing that he took me for the husband of the lady whom he attended, I was about to inform him that I was not, when Harriet interposed :

" You need not go away ! Dr. S. does not desire it, I am sure. He rather wishes you to stay ! "

My position seemed delicate and distressing, but it was not so. The doctor seated himself over against his blooming young patient, and rather near to her, looking at her fixedly ; the bland smile was still upon his countenance, and the ample hat was still upon his head. Nothing was said, either by the lady or by her dumb physician.

Twice, or thrice, the latter murmured softly and inarticulately.

The mute consultation continued about ten minutes, and terminated abruptly. When he had satiated his eyes, and satisfied the demands of science by gazing silently, Dr. S. started suddenly from his chair, as if something had stung him behind, and with a celerity hardly natural in a Quaker, quitted the room, carefully closing the door after him. Harriet appeared to be relieved at being delivered from his silent, searching eye.

"Well ! You see there was no necessity for your going away ; not the least in the world. You might very well stay ! It was Bysshe's wish that Dr. S. should see me, and he has seen me ! "

Shelley continued to reside for some weeks at hotels ; some persons blamed such a course as imprudent, and moreover as being expensive, but his motives were discreet and rational. Next August he would be of age.   It was confidently asserted, and generally believed, that his father would then come to a satisfactory and proper arrangement.   It was thought that a hotel was more convenient for negotiations than lodgings. His father, it was said, would pay his debts, of which the amount was inconsiderable, and make him a moderate, permanent, and suitable allowance.

For some two years I had seen but little of Bysshe, but from this epoch it was my good fortune to see a great deal of him, and to enjoy, off and on, much of the unappreciable pleasure and advantage of his most precious society and familiar and friendly intercourse.   Having consumed many valuable hours in the dull diplomacy of his father's agents, and finding the residence at a hotel, a place where the Muses do not haunt, unfavorable to study, and to assembling a goodly fellowship of ancient books round him, he took lodgings in Half-Moon-Street. I went one day, by invitation, to dine with him there, and on arriving I found Harriet alone.

"Bysshe called on the Duke of Norfolk this morning, who asked him to dinner, and it would have been improper to have refused.   He has just gone, but he will come to us as soon as he can get away."

Harriet and myself dined together, and had tea ; and after tea Harriet was reading aloud to me, as she was wont to do. Her reading was abruptly put an end to by vehement and well-known rapping ; Shelley came tumbling upstairs, with a mighty sound, treading upon his nose, as I accused him of doing, rushed into the room, and throwing off his neckcloth, according to custom, stood staring around for some moments, as wondering why he had been in such a hurry.   He informed us that there was a large party of men at Norfolk House ; he sat near the bottom of the table, and the Earl of Oxford sat next to him.   After dinner, the Earl said to him,—

"Pray, who is that very strange old man at the top of the

table, sitting next to His Grace, who talks so much, so loudly, and in so extraordinary a manner, and all about himself ?

" He is my father, and he is a very strange old man indeed ! The Earl said no more on that head, but we continued to chat together, and he walked with me from St. James's-Square. I have just left him at the door."

Feelings of sympathy and antipathy are various and manifest. Bysshe appeared to be pleased with the Earl of Oxford, because he disliked his father. I did not know the Earl, but I was so fortunate as to meet his lovely and fashionable Countess occasionally, and I was soon able to discover that we had one point of sympathy and strong common feeling,—an intense abhorrence of bores.

THE WOULD-BE SUICIDE.

In London, Bysshe found books and society, and he appeared to rejoice in being delivered from the long-endured, intolerable loneliness of Wales : the good Harriet also rejoiced, and was bright, blooming, calm, and composed, as heretofore ; but she had not renounced her eternal purpose of suicide ; and she still discoursed of some scheme of self-destruction, as coolly as another lady would arrange a visit to an exhibition or a theatre. She told me sometimes that she was very unhappy, but she never said why ; and in particular, she told me frequently, as she had told me formerly, that she had been very unhappy at school, and often intended to kill herself. I asked her again and again the cause of her unhappiness, but she did not know it. It certainly appeared to be mere talk, and I found a festivity in it ; it became jolly, as it were, to laugh at her suicidal schemes, and the solemnity with which she unfolded them : with this she was now and then a little offended. " Mamma is going to have some walnuts pickled next week," a little girl once said to me, a little boy ; and she added, with a grave look and an air of quiet resolution, " and mamma says she is quite determined ! " So poor Harriet was quite determined, and did not choose to be laughed out of it, being displeased with my apologue of the walnuts.

In this strange world one comes across strange people some times, and finds strange kinds of industry, especially when a man lays himself out for strange characters. Dining one day at a hotel in London with Bysshe and Harriet, I met a poor poet there, whose acquaintance they had just made,—how, I know not; I think, through some advertisement in a newspaper. Shelley introduced me to him, and grimly whispered, that he was going to kill himself. " Very well !" " Immediately !" he added. " With all my heart !" The professor of suicide, it must be admitted, had rather a melancholy look. He was pale, cadaverous, and he discoursed during dinner in a grave, pedantic manner, of his inflexible resolution to commit suicide, as it seemed, instantly ; and he talked much, and with due solemnity, of Otho,—of the Otho of Tacitus,—until dinner was over. Otho, he said, was his favorite—his hero ! However, Otho ate his salmon and lobster sauce, and whatever else was put before him, largely and voraciously, and with a prodigious relish ; took his wine very freely, and then a long nap ; and finally departed without having become a felon of himself. When he had taken his leave, Harriet told me with great glee,—"The gentleman is going to kill himself." " Really !" " Directly ; is not that quite delightful ?" " Quite !" " I should not wonder if he is doing it now !" I did not wish to put her out of conceit with this notion, but I should have wondered much if he had been doing anything of the kind. I saw him twice or thrice, there and thereabouts ; his talk was ever in the same self-murderous vein ; so confidently did he speak, so urgent was the necessity, that on leaving the room for five minutes one might expect to return and find him in a pool of blood ; but no, the calamity never happened ; it was plain that suicide was only his stock-in-trade. All people laughed at him, except Harriet, whose sympathies were excited at first ; but after a short time, even she got tired of him ; or possibly she was jealous of Otho's superior confidence of assertion touching impending self-destruction. What ultimately became of the fellow I know not ; I never heard that he cut his throat ; perhaps he hit upon some other mode of getting a dinner, when this dodge was seen through.

NAKEDIZING.

He spoke with enthusiasm of a charming family, whose acquaintance he had lately made, in what manner I do not remember, and he promised to introduce me to them, declaring that I should be as much taken with them as he was himself. He informed me soon afterwards that he had spoken of me to them, that they desired to see me, and the next day he would take me to dine with them. The next day—it was a Sunday, in the summer—we took a walk together, wandering about, as usual, for a long time without plan or purpose. About five o'clock Bysshe stopt suddenly at the door of a house in a fashionable street, ascended the steps hastily, and delivered one of his superb bravura knocks.

" What are we going to do here ? "

" It is here we dine."

He placed me before him, that I might enter first, as the stranger; the door was thrown wide open, and a strange spectacle presented itself. There were five naked figures in the passage advancing rapidly to meet us. The first was a boy of twelve years, the last a little girl of five; the other three children, the two eldest of them being girls, were of intermediate ages, between the two extremes. As soon as they saw me, they uttered a piercing cry, turned round, and ran wildly upstairs, screaming aloud. The stairs presented the appearance of Jacob's Ladder, with the angels ascending it, except that they had no wings, and they moved faster, and made more noise than the ordinary representations of the Patriarch's vision indicate. From the window of the nursery at the top of the house the children had seen the beloved Shelley,—had scampered down stairs in single file to welcome him; me, the killjoy, they had not observed.

I was presented to a truly elegant family, and I found everything in the best taste, and was highly gratified with my reception, and with the estimable acquisition to the number of my friends. Nothing was said about the first strange salutation, nor did I venture to inquire, what it signified. After dinner, Bysshe asked, why the children did not come into the room to the dessert, as usual. The lady of the house colored slightly, and said Shelley should see them bye and-bye, in the nursery, but they did not dare to show themselves in the dining-room. They were all too much ashamed at having been seen, as they were, so unexpectedly, by a stranger!

"LET US SIT UPON THE GROUND."

One summer's evening he had to travel a short distance in his own country, in the county of Sussex ;—such, if I mistake not, for I know the adventure only from Bysshe's account of it, was the scene of his whimsical exploit. He set out on foot, expecting that the stage would soon overtake him. He had not proceeded far when the heavy coach came up. There was no room outside, but the six inside seats were unoccupied ; he got in, and the vehicle rumbled along the dusty road. For a little while it was all very well, but the heavy stage coach stopped suddenly, and a heavy old woman came in to him, reddened with heat, steaming and running down with perspiration. She took her place in the middle seat, like a huge ass between a pair of enormous panniers ; for, on one side was a mighty basket, crammed full of mellow apples, and on the other a like basket, equally well filled with large onions. The odor of the apples and the onions, and the aspect of the heated, melting, smoking old woman, were intolerable to the delicate, sensitive young poet. He bore it, at first, patiently, then impatiently, at last he could endure it no longer ; so, starting up, he seated himself on the floor of the coach, and, fixing his tearful, woeful eyes upon her, he addressed his companion thus, in thrilling accents :

> "For heaven's sake, let us sit upon the ground,
> And tell sad stories of the death of kings !
> How some have been deposed, some slain in war,
> Some haunted by the ghosts they dispossessed ;
> Some poisoned by their wives ; some sleeping killed,
> All murdered !"

"Oh, dear!" exclaimed the terrified old woman. "Dear! dear! Oh, Lord! Oh, Lord!"

But when he shrieked out the two last words, "All murdered!" she ran to the window in an agony, and, thrusting out her head, cried:

"Oh, guard, guard! stop! Oh, guard, guard, guard! let me out!"

The door was opened, she alighted immediately with her strong-smelling wares, and through the united wit of two great poets, that of Shakspeare and his own, he was permitted to finish his journey alone.

He was proud of this achievement, and delighted in it long afterwards.

"Show us, Bysshe, how you got rid of the old woman in Sussex."

He sprang wildly on his feet, and, taking his seat on the floor, with a melancholy air, and in a piteous voice, cried out:

"For heaven's sake, let us sit upon the ground!"

When he had given out the words, "All murdered!" with a fiendish yell, he started up, threw open the window, and began to call, "Guard! guard!" often to the astonishment of persons passing by, whose temperament was less poetic, and less excitable than his own.

So moving were the woes of the gentle Richard Plantagenet, told by the great dramatist, and declaimed by another poet, second to him, at least in time! So drastic was their effect!

SHELLEYAN DINNERS.

At the bare proposal to order dinner, poor Shelley stood aghast, in speechless trance; when he had somewhat recovered from the outrage to his feelings, "Ask Harriet," he shrilly cried, with a desponding, supplicating mien. The good Harriet herself was no proficient in culinary arts; she had never been initiated in the mysteries of housewifery: "Whatever you please," was her ordinary answer.

I was once staying at the house of a country clergyman; the

worthy pastor was eminently skilled in divine things; his not less worthy wife was deeply conversant with human affairs, well versed in all the learning of the kitchen, excellent in ordering the genial board, as became the helpmate of a first-rate theologian. There were usually a few neighbors, guests at dinner. Amongst these, one day, was a lovely young woman; healthy, comely, fair, and plump; the daughter of a substantial farmer of a superior degree.

When the visitors had departed, my kind and notable hostess asked me in confidence what I thought of the handsome, well-fleshed girl?

"I think that she is a beautiful creature! I have seldom seen a prettier young woman of the kind!"

"She is, indeed, and she is as good as she is beautiful—so useful in a house."

"I had heard much about her, but I never saw her before; and I am satisfied that all I heard about her is true. I have had a great deal of talk with her; she seems to understand everything, and to be wonderfully clever in a family. I could not take my eyes off her all the evening; I am afraid she would think me rude, but I could not help it!" "She is so beautiful, it is very difficult to help looking at her; it is not easy to take one's eyes off her!" "No! It is not indeed! I sat looking at her, and thinking what delightful jellies she would make; I could not help looking at her, and saying to myself, how I should like to taste her calves'-foot jelly. And I longed to tell her so!"

Poor Harriet had pledged herself at Keswick to learn of Mrs. Southey to make tea cakes; but Mrs. Southey would not teach, or Harriet would not learn, and she had not redeemed her pledge. It was her only chance, and she lost it, which was unfortunate: it would have been a green spot in a desert. To say, "Whatever you please," is a sorry mode of ordering dinner, and it was all she ever said on that head. Some considerable time after the appointed hour, a roasted shoulder of mutton, of the coarsest, toughest grain, graced, or disgraced the ill-supplied table; the watery gravy that issued from the perverse joint, when it was cut, a duty commonly assigned to me, seemed the most apt of all things to embody the conception of penury and utter destitution. There were potatoes in every respect worthy of the mutton; and the cheese, which was either forgotten or uneatable, closed the ungenial repast. Sometimes there was a huge boiled leg of mutton, boiled till the bone was ready to drop out of the meat, which shrank and started from it on all sides, without any sauce, but with turnips' raw, and manifestly unworthy to be boiled any longer. Sometimes there were impregnable beefsteaks—soles for shooting-shoes. I have dropped a word, a hint, about a pudding; a pudding, Bysshe said dogmatically, is a prejudice. I have wished that the converse of the proposition were true, and that a prejudice was a pudding, and then, according to the judgment of my more enlightened young friends, I should never have been without one.

Bysshe's dietary was frugal and independent; very remarkable and quite peculiar to himself. When he felt hungry he would dash into the first baker's shop, buy a loaf and rush out again, bearing it under his arm; and he strode onwards in his rapid course, breaking off pieces of bread and greedily swallowing them. But however frugal the fare, the waste was considerable, and his path might be tracked, like that of Hop-o'-my-Thumb through the wood, in Mother Goose her tale, by a long line of crumbs.

The spot where he sat reading or writing, and eating his dry bread, was likewise marked out by a circle of crumbs and fragments scattered on the floor. He took with bread, frequently by way of condiment, not water-cresses, as did the Persians of old, according to the fable of Xenophon, but common pudding raisins. These he purchased at some mean little shop, that he might be the more speedily served; and he carried them loose in his waistcoat-pocket, and eat them with his dry bread. He occasionally rolled up little pellets of bread, and, in a sly, mysterious manner, shot them with his thumb, hitting the persons—whom he met in his walks—on the face, commonly on the nose, at which he grew to be very dexterous.

When he was dining at a coffee-house, he would sometimes

amuse himself thus, if that could be an amusement which was done unconsciously.   A person receiving an unceremonious fillip on the nose, after this fashion, started and stared about ; but I never found that anybody, although I was often apprehensive that some one might resent it, perceived or suspected, from what quarter the offending missile had come.   The wounded party seemed to find satisfaction in gazing upwards at the ceiling, and in the belief that a piece of plaster had fallen from thence.   When he was eating his bread alone over his book he would shoot his pellets about the room, taking aim at a picture, at an image, or at any other object which attracted his notice.   He had been taught by a French lady to make panada ; and with this food he often indulged himself.   His simple cookery was performed thus.   He broke a quantity—often, indeed, a surprising quantity—of bread into a large basin, and poured boiling water upon it.   When the bread had been steeped awhile, and had swelled sufficiently, he poured off the water, squeezing it out of the bread, which he chopped up with a spoon ; he then sprinkled pounded loaf sugar over it, and grated nutmeg upon it, and devoured the mass with a prodigious relish.   He was standing one day in the middle of the room, basin in hand, feeding himself voraciously, gorging himself with pap.

" Why, Bysshe," I said, " you lap it up as greedily as the Valkyriæ in Scandinavian story lap up the blood of the slain ! "

" Aye ! " he shouted out, with grim delight, " I lap up the blood of the slain ! "

The idea captivated him ; he was continually repeating the words ; and he often took panada, I suspect, merely to indulge this wild fancy, and say, " I am going to lap up the blood of the slain !   To sup up the gore of murdered kings ! "

Having previously fed himself after his fashion from his private stores, he was independent of dinner, and quite indifferent to it ; the slice of tough mutton would remain untouched upon his plate, and he would sit at table reading some book, often reading aloud, seemingly unconscious of the hospitable rites in which others were engaged, his bread bullets meanwhile being discharged in every direction.

The provisions supplied at lodgings in London were too frequently in those days detestable, and the service which was rendered abominable and disgusting. Meat was procured wherever meat might be bought most cheaply, in order that, being paid for dearly, a more enormous profit might be realized upon it; and those dishes were selected in which the ignorance in cookery of a servant-of-all-work might be least striking.

Our dinners, therefore, were constructive, a dumb show, a mere empty, idle ceremony; our only resource against absolute starvation was tea. "We will have some muffins and crumpets for tea," the famished Harriet would say.. "They will butter them!" Bysshe exclaimed, in a voice thrilling with horror. Harriet sometimes ordered them privily, without consulting him; and when they were brought in silently and appeared smiling upon the tea-table, he dealt with them as remorselessly as with Mrs. Southey's tea-cakes at Keswick. We meekly sought relief in buttered toast; but the butter was too commonly bad, and ill-suited to our palates, but answering admirably the final cause of making the toast; that not being relished in the parlor, there might be more left for the unclean maid to eat. Penny buns were our assured resource. The survivors of those days of peril and hardship are indebted for their existence to the humane interposition and succor of penny buns. A shilling's worth of penny buns for tea. If the purchase was entrusted to the maid, she got such buns as none could believe to have been made on earth, proving thereby incontestably that the girl had some direct communication with the infernal regions, where alone they could have been procured. Shelley was fond of penny buns, but he never bought them unless he was put up to it.

"Get a shilling's worth of penny buns, Bysshe," Harriet said, "at some good confectioner's," the situation of whose shop she described.

He rushed out with incredible alacrity, like a Wind God, and in an instant returned, and was heard stumbling and tumbling upstairs, with the bag of buns, open at the top, in his hand ; and he would sometimes, in his hot haste, drop them on the stairs, and they all rolled down to the bottom, and he picked them up again ; but we were not particular. We had our own tea ; it usually lay spread out on an open paper upon a side table ; others might help themselves, and probably they did so, but there was always some left for us.

"Poor Matilda."

There was a coarse, fat woman, who used to sponge upon him unmercifully under pretence of breaking blood-vessels. It was said that her lungs were her stock in trade ; that she got three hundred a-year by her broken blood-vessels, receiving, as it were, compensation to that amount at least from the credulously charitable.

" Poor Matilda," that was not quite the name, he said to me, one day, horror-stricken with trembling compassion, "poor Matilda has broken a blood-vessel, and is spitting blood!"

" Poor Matilda," I answered, "has broken the cheese-toaster, and is spitting toasted cheese !"

He thought me very inhuman, I am sure, but he laughed ; in truth, the woman was only drunk all the time. He colored and laughed, but relieved her, and she continued to spit blood and to sponge upon the poor fellow, and, in every sense of the word, to spoil him.

Dread of Elephantiasis.

In a crowded stage-coach Shelley once happened to sit opposite an old woman with very thick legs, who, as he imagined, was afflicted with elephantiasis, an exceedingly rare and most terrible disease, in which the legs swell and become as thick as those of an elephant, together with many other distressing symptoms, as the thickening and cracking of the skin, and indeed a whole Iliad of woes, of which he had recently read a formidable description in some medical work, that had taken entire possession of his fanciful and impressible soul. The patient, quite unconscious of her misery, sat dozing quietly

over against him.   He also took it into his head that the disease
is very infectious, and that he had caught it of his corpulent
and drowsy fellow-traveller ; he presently began to discover un-
equivocal symptoms of the fearful contagion in his own person.
I never saw him so thoroughly unhappy as he was, whilst he
continued under the influence of this strange and unaccountable impression.   His female friends tried to laugh him out of
his preposterous whim, bantered him and inquired how he came
to find out that his fair neighbor had such thick legs ?   He did
not relish, or even understand, their jests, but sighed deeply.
By the advice of his friends, he was prevailed upon to consult
a skilful and experienced surgeon, and submitted to a minute
and careful examination : the surgeon of course assured him
that no signs or trace of elephantiasis could be discerned.   He
farther informed him, that the disease is excessively rare, almost unknown, in this part of the world ; that it is not infectious, and that a person really afflicted by it could not bear to
travel in a crowded stage-coach.   Bysshe shook his head,
sighed still more deeply, and was more thoroughly convinced
than ever that he was the victim of a cruel and incurable disease ; and that these assurances were only given with the humane design of soothing one doomed to a miserable and inevitable death.   His imagination was so much disturbed, that he
was perpetually examining his own skin, and feeling and looking at that of others.   One evening, during the access of his
fancied disorder, when many young ladies were standing up for
a country dance, he caused a wonderful consternation amongst
these charming creatures by walking slowly along the row of
girls and curiously surveying them, placing his eyes close to
their necks and bosoms, and feeling their breasts and bare
arms, in order to ascertain whether any of the fair ones had
taken the horrible disease.   He proceeded with so much gravity
and seriousness, and his looks were so woe-begone, that they
did not resist, or resent, the extraordinary liberties, but looked
terrified, and as if they were about to undergo some severe
surgical operation at his hands.   Their partners were standing
opposite in silent and angry amazement, unable to decide in

what way the strange manipulations were to be taken ; yet no-body interrupted his heart-broken handlings, which seemed, from his dejected air, to be preparatory to cutting his own throat.   At last the lady of the house perceived what the young philosopher was about, and by assuring him that not one of the young ladies, as she had herself ascertained, had been infected, and, with gentle expostulations, induced him to desist, and to suffer the dancing to proceed without further examinations.

The monstrous delusion continued for some days ; with the aspect of grim despair he came stealthily and opened the bosom of my shirt several times a day, and minutely inspected my skin, shaking his head, and by his distressed mien plainly sig-nifying that he was not by any means satisfied with the state of my health.   He also quietly drew up my sleeves, and by rubbing it investigated the skin of my arms ; he also measured my legs and ankles, spanning them with a convulsive grasp. " Bysshe, we both have the legs and the skin of an elephant, but neither of us has his sagacity !"   He shook his head in sad, silent disapproval ; to jest in the very jaws of death was hardened insensibility, not genuine philosophy.   He opened in like manner the bosoms and viewed the skin of his other asso-ciates, and even of strangers.   Nor did females escape his curious scrutiny, nor were they particularly solicitous to avoid it ; so impressive were the solemnity and gravity, and the pro-found melancholy of his fear-stricken and awe-inspiring aspect, that there could be no doubt of the innocence and purity of his intentions : and if he had proceeded to more private examina-tions and more delicate investigations, the young ladies would unquestionably have submitted themselves with reverence to his researches, which, however, were arrested by authority in the case of the fair dancers before they had greatly exceeded the bounds of decorum.

This strange fancy continued to afflict him for several weeks, and to divert, or distress, his friends, and then it was forgotten as suddenly as it had been taken up, and gave place to more cheerful reminiscences, or forebodings : he was able to listen to, or even occasionally, but rarely, to relate himself droll stories.

One of them, as it is perfectly innocent, may be repeated without envy or calumny : it had occurred two or three years before.

TAKEN FOR HIS FRIEND.

It is probable that Bysshe was now and then in like manner taken for his friend ; but I never was informed by him that this had actually happened. One misapprehension was of so comical a character that it ought to be related ; and since, most assuredly, the Loves and Graces were not concerned in the matter, there can be no scruples of delicacy in telling the adventure just as it fell out. I called at his lodgings one afternoon in the summer to walk together, as we were wont. He was not at home, but he had left a message for me, that if I went to the residence of a common friend, I should not fail to find him there. I at once repaired thither, and was kindly received, as I invariably was. He had not arrived, but if I would stay to dinner, I should doubtless see him, for he would come, if not to dinner, for certain in the course of the evening. I readily consented to the proposal, and I sat chatting in the drawing-room, hearing the news of the day, and much admiration and many commendations of my incomparable friend, such as I invariably heard wherever he was known. A bell gave warning that dinner would be served in half-an-hour, and I was conducted upstairs into the front bed-room to wash my hands. Whilst I was thus employed two ill-looking fellows burst abruptly into the room ; one of them locked the door and set his back against it, telling me that he arrested me ; that I was his prisoner. He was a short, stout man. The other, a long, lean fellow, showed me a writ, and presented me with a copy of it.

" What does all this mean ? " I asked.

" You know very well, you are Mr. Percy Bysshe Shelley ! "

" You are pleased to say that I am."

" We know very well that you are the defendant ; you need not try to persuade us that you are not ! "

" Then I will not try ! "

Upon this the bailiffs became rather insolent, and were in-

clined to be abusive. I finished washing myself and then sat
down by the window; the men stood in the middle of the room
growling and grumbling. In ten minutes, or a quarter of an
hour, there was a gentle tap at the door; the man who had
locked it opened it,—a spare, white-faced fellow dressed in
black, like an undertaker's man, entered. He looked at me
with surprise, staring hard, and whispered something to the
bailiffs, who seemed still more astonished than he was. They
then threw open the door and told me I was at liberty, and
might depart; it was a mistake. John Doe and Richard Roe,
and their friend in mourning, began to offer excuses, explanations, and apologies, assuring me that they always acted on the
best information, and seldom made mistakes. I did not answer,
but walked down to dinner in silence. How long they remained
in the bed-room, whether they were converted by the influences
of the locality to a vegetable diet, and induced to return to
nature, or what became of these worthies I know not, for I
never fell in with any of the party again.

The arrest, as I afterwards learnt, was for the price of the
good Harriet's fine, new carriage. After such an indignity, and
in order to wipe off the stigma, I ought to have had a ride, and
a good long one, too, in the carriage; but I had not that satisfaction; I never even saw the vehicle, nor heard of it, indeed,
except on this occasion.

EXPECTED AT DINNER.

It was in the year 1813 that I first became acquainted with
William Godwin. I saw him frequently in the course of that
year, and in the year following; and afterwards I met him
more or less frequently, according to circumstances. I had
expressed a wish to know him, and I was soon invited by a
charming family, with whom he was intimate, to dine at their
house, where I should find him and Bysshe. I repaired
thither, to a somewhat early dinner, in accordance with the
habits of the philosopher. I was not on any account to be late,
for it was unpleasant to him to dine later than four o'clock.

It was a fine Sunday. I set out betimes, and arrived at the

appointed place at half-past three. I found a short, stout, thickset old man, of very fair complexion, and with a bald and very large head, in the drawing-room, alone, where he had been for some time by himself, and he appeared to be rather uneasy at being alone. He made himself known to me as William Godwin; it was thus he styled himself. His dress was dark, and very plain, of an old-fashioned cut, even for an old man. His appearance, indeed, was altogether that of a dissenting minister. He informed me that our hospitable host and his family had been called away suddenly into the country, and that we should not have their company, but that Mr. Shelley was expected every moment. He consulted several times a large old silver watch, and wondered greatly that he had not come; but he would doubtless be with us immediately. He spoke confidently on a subject, which, to say the least, was doubtful. Bysshe, as was not uncommonly the case with him, never came near us. Why he made default, nobody ever knew, least of all did he know himself.

"Had Mr. Shelley mistaken the day, the hour? Did he not know the place; surely he must know it, and know it well?"

I could only say, on behalf of my absent friend, that he often failed to observe his engagements and appointments. It was his habit; a disagreeable and most inconvenient one, certainly. Why and how he had formed it, I could not tell, although I was much interrogated and cross-examined on that head. It had been the way with him ever since I had known him, and it was only too probable that it always would be so. I could not explain, excuse, defend, or justify it; I could merely affirm that so it was.

At four o'clock I rang the bell, and ordered dinner. To this order there were objections and expostulations.

"We ought, in common civility, to wait awhile. Mr. Shelley could not fail to be with us shortly."

The objections were overruled, and we two went to dinner; and we two were a multitude, to judge from the number of dishes on the table. Vegetable fare was the rule of the house, and I observed the rule myself; but meat of various kinds had been prepared in various ways for the cannibal guest. He dined carnivorously, but very moderately, paying little attention to the plates of vegetables, which he seemed to contemn, as well as the lore by which they were zealously and learnedly recommended.

William Godwin, according to my observation, always eat meat, and rather sparingly, and little else besides. He drank a glass or two of sherry, wherein I did not join him. Soon after dinner a large cup of very strong green tea,—of gunpowder tea, intensely strong,—was brought to him; this he took with evident satisfaction, and it was the only thing that he appeared to enjoy, although our fare was excellent. Having drunken the tea, he set the cup and saucer forcibly upon the table, at a great distance from him, according to the usages of that old school of manners, to which he so plainly belonged. He presently fell into a sound sleep, sitting very forward in his chair, and leaning forward, so that at times he threatened to fall forward ; but no harm came to him. Not only did the old philosopher sleep soundly, deeply, but he snored loudly.

I got a book, and retiring to the window sat reading for half an hour, or longer, until he awoke. He awoke suddenly, and appeared to be refreshed. "Had Mr. Shelley arrived?" It was his first thought on waking. He would not take any more wine; he would not walk. It was a lovely evening, but he should have quite enough of walking in coming and in returning. He would go to the drawing-room, and we went upstairs.

Sir William Gell's description of the island of Ithaca had just come out ; a handsome quarto volume with engravings ; and it lay upon the table. We looked over it together ; it was new to both of us, and it interested us greatly. He discoursed much of Ithaca, of Greece, of Ulysses, of Troy, of Homer, and of Chapman's "Homer:" it was manifest that his acquaintance with the poems of Homer was chiefly, if not entirely, derived from Chapman's translation. However, he was quite familiar with the story, the characters, the manners of the Odyssey. We spoke nearly all the time we were together of the many extraordinary things, of many things hard to be understood, which are found in that ancient and wonderful poem. The tea-things were brought in. I made tea; I forget whether my companion partook of it. Tea was always most acceptable to me, particularly whilst I was a Pythagorean. Poor dear Pythagoras, with all his wisdom he did not know how to make himself a good cup of tea; or where he might purchase a pound of passable Pekoe, or of satisfactory Souchong. During the whole course of our conversation and operations, my respected associate ever and anon recurred, uneasily and impatiently, to a matter which distressed him sorely—the absence of Mr. Shelley.

Mr. Shelley and William Godwin—such was to be the form of speech: he persisted as pertinaciously in dubbing Bysshe Mister, as in rejecting the title for himself. He questioned me again and again on the subject, and I thought with a certain air of lurking suspicion, as if I knew more than I chose to tell; as if I were privy to the plot, and that there was some deep design in his non-attendance. If he really believed that I was in the confidence of the motives and the secret of his absence, he did me a great injustice.

I ventured to say a few words concerning his famous work on Political Justice; but the topic did not appear to be an agreeable one. The author spoke of it slightingly and disparagingly, either through modesty and politeness, or because he really had come to consider his theories and speculations on government and morals, crude, unformed, and untenable. Whenever that publication had been mentioned to him in my hearing, he uniformly treated the child of his brain like a stepfather. Possibly he felt that his offspring had turned out ill, and had not requited the patience and anxiety that a fond parent had bestowed upon an ingrate. At last he was reluctantly convinced that we should not see the truant. "Perhaps he was unwell? Did I believe that Mr. Shelley had been taken ill?" On the contrary, I firmly believed that he was as well, and as unpunctual, as he had ever been in his life.

William Godwin took leave of me somewhat early, at ten

o'clock precisely by the old watch, charging me earnestly and repeatedly to say a great many things to Mr. Shelley, whom most probably I should see first, by way of reprehension, admonition, and well-merited censure for his unwarrantable neglect. I promised to inform the offender of his disappointment and dissatisfaction. I did not know in what direction the grave reprover's homeward course lay, or whether he might desire any more of my society, and therefore I did not offer to accompany him, as I frequently did at our subsequent meetings. The next morning I saw Bysshe. He was delighted to learn that I had met with William Godwin.

"What did he say? What did we do? What did I think of him? How did I like him?" .

He devoured me with greedy questions, and listened to my answers with eager curiosity and enthusiastic pleasure. But when, to keep my promise with the sage, I reported the proceedings of the preceding day, and inquired, in my turn, why he had been nonsuited at our sittings, and had lost his writ of Nisi Prius, the rocks are never more deaf to naked, shipwrecked mariners than his locked-up ears were to the interrogatories and reproaches which I faithfully conveyed to him.

IANTHE ELIZA SHELLEY.

I never set foot in the house; my visits did not extend beyond the door. They did not remain there long—not above a month, I think. The little girl was named Ianthe Eliza. She received the latter name, doubtless, in honor of the guardian angel who still continued to officiate, occasionally at least, in that capacity. Ianthe, violet flower, or violet, is a name of Greek origin, fetched immediately from Ovid's Metamorphoses, being the name of a girl, to possess whom another girl, Iphis, was transformed into a youth :

"potiturque suâ puer Iphis Ianthe."

The fable is pleasing, and the name pretty ; yet as the young father had so many good old names amongst the ladies of his own family, it is a pity that he did not prefer one of them to so fantastical an appellation. The Yankee Cockney practice of bestowing flowers of fancy names has a vulgarity, affectation, and pretension about it, and was unworthy of him. It was better adapted for the issue of a metropolitan rhymester than for a gentleman's daughter. This accession to his family did not appear to afford him any gratification, or to create an interest. He never spoke of his child to me, and to this hour I never set eyes on her. This I regret, as I believe she is a most estimable person, and in every respect worthy of her parents, and, moreover, suitably married; Ianthe the second having found a second Iphis, it is presumed, without any transformation. I often asked Harriet to let me see her little girl, but she always made some excuse. She was asleep, being dressed, or had gone out, or was unwell. The child had some blemish, though not a considerable one, in one of her eyes; and this, I believe, was the true and only reason why her mother did not choose to exhibit her. She could not bear, herself a beauty, that I should know, such was her weakness, that one so nearly connected with herself was not perfectly beautiful.*

BONNET-SHOPS.

The good Harriet had fully recovered from the fatigues of her first effort of maternity, and, in fact, she had taken it easily. She was now in full force, vigor, and effect; roseate as ever, at times, perhaps, rather too rosy. She had entirely

---

* "Mr. Hogg is mistaken about Shelley's feelings as to his first child. He was extremely fond of it, and would walk up and down a room with it for a long time together, singing to it a monotonous melody of his own making. His song was, 'Yáhmani, Yáhmani, Yáhmani, Yáhmani.' It did not please me, but, what was more important, it pleased the child, and lulled it when it was fretful. Shelley was extremely fond of his children. He was pre-eminently an affectionate father. But to this first born there were accompaniments which did not please him. The child had a wet-nurse whom he did not like, and was much looked after by his wife's sister, whom he intensely disliked. I have often thought that if Harriet had nursed her own child, and if this sister had not lived with them, the link of their married love would not have so readily broken."—*Peacock.*

[This child, a Mrs. Esdaile, died in the present year, at the age of sixty-three.—*S.*]

8*

relinquished her favorite practice of reading aloud, which had been formerly a passion. I do not remember hearing her read even once after the birth of her child; the accustomed exercise of the chest had become fatiguing, or she was weary of it. Neither did she read much to herself; her studies, which had been so constant and exemplary, had dwindled away to nothing, and Bysshe had ceased to express any interest in them, and to urge her, as of old, to devote herself to the cultivation of her mind. When I called upon her, she proposed a walk, if the weather was fine, instead of the vigorous and continuous readings of preceding years.

The walk commonly conducted us to some fashionable bonnet-shop; the reading, it is not to be denied, was sometimes tiresome, the contemplation of bonnets was always so. However, there is a variety, a considerable variety and diversity in the configuration of bonnets. When we descended into the region of caps, their sameness and insipidity I found intolerable. They appeared to me all alike, equally devoid of interest; I could not bring myself to care whether there were two or three more sprigs in the crown, or a little more or less lace on the edge. Besides, a cap was never quite right; it must be altered on the spot, taken in, or let out; that could be done in a minute; the minute was a long one. And, uniformly, too much or too little had been effected by the change; it was to be altered again in another and a longer minute. I rebelled against this, so I was left outside the shop, like a wicked rebel, for one moment.

To loiter in the street on a cold day, for the indefinite and interminable period of one moment, was a punishment too severe even for rebellion and high treason, for treason against a high-crowned cap. So the walking, as well as the reading, came to an end.

When I called on Bysshe, Harriet was often absent; she had gone out with Eliza,—gone to her father's. Bysshe himself was sometimes in London, and sometimes at Bracknell, where he spent a good deal of his time in visiting certain friends, with whom, at that period, he was in very close alliance, and upon terms of the greatest intimacy, and by which connection his subsequent conduct, I think, was much influenced.

" MARY ! " " SHELLEY."

We walked westward, through Newgate Street. When we reached Skinner Street, he said, " I must speak with Godwin ; come in, I will not detain you long."

I followed him through the shop, which was the only entrance, and upstairs. We entered a room on the first floor; it was shaped like a quadrant. In the arc were windows ; in one radius a fireplace, and in the other a door, and shelves with many old books. William Godwin was not at home. Bysshe strode about the room, causing the crazy floor of the ill-built, unowned dwelling-house to shake and tremble under his impatient footsteps. He appeared to be displeased at not finding the fountain of Political Justice. " Where is Godwin ? " he asked me several times, as if I knew. I did not know, and, to say the truth, I did not care. He continued his uneasy promenade ; and I stood reading the names of old English authors on the backs of the venerable volumes, when the door was partially and softly opened. A thrilling voice called " Shelley ! " A thrilling voice answered, " Mary ! " And he darted out of the room, like an arrow from the bow of the far-shooting king. A very young female, fair and fair-haired, pale indeed, and with a piercing look, wearing a frock of tartan, an unusual dress in London at that time, had called him out of the room. He was absent a very short time—a minute or two ; and then returned. " Godwin is out ; there is no use in waiting." So we continued our walk along Holborn.

" Who was that, pray ? " I asked ; " a daughter ? "

" Yes."

" A daughter of William Godwin ? "

" The daughter of Godwin and Mary."

FIELD PLACE.

Let us take one more peep at Field Place ; one more only, and it will be the last, for it was Bysshe's last visit to his paternal hearth and native home. In the beginning of the summer of 1814, he walked one day alone from Bracknell to Horsham. A long and a pleasant walk, I should imagine. He was in an excited state, and had revelations by the way, and saw celestial visions.

A young officer in a marching regiment had been quartered some little time at Horsham ; he met with hospitality and kindness, as others did, at Field Place. He assisted at the brief return of the prodigal son ; he was present at the last visit, and he has given us a written account of it, from which I will extract such particulars as are interesting. It is strangely interlarded with laudations of his benefactors; such rapturous gratitude is creditable to his feelings ; but in mercy to all persons concerned, it is expedient to omit his demonstrations of it. One may infer from the tune and temper of Bysshe's last letter to myself, that his family might have had him then on reasonable, on easy terms, had they known how to negotiate a treaty of peace. They might probably have lured the wild hawk, the peregrine falcon, back to his perch without difficulty. Possibly they did not know it ; certainly they did not know how to set about it ; and the young wanderer was reserved for other, and for higher and more important destinies : man proposes, but man seldom disposes. It is a strange and a sad picture of the fruits of stubborn, intractable, wrong-headed violence to contemplate his mother and sisters timidly entertaining for the last time the divine poet disguised as a soldier. The friendly reception of the young officer at Field Place is related, and the narrative proceeds thus.

" At this time I had not seen Shelley, but the servants, especially the old butler, Laker, had spoken of him to me. He seemed to have won the hearts of the whole household. Mrs. Shelley often spoke to me of her son ; her heart yearned after him with all the fondness of a mother's love. It was during the absence of his father and the three youngest children, that the natural desire of a mother to see her son induced her to propose that he should pay her a short visit. At this time he resided somewhere in the country with his first wife and their

only child, Ianthe.   He walked from his house, until within a
very few miles of Field Place, when a farmer gave him a seat
in his travelling cart.   As he passed along the farmer, ignorant
of the quality of his companion, amused Bysshe with descrip-
tions of the country and its inhabitants.   When Field Place
came in sight, he told whose seat it was ; and as the most
remarkable incident connected with the family, that young
Master Shelley seldom went to church.   The poor fellow arrived at Field Place exceedingly fatigued.   I came there the
following morning to meet him.   I found him with his mother
and his two elder sisters in a small room off the drawing-room,
which they had named Confusion Hall.   He received me with
frankness and kindliness, as if he had known me from childhood,
and at once won my heart.   I fancy I see him now, as he sat
by the window, and hear his voice, the tones of which impressed
me with his sincerity and simplicity.   His resemblance to his
sister, Elizabeth, was as striking as if they had been twins.
His eyes were most expressive, his complexion beautifully
fair ; his features exquisitely fine ; his hair was dark, and no
peculiar attention to its arrangement was manifest.   In person
he was slender and gentleman-like, but inclined to stoop ; his
gait was decidedly not military.   The general appearance indicated great delicacy of constitution.   One would at once pro-
nounce of him, that he was something different from other men.
There was an earnestness in his manner, and such perfect
gentleness of breeding and freedom from everything artificial
as charmed every one.   I never met a man who so immediately won upon me.   The generosity of his disposition and utter
unselfishness imposed upon him the necessity of strict self-
denial in personal comforts.   Consequently he was obliged to be
most economical in his dress.   He one day asked us, how we
liked his coat, the only one he had brought with him.   We said
it was very nice, it looked as if new.   Well, said he, it is an
old black coat, which I have had done up, and smartened with
metal buttons and a velvet collar.   As it was not desirable that
Bysshe's presence in the country should be known, we arranged
that on walking out he should wear my scarlet uniform, and

that I should assume his outer garments. So he donned the soldier's dress, and sallied forth. His head was so remarkably small, that though mine be not large, the cap came down over his eyes, the peak resting on his nose, and it had to be stuffed before it would fit him. His hat just stuck on the crown of my head. He certainly looked like anything but a soldier.

" The metamorphosis was very amusing ; he enjoyed it much, and made himself perfectly at home in his unwonted garb. We gave him the name of Captain Jones, under which name we used to talk of him after his departure ; but, with all our care, Bysshe's visit could not be kept a secret. I chanced to mention the name of Sir James Mackintosh, of whom he expressed the highest admiration. He told me Sir James was intimate with one to whom, as he said, he owed everything; from whose book, Political Justice, he had derived all that was valuable in knowledge and virtue. He discoursed with eloquence and enthusiasm ; but h's views seemed to me exquisitely metaphysical, and by no means clear, precise, or decided. He told me he had already read the Bible in Hebrew four times. He was then only twenty-two years of age. Shelley never learnt Hebrew ; he probably said, in Greek, for he was much addicted to reading the Septuagint. He spoke of the Supreme Being as of infinite mercy and benevolence. He disclosed no fixed views of spiritual things ; all seemed wild and fanciful. He said, that he once thought the surrounding atmosphere was peopled with the spirits of the departed. He reasoned and spoke as a perfect gentleman, and treated my arguments, boy as I was,—I had lately completed my sixteenth year,—with as much consideration and respect as if I had been his equal in ability and attainments. Shelley was one of the most sensitive of human beings ; he had a horror of taking life, and looked upon it as a crime. He read poetry with great emphasis and solemnity : one evening, he read aloud to us a translation of one of Goethe's poems, and at this day I think I hear him. In music he seemed to delight, as a medium of association : the tunes which had been favorites in boyhood charmed him. There was one, which he played several times on the piano with one hand, that seemed to absorb him ; it was an exceedingly simple air, which, I understand, his earliest love was wont to play for him. Poor fellow! He soon left us, and I never saw him afterwards, but I can never forget him. It was his last visit to Field Place. He was an amiable, gentle being."

GROVE'S RECOLLECTIONS OF SHELLEY.

MY DEAR H., TORQUAY, *Feb.* 16, 1857.

It is very difficult, after so long a time, to remember with accuracy events which occurred so long ago. The first time I ever saw Bysshe was when I was at Harrow. I was nine years old ; my brother George, ten. We took him up at Brentford, where he was at school, at Dr. Greenlaw's ; a servant of my father's taking care of us all. He accompanied us to Ferne, and spent the Easter holidays there. The only circumstance I can recollect in connection with that visit was, that Bysshe, who was some few years older than we were, thought it would be good service to play carpenters, and, under his auspices, we got the carpenters' axes, and cut down some of my father's young fir-trees in the park. My father often used to remind me of that circumstance.

I did not meet Bysshe again after that till I was fifteen, the year I left the navy, and then I went to Field Place with my father, mother, Charlotte, and Harriet. Bysshe was there, having just left Eton, and his sister, Elizabeth. Bysshe was at that time more attached to my sister Harriet than I can express, and I recollect well the moonlight walks we four had at Strode, and also at St. Irving's ; that, I think, was the name of the place, then the Duke of Norfolk's, at Horsham. (St. Irving's Hills, a beautiful place, on the right hand side as you go from Horsham to Field Place, laid out by the famous Capability Brown, and full of magnificent forest-trees, waterfalls, and rustic seats. The house was Elizabethan. All has been destroyed.) That was in the year 1810. After our visit at Field Place, we went to my brother's house in Lincoln's Inn Fields, where Bysshe, his mother, and Elizabeth joined us, and a very happy month we spent. Bysshe was full of life and spirits, and very well pleased with his successful devotion to my sister. In the course of that summer, to the best of my recollection, after we had retired into Wiltshire, a continual correspondence was going on, as, I believe, there had been before, between Bysshe and my sister Harriet. But she became uneasy at the tone of his letters on speculative subjects, at first consulting my mother, and subsequently my father also on the subject. This led at last, though I cannot exactly tell how, to the dissolution of an engagement between Bysshe and my sister, which had previously been permitted, both by his father and mine.

In the autumn of 1810 Bysshe went to Oxford, to reside at University College, where he became acquainted with Mr. Hogg, and formed an intimate friendship with him. He found in him a kindred spirit as to his studies and speculations on various subjects, and it was not long ere Bysshe began to write on these. During the Christmas vacation of that year, and in January, 1811, I spent part of it with Bysshe at Field Place, and when we returned to London, his sister Mary sent a letter of introduction with a present to her schoolfellow, Miss Westbrook, which Bysshe and I were to take to her. I recollect we did so, calling at Mr. Westbrook's house. I scarcely know how it came about, but from that time Bysshe corresponded with Miss Westbrook. And not long after, for it was very soon after the Lent term had commenced, a little controversial work was published at Oxford. The pamphlet had not the author's name, but it was suspected in the University who was the author; and the young friends were dismissed from Oxford, for contumaciously refusing to deny themselves to be the authors of the work.

Bysshe and his friend then came to London, his father at that time refusing to receive Bysshe at Field Place. He came, therefore, to my brother's house in Lincoln's-inn Fields. I was then in town, attending Mr. Abernethy's anatomical lectures. The thought of anatomy, especially after a few conversations with my brother, became quite delightful to Bysshe, and he attended a course with me, and sometimes went also to St. Bartholomew's Hospital. At that time Bysshe and his friend took a lodging in Poland-street, where they continued for some time ; I think, a great part of the spring, and I spent a part of every day with them. No particular incident occurred at the time ; at least I do not recollect any. They both, but especially Bysshe, were occupied all the mornings in writing ; and after the anatomical lecture, we used sometimes to walk in St. James's Park, where Bysshe used to express his dislike of soldiers ; objecting to a standing army, as being calculated to fetter the minds of the people.

In the course of the spring, when his father was attending Parliament, an effort was made by the Duke of Norfolk to persuade my cousin to become a politician, under his auspices. By the Duke's invitation Bysshe met his father, at dinner at Norfolk House, to talk over a plan for bringing him in as member for Horsham, and to induce him to exercise his talents in the pursuit of politics. I recollect the indignation Bysshe expressed after that dinner, at what he considered an effort made to shackle his mind, and introduce him into life as a mere follower of the Duke. His father was puzzled what to do when that plan failed.

In the meantime, my brother Thomas, and his first wife, a very nice person, came to town for a few weeks, and became acquainted with Bysshe. He had heard much of Cwm Elan, in Radnorshire (at that time belonging to my brother, but since sold), from my sister Harriet, and wishing much to see the place, he received an invitation from my brother Tom and his wife to go there that summer, which he did. Whilst on the visit, his continued correspondence with Miss W. led to his return to London, and subsequent elopement with her. He corresponded with me also, during this period, and wrote me a letter concerning what he termed, his summons to link his fate with another, closing his communication thus : " Hear it not, Percy, for it is a knell, which summons thee to heaven or to hell ! " I sometimes think I have that letter locked up at S. If I go there in the summer, and find it, I will send it to you.

When Bysshe finally came to town to elope with Miss W.,

he came, as usual, to Lincoln's-inn-Fields, and I was his companion on his visits to her, and finally accompanied them early one morning,—I forget now the month, or the date, but it might have been September,—in a hackney-coach to the Green Dragon, in Gracechurch-street, where we remained all day, till the hour when the mail-coaches start, when they departed in the northern mail for York. The following spring I saw Bysshe and Mrs. Shelley in London. They spent the summer of that year, 1812, with my brother and sister at Cwm Elan. Mrs. G. was very much pleased with Mrs. Shelley, and sorry when they left them. They intended at that time to settle in Wales, but I think they went to the Lakes instead, Bysshe having become acquainted with Southey. From that time I never saw Bysshe again. My brother may have seen something of him, either in town, or in Edinburgh, but I do not quite recollect how that was.

I am afraid I have not been able to remember anything of Bysshe's early life that will prove of use. Though I spent many an afternoon and evening with Bysshe and Mr. H., at almost every coffee-house in London, for they changed their dining place daily for the sake of variety, I cannot recapitulate the conversations, though vividly recollecting the scenes.

Believe me, my dear H.,
Your affectionate cousin,

To H. S.
C. H. G.

My Dear H., Torquay, *Feb.* 25, 1857.

I am indeed glad to hear of the favorable reception given to my few early recollections of Bysshe. I remember on the occasion of our going to the Duke of Norfolk's house, Hills, at Horsham, Bysshe's putting on a working man's dress and coming to my sister as a beggar, and also his taking up one of those very little chests of drawers, peculiar to old houses, such as Hills was, and carrying it off part of the way back to Field Place ; and Elizabeth's being in a state of consternation lest her father should meet with us. But Bysshe had the power of entering so thoroughly into the spirit of his own humor, that nothing could stop him when once his spirits were up, and he carried you along with him in his hilarious flight, and made you a sharer in his mirth, in a manner quite irresistible.

During my intercourse with Bysshe, this was his one happy year. I never saw him after that, but with some care on his mind. I forgot to mention before, that during the early part of the summer which Bysshe spent in town, after leaving Oxford, the Prince Regent gave a splendid fête at Carlton House, in which the novelty was introduced of a stream of water, in imitation of a river, meandering down the middle of a very long table, in a temporary tent erected in Carlton Gardens. This was much commented upon in the papers, and laughed at by the Opposition. Bysshe also was of the number of those who disapproved of the fête and its accompaniments. He wrote a poem on the subject of about fifty lines, which he published immediately, wherein he apostrophized the Prince as sitting on the bank of his tiny river; and he amused himself with throwing copies into the carriages of persons going to Carlton House after the fête.

Believe me, &c.

To H. S.   C. H. G.

THE GODWINS.

The intimacy with Shelley, which was not of Godwin's seeking, was destined to have a far more abiding influence on the lives of both. The first notice of Shelley in the Godwin Diaries is under date Jan. 6, 1811. "Write to Shelly." It is the only time his name is so spelt, his letter was in answer to Shelley's first letter, in which he introduced himself, and was written at once, when he was not quite clear about the name of his correspondent.

Shelley was at this time living at Keswick, in the earlier and happier days of his marriage with Harriet Westbrook, and his eager and restless spirit prompted him to form the acquaintance, by letter, with others whom he believed to be like himself enthusiasts in the cause of humanity, of liberty, and progress.

P. B. Shelley to William Godwin.

" KESWICK, *Jan.* 3, 1811.

" —— You will be surprised at hearing from a stranger. No introduction has, nor in all probability ever will, authorize that which common thinkers would call a liberty. It is, however, a liberty which, although not sanctioned by custom, is so far from being reprobated by reason, that the dearest interests of mankind imperiously demand that a certain etiquette of fashion should no longer keep ' man at a distance from man,' and impose its flimsy barriers between the free communication of intellect. The name of Godwin has been accustomed to excite in me feelings of reverence and admiration. I have been accustomed to consider him as a luminary too dazzling for the darkness which surrounds him, and from the earliest period of my knowledge of his principles, I have ardently desired to share in the footing of intimacy that intellect which I have delighted to contemplate in its emanations. Considering, then, these feelings, you will not be surprised at the inconceivable emotion with which I learned your existence and your dwelling. I had enrolled your name on the list of the honorable dead. I had felt regret that the glory of your being had passed from this earth of ours. It is not so. You still live, and I firmly believe are still planning the welfare of human kind. I have but just entered on the scene of human operations, yet my feelings and my reasonings correspond with what yours were. My course has been short, but eventful. I have seen much of human prejudice, suffered much from human persecution, yet I see no reason hence inferable which should alter my wishes for their renovation. The ill treatment I have met with has more than ever impressed the truth of my principles on my judgment. I am young : I am ardent in the cause of philanthropy and truth : do not suppose that this is vanity. I am not conscious that it influences the portraiture. I imagine myself dispassionately describing the state of my mind. I am young : you have gone before me, I doubt not are a veteran to me in the years of persecution. Is it strange that, defying persecution as I have done, I should outstep the limits of custom's prescription, and endeavor to make my desire useful by friendship with William Godwin? I pray you to answer this letter. Imperfect as it may be, my capacity, my desire, is ardent, and unintermitted. Half-an-hour would be at least humanity employed in the experiment. I may mistake your residence. Certain feelings, of which I may be an inadequate arbiter, may induce you to desire concealment. I may not in fine have an answer to this letter. If I do not, when I come to London I shall seek for you. I am convinced I could represent myself to you in such terms as not to be thought wholly unworthy of your friendship. At least, if any desire for universal happiness has any claim upon your preference, that desire I can exhibit. Adieu. I shall earnestly await your answer.

"P. B. SHELLEY."

When arranging his usual short summer excursion in 1812, Godwin determined to combine this with a visit to the Shelleys. They had asked him to visit him, but no time had been fixed for his arrival; indeed the invitation had not been pressed when Godwin first thought of making his tour westward, for the Shelleys feared they could scarcely make him quite comfortable in the limited accommodation they could offer him. But on his arrival at Lynmouth, the Shelleys were gone, and had taken up their abode at Tanyrallt in North Wales.

William Godwin to Mrs. Godwin.

"LYNMOUTH, VALLEY OF STONES, Sep. 19th, 1812.

"MY DEAR LOVE,—The Shelleys are gone! have been gone these three weeks. I hope you hear the first from me; I dread lest every day may have brought you a letter from them, conveying this strange intelligence. I know you would conjure up a thousand frightful ideas of my situation under this disappointment. I have myself a disposition to take quietly any evil, when it can no longer be avoided, when it ceases to be attended with uncertainty, and when I can already compute the amount of it.   I heard this news instantly on my arrival at this place, and therefore walked immediately (that is, as soon as I had dined) to the Valley of Stones, that, if I could not have what was gone away, I might at least not fail to visit what remained.

" You advise me to return by sea; I thank you a thousand times for your kind and considerate motive in this, but certainly nothing more could be proposed to me at this moment than a return by sea.   I left Bristol at one o'clock on Wednesday, and arrived here at four o'clock on Friday, after a passage of fifty-one hours.   We had fourteen passengers, and only four berths, therefore I lay down only once for a few hours.   We had very little wind, and accordingly regularly tided it for six hours, and lay at anchor for six, till we reached this place. This place is fifteen miles short of Ilfracombe.   If the captain, after a great entreaty from the mate and one of his passengers (for I cannot entreat for such things) [had not] lent me his own boat to put me ashore, I really think I should have died with *ennui.*   We anchored, Wednesday night, somewhere within sight of the Holmes (small islands, so called, in the British Channel).   The next night we came within sight of Minehead, but the evening set in with an alarming congregation of black clouds, the sea rolled vehemently without a wind (a phenomenon which is said to portend a storm) and the captain in a fright put over to Penarth, near Cardiff, and even told us he should put us ashore there for the night.   At Penarth, he said, there was but one house, but it had a fine large barn annexed to it capable of accommodating us all.   This was a cruel reverse to me and my fellow-passengers, who had never doubted that we should reach the end of our voyage some time in the second day.   By the time, however, we had made the Welsh coast, the frightful symptoms disappeared, the night became clear and serene, and I landed here happily—that is, without further accident—the next day.   These are small events to a person accustomed to a seafaring life, but they were not small to me, and you will allow that they were not much mitigated by the elegant and agreeable accommodations of our crazed vessel. I was not decisively seasick, but had qualmish and discomforting sensations from the time we left the Bristol river, particularly after having lain down a few hours of Wednesday night.

"Since writing the above I have been to the house where Shelley lodged, and I bring good news. I saw the woman of the house, and I was delighted with her. She is a good creature, and quite loved the Shelleys. They lived here nine weeks and three days. They went away in a great hurry, in debt to her and two more. They gave her a draft upon the Honorable Mr. Lawless, brother to Lord Cloncurry, and they borrowed of her twenty-nine shillings, besides £3 that she got for them from a neighbor, all of which they faithfully returned when they got to Ilfracombe, the people not choosing to change a bank-note which had been cut in half for safety in sending it by the post. But the best news is that the woman says they will be in London in a fortnight. This quite comforts my heart."

The Shelleys arrived in London after their stay at Tanyrallt on October 4th, and dined with Godwin. They remained in London just six weeks, during which time Shelley and Godwin met almost daily, and he with his wife and her sister, Miss Westbrook, were frequent visitors in Skinner street. Of the two persons who were most to influence Shelley's life in after years, Mary Wollstonecraft Godwin and Jane Clairmont, who made her home with him and his second wife, he saw but little. Mary Godwin was just fifteen, was still a child, and considered as such in her family. Her half-sister Fanny was Miss Godwin, and was, after this visit, Shelley's friend and occasional correspondent. Jane Clairmont was only at home for two nights during the six weeks Shelley spent in London. She was several years older than Fanny, and even then led a somewhat independent life apart from her mother and step-father, presumably as a governess, since that was the occupation she afterwards followed in Italy, during the intervals of her residence with the Shelleys. In those later days, however, it seemed more poetical to an imaginative mind to call herself

" Clair" instead of Jane, by which self-chosen name she appears in the Shelley Diaries. Godwin, however,. preferring blunt reality, sticks to her true name.

When Mary Godwin was fifteen her father received a letter from an unknown correspondent, who took a deep interest in the theories of education which had been held by Mary Wollstonecraft, and who was anxious to know how far these were carried out in regard to the children she had left. An extract from Godwin's reply paints his daughter as she was at that period :—

" Your inquiries relate principally to the two daughters of Mary Wollstonecraft. They are neither of them brought up with an exclusive attention to the system and ideas of their mother. I lost her in 1797, and in 1801 I married a second time. One among the motives which led me to choose this was the feeling I had in myself of an incompetence for the education of daughters. The present Mrs. Godwin has great strength and activity of mind, but is not exclusively a follower of the notions of their mother ; and indeed, having formed a family establishment without having a previous provision for the support of a family, neither Mrs. Godwin nor I have leisure enough for reducing novel theories of education to practice, while we both of us honestly endeavor, as far as our opportunities will permit, to improve the mind and characters of the younger branches of our family.

" Of the two persons to whom your inquiries relate, my own daughter is considerably superior in capacity to the one her mother had before. Fanny, the eldest, is of a quiet, modest, unshowy disposition, somewhat given to indolence, which is her greatest fault, but sober, observing, peculiarly clear and distinct in the faculty of memory, and disposed to exercise her own thoughts and follow her own judgment. Mary, my daughter, is the reverse of her in many particulars. She is singularly bold, somewhat imperious, and active of mind. Her desire of knowledge is great, and her perseverance in everything she undertakes almost invincible. My own daughter is, I believe, very pretty; Fanny is by no means handsome, but in general prepossessing."

In 1813 Shelley was again in London for a short time during the summer, but Mary was absent in Scotland. She was not strong, and as a growing girl needed purer air than Skinner Street could offer; she had therefore gone to Dundee with her father's friends, Mr. Baxter and his daughter; and remained with them six months. It was not until the summer of 1814 that Shelley and Mary Godwin became really acquainted, when he found the child whom he had scarcely noticed two years before had grown into the woman of nearly seventeen summers.

The story has often been told, and told in different ways; but the facts as far as they can be gleaned from the scanty entries in Godwin's Diary are these. Shelley came to London on May 18th, leaving his wife at Binfield, certainly without the least idea that it was to be a final separation from him, though the relations between husband wife had for some time been increasingly unhappy. He was of course received in Godwin's house on the old footing of close intimacy, and rapidly fell in love with Mary. Fanny Godwin was away from home visiting some of the Wollstonecrafts, or she, three years older than Mary, might have discouraged the romantic attachment which sprang up between her sister and their friend. Jane Clairmont's influence was neither then, nor at any other time, used, or likely to be used, judiciously.

It was easy for the lovers, for such they became before they were aware of it, to meet without the attention of the parents being drawn to the increasing intimacy, and yet without any such sense of clandestine interviews, as might have disclosed to themselves whither they were drifting. Mary was unhappy at home; she thoroughly disliked Mrs. Godwin, to whom Fanny was far more tolerant; her desire for knowledge and love for reading were discouraged, and when seen with a book in her hand, she was wont to hear from her step-mother that her proper sphere was the storeroom. Old St. Pancras churchyard was then a quiet and secluded spot, where Mary Wollstonecraft's grave was shaded by a fine weeping willow. Here Mary Godwin used to take her books in the warm days of June, to spend every hour she could call her own. Here her intimacy with Shelley ripened, and here, in Lady Shelley's words, "she placed her hand in his, and linked her fortunes with his own."

It was not till July 8th that Godwin saw in any degree what was going on. The Diary records a "Talk with Mary," and a letter to Shelley. The explanation was satisfactory—it was before the mutual confession in St. Pancras churchyard—and Godwin and Shelley still met daily; but the latter did not dine again in Skinner Street. On July 14th Harriet Shelley arrived in London. The entries in the Diary for that and the following day are :—

> "15, *F.* M[arshal] and Shelley for Nash : Balloon : P. B. and H. Shelley to call n ; M. and F. Jones call, for Miss White : call on H. Shelley.
> "16, *Sa.* C. Turner (fr. Macintosh and Dadley) call : call on Shelleys ; coach w. P. B. S."

It is quite certain that Godwin used all his influence to restore the old relations between husband and wife; and on the 22d "Talk with Jane, letter fr. do. Write to H. S.," evidently refer to his dislike of the attention which Shelley now paid his daughter. But it was too late ; for on July 28th, early in the morning, Mary Godwin left her father's house, accompanied by Jane Clairmont. They joined Shelley, posted to Dover, and crossed in an open boat to Calais during a violent storm, during which they were in considerable danger. As soon as the elopement was discovered Mrs. Godwin pursued the party.

Godwin's Diary is here also extremely brief :—

> "28, *Th. Five in the morning.* Macmillan calls. M. J. for Dover."

Charles Clairmont wrote to break the news to Fanny, and devoted himself to his step-father during the three days of uncertainty, till Mrs. Godwin returned from Calais on July 31st.

On the evening of their arrival at Calais, Shelley and Mary began a joint diary, which was continued by one or the other through the remainder of Shelley's life. The entry for the second day gives an account of the entrance into their room of the landlord of the Calais Hotel to say that " a fat lady had arrived who said that I had run away with her daughter." As all the world knows, her persuasions had no avail, and she returned alone ; Jane Clairmont, in spite of her mother's remonstrances, determined to stay with Shelley and Mary. The three went to Paris, where they bought a donkey, and rode him in turns to Geneva, the others walking. He was bought for Mary as the weakest of the party, but Shelley's feet were soon blistered, and he was glad to ride now and then, not without the jeers of the passers by, in the spirit of those who scoffed in the Fable of the " Old Man and his Ass."

Sleeping now in a cabaret and now in a cottage, they at last finished this strange honeymoon, and the strangest sentimental journey ever undertaken since Adam and Eve went forth with all the world before them where to choose.

Godwin's irritation and displeasure at the step his daughter had taken were extreme. His own views on the subject of marriage had undergone a considerable change, and he was more alive than in former years to the strictures of the world. Nor is it possible for the most enthusiastic admirers of Shelley to palliate materially his conduct in the matter. On any view of the relations between the sexes, on any view of the desirableness of divorce, the breach with Harriet was far too recent to justify his conduct. In spite of her after-conduct our sympathies cannot but be in some measure with the discarded wife. But neither need they be refused to Mary Godwin. Let it be remembered that she was not seventeen, that her whole sympathies were with her mother, who had held views on marriage, different indeed to those which her daughter was upholding by her action, but which a young inexperienced girl might easily confuse with them, that her home was unhappy, and that she had met one who was to her then, and through all her married life, as one almost divine, last and not least that she was upheld in all that she did by an astute and worldly woman, who, though no relation, stood to Mary in the place of an elder sister. For Miss Clairmont indeed it is difficult to find excuse.

HARRIET SHELLEY.

[Why did Shelley marry Harriet Westbrook, and why did he desert Harriet Shelley? These two questions force themselves on the readers of his biography, and demand answers, particularly the second one. I doubt whether Shelley could have answered it satisfactorily: he could not have justified himself, even to himself. Let us see what some of his biographers have to say about this ugliest episode of his erratic life. We will begin with Lady Shelley : " Towards the close of 1813, estrangements, which for some time had been slowly growing between Mr. and Mrs. Shelley, came to a crisis. Separation ensued ; and Mrs. Shelley returned to her father's house. Here she gave birth to her second child,—a son, who died in 1826. The occurences of this painful epoch in Shelley's life, and of the causes which led to them, I am spared from relating. In Mary Shelley's own words :—' This is not the time to relate the truth ; and I should reject any coloring of the truth. No account of these events has ever been given at all approaching reality in their details, either as regards himself or others ; nor shall I further allude to them than to remark that the errors of action committed by a man as noble and generous as Shelley, may, as far as he only is concerned, be fearlessly avowed by those who loved him, in the firm conviction that, were they judged impartially, his character would stand in fairer and brighter light than that of any contemporary.' Of those remaining who were intimate with Shelley at this time, each has given us a different version of the sad event, colored by his own views and personal feelings. Evidently Shelley confided to none of these friends. We, who bear his name, and are of his family, have in our possession papers written by his own hand, which in after years may make the story of his life complete, and which few now living, except Shelley's own children, have ever perused. One mistake which has gone forth to the world, we feel ourselves positively called upon to contradict. Harriet's death has sometimes been ascribed to Shelley. This is entirely false. There was no immediate connection between her tragic end and any conduct on the part of her husband. It is true, however, that it was a permanent source of the deepest sorrow to him ; for never during all his after life did the dark shade depart which had fallen on his gentle and sensitive nature from the self-sought grave of the companion of his early youth." Thus wrote Lady Shelley in 1859. Mr. Peacock dissents from Lady Shelley respecting the separation of Shelley and Harriet, and remarks that whatever degree of confidence Shelley may have placed in his several friends, there are some facts which speak for themselves, and admit of no misunderstanding. He shows, by an extract from one of Shelley's letters, that no estrangement had taken place to the end of 1812, and states his memory sufficiently attests that there was none in 1813. "Shelley returned to London shortly before Christmas, then took a furnished house for two or three months at Windsor, visiting London occasionally. In March, 1814, he married Harriet a second time, according to the following certificate :—

'*Marriages in March*, 1814.

164. Percy Bysshe Shelley and Harriet Shelley (formerly Harriet Westbrook, Spinster, a Minor), both of this Parish, were re-married in this Church by Licence (the parties having been already married to each other according to the Rites and Ceremonies of the Church of Scotland), in order to obviate all doubts that have arisen, or shall or may arise, touching or concerning the validity of the aforesaid Marriage (by and with the consent of John Westbrook, the paternal

and lawful father of the said Minor) the twenty-fourth day of March, in the Year 1814.—By me,

EDWARD WILLIAMS, Curate.

This marriage { PERCY BYSSHE SHELLEY,
was solemnized { HARRIET SHELLEY, formerly
between us   {   Harriet Westbrook.

In presence of { JOHN WESTBROOK,
              { JOHN STANLY.

The above is a true extract from the Register Book of Marriages belonging to the Parish of Saint George, Hanover-square ; extracted this eleventh day of April 1859.—By me,

H. WEIGHTMAN, Curate.'

" It is therefore not correct to say that ' estrangements which had been slowly growing came to a crisis towards the end of 1813.' The date of the above certificate is conclusive on the point. The second marriage could not have taken place under such circumstances. Divorce would have been better for both parties, and the dissolution of the first marriage could have been easily obtained in Scotland. There was no estrangement, no shadow of a thought of separation, till Shelley became acquainted, not long after his second marriage, with the lady who was subsequently his second wife. The separation did not take place by mutual consent. I cannot think that Shelley ever so represented it. He never did so to me : and the account which Harriet gave me of the entire proceedings was decidedly contradictory of any such supposition. He might well have said, after first seeing Mary Wollstonecraft Godwin, ' *Ut vidi! ut perii!* ' Nothing that I ever read in tale or history could present a more striking image of a sudden, violent, irresistible, uncontrollable passion, than that under which I found him laboring when, at his request, I went up from the country to call on him in London. Between his old feelings towards Harriet, *from whom he was not then separated*, and his new passion for Mary he showed in his looks, in his gestures, in his speech, the state of a mind ' suffering, like a little kingdom, the nature of

an insurrection.'   His eyes were bloodshot, his hair and dress
disordered.   He caught up a bottle of laudanum, and said, 'I
never part from this.'   He added, 'I am always repeating to
myself your lines from Sophocles :

> Man's happiest lot is not to be :
>   And when we tread life's thorny steep,
> Most blest are they, who earliest free,
>   Descend to death's eternal sleep.'

Again he said, more calmly, ' Every one who knows me must
know that the partner of my life should be one who can feel
poetry and understand philosophy.   Harriet is a noble animal,
but she can do neither.'   I said, ' It always appeared to me
that you were very fond of Harriet.'   Without affirming or
denying this, he answered, ' But you did not know how I hated
her sister.'   The term ' noble animal' he applied to his wife, in
conversation with another friend now living, intimating that the
nobleness which he thus ascribed to her would induce her to
acquiesce in the inevitable transfer of his affections to their new
shrine.   She did not so acquiesce, and he cut the Gordian knot
of the difficulty by leaving England with Miss Godwin on the
28th of July, 1814.   Shortly after this 1 received a letter from
Harriet, wishing to see me.   I called on her at her father's
house in Chapel street, Grosvenor square.   She then gave me
her own account of the transaction, which, as I have said, decidedly contradicted the supposition of anything like separation
by mutual consent.   She at the same time gave me a description, by no means flattering, of Shelley's new love, whom I had
not then seen.   I said, ' If you have described her correctly,
what could he see in her ? '   ' Nothing,' she said, ' but that her
name was Mary, and not only Mary, but Mary Wollstonecraft.'
The lady had nevertheless great personal and intellectual at-
tractions, though it is not to be wondered at that Harriet could
not see them.   I feel it due to the memory of Harriet to state
my most decided conviction that her conduct as a wife was as
pure, as true, as absolutely faultless, as that of any who for
such conduct are held most in honor."   Thus wrote Mr. Peacock in 1860.

He proves pretty conclusively, I think, that no serious estrangements existed between Shelley and Harriet in 1813, or that if any did exist they were healed by their second marriage, concerning which we cannot but ask if Lady Shelley was aware that it had occurred when she was writing her *Memorials?* She does not refer to it in the first edition of that work, nor does she refer to it in her last·edition, which was published only last year. One would think that her Ladyship must have heard of it in seventeen years! Clearly she does not share Mr. Peacock's enthusiasm for the memory of her husband's father's first wife. "Few are now living who remember Harriet Shelley," Mr. Peacock continues. "I remember her well, and will describe her to the best of my recollection. She had a good figure, light, active, and graceful. Her features were regular and well-proportioned. Her hair was light brown, and dressed with taste and simplicity. In her dress she was truly *simplex munditiis.* Her complexion was beautifully transparent; the tint of the blush rose shining through the lily. The tone of her voice was pleasant; her speech the essence of frankness and cordiality; her spirits always cheerful; her laugh spontaneous, hearty, and joyous. She was well educated. She read agreeably and intelligently. She wrote only letters, but she wrote them well. Her manners were good ; and her whole aspect and demeanor such manifest emanations of pure and truthful nature, that to be once in her company was to know her thoroughly. She was fond of her husband, and accommodated herself in every way to his tastes. If they mixed in society, she adorned it; if they lived in retirement, she was satisfied ; if they travelled, she enjoyed the change of scene." It is a pity that this "noble animal" could not feel poetry and understand philosophy! Mr. Garnett, who writes in the interest of the Shelley family, undertakes to show a silver lining to this dark cloud upon the poet's fame, and refers to certain documents in possession of the family which refute Mr. Peacock's assertions. "The time cannot be distant when these assertions must be refuted by the publication of documents hitherto withheld, and Shelley's family have doubted whether it be worth which to anticipate it." So he wrote in 1862, and Lady Shelley wrote to the same effect in 1874, " The time, however, has not arrived at which it is desirable that facts already known to the poet's own family and a few private friends should be disclosed. Now, as when this book was first issued, we feel confident that the more is really known the more will all mists of false aspersion and misconception clear away Shelley's memory ; and now, as then, we feel that we obey the wishes of the dead in keeping silence of all beyond what here is told." This is pretty writing, the answer to which is, that the reputation of a famous poet is at stake, and that the papers which are to clear it ought not to be withheld from the world forever. Sixty-two years have passed since he abandoned the wife of his youth, and fifty-four years since he went to his watery grave—how much longer time must elapse before his memory is vindicated? Mr. Peacock doubted the existence of the wonderful papers in question, but Mr. Garnett declares that he has seen them, and that they " demonstrate that Shelley and Harriet corresponded, both during the former's absence on the Continent and afterwards ; that he visited her repeatedly after his return to England ; that so late, at least, as December, 1814, he continued to take an affectionate interest in her, gave her much good advice, or what he regarded as such, and exposed himself to no little inconvenience and danger of misconstruction in a generous endeavor to promote her welfare ; that previous to his departure from England he had given instructions that deeds should be prepared and a settlement executed for her benefit." It is difficult to put one's self, at least I find it difficult to put myself, in the place of Shelley, or indeed of either of the other combatants in this triangular duel of love and sorrow : I cannot understand the morals of the Divine Poet, as Mr. Hogg calls him, and his Divine Mistress, and the want of spirit in his twice-wedded, abandoned wife. These good people are beyond my comprehension. There was something comical about them, too, if Mr. Rossetti was correctly informed. " I am told," he writes, " that, at some time after the return of Shelley and Mary from the Continent in the year 1814, he consulted a legal friend with a view to intro-

9*

ducing Harriet into his household as a permanent inmate—it is to be presumed, as strictly and solely a friend of the connubial pair, Mary and himself; and it required some little cogency of demonstration on the part of the lawyer to convince the primeval intellect of Shelley that such an arrangement had its weak side." The Shelleyan life of Harriet was divided into two episodes. The first consisted of less than three years of marriage, the last of a little more than two years of desertion. Hogg and others have furnished, as we have seen, materials for a history of the one; the other is wrapt in obscurity. Mr. Rossetti shall tell us the little that is known about it : " The exact course of Harriet's life since June, 1814, has never been accurately disclosed ; and there is plenty of reason why, even if one had at command (which I have not) details as yet unpublished, one should hesitate to bring them forward. I shall confine myself to producing the most definite statement yet made on the subject—that of Mr. Thornton Hunt; omitting only one unpleasant expression, which I have reason (from two independent and unbiassed sources of information) to suppose overcharged. He unreservedly allows, with other biographers, that there was nothing to censure in Harriet's conjugal conduct before the separation; 'but subsequently she forfeited her claims to a return, even in the eye of the law. If she left [Shelley*], it would appear that she herself was deserted in turn by a man in a very humble grade of life, and it was in consequence of this desertion that she killed herself.' The same author says that, before this event, Mr. Westbrook's faculties had begun to fail; he had treated Harriet with harshness, 'and she was driven from the paternal roof.† This Shelley did not know at the time.' Another writer affirms that Harriet—poor, uncared-for young creature—suffered great privations, and sank to the

---

* I do not see the force of this expression. It is certain, in one sense, that Harriet did leave Shelley ; and equally certain that (to say the very least) her leaving him was *less* of a voluntary act on her part than his leaving her was on his.

† "The immediate cause of her death was that her father's door was shut against her, though he had at first sheltered her and her children. This was done by order of her sister, who would not allow Harriet access to the bed-side of her dying father."— *Paul.*

lowest grade of misery.   DeQuincey says she was stung by cal-
umnies incidental to the position of a woman separated from
her husband, and was oppressed by the lonesomeness of her
abode—which seems to be rather a vague version of the facts.
In any case we will be very little inclined to cast stones at the
forlorn woman who sought and found an early cleansing in the
waters of death—a final refuge from all the pangs of desertion
or of self-scorn.   I find nothing to suggest otherwise than that
Shelley had lost sight of Harriet for several months preceding
her suicide ; though it might seem natural to suppose that he
continued to keep up some sort of knowledge just how *she* went
on, at least of the state of his young children Ianthe and Charles.
At all events, be he blameworthy or not in the original matter
of the separation, or on the ground of recent obliviousness of
Harriet or his children, it is an ascertained fact that her suicide
was in no way immediately connected with any act or default of
his, but with a train of circumstances for which the responsibility
lay with Harriet herself, or had to be divided between her and
the antecedent conditions of various kinds."   The end came
before she was twenty-two, when she drowned herself in the
Serpentine.   Mr. Peacock thinks it was in December, 1816; but
he was mistaken.   Mr. Rossetti says it was in November of
that year, and fixes the date as the 10th, on the authority of an
American edition of Shelley's works.   I fixed upon the 9th myself, fourteen years ago, I forget now on what authority.*   On
one of these days the body of Harriet Shelley was borne to the
house of her father in Chapel street, and intelligence of her
death was sent to Shelley, who was at Bath, Mr. Rossetti thinks.
If so, he did not remain long, for by the 19th of November he
was at Marlow, whence he wrote to Godwin.   No biographer
of Shelley, so far as I am aware, has ever seen the following
letter, which was formerly in my possession.   It was sealed with
a black seal.   The wax had not taken sharply, but as far as I

---

* [Mr. Paul agrees with me in thinking that Harriet drowned herself on the 9th of
November, but says that the body was not found till December 10th, and that Godwin received a letter on the subject from Shelley on the 16th.   That he is mistaken in
regard to the two dates last named is evident from the letter of Shelley's referred
to above.—*S.*]

could make out it contained the impression of some mythological figure, apparently a Hindu goddess, rampant on a barge, or boat, with a peacock's tail, and a dagger in her hand. The post-mark was ' Marlow, Nov. 19, 1816.'

" 'MY DEAR SIR,   " MARLOW, Wednesday morning.
 , " ' In the legend of St. Colombanus we are told that he performed a miracle by hanging his garment on a sunbeam.

" ' I, too, have tried to discover a ray of light to fasten hope on it. The casualties of this life come on like waves, one succeeding the other. We may escape the heavy roll of the mighty ocean, and be wrecked on the still, smooth waters of the land-locked bay. We dread the storm and the hurricane, and forget how many have perished within sight of shore. However the human mind may have a natural desire to blot out from memory objects that are hopeless, oblivion does not always descend upon the sorrowing soul. How much in every man's heart dies away unuttered ! How many chords of the lyre in the poet's heart have been dumb in the world's ear ! I am bowed down with grief, though relieved of part of the load which the sad event has brought upon me ; yet sufficient anxiety remains on my mind to give me ample subject for thought and sorrowful reflection. With how many garlands we can beautify the tomb ! If we begin betimes we can learn to make the prospect of the grave the most seductive of human visions ; by little and little we hive therein all the most pleasing of our dreams. Surely if any spot in the world be sacred, it is that in which grief ceases, and from which, if the voice within our hearts mocks us not with an everlasting lie, we spring upon the untiring wings of a painless and seraphic life, those we love around, our nature, universal intelligence, our atmosphere, eternal love. Mary sends kisses. Believe me ever yours.

" ' P. B. SHELLEY.' "

The epilogue to this tragedy was spoken on the 30th of December, 1816. Six days before that time Godwin wrote a letter to his daughter, which, Mr. Paul says, was the first that had passed between them since she left her home. Godwin kept a diary, and a singular one it was. She is carefully described in the diary as *M. W. G.* Shelley's second marriage took place on Monday, December 30; the entries relating to it in Godwin's diary are extremely curious, as though intended to mislead any one who might, without sufficient information, glance at his book. It is probable that the diary in use during the year always lay on his desk, obvious to prying eyes, while those not in use were locked away. However this may be, the entries are as follows :—

"*Der.* 29, *Su.* Mandeville ca la. P. B. S. and M. W. G. dine and sup.
"30, *M.* Write to Hume. Call on Mildred w. P. B. S., M. W. G., and M. J.; they dine and sup; tea Constable's w. Wells, Wallace, Patrick, and Miss C.
See No. XVIII. *infra pag ult.*
"31, *Tu.* They breakfast, dine, and sup. Holinshead, Ric. iii."

On turning to the last page of Diary, vol. xviii., the last but one used, and containing entries of two years before the present date, the words "Call on Mildred" are explained. On the blank page at the end of that volume is written :—

"Percy Bysshe Shelley married to Mary Wollstonecraft Godwin at St. Mildred's Church, Bread Street, Dec. 30, 1816.
"Haydon, *Curate.*
"Spire, *Clerk.*
"*Present*—William Godwin.
"Mary Jane Godwin."]

MISS JANE CLAIRMONT.

[Mr. Percy Bysshe Shelley, Miss Mary Wollstonecraft Godwin, and Miss Jane Clairmont returned to England in September, 1814. In the beginning of May, 1816, the same party, with the addition of a child, a little boy named William which Miss Godwin had borne to Mr. Shelley, departed for the Continent again. They reached Sicheron near Geneva, on the 17th of May. "On the 25th, Lord Byron with his travelling physician, Dr. Polidori, arrived at the same hotel; and the two parties encountered on the 27th, if not before." His Lordship had been abandoned by his wife about four months earlier, and was out of humor with his countrymen, but willing to be pleased with his countrywomen, as his admirers well remember. Mr. Rosetti shall tell the story of one of the latter. "Byron and Shelley had not previously met; they now found themselves in daily and intimate intercourse. One of the Shelley party, however, Miss Clairmont, was already known to Byron, for she had, not long before, called upon him as connected with the management of Drury Lane Theatre, and had sought an engagement on the stage, which did not take effect. Byron possibly—indeed, probably—had then admired her; if not, he did so now. The result was the birth, on the following January, of the daughter known to Byronic biographers as Allegra, or Alba. Shelley and Mary knew nothing of this fleeting outburst of passion at the time, and were by no means pleased when its results became apparent. But they acted with perfect good feeling, and did everything for Allegra and her mother. For the latter, Byron, from first to last, did nothing; a shameful blot on his honor, unless, indeed, we surmise that neither Miss Clairmont nor her friends would accede to any proffer on his part." The Shelley party returned to England in September. In the spring of 1818 Shelley and his wife and two children, and Miss Clairmont and Lord Byron's child, left England for Italy, and, as Mr. Rosetti puts it, the archangelic feet and brain and heart were never again to be repelled by that grudging and unwitting step-mother. They proceeded to Milan, and Allegra was sent on to her noble papa at Venice. Thus much about Miss Clairmont and the whereabouts of the Shelleys. And now

for Mr. Trelawney and his mingled recollections of Shelley
and Byron.]

WORDSWORTH'S OPINION OF SHELLEY.

In the summer of 1819 I was at Ouchy, a village on the
margin of the lake of Geneva, in the Canton de Vaux! The
most intelligent person I could find in the neighborhood to
talk to, was a young bookseller at Lausanne, educated at a
German University ; he was familiar with the works of many
most distinguished writers ; his reading was not confined, as
it generally is with men of his craft, to catalogues and indexes,
for he was an earnest student, and loved literature more than
lucre.

As Lausanne is one of the inland harbors of refuge in which
wanderers from all countries seek shelter, his shelves contained
works in all languages ; he was a good linguist, and read the
most attractive of them. " The elevation of minds," he said,
" was more important than the height of mountains (I was
looking at a scale of the latter), and books are the standards to
measure them by." He used to translate for me passages
from the works of Schiller, Kant, Goëthe, and others, and
write comments on their paradoxical, mystical, and metaphysical theories. One morning I saw my friend sitting under the
acacias on the terrace in front of the house in which Gibbon
had lived, and where he wrote the " Decline and Fall." He
said, " I am trying to sharpen my wits in this pungent air
which gave such a keen edge to the great historian, so that I
may fathom this book. Your modern poets, Byron, Scott, and
Moore, I can read and understand as I walk along, but I have
got hold of a book by one now that makes me stop to take
breath and think." It was Shelley's " Queen Mab." As I
had never heard that name or title, I asked how he got the
volume. " With a lot of new books in English, which I took
in exchange for old French ones. Not knowing the names of
the authors, I might not have looked into them, had not a
pampered, prying priest smelt this one in my lumber-room,
and, after a brief glance at the notes, exploded in wrath,

shouting out 'Infidel, jacobin leveller : nothing can stop this spread of blasphemy but the stake and the fagot ; the world is retrograding into accursed heathenism and universal anarchy!' When the priest had departed, I took up the small book he had thrown down, saying, 'Surely there must be something here worth tasting.' You know the proverb 'No person throws a stone at a tree that does not bear fruit.'"

"Priests do not," I answered ; "so I, too, must have a bite of the forbidden fruit. What do you think of it ?"

"To my taste," said the bookseller, "the fruit is crude, but well flavored ; it requires a strong stomach to digest it ; the writer is an enthusiast, and has the true spirit of a poet ; he aims at regenerating, not like Byron and Moore, levelling mankind. They say he is but a boy, and this his first offering : if that be true, we shall hear of him again."

Some days after this conversation I walked to Lausanne, to breakfast at the hotel with an old friend, Captain Daniel Roberts, of the Navy. He was out, sketching, but presently came in accompanied by two English ladies, with whom he had made acquaintance whilst drawing, and whom he brought to our hotel. The husband of one of them soon followed. I saw by their utilitarian garb, as well as by the blisters and blotches on their cheeks, lips, and noses, that they were pedestrian tourists, fresh from the snow-covered mountains, the blazing sun and frosty air having acted on their unseasoned skins, as boiling water does on the lobster, by dyeing his dark coat scarlet. The man was evidently a denizen of the north, his accent harsh, skin white, of an angular and bony build, and self-confident and dogmatic in his opinions. The precision and quaintness of his language, as well as his eccentric remarks on common things, stimulated my mind. Our icy islanders thaw rapidly when they have drifted into warmer latitudes : broken loose from its anti-social system, mystic casts, coteries, sets, and sects, they lay aside their purse-proud tuft-hunting, and toadying ways, and are very apt to run riot in the enjoyment of all their senses. Besides, we are compelled to talk in strange company, if not from good breeding, to prove our breed, as the gift of speech is often our principal if not sole distinction from the rest of the brute animals.

To return to our breakfast. The travellers, flushed with health, delighted with their excursion, and with appetites earned by bodily and mental activity, were in such high spirits, that Roberts and I caught the infection of their mirth ; we talked as loud and fast as if under the exhilarating influence of champagne, instead of such a sedative compound as *café au lait*. I can rescue nothing out of oblivion but a few last words. The stranger expressed his disgust at the introduction of carriages into the mountain districts of Switzerland, and at the old fogies who used them.

" As to the arbitrary, pitiless, Godless wretches," he exclaimed, " who have removed nature's landmarks by cutting roads through Alps and Apennines, until all things are reduced to the same dead level, they will be arraigned hereafter with the unjust ; they have robbed the best specimens of what men should be, of their freeholds in the mountains ; the eagle, the black cock, and the red deer, they have tamed or exterminated. The lover of nature can nowhere find a solitary nook to contemplate her beauties. Yesterday," he continued, " at the break of day, I scaled the most rugged height within my reach ; it looked inaccessible ; this pleasant delusion was quickly dispelled ; I was rudely startled out of a deep reverie by the accursed jarring, jingling, and rumbling of a calêche, and harsh voices that drowned the torrent's fall."

The stranger, now hearing a commotion in the street, sprang on his feet, looked out of the window, and rang the bell violently.

" Waiter," he said, " is that our carriage ? Why did you not tell us ? Come, lasses, be stirring, the freshness of the day is gone. You may rejoice in not having to walk ; there is a chance of saving the remnants of skin the sun has left on our chins and noses,—to-day we shall be stewed instead of barbecued."

On their leaving the room to get ready for their journey, my

friend Roberts told me the strangers were the poet Wordsworth, his wife, and sister.

Who could have divined this? I could see no trace, in the
hard features and weather-stained brow of the outer-man, of
the divinity within him. In a few minutes the travellers reappeared; we cordially shook hands, and agreed to meet again
at Geneva. Now that I knew that I was talking to one of the
veterans of the gentle craft, as there was no time to waste in
idle ceremony, I asked him abruptly what he thought of Shelley
as a poet?

"Nothing," he replied, as abruptly.

Seeing my surprise, he added, "A poet who has not produced a good poem before he is twenty-five, we may conclude
cannot, and never will do so."

"The Cenci!" I said eagerly.

"Won't do," he replied, shaking his head, as he got into
the carriage; a rough-coated Scotch terrier followed him.

"This hairy fellow is our flea-trap," he shouted out, as they
started off.

When I recovered from the shock of having heard the harsh
sentence passed by an elder bard on a younger brother of the
Muses, I exclaimed,

"After all, poets are but earth. It is the old story,—Envy—
Cain and Abel. Professions, sects, and communities in
general, right or wrong, hold together, men of the pen excepted; if one of their guild is worsted in the battle, they do
as the rooks do by their inky brothers, fly from him, cawing
and screaming; if they don't fire the shot, they sound the
bugle to charge."

I did not then know that the full-fledged author never reads
the writings of his contemporaries, except to cut them up in a
review,—that being a work of love. In after-years, Shelley
being dead, Wordsworth confessed this fact; he was then induced to read some of Shelley's poems, and admitted that
Shelley was the greatest master of harmonious verse in our
modern literature.

MR. WILLIAMS' DESCRIPTION OF SHELLEY.

Shortly after I went to Geneva. In the largest country-house (Plangeau) near that city lived a friend of mine, a Cornish baronet, a good specimen of the old school; well read, and polished by long intercourse with intelligent men of many nations. He retained a custom of the old barons, now obsolete,—his dining-hall was open to all his friends; you were welcomed at his table as often as it suited you to go there, without the ceremony of inconvenient invitations.

At this truly hospitable house, I first saw three young men, recently returned from India. They lived together at a pretty villa (*Maison aux Grênades*, signifying the House of Pomegranates), situated on the shores of the lake, and at an easy walk from the city of Geneva and the baronet's. Their names were George Jervoice, of the Madras Artillery; E. E. Williams, and Thomas Medwin, the two last, lieutenants on half-pay, late of the 8th Dragoons. Medwin was the chief medium that impressed us with a desire to know Shelley; he had known him from childhood; he talked of nothing but the inspired boy, his virtues and his sufferings, so that, irrespective of his genius, we all longed to know him. From all I could gather from him, Shelley lived as he wrote, the life of a true poet, loving solitude, but by no means a cynic. In the two or three months I was at Geneva, I passed many agreeable days at the two villas I have mentioned. Late in the autumn I was unexpectedly called to England; Jervoice and Medwin went to Italy; the Williams's determined on passing the winter at Chalons sur Saône. I offered to drive them there, in a light Swiss carriage of my own; and in the spring to rejoin them, and to go on to Italy together in pursuit of Shelley.

Human animals can only endure a limited amount of pain or pleasure, excess of either is followed by insensibility. The Williams's, satiated with felicity at their charming villa on the cheerful lake of Geneva, resolved to leave it, and see how long they could exist deprived of everything they had been accustomed to. With such an object, a French provincial town was just the place to try the experiment. Chalons sur Saône was decided on. We commenced our journey in November, in an open carriage. After four days' drive through wind, rain, and mud, we arrived at Chalons in a sorry plight. The immense plain which surrounded the town was flooded; we took up our quarters at an hotel on the slimy banks of the Saône. What a contrast to the villa of pomegranates we had left, we all thought —but said nothing.

When I left them by the *malle poste*, on my way to Paris, I felt as a man should feel when, stranded on a barren rock, he seizes the only boat and pushes off to the nearest land, leaving his forlorn comrades to perish miserably. After a course of spare diet of soup maigre, bouilli, sour wine, and solitary confinement had restored their senses, they departed in the spring for the south, and never looked behind them until they had crossed the Alps. They went direct to the Shelleys; and amongst Williams's letters I find his first impressions of the poet, which I here transcribe :—

My dear Trelawny,   Pisa, *April*, 1821.

We purpose wintering in Florence, and sheltering ourselves from the summer heat at a castle of a place, called Villa Poschi, at Pugnano, two leagues from hence, where, with Shelley for a companion, I promise myself a great deal of pleasure, sauntering in the shady retreats of the olive and chestnut woods that grow above our heads up the hill sides. He has a small boat building, only ten or twelve feet long, to go adventuring, as he calls it, up the many little rivers and canals that intersect this part of Italy; some of which pass through the most beautiful scenery imaginable, winding among the terraced gardens at the base of the neighboring mountains, and opening into such lakes as Beintina, etc.

Shelley is certainly a man of most astonishing genius in appearance, extraordinarily young, of manners mild and amiable, but withal full of life and fun. His wonderful command of language, and the ease with which he speaks on what are generally considered abstruse subjects, are striking; in short, his ordinary conversation is akin to poetry, for he sees things in the most singular and pleasing lights : if he wrote as he talked, he would be popular enough. Lord Byron and others think him by far the most imaginative poet of the day. The style of his lordship's letters to him is quite that of a pupil, such as asking his opinion, and demanding his advice on certain points, etc. I must tell you, that the idea of the tragedy of Manfred, and many of the philosophical, or rather metaphysical, notions interwoven in the composition of the fourth Canto of Childe Harold, are of his suggestion ; but this, of course, is between ourselves. A few nights ago I nearly put an end to the Poet and myself. We went to Leghorn, to see after the little boat, and, as the wind blew excessively hard, and fair, we resolved upon returning to Pisa in her, and accordingly started with a huge sail, and at 10 o'clock P.M. capsized her.

I commenced this letter yesterday morning, but was prevented from continuing it by the very person of whom I am speaking, who, having heard me complain of a pain in my chest since the time of our ducking, brought with him a doctor, and I am now writing to you in bed, with a blister on the part supposed to be affected. I am ordered to lie still and try to sleep, but I prefer sitting up and bringing this sheet to a conclusion. A General R., an Englishman, has been poisoned by his daughter and her paramour, a Venetian servant, by small doses of arsenic, so that the days of the Cenci are revived, with this difference, that crimes seem to strengthen with keeping. Poor Beatrice was driven to parricide by long and unendurable outrages : in this last case, the parent was sacrificed by the lowest of human passions, the basis of many crimes. By the by, talking of Beatrice and the Cenci, I have a horrid history to tell you of that unhappy girl, that it is impossible to put on paper : you will not wonder at the act, but admire the virtue (an odd expression, you will perhaps think) that inspired the blow. Adieu. Jane desires to be very kindly remembered, and believe me,

Very sincerely yours,
E. E. WILLIAMS.

"Come in, Shelley."

I was not accustomed to the town life I was then leading, and became as tired of society as townfolks are of solitude. The great evil in solitude is, that your brain lies idle ; your muscles expand by exercise, and your wits contract from the want of it.

To obviate this evil, and maintain the just equilibrium between the body and the brain, I determined to pass the coming winter in the wildest part of Italy, the Maremma, in the midst of the marshes and malaria, with my friends Roberts and Williams ; keen sportsmen both—that part of the country being well stocked with woodcocks and wild fowl. For this purpose, I shipped an ample supply of dogs, guns, and other implements of the chase to Leghorn. For the exercise of my brain, I proposed passing my summer with Shelley and Byron, boating in the Mediterranean. After completing my arrangements, I started in the autumn by the French malle-post, from Paris to Chalons, regained possession of the horse and cabriolet I had left with Williams, and drove myself to Geneva, where Roberts was waiting for me. After a short delay, I continued my journey south with Roberts in my Swiss carriage, so that we could go on or stop, where and when we pleased. By our method of travelling, we could sketch, shoot, fish, and observe everything at our leisure. If our progress was slow, it was most pleasant. We crossed Mount Cenis, and in due course arrived at Genoa. After a long stop at that city of painted palaces, anxious to see the Poet, I drove to Pisa alone. I arrived late, and after putting up my horse at the inn and dining, hastened to the Tre Palazzi, on the Lung 'Arno, where the Shelleys and Williams's lived on different flats under the same roof, as is the custom on the Continent. The Williams's received me in their earnest cordial manner ; we had a great deal to communicate to each other, and were in loud and animated conversation, when I was rather put out by observing in the passage near the open door, opposite to where I sat, a pair of glittering eyes steadily fixed on mine ; it was too dark to make out whom they belonged to. With the acuteness of a woman, Mrs. Williams's eyes followed the direction of mine, and going to the doorway, she laughingly said,

" Come in, Shelley, it's only our friend Tre just arrived."

Swiftly gliding in, blushing like a girl, a tall thin stripling held out both his hands ; and although I could hardly believe as I looked at his flushed, feminine, and artless face that it could be the Poet, I returned his warm pressure. After the ordinary greetings and courtesies he sat down and listened. I was silent from astonishment : was it possible this mild-looking beardless boy could be the veritable monster at war with all the world ?—excommunicated by the Fathers of the Church, deprived of his civil rights by the fiat of a grim Lord Chancellor, discarded by every member of his family, and denounced by the rival sages of our literature as the founder of a Satanic school ? I could not believe it ; it must be a hoax. · He was habited like a boy, in a black jacket and trousers, which he seemed to have outgrown, or his tailor, as is the custom, had most shamefully stinted him in his " sizings." Mrs. Williams saw my embarrassment, and to relieve me asked Shelley what book he had in his hand ? His face brightened, and he answered briskly :

" Calderon's Magico Prodigioso, I am translating some passages in it."

" Oh, read it to us ! "

Shoved off from the shore of common-place incidents that could not interest him, and fairly launched on a theme that did, he instantly became oblivious of everything but the book in his hand. The masterly manner in which he analyzed the genius of the author, his lucid interpretation of the story, and the ease with which he translated into our language the most subtle and imaginative passages of the Spanish poet, were marvellous, as was his command of the two languages. After this touch of his quality I no longer doubted his identity ; a dead silence ensued ; looking up, I asked,

" Where is he ? "

Mrs. Williams said, " Who ? Shelley ? Oh, he comes and goes like a spirit, no one knows when or where."

Presently he reappeared with Mrs. Shelley. She brought us back from the ideal world Shelley had left us in, to the real one, welcomed me to Italy, and asked me the news of London and Paris, the new books, operas, and bonnets, marriages, murders, and other marvels. The Poet vanished, and tea appeared. Mary Wollstonecraft (the authoress), the wife of William Godwin, died in 1797, in giving birth to their only child, Mary, married to the poet Shelley ; so that at the time I am speaking of Mrs. Shelley was twenty-four. Such a rare pedigree of genius was enough to interest me in her, irrespective of her own merits as an authoress. The most striking feature in her face was her calm, gray eyes ; she was rather under the English standard of woman's height, very fair and light, haired, witty, social, and animated in the society of friends, though mournful in solitude ; like Shelley, though in a minor degree, she had the power of expressing her thoughts in varied and appropriate words, derived from familiarity with the works of our vigorous old writers. Neither of them used obsolete or foreign words. This command of our language struck me the more as contrasted with the scanty vocabulary used by ladies in society, in which a score of poor hackneyed phrases suffice to express all that is felt or considered proper to reveal.

SHELLEY'S INFLUENCE ON BYRON.

At two o'clock on the following day, in company with Shelley, I crossed the Ponte Vecchio, and went on the Lung 'Arno to the Palazzo Lanfranchi, the residence of Lord Byron. We entered a large marble hall, ascended a giant staircase, passed through an equally large room over the hall, and were shown into a smaller apartment which had books and a billiard-table in it. A surly-looking bull-dog (Moretto) announced us, by growling, and the Pilgrim instantly advanced from an inner chamber, and stood before us. His halting gait was apparent, but he moved with quickness ; and although pale, he looked as fresh, vigorous, and animated as any man I ever saw. His pride, added to his having lived for many years alone, was the cause I suppose that he was embarrassed at first meeting with strangers ; this he tried to conceal by an affectation of ease. After the interchange of common-place question and answer, he regained his self-possession, and turning to Shelley, said,

" As you are addicted to poesy, go and read the versicles I was delivered of last night, or rather this morning—that is, if you can. I am posed. I am getting scurrilous. There is a letter from Tom Moore ; read, you are blarneyed in it ironically."

He then took a cue, and asked me to play billiards ; he struck the balls and moved about the table briskly, but neither played the game nor cared a rush about it, and chatted after this idle fashion :—

" The purser of the frigate I went to Constantinople in called an officer *scurrilous* for alluding to his wig. Now, the day before I mount a wig—and I shall soon want one—I'll ride about with it on the pummel of my saddle, or stick it on my cane.

" In that same frigate, near the Dardanelles, we nearly ran down an American trader with his cargo of notions. Our captain, old Bathurst, hailed, and with the dignity of a lord, asked him where he came from, and the name of his ship. The Yankee captain bellowed,—

" ' You copper-bottomed sarpent, I guess you'll know when I've reported you to Congress.' "

The surprise I expressed by my looks was not at what he said, but that he could register such trifles in his memory. Of course with other such small anecdotes, his great triumph at having swum from Sestos to Abydos was not forgotten. I had come prepared to see a solemn mystery, and so far as I could judge from the first act it seemed to me very like a solemn farce. I forgot that great actors when off the stage are dull dogs ; and that even the mighty Prospero, without his book and magic mantle, was but an ordinary mortal. At this juncture Shelley joined us ; he never laid aside his book and magic mantle ; he waved his wand, and Byron, after a faint show of defiance,

10

stood mute ; his quick perception of the truth of Shelley's comments on his poem transfixed him, and Shelley's earnestness and just criticism held him captive.

I was however struck with Byron's mental vivacity and wonderful memory ; he defended himself with a variety of illustrations, precedents, and apt quotations from modern authorities, disputing Shelley's propositions, not by denying their truth as a whole, but in parts, and the subtle questions he put would have puzzled a less acute reasoner than the one he had to contend with. During this discussion I scanned the Pilgrim closely.

In external appearance Byron realized that ideal standard with which imagination adorns genius. He was in the prime of life, thirty-five ; of middle height, five feet eight and a half inches ; regular features, without a stain or furrow on his pallid skin, his shoulders broad, chest open, body and limbs finely proportioned. His small, highly-finished head and curly hair, had an airy and graceful appearance from the massiveness and length of his throat : you saw his genius in his eyes and lips. In short, Nature could do little more than she had done for him, both in outward form and in the inward spirit she had given to animate it. But all these rare gifts to his jaundiced imagination only served to make his one personal defect (lameness) the more apparent, as a flaw is magnified in a diamond when polished ; and he brooded over that blemish as sensitive minds will brood until they magnify a wart into a wen.

His lameness certainly helped to make him skeptical, cynical, and savage. There was no peculiarity in his dress, it was adapted to the climate ; a tartan jacket braided,—he said it was the Gordon pattern, and that his mother was of that ilk. A blue velvet cap with a gold band, and very loose nankeen trousers, strapped down so as to cover his feet : his throat was not bare, as represented in drawings. At three o'clock, one of his servants announced that his horses were at the door, which broke off his discussion with Shelley, and we all followed him to the hall. At the outer door, we found three or four very ordinary-looking horses ; they had holsters on the saddles, and

many other superfluous trappings, such as the Italians delight in, and Englishmen eschew. Shelley, and an Irish visitor just announced, mounted two of these sorry jades. I luckily had my own cattle. Byron got into a calêche, and did not mount his horse until we had cleared the gates of the town, to avoid, as he said, being stared at by the "d—d Englishers," who generally congregated before his house on the Arno. After an hour or two of slow riding and lively talk,—for he was generally in good spirits when on horseback,—we stopped at a small *podere* on the roadside, and dismounting went into the house, in which we found a table with wine and cakes. From thence we proceeded into the vineyard at the back; the servant brought two brace of pistols, a cane was stuck in the ground and a five paul-piece, the size of half-a-crown, placed in a slit at the top of the cane. Byron, Shelley, and I, fired at fifteen paces, and one of us generally hit the cane or the coin : our firing was pretty equal; after five or six shots each, Byron pocketed the battered money and sauntered about the grounds. We then remounted. On our return homewards, Shelley urged Byron to complete something he had begun. Byron smiled and replied,

"John Murray, my patron and paymaster, says my plays won't act. I don't mind that, for I told him they were not written for the stage—but he adds, my poesy won't sell : that I do mind, for I have an 'itching palm.' He urges me to resume my old 'Corsair style, to please the ladies.'"

Shelley indignantly answered,

"That is very good logic for a bookseller, but not for an author : the shop interest is to supply the ephemeral demand of the day. It is not for him but you 'to put a ring in the monster's nose' to keep him from mischief."

Byron smiling at Shelley's warmth, said,

"John Murray is right, if not righteous : all I have yet written has been for woman-kind ; you must wait until I am forty, their influence will then die a natural death, and I will show the men what I can do."

Shelley replied,

"Do it now—write nothing but what your conviction of its truth inspires you to write; you should give counsel to the wise, and not take it from the foolish. Time will reverse the judgment of the vulgar. Contemporary criticism only represents the amount of ignorance genius has to contend with."

I was then and afterwards pleased and surprised at Byron's passiveness and docility in listening to Shelley—but all who heard him felt the charm of his simple, earnest manner; while Byron knew him to be exempt from the egotism, pedantry, coxcombry, and, more than all, the rivalry of authorship, and that he was the truest and most discriminating of his admirers.

Byron, looking at the western sky, exclaimed,

"Where is the green your friend the Laker talks such fustian about," meaning Coleridge—

> "'Gazing on the western sky,
> And its peculiar tint of yellow green.'
>
> *Dejection: an Ode.*

"Who ever," asked Byron, "saw a green sky?"

Shelley was silent, knowing that if he replied, Byron would give vent to his spleen. So I said, "The sky in England is oftener green than blue."

"Black, you mean," rejoined Byron; and this discussion brought us to his door.

As he was dismounting he mentioned two odd words that would rhyme. I observed on the felicity he had shown in this art, repeating a couplet out of Don Juan; he was both pacified and pleased at this, and putting his hand on my horse's crest, observed,

"If you are curious in these matters, look in Swift. I will send you a volume; he beats us all hollow, his rhymes are wonderful."

And then we parted for that day, which I have been thus particular in recording, not only as it was the first of our acquaintance, but as containing as fair a sample as I can give of his appearance, ordinary habits, and conversation.

THE SNAKE.

In his perverse and moody humors, Byron would give vent to his Satanic vein. After a long silence, one day on horseback, he began :—

"I have a conscience, although the world gives me no credit for it; I am now repenting, not of the few sins I have committed, but of the many I have not committed. There are things, too, we should not do, if they were not forbidden. My Don Juan was cast aside and almost forgotten, until I heard that the pharisaic synod in John Murray's back parlor had pronounced it as highly immoral, and unfit for publication. 'Because thou art virtuous thinkest thou there shall be no more cakes and ale?' Now my brain is throbbing and must have vent. I opined gin was inspiration, but cant is stronger. To-day I had another letter warning me against the Snake (Shelley). He, alone, in this age of humbug, dares stem the current, as he did to-day the flooded Arno in his skiff, although I could not observe he made any progress. The attempt is better than being swept along as all the rest are, with the filthy garbage scoured from its banks."

Taking advantage of this panegyric on Shelley I observed, he might do him a great service at little cost, by a friendly word or two in his next work, such as he had bestowed on authors of less merit.

Assuming a knowing look, he continued,

"All trades have their mysteries ; if we crack up a popular author, he repays us in the same coin, principal and interest. A friend may have repaid money lent,—can't say any of mine have ; but who ever heard of the interest being added thereto ? "

I rejoined,

"By your own showing you are indebted to Shelley; some of his best verses are to express his admiration of your genius."

"Ay," he said, with a significant look, "who reads them ? If we puffed the Snake, it might not turn out a profitable investment. If he cast off the slough of his mystifying metaphysics, he would want no puffing."

Seeing I was not satisfied, he added,

" If we introduced Shelley to our readers, they might draw comparisons, and they are ' *odorous.*' "

After Shelley's death, Byron, in a letter to Moore, of the 2d of August, 1822, says,

" There is another man gone, about whom the world was ill-naturedly, and ignorantly, and brutally mistaken. It will, perhaps, do him justice *now*, when he can be no better for it."

In a letter to Murray of an earlier date, he says,

" You were all mistaken about Shelley, who was, without exception, the best and least selfish man I ever knew."

And, again, he says, " You are all mistaken about Shelley; you do not know how mild, how tolerant, how good he was."

What Byron says of the world, that it will, perhaps, do Shelley justice when he can be no better for it, is far more applicable to himself. If the world erred, they did so in ignorance; Shelley was a myth to them. Byron had no such plea to offer, but he was neither just nor generous, and never drew his weapon to redress any wrongs but his own.

In the annals of authors I cannot find one who wrote under so many discouragements as Shelley; for even Bunyan's dungeon walls echoed the cheers of hosts of zealous disciples on the outside, whereas Shelley could number his readers on his fingers. He said, " I can only print my writings by stinting myself in food ! " Published, or sold openly, they were not.

The utter loneliness in which he was condemned to pass the largest portion of his life would have paralyzed any brains less subtilized by genius than his were. Yet he was social and cheerful, and, although frugal himself, most liberal to others, while to serve a friend he was ever ready to make any sacrifice. It was, perhaps, fortunate he was known to so few, for those few kept him close shorn. He went to Ravenna in 1821 on Byron's business, and, writing to his wife, makes this comment on the Pilgrim's asking him to execute a delicate commission : " But it seems destined that I am always to have some active part in the affairs of everybody whom I approach." And so he had.

Shelley, in his elegy on the death of Keats, gives this picture of himself :

> "'Midst others of less note, came one frail Form,
> A phantom amongst men ; companionless
> As the last cloud of an expiring storm,
> Whose thunder is its knell ; he, as I guess,
> Had gazed on Nature's naked loveliness,
> Actæon-like, and now he fled astray
> With feeble steps o'er the world's wilderness,
> And his own thoughts, along that rugged way,
> Pursued, like raging hounds, their father and their prey."

Every day I passed some hours with Byron, and very often my evenings with Shelley and Williams, so that when my memory summons one of them to appear, the others are sure to follow in his wake. If Byron's reckless frankness and apparent cordiality warmed your feelings, his sensitiveness, irritability, and the perverseness of his temper, cooled them. I was not then thirty, and the exigences of my now full-blown vanities were unsated, and my credulity unexhausted. I believed in many things then, and believe in some now; I could not sympathize with Byron, who believed in nothing.

"As for love, friendship, and your *entusamusy*," said he, "they must run their course. If you are not hanged or drowned before you are forty, you will wonder at all the foolish things they have made you say and do,—as I do now."

"I will go over to the Shelleys," I answered, "and hear their opinions on the subject."

"Ay, the Snake has fascinated you ; I am for making a man of the world of you ; they will mould you into a Frankenstein monster: so good-night !"

Goëthe's Mephistopheles calls the serpent that tempted Eve, "My Aunt—the renowned snake ;" and as Shelley translated and repeated passages of "Faust"—to, as he said, impregnate Byron's brain,—when he came to that passage, "My Aunt, the renowned snake," Byron said, "Then you are her nephew," and henceforth he often called Shelley the Snake ; his bright eyes, slim figure, and noiseless movements, strengthened, if it did not suggest, the comparison. Byron was the real snake—a dangerous mischief-maker; his wit or humor might force a grim smile, or hollow laugh, from the standers by, but they savored more of pain than playfulness, and made you dissatisfied with yourself and him. When I left his gloomy hall, and the echoes of the heavy iron-plated door died away, I could hardly refrain from shouting with joy as I hurried along the broad-flagged terrace which overhangs the pleasant river, cheered on my course by the cloudless sky, soft air, and fading light, which close an Italian day.

SHELLEY'S AVERSION TO COMPANY.

After a hasty dinner at my albergo, I hastened along the Arno to the hospitable and cheerful abode of the Shelleys. There I found those sympathies and sentiments which the Pilgrim denounced as illusions believed in as the only realities.

Shelley's mental activity was infectious; he kept your brain in constant action. Its effect on his comrade was very striking. Williams gave up all his accustomed sports for books, and the bettering of his mind; he had excellent natural ability; and the Poet delighted to see the seeds he had sown, germinating. Shelley said he was the sparrow educating the young of the cuckoo. After a protracted labor, Ned was delivered of a five-act play. Shelley was sanguine that his pupil would succeed as a dramatic writer. One morning I was in Mrs. Williams's drawing-room, by appointment, to hear Ned read an act of his drama. I sat with an aspect as caustic as a critic who was to decide his fate. Whilst thus intent Shelley stood before us with a most woeful expression.

Mrs. Williams started up, exclaiming, "What's the matter, Percy?"

"Mary has threatened me."

"Threatened you with what?"

He looked mysterious and too agitated to reply.

Mrs. Williams repeated, "With what? to box your ears?"

"Oh, much worse than that; Mary says she will have a party; there are English singers here, the Sinclairs, and she will ask them, and every one she or you know—oh, the horror!"

We all burst into a laugh except his friend Ned.

" It will kill me."

" Music, kill you ! " said Mrs. Williams. " Why, you have told me, you flatterer, that you loved music."

" So I do. It's the company terrifies me. For pity go to Mary and intercede for me ; I will submit to any other species of torture than that of being bored to death by idle ladies and gentlemen."

After various devices it was resolved that Ned Williams should wait upon the lady,—he being gifted with a silvery tongue, and sympathizing with the Poet in his dislike of fine ladies,—and see what he could do to avert the threatened invasion of the Poet's solitude. Meanwhile, Shelley remained in a state of restless ecstasy ; he could not even read or sit. Ned returned with a grave face ; the Poet stood as a criminal stands at the bar, whilst the solemn arbitrator of his fate decides it. " The lady," commenced Ned, has " set her heart on having a party, and will not be baulked ; " but, seeing the Poet's despair, he added, " It is to be limited to those here assembled, and some of Count Gamba's family ; and instead of a musical feast —as we have no souls—we are to have a dinner." The Poet hopped off, rejoicing, making a noise I should have thought whistling, but that he was ignorant of that accomplishment.

SHELLEY AND BYRON CONTRASTED.

I have seen Shelley and Byron in society, and the contrast was as marked as their characters. The former, not thinking of himself, was. as much at ease as in his own home, omitting no occasion of obliging those whom he came in contact with, readily conversing with all or any who addressed him, irrespective of age or rank, dress or address. To the first party I went with Byron, as we were on our road, he said,

" It's so long since I have been in English society, you must tell me what are their present customs. Does rank lead the way, or does the ambassadress pair us off into the dining-room ? Do they ask people to wine ? Do we exit with the women, or stick to our claret ? "

10*

On arriving, he was flushed, fussy, embarrassed, over cere-
monious, and ill at ease, evidently thinking a great deal of himself and very little of others.   He had learnt his manners, as I
have said, during the Regency, when society was more exclusive than even now, and consequently more vulgar.

To know an author, personally, is too often but to destroy
the illusion created by his works ; if you withdraw the veil of
your idol's sanctuary, and see him in his night-cap, you discover a querulous old crone, a sour pedant, a supercilious cox-
comb, a servile tuft-hunter, a saucy snob, or, at best, an ordinary moital.   Instead of the high-minded seeker after truth
and abstract knowledge, with a nature too refined to bear the
vulgarities of life, as we had imagined, we find him full of egotism and vanity, and eternally fretting and fuming about trifles.
As a general rule, therefore, it is wise to avoid writers whose
works amuse or delight you, for when you see them they will
delight you no more.   Shelley was a grand exception to this
rule.   To form a just idea of his poetry, you should have witnessed his daily life ; his words and actions best illustrated his
writings.   If his glorious conception of Gods and men constituted an atheist, I am afraid all that listened were little better.
Sometimes he would run through a great work on science, con-
dense the author's labored exposition, and by substituting
simple words for the jargon of the schools, make the most abstruse subject transparent.   The cynic Byron acknowledged
him to be the best and ablest man he had ever known.

SHELLEY NOT A SWIMMER.

The truth was, Shelley loved everything better than himself.
Self-preservation is, they say, the first law of nature, with him
it was the last ; and the only pain he ever gave his friends arose
from the utter indifference with which he treated everything
concerning himself.   I was bathing one day in a deep pool in
the Arno, and astonished the Poet by performing a series of
aquatic gymnastics, which I had learnt from the natives of the
South Seas.   On my coming out, whilst dressing, Shelley said,
mournfully,

" Why can't I swim, it seems so very easy ? "

I answered, " Because you think you can't. If you determine, you will ; take a header off this bank, and when you rise
turn on your back, you will float like a duck ; but you must
reverse the arch in your spine, for it's now bent the wrong
way."

He doffed his jacket and trousers, kicked off his shoes and
socks, and plunged in ; and there he lay stretched out on the
bottom like a conger eel, not making the least effort or struggle
to save himself. He would have been drowned if I had not
instantly fished him out. When he recovered his breath, he
said :

" I always find the bottom of the well, and they say Truth
lies there. In another minute I should have found it, and you
would have found an empty shell. It is an easy way of getting
rid of the body."

" What would Mrs. Shelley have said to me if I had gone
back with your empty cage ? "

" Don't tell Mary—not a word ! " he rejoined, and then continued, " It's a great temptation ; in another minute, I might
have been in another planet."

" But as you always find the bottom," I observed, " you
might have sunk ' deeper than did ever plummet sound.' "

" I am quite easy on that subject," said the Bard. " Death
is the veil, which those who live call life : they sleep, and it is
lifted. Intelligence should be imperishable ; the art of printing
has made it so in this planet."

" Do you believe in the immortality of the spirit ? "

He continued, " Certainly not ; how can I ? We know nothing ; we have no evidence ; we cannot express our inmost
thoughts. They are incomprehensible even to ourselves."

" Why," I asked, " do you call yourself an atheist ? it anni-
hilates you in this world."

" It is a word of abuse to stop discussion, a painted devil to
frighten the foolish, a threat to intimidate the wise and good.
I used it to express my abhorrence of superstition ; I took up
the word, as a knight took up a gauntlet, in defiance of injus-

tice.   The delusions of Christianity are fatal to genius and originality : they limit thought."

SHELLEY'S FORGETFULNESS.

Shelley's thirst for knowledge was unquenchable.   He set to work on a book, or a pyramid of books ; his eyes glistening with an energy as fierce as that of the most sordid gold-digger who works at a rock of quartz, crushing his way through all impediments, no grain of the pure ore escaping his eager scrutiny.   I called on him one morning at ten, he was in his study with a German folio open, resting on the broad marble mantelpiece, over an old-fashioned fire place, and with a dictionary in his hand.   He always read standing if possible.   He had promised over night to go with me, but now begged me to let him off.   I then rode to Leghorn, eleven or twelve miles distant, and passed the day there ; on returning at six in the evening to dine with Mrs. Shelley and the Williams's, as I had engaged to do, I went into the Poet's room and found him exactly in the position in which I had left him in the morning, but looking pale and exhausted.

"Well," I said, "have you found it ? "

Shutting the book and going to the window, he replied, " No, I have lost it : " with a deep sigh : " ' I have lost a day.' "

"Cheer up, my lad, and come to dinner."

Putting his long fingers through his masses of wild tangled hair, he answered faintly, "You go, I have dined—late eating don't do for me."

"What is this ? " I asked as I was going out of the room, pointing to one of his bookshelves with a plate containing bread and cold meat on it.

" That,"—coloring,—" why that must be my dinner.   It's very foolish ; I thought I had eaten it."

Saying I was determined that he should for once have a regular meal, I lugged him into the dining-room, but he brought a book with him and read more than he ate.   He seldom ate at stated periods, but only when hungry,—and then like the birds, if he saw something edible lying about,—but the cupboards of literary ladies are like Mother Hubbard's, bare. His drink was water, or tea if he could get it, bread was literally his staff of life ; other things he thought superfluous. An Italian who knew his way of life, not believing it possible that any human being would live as Shelley did, unless compelled by poverty, was astonished when he was told the amount of his income, and thought he was defrauded or grossly ignorant of the value of money. He, therefore, made a proposition which much amused the Poet, that he, the friendly Italian, would undertake for ten thousand crowns a-year to keep Shelley like a grand Seigneur, to provide his table with luxuries, his house with attendants, a carriage and opera box for my lady, besides adorning his person after the most approved Parisian style. Mrs. Shelley's toilette was not included in the wily Italian's estimates. The fact was, Shelley stinted himself to bare necessaries, and then often lavished the money, saved by unprecedented self-denial, on selfish fellows who denied themselves nothing ; such as the great philosopher had in his eye when he said, " It is the nature of extreme self-lovers, as they will set a house on fire, an' it were only to roast their own eggs."

Byron on our voyage to Greece, talking of England, after commenting on his own wrongs, said, " And Shelley, too, the best and most benevolent of men ; they hooted him out of his country like a mad-dog, for questioning a dogma. Man is the same rancorous beast now that he was from the beginning, and if the Christ they profess to worship reappeared, they would again crucify him."

THE PINE FOREST OF PISA.

His pride was spiritual. When attacked, he neither fled nor stood at bay, nor altered his course, but calmly went on with heart and mind intent on elevating his species. Whilst men tried to force him down to their level, he toiled to draw their minds upwards. His words were, " I always go on until I am stopped, and I never am stopped." Like the Indian palms, Shelley never flourished far from water. When compelled to take up his quarters in a town, he every morning with the instinct that guides the water-birds, fled to the nearest lake, river, or seashore, and only returned to roost at night. If debarred from this, he sought out the most solitary places. Towns and crowds distracted him. Even the silent and half-deserted cities of Italy, with their temples, palaces, paintings, and sculpture, could not make him stay, if there was a wood or water within his reach. At Pisa, he had a river under his window, and a pine forest in the neighborhood.

I accompanied Mrs. Shelley to this wood in search of the Poet, on one of those brilliant spring mornings we on the wrong side of the Alps are so rarely blessed with. A calêche took us out of Pisa through the gate of the Cascine ; we drove through the Cascine and onwards for two or three miles, traversing the vineyards and farms, on the Grand Ducal estate. On approaching some farm buildings, near which were a hunting-palace and chapel, we dismissed the carriage, directing the driver to meet us at a certain spot in the afternoon. We then walked on, not exactly knowing what course to take, and were exceedingly perplexed on coming to an open space, from which four roads radiated. There we stopped until I learnt from a Contadino, that the one before us led directly to the sea, which was two or three miles distant, the one on the right, led to the Serchio, and that on the left, to the Arno : we decided on taking the road to the sea. We proceeded on our journey over a sandy plain ; the sun being near its zenith. Walking was not included among the number of accomplishments in which Mrs. Shelley excelled ; the loose sand and hot sun soon knocked her up. When we got under the cool canopy of the pines, she stopped and allowed me to hunt for her husband. I now strode along ; the forest was on my right hand, and extensive pastures on my left, with herds of oxen, camels, and horses grazing thereon. I came upon the open sea at a place called Gombo, from whence I could see Via Reggio, the Gulf of Spezzia, and the mountains beyond. After bathing, seeing nothing of the Poet, I penetrated the densest part of the forest, ever and anon making the woods ring with the name of Shelley, and scaring the herons and water-birds from the chain of stagnant pools which impeded my progress.

With no landmarks to guide me, nor sky to be seen above, I was bewildered in this wilderness of pines and ponds; so I sat down, struck a light, and smoked a cigar. A red man would have known his course by the trees themselves, their growth, form, and color; or if a footstep had passed that day, he would have hit upon its trail. As I mused upon his sagacity and my own stupidity, the braying of a brother jackass startled me. He was followed by an old man picking up pine cones. I asked him if he had seen a stranger?

"L'Inglese malincolico haunts the woods maledetta. I will show you his nest."

As we advanced, the ground swelled into mounds and hollows. By-and-by the old fellow pointed with his stick to a hat, books, and loose papers lying about, and then to a deep pool of dark glimmering water, saying, "Eccolo!" I thought he meant that Shelley was in or under the water. The careless, not to say impatient, way in which the Poet bore his burden of life, caused a vague dread amongst his family and friends that he might lose or cast it away at any moment.

The strong light streamed through the opening of the trees. One of the pines, undermined by the water, had fallen into it. Under its lee, and nearly hidden, sat the Poet, gazing on the dark mirror beneath, so lost in his bardish reverie that he did not hear my approach. There the trees were stunted and bent, and their crowns were shorn like friars by the sea breezes, excepting a cluster of three, under which Shelley's traps were lying; these overtopped the rest. To avoid startling the Poet out of his dream, I squatted under the lofty trees, and opened his books. One was a volume of his favorite Greek dramatist, Sophocles,—the same that I found in his pocket after his death—and the other was a volume of Shakspeare. I then hailed him, and, turning his head, he answered faintly,

"Hollo, come in."

"Is this your study?" I asked.

"Yes," he answered, "and these trees are my books—they

tell no lies. You are sitting on the stool of inspiration," he exclaimed. "In those three pines the weird sisters are imprisoned, and this," pointing to the water, "is their cauldron of black broth. The Pythian priestesses uttered their oracles from below—now they are muttered from above. Listen to the solemn music in the pine-tops—don't you hear the mournful murmurings of the sea? Sometimes they rave and roar, shriek and howl, like a rabble of priests. In a tempest, when a ship sinks, they catch the despairing groans of the drowning mariners. Their chorus is the eternal wailing of wretched men."

"They, like the world," I observed, "seem to take no note of wretched women. The sighs and wailing you talk about are not those of wretched men afar off, but are breathed by a woman near at hand—not from the pine-tops, but by a forsaken lady."

"What do you mean?" he asked.

"Why, that an hour or two ago I left your wife, Mary Shelley, at the entrance of this grove, in despair at not finding you."

He started up, snatched up his scattered books, and papers, thrust them into his hat and jacket pockets, sighing "Poor Mary! hers is a sad fate. Come along; she can't bear solitude, nor I society—the quick coupled with the dead."

He glided along with his usual swiftness, for nothing could make him pause for an instant when he had an object in view, until he had attained it. On hearing our voices, Mrs. Shelley joined us; her clear gray eyes and thoughtful brow expressing the love she could not speak. To stop Shelley's self-reproaches, or to hide her own emotions, she began in a bantering tone, chiding and coaxing him :—

"What a wild-goose you are, Percy; if my thoughts have strayed from my book, it was to the opera, and my new dress from Florence—and especially the ivy wreath so much admired for my hair, and not to you, you silly fellow! When I left home, my satin slippers had not arrived. These are serious matters to gentlewomen, enough to ruffle the serenest tempered. As to you and your ungallant companion, I had forgotten that such things are ; but as it is the ridiculous custom to have men at balls and operas, I must take you with me, though, from your uncouth ways, you will be taken for Valentine and he for Orson."

Shelley, like other students, would, when the spell that bound his faculties was broken, shut his books, and indulge in the wildest flights of mirth and folly. As this is a sport all can join in, we talked and laughed, and shrieked, and shouted, as we emerged from under the shadows of the melancholy pines and their nodding plumes, into the now cool purple twilight and open country. The cheerful and graceful peasant girls, returning home from the vineyards and olive groves, stopped to look at us. The old man I had met in the morning gathering pine cones, passed hurriedly by with his donkey, giving Shelley a wide berth, and evidently thinking that the melancholy Englishman had now become a raving maniac. Sancho says, " Blessings on the man who invented sleep ; " the man who invented laughing deserves no less.

The day I found Shelley in the pine forest, he was writing verses on a guitar. I picked up a fragment, but could only make out the first two lines :—

> " Ariel, to Miranda take
> This slave of music."

It was a frightful scrawl; words smeared out with his finger, and one upon the other, over and over in tiers, and all run together in most " admired disorder ; " it might have been taken for a sketch of a marsh overgrown with bulrushes, and the blots for wild ducks; such a dashed off daub as self-conceited artists mistake for a manifestation of genius. On my observing this to him, he answered,

" When my brain gets heated with thought, it soon boils, and throws off images and words faster than I can skim them off. In the morning, when cooled down, out of the rude sketch as you justly call it, I shall attempt a drawing. If you ask me why I publish what few or none will care to read, it is that the spirits I have raised haunt me until they are sent to the devil of a printer. All authors are anxious to breech their bantlings."

Shelley's Dramatic Aspirations.

One day I drove the Poet to Leghorn. In answer to my questions, Shelley said, "In writing the Cenci my object was to see how I could succeed in describing passions I have never felt, and to tell the most dreadful story in pure and refined language. The image of Beatrice haunted me after seeing her portrait. The story is well authenticated, and the details far more horrible than I have painted them. The Cenci is a work of art; it is not colored by my feelings, nor obscured by my metaphysics. I don't think much of it. It gave me less trouble than anything I have written of the same length.

"I am now writing a play for the stage. It is affectation to say we write a play for any other purpose. The subject is from English history; in style and manner I shall approach as near our great dramatist as my feeble powers will permit. King Lear is my model, for that is nearly perfect. I am amazed at my presumption. Poets should be modest. My audacity savors of madness.

"Considering the labor requisite to excel in composition, I think it would be better to stick to one style. The clamor for novelty is leading us all astray. Yet, at Ravenna, I urged Byron to come out of the dismal 'wood of error' into the sun, to write something new and cheerful. Don Juan is the result. The poetry is superior to Childe Harold, and the plan, or rather want of plan, gives scope to his astonishing natural powers.

"My friends say my Prometheus is too wild, ideal, and perplexed with imagery. It may be so. It has no resemblance to the Greek Drama. It is original; and cost me severe mental labor. Authors, like mothers, prefer the children who have given them most trouble. Milton preferred his Paradise Regained, Petrarch his Africa, and Byron his Doge of Venice.

"I have the vanity to write only for poetical minds, and

must be satisfied with few readers. Byron is ambitious; he writes for all, and all read his works.

" With regard to the great question, the System of the Universe, I have no curiosity on the subject. I am content to see no farther into futurity than Plato and Bacon. My mind is tranquil; I have no fears and some hopes. In our present gross material state our faculties are clouded;—when Death removes our clay coverings the mystery will be solved."

He thought a play founded on Shakspeare's " Timon " would be an excellent mode of discussing our present social and political evils dramatically, and of descanting on them.

.How Shelley Impressed Strangers.

After we had done our business, I called on a Scotch family and lured my companion in. He abhorred forcing himself on strangers—so I did not mention his name, merely observing,

" As you said you wanted information about Italy, here is a friend of mine can give it you—for I cannot."

The ladies—for there was no man there—were capital specimens of Scotchwomen, fresh from the land of cakes,—frank, fair, intelligent, and of course, pious. After a long and earnest talk we left them, but not without difficulty, so pressing were they for us to stop to dinner.

When I next visited them, they were disappointed at the absence of my companion; and when I told them it was Shelley, the young and handsome mother clasped her hands, and exclaimed,

" Shelley! That bright-eyed youth;—so gentle, so intelligent—so thoughtful for us. Oh, why did you not name him ? "

" Because he thought you would have been shocked."

" Shocked !—why I would have knelt to him in penitence for having wronged him even in my thoughts. If he is not pure and good—then there is no truth and goodness in this world. His looks reminded me of my own blessed baby,—so innocent—so full of love and sweetness."

" So is the serpent that tempted Eve described," I said.

" Oh, you wicked scoffer ! " she continued. " But I know you love him. I shall have no peace of mind until you bring him here. You remember, sister, I said his young face had lines of care and sorrow on it—when he was showing us the road to Rome on the map and the sun shone on it ;—poor boy ! Oh, tell us about his wife,—is she worthy of him ? She must love him dearly—and so must all who know him."

To palliate the warm-hearted lady's admiration of the Poet —as well as my own—I must observe, that all on knowing him sang the same song ; and as I have before observed, even Byron in his most moody and cynical vein, joined in the chorus, echoing my monotonous notes. The reason was, that after having heard or read the rancorous abuse heaped on Shelley by the mercenary literature of the day,—in which he was described as a monster more hideous than Caliban,—the revulsion of feeling on seeing the man was so great, that he seemed as gentle a spirit as Ariel. There never has been nor can be any true likeness of him. Desdemona says, " I saw Othello's visage in his mind," and Shelley's "visage" as well as his mind are to be seen in his works.

SHELLEY ON THE SAN SPIRIDIONE.

When I was at Leghorn with Shelley, I drew him towards the docks, saying,

" As we have a spare hour let's see if we can't put a girdle round about the earth in forty minutes." In these docks are living specimens of all the nationalities of the world ; thus we can go round it, and visit and examine any particular nation we like, observing their peculiar habits, manners, dress, language, food, productions, arts, and naval architecture ; for see how varied are the shapes, build, rigging, and decoration of the different vessels. There lies an English cutter, a French chasse marée, an American clipper, a Spanish tartan, an Austrian trabacolo, a Genoese felucca, a Sardinian zebeck, a Neapolitan brig, a Sicilian sparanza, a Dutch galleot, a Danish snow, a Russian hermaphrodite, a Turkish sackalever, a Greek bombard. I don't see a Persian Dow, an Arab grab, or a Chinese junk ; but there are enough for our purpose and to spare.

As you are writing a poem, ' Hellas,' about the modern Greeks, would it not be as well to take a look at them amidst all the din of the docks ?   I hear their shrill nasal voices, and should like to know if you can trace in the language or lineaments of these Greeks of the nineteenth century, A. D., the faintest resemblance to the lofty and sublime spirits who lived in the fourth century, B. C. An English merchant who has dealings with them, told me he thought these modern Greeks were, if judged by their actions, a cross between the Jews and gypsies ; —but here comes the Capitano Zarita ; I know him."

So dragging Shelley with me I introduced him, and asking to see the vessel, we crossed the plank from the quay and stood on the deck of The San Spiridione in the midst of her chattering irascible crew.   They took little heed of the skipper, for in these trading vessels each individual of the crew is part owner, and has some share in the cargo ; so they are all interested in the speculation—having no wages. They squatted about the decks in small knots, shrieking, gesticulating, smoking, eating, and gambling like savages.

"Does this realize your idea of Hellenism, Shelley ? " I said.

"No ! but it does of Hell," he replied.

The captain insisted on giving us pipes and coffee in his cabin, so I dragged Shelley down.   Over the rudder-head facing us, there was a gilt box enshrining a flaming gaudy daub of a saint, with a lamp burning before it ; this was Il Padre Santo Spiridione, the ship's godfather. The skipper crossed himself and squatted on the dirty divan. Shelley talked to him about the Greek revolution that was taking place, but from its interrupting trade the captain was opposed to it.

"Come away !" said Shelley. "There is not a drop of the old Hellenic blood here. These are not the men to rekindle the ancient Greek fire ; their souls are extinguished by traffic and superstition. Come away ! "—and away we went.

SHELLEY AND THE AMERICAN MATE.

"It is but a step," I said, "from these ruins of worn-out Greece to the New World, let's board the American clipper."

" I had rather not have any more of my hopes and illusions mocked by sad realities," said Shelley.

" You must allow," I answered, " that graceful craft was designed by a man who had a poet's feeling for things beautiful ; let's get a model and build a boat like her."

The idea so pleased the Poet that he followed me on board her. The Americans are a social, free-and-easy people, accustomed to take their own way, and to readily yield the same privilege to all others, so that our coming on board, and examination of the vessel, fore and aft, were not considered as intrusion. The captain was on shore, so I talked to the mate, a smart specimen of a Yankee. When I commended her beauty, he said,

" I do expect, now we have our new copper on, she has a look of the brass sarpent, she has as slick a run, and her bearings are just where they should be."

I said we wished to build a boat after her model.

" Then I calculate you must go to Baltimore or Boston to get one ; there is no one on this side the water can do the job. We have our freight all ready, and are homeward-bound ; we have elegant accommodation, and you will be across before your young friend's beard is ripe for a razor. Come down, and take an observation of the state cabin."

It was about seven and a half feet by five ; " plenty of room to live or die comfortably in," he observed, and then pressed us to have a chaw of real old Virginian cake, *i. e.* tobacco, and a cool drink of peach brandy. I made some observation to him about the Greek vessel we had visited.

" Crank as an eggshell," he said ; " too many sticks and top hamper, she looks like a bundle of chips going to hell to be burnt."

I seduced Shelley into drinking a wine-glass of weak grog, the first and last he ever drank. The Yankee would not let us go until we had drunk, under the star-spangled banner, to the memory of Washington, and the prosperity of the American commonwealth.

" As a warrior and statesman," said Shelley, " he was righteous in all he did, unlike all who lived before or since ; he never used his power but for the benefit of his fellow-creatures,

> ' He fought,
> For truth and wisdom, foremost of the brave ;
> Him glory's idle glances dazzled not ;
> 'Twas his ambition, generous and great,
> A life to life's great end to consecrate.' "

"Stranger," said the Yankee, "truer words were never spoken ; there is dry rot in all the main timbers of the Old World, and none of you will do any good till you are docked, refitted, and annexed to the New. You must log that song you sang ; there ain't many Britishers that will say as much of the man that whipped them ; so just set these lines down in the log, or it won't go for nothing."

Shelley wrote some verses in the book, but not those he had quoted ; and so we parted.

SHELLEY AND HIS LITERARY BRETHREN.

Like many other over-sensitive people, he thought everybody shunned him, whereas it was he who stood aloof. To the few who sought his acquaintance, he was frank, cordial, and, if they appeared worthy, friendly in the extreme ; but he shrank like a maiden from making the first advances. At the beginning of his literary life, he believed all authors published their opinions as he did his from a deep conviction of their truth and importance, after due investigation. When a new work appeared, on any subject that interested him, he would write to the authors expressing his opinion of their books, and giving his reasons for his judgment, always arguing logically, and not for display ; and, with his serene and imperturbable temper, variety of knowledge, tenacious memory, command of language, or rather of all the languages of literature, he was a most subtle critic ; but, as authors are not the meekest or mildest of men, he occasionally met with rude rebuffs, and retired into his own shell.

In this way he became acquainted with Godwin, in early life ; and in his first work, " Queen Mab," or rather in the notes appended to that poem, the old philosopher's influence on the beardless boy is strongly marked. For publishing these notes Shelley was punished as the man is stated to have been who committed the first murder : " every man's hand was against him." Southey, Wordsworth, Coleridge, Keats, and others he had either written to, corresponded with, or personally known ; but in their literary guild he found little sympathy; their enthusiasm had burnt out whilst Shelley's had waxed stronger. Old Rothschild's sage maxim perhaps influenced them, " Never connect yourself with an unlucky man." However that may be, all intercourse had long ceased between Shelley and any of the literary fraternity of the day, with the exception of Peacock, Keats, Leigh Hunt, and the Brothers Smith, of the " Rejected Addresses."

Resolves to Build a Boat.

I will now return to our drive home from visiting the ships in the docks of Leghorn. Shelley was in high glee, and full of fun, as he generally was after these " distractions," as he called them. The fact was his excessive mental labor impeded, if it did not paralyze, his bodily functions. When his mind was fixed on a subject, his mental powers were strained to the utmost. If not writing or sleeping, he was reading ; he read whilst eating, walking, or travelling—the last thing at night, and the first thing in the morning—not the ephemeral literature of the day, which requires little or no thought, but the works of the old sages, metaphysicians, logicians, and philosophers, of the Grecian and Roman poets, and of modern scientific men, so that anything that could diversify or relax his overstrained brain was of the utmost benefit to him. Now he talked of nothing but ships, sailors, and the sea ; and, although he agreed with Johnson that a man who made a pun would pick a pocket, yet he made several in Greek, which he at least thought good, for he shrieked with laughter as he uttered them. Fearing his phil-Hellenism would end by making him serious, as it always did, I brought his mind back by repeating some lines of Sedley's beginning,

> "Love still has something of the sea
> From whence his mother rose."

During the rest of our drive we had nothing but sea yarns. He regretted having wasted his life in Greek and Latin, instead of learning the useful arts of swimming and sailoring. He resolved to have a good-sized boat forthwith. I proposed we should form a colony at the Gulf of Spezzia, and I said—" You get Byron to join us, and with your family and the Williams's, and books, horses, and boats, undisturbed by the botherations of the world, we shall have all that reasonable people require."

This scheme enchanted him. " Well," I said, " propose this to Byron to-morrow."

" No !" he answered, " you must do that. Byron is always influenced by his last acquaintance. You are the last man, so do you pop the question."

" I understand that feeling," I observed. " When well known neither men nor women realize our first conception of them, so we transfer our hopes to the new men or women who make a sign of sympathy, only to find them like those who have gone before, or worse." I quoted his own lines as exemplifying my meaning—

> "Where is the beauty, love, and truth we seek,
> But in our minds !"

SHELLEY'S HOUSE ON THE GULF OF SPEZZIA.

The following morning I told Byron our plan. Without any suggestion from me he eagerly volunteered to join us, and asked me to get a yacht built for him, and to look out for a house as near the sea as possible. I allowed some days to pass before I took any steps in order to see if his wayward mind would change. As he grew more urgent I wrote to an old naval friend, Captain Roberts, then staying at Genoa, a man peculiarly fitted to execute the order, and requested him to send plans and estimates of an open boat for Shelley, and a

I I

large decked one for Byron. Shortly after, Williams and I rode along the coast to the Gulf of Spezzia. Shelley had no pride or vanity to provide for, yet we had the greatest difficulty in finding any house in which the humblest civilized family could exist.

On the shores of this superb bay, only surpassed in its natural beauty and capability by that of Naples, so effectually has tyranny paralyzed the energies and enterprise of man, that the only indication of human habitation was a few most miserable fishing villages scattered along the margin of the bay. Near its centre, between the villages of Sant' Arenzo and Lerici, we came upon a lonely and abandoned building called the Villa Magni, though it looked more like a boat or bathing-house than a place to live in. It consisted of a terrace or ground floor unpaved, and used for storing boat-gear and fishing-tackle, and of a single story over it divided into a hall or saloon and four small rooms which had once been whitewashed; there was one chimney for cooking. This place, we thought the Shelleys might put up with for the summer. The only good thing about it was a veranda facing the sea, and almost over it. So we sought the owner and made arrangements, dependent on Shelley's approval, for taking it for six months. As to finding a palazzo grand enough for a Milordo Inglese, within a reasonable distance of the bay, it was out of the question.

Williams returned to Pisa; I rode on to Genoa, and settled with Captain Roberts about building the boats. He had already, with his usual activity, obtained permission to build them in the government dock-yards, and had his plans and estimates made out. I need hardly say that though the Captain was a great arithmetician, this estimate, like all the estimates as to time and cost that were ever made, was a mere delusion, which made Byron wroth, but did not ruffle Shelley's serenity.

HABITS OF SHELLEY AND BYRON.

On returning to Pisa I found the two Poets going through the same routine of habits they had adopted before my departure;

the one getting out of bed after noon, dawdling about until two or three, following the same road on horseback, stopping at the same Podere, firing his pop-guns, and retracing his steps at the same slow pace ;—his frugal dinner followed by his accustomed visit to an Italian family, and then—the midnight lamp, and the immortal verses.

The other was up at six or seven, reading Plato, Sophocles, or Spinoza, with the accompaniment of a hunch of dry bread ; then he joined Williams in a sail on the Arno, in a flat-bottomed skiff, book in hand, and from thence he went to the pine-forest, or some out-of-the-way place. When the birds went to roost he returned home, and talked and read until midnight. The monotony of this life was only broken at long intervals by the arrival of some old acquaintances of Byron's : Rogers, Hob-house, Moore, Scott—not Sir Walter,—and these visits were brief. John Murray, the publisher, sent out new books, and wrote amusing gossiping letters, as did Tom Moore and others. These we were generally allowed to read, or hear read, Byron archly observing, " My private and confidential letters are better known than any of my published works."

THE NEW TOY.

Shelley's boyish eagerness to possess the new toy, from which he anticipated never-failing pleasure in gliding over the azure seas, under the cloudless skies of an Italian summer, was pleasant to behold. His comrade Williams was inspired by the same spirit. We used to draw plans on the sands of the Arno of the exact dimensions of the boat, dividing her into compartments (the forepart was decked for stowage), and then, squatting down within the lines, I marked off the imaginary cabin. With a real chart of the Mediterranean spread out before them, and with faces as grave and anxious as those of Columbus and his companions, they held councils as to the islands to be visited, coasts explored, courses steered, the amount of armament, stores, water, and provisions which would be necessary. Then we would narrate instances of the daring of the old navigators, as when Diaz discovered the Cape of Good Hope in 1446, with two vessels each of fifty tons burden; or when Drake went round the world, one of his craft being only thirty tons; and of the extraordinary runs and enterprises accomplished in open boats of equal or less tonnage, than the one we were building from the earliest times to those of Commodore Bligh. Byron, with the smile of a Mephistopheles standing by, asked me the amount of salvage we, the salvors, should be entitled to in the probable event of our picking up and towing Shelley's water-logged craft into port.

As the world spun round, the sandy plains of Pisa became too hot to be agreeable, and the Shelleys, longing for the sea-breezes, departed to their new abode. Byron could not muster energy enough to break through his dawdling habits, so he lingered on under the fair plea of seeing the Leigh Hunts settled in his ground-floor, which was prepared for them. I rode on to Genoa to hasten the completion and despatch of the long-promised boat-flotilla. I found Captain Roberts had nearly finished Shelley's boat. Williams had brought with him, on leaving England, the section of a boat as a model to build from, designed by a naval officer, and the two friends had so often sat contemplating this toy, believing it to be a marvel of nautical architecture, that nothing would satisfy them but that their craft should be built exactly on the same lines. Roberts, and the builder at Genoa, not approving, protested against it. You might as well have attempted to persuade a young man after a season of boating, or hunting, that he was not a thorough seaman and sportsman; or a youngster flushed with honors from a university that he was not the wisest of men. Williams was on ordinary occasions as humble-minded as Shelley, but having been two or three years in the navy, and then in the cavalry, he thought there was no vanity in his believing that he was as good a judge of a boat or horse as any man. In these small conceits we are all fools at the beginning of life, until time, with his sledge-hammer, has let the daylight into our brain-boxes; so the boat was built according to his cherished model. When it was finished, it took two tons of iron ballast to bring her down to her bearings, and then she was very crank in a breeze, though not deficient in beam. She was fast, strongly built, and Torbay rigged. I despatched her under charge of two steady seamen, and a smart sailor lad, aged eighteen, named Charles Vivian. Shelley sent back the two sailors and only retained the boy; they told me on their return to Genoa, that they had been out in a rough night, that she was a ticklish boat to manage, but had sailed and worked well, and with two good seamen she would do very well; and that they had cautioned the gents accordingly.

LETTERS TO TRELAWNY.

I shortly after received the following letter from Shelley:

MY DEAR TRELAWNY,   LERICI, *May* 16, 1822.

The "Don Juan" is arrived, and nothing can exceed the admiration she has excited; for we must suppose the name to have been given her during the equivocation of sex which her god-father suffered in the harem. Williams declares her to be perfect, and I participate in his enthusiasm, inasmuch as would be decent in a landsman. We have been out now several days, although we have sought in vain for an opportunity of trying her against the feluccas or other large craft in the bay; she passes the small ones as a comet might pass the dullest planet of the heavens. When do you expect to be here in the "Bolivar?" If Roberts's 50*l.* grow into a 500*l.*, and his ten days into months, I suppose I may expect that I am considerably in your debt, and that you will not be round here until the middle of the summer. I hope that I shall be mistaken in the last of these conclusions; as to the former, whatever may be the result, I have little reason and less inclination to complain of my bargain. I wish you could express from me to Roberts, how excessively I am obliged to him for the time and trouble he has expended for my advantage, and which I wish could be as easily repaid as the money which I owe him, and which I wait your orders for remitting.

I have only heard from Lord Byron once, and solely upon

that subject. Tita is with me, and I suppose will go with you in the schooner to Leghorn. We are very impatient to see you, and although we cannot hope that you will stay long on your *first* visit, we count upon you for the latter part of the summer, as soon as the novelty of Leghorn is blunted. Mary desires her best regards to you, and unites with me in a sincere wish to renew an intimacy from which we have already experienced so much pleasure.

Believe me, my dear Trelawny,
Your very sincere friend,
P. B. SHELLEY.

MY DEAR TRELAWNY, LERICI, *June* 18, 1822.

I have written to Guelhard, to pay you 154 Tuscan crowns, the amount of the balance against me according to Roberts's calculation, which I keep for your satisfaction, deducting sixty, which I paid the aubergiste at Pisa, in all 214. We saw you about eight miles in the offing this morning; but the abatement of the breeze leaves us little hope that you can have made Leghorn this evening. Pray write us a full, true, and particular account of your proceedings, etc.—How Lôrd Byron likes the vessel; what are your arrangements and intentions for the summer; and when we may expect to see you or him in this region again; and especially whether there is any news of Hunt.

Roberts and Williams are very busy in refitting the "Don Juan;" they seem determined that she shall enter Leghorn in style. I am no great judge of these matters; but am excessively obliged to the former, and delighted that the latter should find amusement, like the sparrow, in educating the cuckoo's young.

You, of course, enter into society at Leghorn; should you meet with any scientific person, capable of preparing the *Prussic Acid, or essential oil of bitter almonds,* I should regard it as a great kindness if you could procure me a small quantity It requires the greatest caution in preparation, and ought to be highly concentrated; I would give any price for this medicine; you remember we talked of it the other night, and we both expressed a wish to possess it; my wish was serious, and sprung from the desire of avoiding needless suffering. I need not tell you I have no intention of suicide at present, but I confess it would be a comfort to me to hold in my possession that golden key to the chamber of perpetual rest. *The Prussic Acid* is used in medicine in infinitely minute doses; but that preparation is weak, and has not the concentration necessary to medicine all ills infallibly. A single drop, even less, is a dose, and it acts by paralysis.

I am curious to hear of this publication about Lord Byron and the Pisa circle. I hope it will not annoy him, as to me I am supremely indifferent. If you have not shown the letter I sent you, don't, until Hunt's arrival, when we shall certainly meet.   Your very sincere friend,

P. B. SHELLEY.

Mary is better, though still excessively weak.

SHELLEY'S SEAMANSHIP.

Not long after, I followed in Byron's boat, the "Bolivar" schooner. There was no fault to find with her; Roberts and the builder had fashioned her after their own fancy, and she was both fast and safe. I manned her with five able seamen, four Genoese and one Englishman. I put into the Gulf of Spezzia, and found Shelley in ecstasy with his boat, and Williams as touchy about her reputation as if she had been his wife. They were hardly ever out of her, and talked of the Mediterranean as a lake too confined and tranquil to exhibit her sea-going excellence. They longed to be on the broad Atlantic, scudding under bare poles in a heavy sou'wester, with plenty of sea room. I went out for a sail in Shelley's boat to see how they would manage her. It was great fun to witness Williams teaching the Poet how to steer, and other points of seamanship. As usual, Shelley had a book in hand, saying he could read and steer at the same time, as one was mental, the other mechanical.

" Luff! " said Williams.

Shelley put the helm the wrong way. Williams corrected him.

"Do you see those two white objects a-head? keep them in a line, the wind is heading us." Then turning to me, he said : "Lend me a hand to haul in the main-sheet, and I will show you how close she can lay to the wind to work off a lee-shore."

"No," I answered; "I am a passenger, and won't touch a rope."

"Luff!" said Williams, as the boat was yawning about. "Shelley, you can't steer, you have got her in the wind's eye; give me the tiller, and you attend the main-sheet. Ready about!" said Williams. "Helms down—let go the fore-sheet —see how she spins round on her heel—is not she a beauty? Now, Shelley, let go the main-sheet, and boy, haul aft the jib-sheet!"

The main-sheet was jammed, and the boat unmanageable, or as sailors express it, in irons; when the two had cleared it, Shelley's hat was knocked overboard, and he would probably have followed, if I had not held him. He was so uncommonly awkward, that when they had things ship-shape, Williams, somewhat scandalized at the lubberly manœuvre, blew up the Poet for his neglect and inattention to orders. Shelley was, however, so happy, and in such high glee, and the nautical terms so tickled his fancy, that he even put his beloved "Plato" in his pocket, and gave his mind up to fun and frolic.

"You will do no good with Shelley," I said, "until you heave his books and papers overboard; shear the wisps of hair that hang over his eyes; and plunge his arms up to the elbow in a tar-bucket. And you, captain, will have no authority, until you dowse your frock coat and cavalry boots. You see I am stripped for a swim, so please, whilst I am on board, to keep within swimming distance of the land."

The boy was quick and handy, and used to boats. Williams was not as deficient as I anticipated, but over-anxious and wanted practice, which alone makes a man prompt in emergency. Shelley was intent on catching images from the ever-changing sea and sky, he heeded not the boat. On my suggesting the addition to their crew of a Genoese sailor accustomed to the coast—such as I had on board the "Bolivar,"—Williams, thinking I undervalued his efficiency as a seaman, was scandalized—"as if we three seasoned salts were not enough to manage an open boat, when lubberly sloops and cutters of fifty or sixty tons were worked by as few men on the rough seas and iron-bound coast of Scotland!"

"Yes," I answered, "but what a difference between those sea-lions and you and our water-poet! A decked cutter besides, or even a frigate is easier handled in a gale or squall, and out-and-out safer to be on board of than an open boat. If we had been in a squall to-day with the main-sheet jammed, and the tiller put starboard instead of port, we should have had to swim for it."

"Not I: I should have gone down with the rest of the pigs in the bottom of the boat," said Shelley, meaning the iron pig-ballast.

When I took my departure for Leghorn on board the "Bolivar," they accompanied me out of the bay, and then we parted.

SHELLEY, BYRON, AND THE HUNTS.

Shelley, with his friend Williams, soon came in their boat, scudding into the harbor of Leghorn. They went with the Hunts to Pisa, and established them in Lord Byron's palace, Shelley having furnished a floor there for them. In a few days Shelley returned to Leghorn, and found Williams eager to be off. We had a sail outside the port in the two boats. Shelley was in a mournful mood; his mind depressed by a recent interview with Byron.

Byron, at first, had been more eager than Shelley for Leigh Hunt's arrival in Italy to edit and contribute to the proposed new Review, and so continued until his English correspondents had worked on his fears. They did not oppose, for they knew his temper too well, but artfully insinuated that he was jeopardizing his fame and fortune, &c., &c., &c. Shelley found

11*

Byron so irritable, so shuffling and equivocating, whilst talking with him on the fufilment of his promises with regard to Leigh Hunt,—that, but for imperilling Hunt's prospects, Shelley's intercourse with Byron would then have abruptly terminated ; it was doomed to be their last meeting.

On Saturday, the 6th, Williams wrote the following letter to his wife at the Villa Magni :

" I have just left the quay, my dearest girl, and the wind blows right across to Spezzia, which adds to the vexation I feel at being unable to leave this place. For my own part, I should have been with you in all probability on Wednesday evening, but I have been kept day after day, waiting for Shelley's definitive arrangements with Lord B. relative to poor Hunt, whom, in my opinion, he has treated vilely. A letter from Mary, of the most gloomy kind, reached S. yesterday, and this mood of hers aggravated my uneasiness to see you ; for I am proud, dear girl, beyond words to express, in the conviction, that *wherever* we may be together you could be cheerful and contented.

" Would I could take the present gale by the wings and reach you to-night ; hard as it blows I would venture across for *such* a reward. However, to-morrow something decisive shall take place ; and if I am detained, I shall depart in a felúca, and leave the boat to be brought round in company with Tre-lawny in the ' Bolivar.' He talks of visiting Spezzia again in a few days. I am tired to death of waiting—this is our longest separation, and seems a year to me. Absence alone is enough to make me anxious, and indeed, unhappy; but I think if I had left you in our own house in solitude, I should feel it less than I do now. What can I do ? Poor S. desires that I should return to you, but I know secretly wishes me not to leave him in the lurch. He too, by his manner, is as anxious to see you almost as I could be, but the interests of poor H. keep him here ;—in fact, with Lord B. it appears they cannot do any-thing,—who actually said as much as that he did not wish (?) his name to be attached to the work, and of course to theirs.

"In Lord Byron's family all is confusion;—the cut-throats he is so desirous to have about him, have involved him in a second row; and although the present banishment of the Gambas from Tuscany is attributed to the first affair of the dragoon, the continued disturbances among his and their servants is, I am sure, the principal cause for its being carried into immediate effect. Four days (commencing from the day of our arrival at Leghorn) were only given them to find another retreat; and as Lord B. considers this a personal, though tacit attack upon himself, he chooses to follow their fortunes in another country. Genoa was first selected,—of that government they could have no hope;—Geneva was then proposed, and this proved as bad if not worse. Lucca is now the choice, and Trelawny was despatched last night to feel their way with the governor, to whom he carried letters. All this time Hunt is shuffled off from day to day, and now, heaven knows, when or how it will end.

"Lord B.'s reception of Mrs. H. was—as S. tells me—most shameful. She came into his house sick and exhausted, and he scarcely deigned to notice her; was silent, and scarcely bowed. This conduct cut. H. to the soul; but the way in which he received our friend Roberts, at Dunn's door, shall be described when we meet:—it must be acted. How I long to see you; I had written *when*, but I will make no promises, for I too well know how distressing it is to both of us to break them. Tuesday evening at furthest, unless kept by the weather, I *will* say, ' Oh, Jane! how fervently I press you and our little ones to my heart.'

"Adieu!—Take body and soul; for you are at once my heaven and earth;—that is all I ask of both.

"E. Elk. W—.

"S. is at Pisa, and will write to-night to me."

The last entry in Williams's Journal is dated July 4, 1822, Leghorn.

" Processions of priests and religiosi have been for several days past praying for rain ; but the gods are either angry, or nature too powerful."

ROW WITH SOLDIERS.

The affair of the dragoon alluded to in Williams's letter, as connected with the Gambas, was this: As Byron and his companions were returning to Pisa on horseback, the road being blocked up by the party,—a sergeant-major on duty in their rear trotted his horse through the cavalcade.   One of the awkward literary squad,—a resolute bore, but timid rider,—was nearly spilt, from his nag shying.   To divert the jeers from his own bad riding, he appealed pathetically to Byron, saying :—

"Shall we endure this man's insolence ?"

Byron said : "No, we will bring him to an account ;" and instantly galloped after the dragoon into Pisa, his party following.   The guard at the gate turned out with drawn swords, but could not stop them.   Some of the servants of Byron and the Gambas were idling on the steps of his palace ; getting a glimpse of the row, one of them armed himself with a stable-fork, rushed at the dragoon as he passed Byron's palace, and wounded him severely in the side.   This scene was acted in broad daylight on the Lung 'Arno, the most public place in the city, scores of people looking on ! yet the police, with their host of spies and backed by the power of a despotic government, could never ascertain who struck the blow.

Not liking to meddle with the Poet, they imprisoned two of his servants, and exiled the family of Count Gamba.   Byron chose to follow them.   Such is the hatred of the Italians to their rulers and all who have authority over them, that the blind beggars at the corners of the streets,—no others are permitted to beg in Tuscany,—hearing that the English were without arms, sidled up to some of them, adroitly putting into their hands formidable stilettos, which they had concealed in the sleeves of their ragged gaberdines.

Shelley wrote me the following note about the dragoon.

MY DEAR T.

Gamba is with me, and we are drawing up a paper demanded of us by the police. Mary tells me that you have an account from Lord Byron of the affair, and we wish to see it before ours is concluded. The man is severely wounded in the side, and his life is supposed to be in danger from the weapon having grazed the liver. It were as well if you could come here, as we shall decide on no statement without you.

Ever yours truly,
SHELLEY.

Mrs. Shelley, writing an account of the row, says :

"Madame G. and I happened to be in the carriage, ten paces behind, and saw the whole. Taaffe kept at a safe distance during the fray, but fearing the consequence, he wrote such a report that Lord Byron quarrelled with him ; and what between insolence and abject humility he has kept himself in hot water, when, in fact, he had nothing to fear."

THAT FATAL AND PERFIDIOUS BARK.

On Monday, the 8th of July, 1822, I went with Shelley to his bankers, and then to a store. It was past one P. M. when we went on board our respective boats,—Shelley and Williams to return to their home in the Gulf of Spezzia ; I in the "Bolivar," to accompany them into the offing. When we were under weigh, the guard-boat boarded us to overhaul our papers. I had not got my port clearance, the captain of the port having refused to give it to the mate, as I had often gone without. The officer of the Health Office consequently threatened me with forty days' quarantine. It was hopeless to think of detaining my friends. Williams had been for days fretting and fuming to be off ; they had no time to spare, it was past two o'clock, and there was very little wind.

Sullenly and reluctantly I re-anchored, furled my sails, and with a ship's glass watched the progress of my friends' boat.

My Genoese mate observed,—" They should have sailed this morning at three or four A. M., instead of three P. M.   They are standing too much in shore; the current will set them there."

I said, " They will soon have the land-breeze."

" May-be," continued the mate, " she will soon have too much breeze; that gaff top-sail is foolish in a boat with no deck and no sailor on board."   Then pointing to the S.W., " Look at those black lines and the dirty rags hanging on them out of the sky—they are a warning; look at the smoke on the water; the devil is brewing mischief."

There was a sea-fog, in which Shelley's boat was soon after enveloped, and we saw nothing more of her.

Although the sun was obscured by mists, it was oppressively sultry.   There was not a breath of air in the harbor.   The heaviness of the atmosphere and an unwonted stillness be-numbed my senses.   I went down into the cabin and sank into a slumber.   I was roused up by a noise over-head and went on deck.   The men were getting up a chain cable to let go another anchor.   There was a general stir amongst the shipping; shifting berths, getting down yards and masts, veering out cables, hauling in of hawsers, letting go anchors, hailing from the ships and quays, boats sculling rapidly to and fro.   It was almost dark, although only half-past six o'clock.   The sea was of the color, and looked as solid and smooth as a sheet of lead, and covered with an oily scum.   Gusts of wind swept over without ruffling it, and big drops of rain fell on its surface, rebounding, as if they could not penetrate it.   There was a commotion in the air, made up of many threatening sounds, coming upon us from the sea.   Fishing-craft and coasting-vessels under bare poles rushed by us in shoals, running foul of the ships in the harbor.   As yet the din and hubbub was that made by men, but their shrill pipings were suddenly silenced by the crashing voice of a thunder squall that burst right over our heads.   For some time no other sounds were to be heard than the thunder, wind, and rain.   When the fury of the storm, which did not last for more than twenty minutes, had abated, and the horizon was in some degree cleared, I looked to seaward anxiously, in the hope of descrying Shelley's boat, amongst the many small craft scattered about. I watched every speck that loomed on the horizon, thinking that they would have borne up on their return to the port, as all the other boats that had gone out in the same direction had done.

I sent our Genoese mate on board some of the returning craft to make inquiries, but they all professed not to have seen the English boat. So remorselessly are the quarantine laws enforced in Italy, that, when at sea, if you render assistance to a vessel in distress, or rescue a drowning stranger, on returning to port you are condemned to a long and rigorous quarantine of fourteen or more days. The consequence is, should one vessel see another in peril, or even run it down by accident, she hastens on her course, and by general accord, not a word is said or reported on the subject. But to resume my tale. I did not leave the " Bolivar " until dark. During the night it was gusty and showery, and the lightning flashed along the coast ; at daylight I returned on board, and resumed my examinations of the crews of the various boats which had returned to the port during the night. They either knew nothing, or would say nothing. My Genoese, with the quick eye of a sailor, pointed out, on board a fishing-boat, an English-made oar, that he thought he had seen in Shelley's boat, but the entire crew swore by all the saints in the calendar that this was not so. Another day was passed in horrid suspense. On the morning of the third day I rode to Pisa. Byron had returned to the Lanfranchi Palace. I hoped to find a letter from the Villa Magni ; there was none. I told my fears to Hunt, and then went upstairs to Byron. When I told him, his lip quivered, and his voice faltered as he questioned me. I sent a courier to Leghorn to despatch the " Bolivar," to cruise along the coast, whilst I mounted my horse and rode in the same direction. I also despatched a courier along the coast to go as far as Nice. On my arrival at Via Reggio, I heard that a punt, a water-keg, and some bottles had been found on the beach. These things I recognized as having been in Shelley's boat when he left Leghorn.

THE BODIES FOUND.

Nothing more was found for seven or eight days, during which time of painful suspense, I patrolled the coast with the coast-guard, stimulating them to keep a good look-out by the promise of a reward. It was not until many days after this that my worst fears were confirmed. Two bodies were found on the shore,—one near Via Reggio, which I went and examined. The face and hands, and parts of the body not protected by the dress, were fleshless. The tall, slight figure, the jacket, the volume of Sophocles in one pocket, and Keats's poems in the other, doubled back, as if the reader, in the act of reading, had hastily thrust it away, were all too familiar to me to leave a doubt on my mind that this mutilated corpse was any other than Shelley's. The other body was washed on shore three miles distant from Shelley's, near the tower of Migliarino, at the Bocca Lericcio. I went there at once. This corpse was much more mutilated; it had no other covering than the shreds of a shirt, and that partly drawn over the head, as if the wearer had been in the act of taking it off,—a black silk handkerchief, tied sailor-fashion, round the neck,—socks,— and one boot, indicating also that he had attempted to strip. The flesh, sinews, and muscles hung about in rags, like the shirt, exposing the ribs and bones. I had brought with me from Shelley's house a boot of Williams's, and this exactly matched the one the corpse had on. That, and the handkerchief, satisfied me that it was the body of Shelley's comrade. Williams was the only one of the three who could swim, and it is probable that he was the last survivor. It is likewise possible, as he had a watch and money, and was better dressed than the others, that his body might have been plundered when found. Shelley always declared that in case of wreck he would vanish instantly, and not imperil valuable lives by permitting others to aid in saving his, which he looked upon as valueless.

It was not until three weeks after the wreck of the boat that a third body was found—four miles from the other two. This I concluded to be that of the sailor boy, Charles Vivian, although it was a mere skeleton, and impossible to be identified. It was buried in the sand, above the reach of the waves.

THE TWO WIDOWS.

I mounted my horse, and rode to the Gulf of Spezzia, put up my horse, and walked until I caught sight of the lone house on the sea-shore in which Shelley and Williams had dwelt, and where their widows still lived. Hitherto in my frequent visits —in the absence of direct evidence to the contrary, I had buoyed up their spirits by maintaining that it was not impossible but that the friends still lived ; now I had to extinguish the last hope of these forlorn women. I had ridden fast, to prevent any ruder messenger from bursting in upon them. As I stood on the threshold of their house, the bearer, or rather confirmer, of news which would rack every fibre of their quivering frames to the utmost, I paused, and, looking at the sea, my memory reverted to our joyous parting only a few days before.

The two families, then, had all been in the veranda, overhanging a sea so clear and calm, that every star was reflected on the water, as if it had been a mirror; the young mothers singing some merry tune, with the accompaniment of a guitar. Shelley's shrill laugh—I heard it still—rang in my ears, with Williams's friendly hail, the general *buona notte* of all the joyous party, and the earnest entreaty to me to return as soon as possible, and not to forget the commissions they had severally given me. I was in a small boat beneath them, slowly rowing myself on board the " Bolivar," at anchor in the bay, loath to part from what I verily believed to have been at that time the most united, and happiest, set of human beings in the whole world. And now by the blow of an idle puff of wind the scene was changed. Such is human happiness.

My reverie was broken by a shriek from the nurse Caterina, as, crossing the hall, she saw me in the doorway. After asking her a few questions, I went up the stairs, and, unannounced, entered the room.   I neither spoke, nor did they question me. Mrs. Shelley's large gray eyes were fixed on my face.   I turned away.   Unable to bear this horrid silence, with a convulsive effort she exclaimed—

"Is there no hope?"

I did not answer, but left the room, and sent the servant with the children to them.   The next day I prevailed on them to return with me to Pisa.   The misery of that night and the journey of the next day, and of many days and nights that followed, I can neither describe nor forget.

DISPOSITION OF SHELLEY'S REMAINS.

It was ultimately determined by those most interested, that Shelley's remains should be removed from where they lay, and conveyed to Rome, to be interred near the bodies of his child, and of his friend Keats, with a suitable monument, and that Williams's remains should be taken to England.   To do this, in their then far advanced state of decomposition, and to obviate the obstacles offered by the quarantine laws, the ancient custom of burning and reducing the body to ashes was suggested.   I wrote to our minister at Florence, Dawkins, on the subject, and solicited his friendly intercession with the Lucchese and Florentine governments, that I might be furnished with authority to accomplish our purpose.

The following was his answer :—

DEAR SIR,

An order was sent yesterday from hence to the Governor of Via Reggio, to deliver up the remains of Mr. Shelley to you, or any person empowered by you to receive them.

I said they were to be removed to Leghorn for interment, but that need not bind you.   If they go by sea, the governor will give you the papers necessary to insure their admittance elsewhere.   If they travel by land, they must be accompanied by a guard as far as the frontier,—a precaution always taken to prevent the possibility of infection. Quicklime has been thrown into the graves, as is usual in similar cases.

With respect to the removal of the other corpse, I can tell you nothing till I hear from Florence. I applied for the order as soon as I received your letter, and I expect an answer to my letter by to-morrow's post.

I am very sensible of Lord Byron's kindness, and should have called upon him when I passed through Pisa, had he been anybody but Lord Byron. Do not mention trouble ; I am here to take as much as my countrymen think proper to give me ; and all I ask in return is fair play and good humor, which I am sure I shall always find in the S. S. S.

Believe me, dear sir,
Yours very faithfully,
W. DAWKINS.

Such were his subsequent influence and energy, that he ultimately overcame all the obstacles and repugnance of the Italians to sanction such an unprecedented proceeding in their territories.

PREPARATIONS FOR THE BURNING.

I got a furnace made at Leghorn, of iron-bars and strong sheet-iron, supported on a stand, and laid in a stock of fuel, and such things as were said to be used by Shelley's much loved Hellenes on their funeral pyres.

On the 13th of August, 1822, I went on board the " Bolivar," with an English acquaintance, having written to Byron and Hunt to say I would send them word when everything was ready, as they wished to be present. I had previously engaged two large feluccas, with drags and tackling, to go before, and endeavor to find the place where Shelley's boat had foundered ; the captain of one of the feluccas having asserted that he was out in the fatal squall, and had seen Shelley's boat go down off Via Reggio, with all sail set. With light and fitful breezes we were eleven hours reaching our destination—the tower of Migliarino, at the Bocca Lericcio, in the Tuscan States. There was a village there, and about two miles from that place Williams was buried. So I anchored, landed, called on the officer in command, a major, and told him my object in coming, of which he was already apprised by his own government. He assured me I should have every aid from him. As it was too late in the day to commence operations, we went to the only inn in the place, and I wrote to Byron to be with us next day at noon. The major sent my letter to Pisa by a dragoon, and made arrangements for the next day. In the morning he was with us early, and gave me a note from Byron, to say he would join us as near noon as he could. At ten we went on board the commandant's boat, with a squad of soldiers in working dresses, armed with mattocks and spades, an officer of the quarantine service, and some of his crew. They had their peculiar tools, so fashioned as to do their work without coming into personal contact with things that might be infectious—long-handled tongs, nippers, poles with iron hooks and spikes, and divers others that gave one a lively idea of the implements of torture devised by the holy inquisitors. Thus freighted, we started, my own boat following with the furnace, and the things I had brought from Leghorn. We pulled along the shore for some distance, and landed at a line of strong posts and railings which projected into the sea—forming the boundary dividing the Tuscan and Lucchese States. We walked along the shore to the grave, where Byron and Hunt soon joined us : they, too, had an officer and soldiers from the tower of Migliarino, an officer of the Health Office, and some dismounted dragoons, so we were surrounded by soldiers, but they kept the ground clear, and readily lent their aid. There was a considerable gathering of spectators from the neighborhood, and many ladies richly dressed were amongst them. The spot where the body lay was marked by the gnarled root of a pine tree.

Opening the Grave.

A rude hut, built of young pine-tree stems, and wattled with their branches, to keep the sun and rain out, and thatched with reeds, stood on the beach to shelter the look-out man on duty. A few yards from this was the grave, which we commenced opening—the Gulf of Spezzia and Leghorn at equal distances of twenty-two miles from us. As to fuel, I might have saved myself the trouble of bringing any, for there was an ample supply of broken spars and planks cast on the shore from wrecks, besides the fallen and decaying timber in a stunted pine forest close at hand. The soldiers collected fuel whilst I erected the furnace, and then the men of the Health Office set to work, shovelling away the sand which covered the body, while we gathered round, watching anxiously. The first indication of their having found the body, was the appearance of the end of a black silk handkerchief—I grubbed this out with a stick, for we were not allowed to touch anything with our hands—then some shreds of linen were met with, and a boot with the bone of the leg and the foot in it. On the removal of a layer of brushwood, all that now remained of my lost friend was exposed—a shapeless mass of bones and flesh. The limbs separated from the trunk on being touched.

"Is that a human body?" exclaimed Byron; "why it's more like the carcase of a sheep, or any other animal, than a man : this is a satire on our pride and folly."

I pointed to the letters E. E. W. on the black silk handkerchief.

Byron looking on, muttered, "The entrails of a worm hold together longer than the potter's clay, of which man is made. Hold! let me see the jaw," he added, as they were removing the skull, "I can recognize any one by the teeth, with whom I have talked. I always watch the lips and mouth : they tell what the tongue and eyes try to conceal."

I had a boot of Williams's with me ; it exactly corresponded with the one found in the grave. The remains were removed piecemeal into the furnace.

"Don't repeat this with me," said Byron; "let my carcase rot where it falls."

The Burning of Williams.

The funereal pyre was now ready; I applied the fire, and the materials. being dry and resinous, the pine-wood burnt furiously, and drove us back. It was hot enough before, there was no breath of air, and the loose sand scorched our feet. As soon as the flames became clear, and allowed us to approach we threw frankincense and salt into the furnace, and poured a flask of wine and oil over the body. The Greek oration was omitted, for we had lost our Hellenic bard. It was now so insufferably hot that the officers and soldiers were all seeking shade.

"Let us try the strength of these waters that drowned our friends," said Byron, with his usual audacity. "How far out do you think they were when their boat sank?"

"If you don't wish to be put into the furnace, you had better not try; you are not in condition."

He stripped, and went into the water, and so did I and my companion. Before we got a mile out, Byron was sick, and persuaded to return to the shore. My companion, too, was seized with cramp, and reached the land by my aid. At four o'clock the funereal pyre burnt low, and when we uncovered the furnace, nothing remained in it but dark-colored ashes, with fragments of the larger bones. Poles were now put under the red-hot furnace, and it was gradually cooled in the sea. I gathered together the human ashes, and placed them in a small oak-box, bearing an inscription on a brass plate, screwed it down, and placed it in Byron's carriage. He returned with Hunt to Pisa, promising to be with us on the following day at Via Reggio. I returned with my party in the same way we came, and supped and slept at the inn.

The Burning of Shelley.

On the following morning we went on board the same boats, with the same things and party, and rowed down the little river near Via Reggio to the sea, pulled along the coast towards Massa, then landed, and began our preparations as before.

Three white wands had been stuck in the sand to mark the Poet's grave, but as they were at some distance from each other, we had to cut a trench thirty yards in length, in the line of the sticks, to ascertain the exact spot, and it was nearly an hour before we came upon the grave.

In the mean time Byron and Leigh Hunt arrived in the carriage, attended by soldiers, and the Health Officer, as before. The lonely and grand scenery that surrounded us so exactly harmonized with Shelley's genius, that I could imagine his spirit soaring over us. The sea, with the islands of Gorgona, Capraji, and Elba, was before us; old battlemented watch-towers stretched along the coast, backed by the marble-crested Apennines glistening in the sun, picturesque from their diversified outlines, and not a human dwelling was in sight. As I thought of the delight Shelley felt in such scenes of loneliness and gran-deur whilst living, I felt we were no better than a herd of wolves or a pack of wild dogs, in tearing out his battered and naked body from the pure yellow sand that lay so lightly over it, to drag him back to the light of day; but the dead have no voice, nor had I power to check the sacrilege—the work went on silently in the deep and unresisting sand, not a word was spoken, for the Italians have a touch of sentiment, and their feelings are easily excited into sympathy. Even Byron was silent and thoughtful. We were startled and drawn together by a dull hollow sound that followed the blow of a mattock; the iron had struck a skull, and the body was soon uncovered. Lime had been strewn on it; this, or decomposition, had the effect of staining it of a dark and ghastly indigo color. Byron asked me to preserve the skull for him; but remembering that he had formerly used one as a drinking-cup, I was determined Shelley's should not be so profaned. The limbs did not separate from the trunk, as in the case of Williams's body, so that the corpse was removed entire into the furnace. I had taken the precaution of having more and larger pieces of timber, in consequence of my experience of the day before of the difficulty of consuming a corpse in the open air with our apparatus. After the fire was well kindled we repeated the ceremony of the previous day; and more wine was poured over Shelley's dead body than he had consumed during his life. This with the oil and salt made the yellow flames glisten and quiver. The heat from the sun and fire was so intense that the atmosphere was tremulous and wavy. The corpse fell open and the heart was laid bare. The frontal bone of the skull, where it had been struck with the mattock, fell off; and, as the back of the head rested on the red-hot bottom bars of the furnace, the brains literally seethed, bubbled, and boiled as in a cauldron, for a very long time.

Byron could not face this scene, he withdrew to the beach and swam off to the " Bolivar." Leigh Hunt remained in the carriage. The fire was so fierce as to produce a white heat on the iron, and to reduce its contents to gray ashes. The only portions that were not consumed were some fragments of bones, the jaw, and the skull, but what surprised us all, was that the heart remained entire. In snatching this relic from the fiery furnace, my hand was severely burnt; and had any one seen me do the act I should have been put into quarantine.

After cooling the iron machine in the sea, I collected the human ashes and placed them in a box, which I took on board the " Bolivar." Byron and Hunt retraced their steps to their home, and the officers and soldiers returned to their quarters. I liberally rewarded the men for the admirable manner in which they behaved during the two days they had been with us.

As I undertook and executed this novel ceremony, I have been thus tediously minute in describing it.

Byron's idle talk, during the exhumation of Williams's re- mains, did not proceed from want of feeling, but from his anxiety to conceal what he felt from others. When confined to his bed and racked by spasms, which threatened his life, I have heard him talk in a much more unorthodox fashion, the instant he could muster breath to banter. He had been taught during his town-life, that any exhibition of sympathy or feeling was maudlin and unmanly, and that the appearance of daring and indifference, denoted blood and high breeding.

SHELLEY'S GRAVE.

When I arrived at Leghorn, as I could not immediately go
on to Rome, I consigned Shelley's ashes to our Consul at Rome,
Mr. Freeborn, requesting him to keep them in his custody until
my arrival. When I reached Rome, Freeborn told me that to
quiet the authorities there, he had been obliged to inter the
ashes with the usual ceremonies in the Protestant burying-place.
When I came to examine the ground with the man who had the
custody of it, I found Shelley's grave amidst a cluster of others.
The old Roman wall partly inclosed the place, and there was a
niche in the wall formed by two buttresses—immediately under
an ancient pyramid, said to be the tomb of Caius Cestius.
There were no graves near it at that time. This suited my
taste, so I purchased the recess, and sufficient space for plant-
ing a row of the Italian upright cypresses. As the souls of
heretics are foredoomed by the Roman priests, they do not
affect to trouble themselves about their bodies. There was no
" faculty " to apply for nor bishop's license to exhume the body.
The custode or guardian who dwelt within the inclosure and
had the key of the gate, seemed to have uncontrolled power
within his domain, and scudi, impressed with the image of
Saint Peter with the two keys, ruled him. Without more ado,
masons were hired, and two tombs built in the recess. In one
of these, when completed, I deposited the box, with Shelley's
ashes, and covered it in with solid stone, inscribed with a Latin
epitaph, written by Leigh Hunt. I received the following note
at Leghorn previous to burning the body :—

" DEAR TRELAWNY,   " PISA, 1st *August*, 1822.

" You will of course call upon us in your way to your melancholy task ; but I write to say, that you must not reckon upon
passing through Pisa in a very great hurry, as the ladies particularly wish to have an evening, while you are here, for consulting further with us ; and I myself mean, at all events, to
accompany you on your journey, if you have no objection.

" I subjoin the inscriptions—mere matter-of-fact memor-

12

andums—according to the wish of the ladies. It will be for the other inscriptions to say more.

"Yours sincerely,
"LEIGH HUNT.

"P.S.—Mrs. Shelley wishes very much that Capt. Roberts would be kind enough to write to his uncle about her desk, begging it to be forwarded as speedily as possible. If it is necessary to be opened, the best way will be to buy a key for that purpose ; but if a key is not to be had, of course it must be broken open. As there is something in the secret drawers, it will be extremely desirable that as few persons meddle with it as possible."

"PERCY BYSSHE SHELLEY, ANGLUS, ORAM ETRUSCAM LEGENS IN NAVIGIOLO INTER LIGURNUM PORTUM ET VIAM REGIAM, PROCELLÂ PERIIT VIII. NON. JUL. MDCCCXXII. ÆTAT. SUÆ XXX.

"EDVARDUS ELLIKER WILLIAMS, ANGLICÂ STIRPE ORTUS, INDIÂ ORIENTALI NATUS, A LIGURNO PORTU IN VIAM REGIAM NAVIGIOLO PROFICISCENS, TEMPESTATE PERIIT VIII. NON. JUL. MDCCCXXII. ÆTAT. SUÆ XXX."

"IO, SOTTOSCRITTA, PREGO LE AUTORITÀ DI VIA REGGIO O LIVORNO DI CONSEGNARE AL SIGNORE ODOARDO TRELAWNY, INGLESE, LA BARCA NOMINATA IL DON JUAN, E TUTTA LA SUA CARICA, APPARTENENTE AL MIO MARITO, PER ESSERE ALLA SUA DISPOZIZIONE. MARIA SHELLEY.

"GENOVA, 16 SETT^bre 1822."

To which I added two lines from Shelley's favorite play "The Tempest,"

> "Nothing of him that doth fade,
> But doth suffer a sea change
> Into something rich and strange."

The other tomb built merely to fill up the recess, was likewise covered in in the same way—but blank without as within. I planted eight seedling cypresses. When I last saw them in 1844, the seven which remained were about thirty-five feet in height. I added flowers as well. The ground I had purchased, I enclosed, and so ended my task.

RAISING SHELLEY'S BOAT.

It is mentioned in my narrative, that when I left Leghorn, in the " Bolivar," to burn the bodies, I despatched two large feluccas, with ground-tackling to drag for Shelley's foundered boat, having previously ascertained the spot in which she had been last seen afloat. This was done for five or six days, and they succeeded in finding her, but failed in getting her up. I then wrote the particulars to my friend Capt. Roberts, who was still at Genoa, asking him to complete the business. He did so, whilst I went on to Rome, and, as will be seen by the following letters, he not only found, but got her up, and brought her into the harbor of Leghorn.

DEAR T.   PISA, *Sept.* 1822.

We have got fast hold of Shelley's boat, and she is now safe at anchor off Via Reggio. Everything is in her, and clearly proves, that she was not capsized. I think she must have been swamped by a heavy sea; we found in her, two trunks, that of Williams containing money and clothes, and Shelley's, filled with books and clothes.

Yours, very sincerely,

DAN ROBERTS.

DEAR T.   *Sept.* 18, 1822.

I consulted Ld. B., on the subject of paying the crews of the felucca employed in getting up the boat. He advised me to sell her by auction, and to give them half the proceeds of the sale. I rode your horse to Via Reggio. On Monday we had the sale, and only realized a trifle more than two hundred dollars.

The two masts were carried away just above board, the bowsprit broken off close to the bows, the gunwale stove in, and the hull half full of blue clay, out of which we fished clothes, books, spy-glass, and other articles. A hamper of wine that Shelley bought at Leghorn, a present for the harbormaster of Lerici, was spoilt, the corks forced partly out of the bottles, and the wine mixed with the salt-water. You know, this is effected by the pressure of the cold sea-water.

We found in the boat two memorandum-books of Shelley's, quite perfect, and another damaged, a journal of Williams's, quite perfect, written up to the 4th of July. I washed the printed books, some of them were so glued together by the slimy mud, that the leaves could not be separated; most of these things are now in Ld. B.'s custody. The letters, private papers, and Williams's journal, I left in charge of Hunt, as I saw there were many severe remarks on Ld. B.

Ld. B. has found out, that you left at Genoa some of the ballast of the "Bolivar," and he asked me to sell it for him. What a damned close calculating fellow he is. You are so bigoted in his favor that I will say no more, only God defend me from ever having anything more to do with him.

P. S.—On a close examination of Shelley's boat, we find many of the timbers on the starboard quarter broken, which makes me think for certain, that she must have been run down by some of the feluccas in the squall.

DAN ROBERTS.

Byron's Shabbiness to Mrs. Shelley.

All that were now left of our Pisan circle established themselves at Albaro—Byron, Leigh Hunt, and Mrs. Shelley. I took up my quarters in the city of palaces. The fine spirit that had animated and held us together was gone! Left to our own devices, we degenerated apace. Shelley's solidity had checked Byron's flippancy, and induced him occasionally to act justly, and talk seriously; now he seemed more sordid and selfish than ever. He behaved shabbily to Mrs. Shelley; I might use a harsher epithet. In all the transactions between Shelley and Byron in which expenses had occurred, and there were many, the former, as was his custom, had paid all, the latter promising to repay; but as no one ever repaid Shelley, Byron did not see the necessity of his setting the example;

and now that Mrs. Shelley was left destitute by her husband's death, Byron did nothing for her. He regretted this when too late, for in our voyage to Greece, he alluded to Shelley, saying, "Tre, you did what I should have done, let us square accounts to-morrow; I must pay my debts." I merely observed, "Money is of no use at sea, and when you get on shore you will find you have none to spare;" he probably thought so too, for he said nothing more on the subject.

MRS. SHELLEY'S JOURNAL.

"*October 2d*, 1822.—On the 8th of July I finished my journal. This is a curious coincidence. The date still remains—the fatal 8th—a monument to show that all ended then. And I begin again? Oh, never! But several motives induce me, when the day has gone down, and all is silent around me, steeped in sleep, to pen, as occasion wills, my reflections and feelings. First, I have no friend. For eight years I communicated, with unlimited freedom, with one whose genius far transcending mine, awakened and guided my thoughts. I conversed with him; rectified errors of judgment; obtained new lights from him; and my mind was satisfied. Now I am alone—oh, how alone. The stars may behold my tears, and the winds drink my sighs; but my thoughts are a sealed treasure, which I can confide to none. But can I express all I feel? Can I give words to thoughts and feelings that as a tempest hurry me along? Is this the sand that the ever-flowing sea of thought would impress indelibly? Alas! I am alone. No eye answers mine; my voice can with none assume its natural modulation. What a change! Oh, my beloved Shelley! how often during those happy days—happy, though checkered—I thought how superiorly gifted I had been in being united to one to whom I could unveil myself, and who could understand me! Well, then, I am now reduced to these white pages, which I am to blot with dark imagery. As I write, let me think what he would have said if, speaking thus to him, he could have answered me. Yes, my own heart, I would fain know what you think of my desolate state; what you think I ought to do, what to think. I guess you would answer thus :—'Seek to know your own heart, and, learning what it best loves, try to enjoy that.' Well, I cast my eyes around, and looking forward to the bounded prospect in view, I ask myself what pleases me there. My child ;—so many feelings arise when I think of him, that I turn aside to think no more. Those I most loved are gone forever ; those who held the second rank are absent ; and among those near me as yet, I trust to the disinterested kindness of one alone. Beneath all this, my imagination ever flags. Literary labors, the improvement of my mind, and the enlargement of my ideas, are the only occupations that elevate me from my lethargy ; all events seem to lead me to that one point, and the coursers of destiny having dragged me to that single resting-place, have left me. Father, mother, friend, husband, children—all made, as it were, the team that conducted me here ; and now all except you, my poor boy (and you are necessary to the continuance of my life), all are gone, and I am left to fulfil my task. So be it !

" *October* 5*th.*—Well, they are come ; * and it is all as I said. I awoke as from sleep, and thought how I had vegetated these last days ; for feeling leaves little trace on the memory if it be, like mine, unvaried. I have felt for and with myself alone, and I awake now to take a part in life. As far as others are concerned, my sensations have been most painful. I must work hard amidst the vexations that I perceive are preparing for me—to preserve my peace and tranquillity of mind. I must preserve some, if I am to live ; for since I bear at the bottom of my heart a fathomless well of bitter waters, the workings of which my philosophy is ever at work to repress, what will be my fate if the petty vexations of life are added to this sense of eternal and infinite misery ?

"Oh, my child ! what is your fate to be ? You alone reach me ; you are the only chain that links me to time ; but for you I should be free. And yet I cannot be destined to live long !

* Leigh Hunt and his family.—ED.

Well, I shall commence my task, commemorate the virtues of the only creature worth loving or living for, and then, may be, I may join him. Moonshine may be united to her planet, and wander no more, a sad reflection of all she loved on earth.

"*October 7th.*—I have received my desk to-day, and have been reading my letters to mine own Shelley during his absences at Marlow. What a scene to recur to! My William, Clara, Allegra, are all talked of. They lived then, they breathed this air, and their voices struck on my sense; their feet trod the earth beside me, and their hands were warm with blood and life when clasped in mine. Where are they all? This is too great an agony to be written about. I may express my despair, but my thoughts can find no words.

*   *   *   *   *   *

"I would endeavor to consider myself a faint continuation of his being, and, as far as possible, the revelation to the earth of what he was. Yet, to become this, I must change much, and above all I must acquire that knowledge, and drink at those fountains of wisdom and virtue, from which he quenched his thirst. Hitherto I have done nothing; yet I have not been discontented with myself. I speak of the period of my residence here. For, although unoccupied by those studies which I have marked out for myself, my mind has been so active, that its activity, and not its indolence, has made me neglectful. But now the society of others causes this perpetual working of my ideas somewhat to pause; and I must take advantage of this to turn my mind towards its immediate duties, and to determine with firmness to commence the life I have planned. You will be with me in all my studies, dearest love! Your voice will no longer applaud me, but in spirit you will visit and encourage me; I know you will. What were I, if I did not believe that you still exist? It is not with you as with another. I believe that we all live hereafter; but you, my only one, were a spirit caged, an elemental being, enshrined in a frail image, now shattered. Do they not all with one voice assert the same? Trelawny, Hunt, and many others; and so at last you

quitted this painful prison, and you are free, my Shelley—
while I, your poor chosen one, am left to live as I may.

"What a strange life mine has been! Love, youth, fear,
and fearlessness led me early from the regular routine of life,
and I united myself to this being, who not one of *us*, though
like to us, was pursued by numberless miseries and annoyances, in all which I shared. And then I was the mother of
beautiful children ; but these stayed not by me. Still he was
there ; and though, in truth, after my William's death, this
world seemed only a quicksand, sinking beneath my feet, yet
beside me was this bank of refuge—so tempest-worn and frail,
that methought its very weakness was strength—and since
Nature had written destruction on its brow, so the Power that
rules human affairs had determined, in spite of Nature, that
it should endure. But that is gone. His voice can no longer
be heard ; the earth no longer receives the shadow of his form ;
annihilation has come over the earthly appearance of the most
gentle creature that ever yet breathed this air ; and I am still
here—still thinking, existing, all but hoping. Well, I will close
my book ; to-morrow I must begin this new life of mine.

" *October* 19*th.*—How painful all change becomes to one who,
entirely and despotically engrossed by their own feelings, leads
as it were an *internal* life, quite different from the outward and
apparent one. Whilst my life continues its monotonous course
within sterile banks, an undercurrent disturbs the smooth face
of the waters, distorts all objects reflected in it, and the mind
is no longer a mirror in which outward events may reflect themselves, but becomes itself the painter and creator. If this perpetual activity has power to vary with endless change the every-
day occurrences of a most monotonous life, it appears to be
animated with the spirit of tempest and hurricane when any
real occurrence diversifies the scene. Thus, to-night, a few
bars of a known air seemed to be as a wind to rouse from its
depths every deep-seated emotion of my mind. I would have
given worlds to have sat, my eyes closed, and listened to them
for years. The restraint I was under caused these feelings to

vary with rapidity; but the words of the conversation, uninteresting as they might be, seemed all to convey two senses to me, and, touching a chord within me, to form a music of which the speaker was little aware. I do not think that any person's voice has the same power of awakening melancholy in me as Albè's.* I have been accustomed, when hearing it, to listen and to speak little; another voice, not mine, ever replied—a voice whose strings are broken. When Albè ceases to speak, I expect to hear *that other* voice, and, when I hear another instead, it jars strangely with every association. I have seen so little of Albè since our residence in Switzerland, and, having seen him there every day, his voice—a peculiar one—is engraved on my memory with other sounds and objects from which it can never disunite itself. I have heard Hunt in company and conversation with many, when my own one was not there. Trelawny, perhaps, is associated in my mind with Edward more than with Shelley. Even our older friends, Peacock and Hogg, might talk together, or with others, and their voices would suggest no change to me. But, since incapacity and timidity always prevented my mingling in the nightly conversations of Diodati, they were, as it were, entirely *tête-à-tête* between my Shelley and Albè; and thus, as I have said, when Albè speaks and Shelley does not answer, it is as thunder without rain—the form of the sun without heat or light —as any familiar object might be shorn of its best attributes; and I listen with an unspeakable melancholy that yet is not all pain.

"The above explains that which would otherwise be an enigma, why Albè, by his mere presence and voice, has the power of exciting such deep and shifting emotions within me. For my feelings have no analogy either with my opinion of him, or the subject of his conversation. With another I might talk, and not for the moment think of Shelley—at least not think of him with the same vividness as if I were alone; but, when in company with Albè, I can never cease for a second to have

---

* Lord Byron.—Ed.

12*

Shelley in my heart and brain, with a clearness that mocks reality—interfering, even, by its force, with the functions of life—until, if tears do not relieve me, the hysterical feeling, analogous to that which the murmur of the sea gives me, presses painfully upon me.

" Well, for the first time for about a month, I have been in company with Albè for two hours, and, coming home, I write this, so necessary is it for me to express in words the force of my feelings. Shelley, beloved! I look at the stars and at all nature, and it speaks to me of you in the clearest accents. Why cannot you answer me, my own one? Is the instrument so utterly destroyed? I would endure ages of pain to hear one tone of your voice strike on my ear.

" *November* 10*th.*—I have made my first probation in writing, and it has done me much good, and I get more calm; the stream begins to take to its new channel inasmuch as to make me fear change. But people must know little of me who think that, abstractedly, I am content with my present mode of life. Activity of spirit is my sphere. But we cannot be active of mind without an object; and I have none. I am allowed to have some talent—that is sufficient, methinks, to cause my irreparable misery; for, if one has genius, what a delight it is to associate with a superior. Mine own Shelley! the sun knows of none to be likened to you—brave, wise, gentle, noble-hearted, full of learning, tolerance, and love. Love! what a word for me to write! Yet, my miserable heart, permit me yet to love—to see him in beauty, to feel him in beauty; to be interpenetrated by the sense of his excellence; and thus to love, singly, eternally, ardently, and not fruitlessly; for I am still his—still the chosen one of that blessed spirit—still vowed to him forever and ever!

" *November* 11*th.*—It is better to grieve than not to grieve. Grief at least tells me that I was not always what I am now. I was once selected for happiness; let the memory of that abide by me. You pass by an old ruined house in a desolate lane, and heed it not. But, if you hear that that house is haunted by a wild and beautiful spirit, it acquires an interest and beauty of its own.

"I shall be glad to be more alone again; one ought to see no one, or many; and, confined to one society, I shall lose all energy except that which I possess from my own resources; and I must be alone for these to be put in activity.

"A cold heart! Have I a cold heart? God knows! But none need envy the icy region this heart encircles; and at least the tears are hot which the emotions of this cold heart forces me to shed. A cold heart! Yes, it would be cold enough if all were as I wished it—cold, or burning in that flame for whose sake I forgive this, and would forgive every other imputation—that flame in which your heart, beloved, lay unconsumed. My heart is very full to-night!

"I shall write his life, and thus occupy myself in the only manner from which I can derive consolation. That will be a task that may convey some balm. What though I weep? All is better than inaction and—not forgetfulness—that never is—but an inactivity of remembrance.

"And you, my own boy! I am about to begin a task which, if you live, will be an invaluable treasure to you in after times. I must collect my materials, and then, in the commemoration of the divine virtues of your father, I shall fulfil the only act of pleasure there remains for me, and be ready to follow you, if you leave me, my task being fulfilled. I have lived; rapture, exultation, content,—all the varied changes of enjoyment,— have been mine. It is all gone; but still, the airy paintings of what it has gone through float by, and distance shall not dim them. If I were alone, I had already begun what I have determined to do; but I must have patience, and for those events my memory is brass, my thoughts a never tired engraver. France—Poverty—A few days of solitude, and some uneasiness—A tranquil residence in a beautiful spot—Switzerland— Bath—Marlow—Milan—The Baths of Lucerne—Este—Venice —Rome—Naples—Rome and misery—Leghorn—Florence—

—Pisa—Solitude—The Williamses—The Baths—Pisa : these are the heads of chapters, and each containing a tale romantic beyond romance.

"I no longer enjoy, but I love! Death cannot deprive me of that living spark which feeds on all given it, and which is now triumphant in sorrow. I love, and shall enjoy happiness again ; I do not doubt that—but when?

"*December* 31*st.*—So, this year has come to an end! Shelley, beloved! the year has a new name from any thou knewest. When spring arrives, leaves you never saw will shadow the ground, and flowers you never beheld will star it ; the grass will be of another growth, and the birds sing a new song ; the aged earth dates with a new number.

"I trust in a hereafter—I have ever done so. I know that that shall be mine—even with thee, glorious spirit! who surely lookest on, pitiest, and lovest thy Mary.

"I love thee, my only one ; I love nature ; and I trust that I love all that is good in my fellow-creatures. But how changed I am! Last year, having you, I sought for the affection of others, and loved them even when unjust and cold ; but now my heart is truly iced. If they treat me well, I am grateful. Yes, when that is, I call thee to witness in how warm a gush my blood flows to my heart, and tears to my eyes. But I am a lonely, unloved thing, serious and absorbed. None care to read my sorrow.

"Sometimes I thought that fortune had relented towards us —that your health would have improved, and that fame and joy would have been yours ; for, when well, you extracted from nature alone an endless delight. The various threads of our existence seemed to be drawing to one point, and there to assume a cheerful hue.

"Again I think that your gentle spirit was too much wounded by the sharpnesses of this world ; that your disease was incurable ; and that, in a happy time, you became the partaker of cloudless day, ceaseless hours, and infinite love.

"Thy name is added to the list which makes the earth bold

in her age, and proud of what has been. Time, with unwearied but slow feet, guides her to the goal that thou hast reached ; and I, her unhappy child, am advanced still nearer the hour when my earthly dress shall repose near thine, beneath the tomb of Cestius.

"*February* 2*d*, 1823.—On the 21st of January, those rites were fulfilled. Shelley! my own beloved! You rest beneath the blue sky of Rome ; in that, at least, I am satisfied.

"What matters it that they cannot find the grave of my William? That spot is sanctified by the presence of his pure earthly vesture, and that is sufficient—at least, it must be. I am too truly miserable to dwell on what, at another time, might have made me unhappy. He is beneath the tomb of Cestius. I see the spot.

"*February* 3*d*.—A storm has come across me—a slight circumstance has disturbed the deceitful calm of which I boasted. I thought I heard my Shelley call me—not my Shelley in Heaven, —but my Shelley, my companion in my daily tasks. I was reading; I heard a voice say, 'Mary!' 'It is Shelley,' I thought ; the revulsion was of agony. Never more——

"But I have better hopes and other feelings. Your earthly shrine is shattered, but your spirit ever hovers over me, or awaits me, when I shall be worthy to join it. To that spirit, which, when imprisoned here, yet showed by its exalted nature its superior derivation——*

"*February* 24*th*.—Evils throng around me, my beloved, and I have indeed lost all in losing thee. Were it not for my child, this would rather be a soothing reflection, and, if starvation were my fate, I should fulfil that fate without a sigh. But our child demands all my care, now that you have left us. I must be all to him : the father, death has deprived him of ; the relations, the bad world permits him not to have. What is yet

---

* This sentence, like that at the end of the preceding paragraph, appears to have been left incomplete.—ED.

in store for me ?   Am I to close the eyes of our boy, and then join you ?

" The last weeks have been spent in quiet.   Study could not give repose to, but somewhat regulated, my thoughts.   I said : ' I lead an innocent life, and it may become a useful one.   I have talent, I will improve that talent; and if, while meditating on the wisdom of ages, and storing my mind with all that has been recorded of it, any new light bursts upon me, or any discovery occurs that may be useful to my fellows, then the balm of utility may be added to innocence.'

" What is it that moves up and down in my soul, and makes me feel as if my intellect could master all but my fate ?   I fear it is only youthful ardòr—the yet untamed spirit, which, wholly withdrawn from the hopes, and almost from the affections, of life, indulges itself in the only walk free to it, and, mental exertion being all my thought, except regret, would make me place my hopes in that.   I am, indeed, become a recluse in thought and act; and my mind, turned Heavenward, would, but for my only tie, lose all commune with what is around me.   If I be proud, yet it is with humility that I am so.   I am not vain. My heart shakes with its suppressed emotions, and I flag beneath the thoughts that possess me.

" Each day, as I have taken my solitary walk, I have felt myself exalted with the idea of occupation, improvement, knowledge, and peace.   Looking back to my past life as a delicious dream, I steeled myself, as well as I could, against such severe regrets as should overthrow my calmness.   Once or twice, pausing in my walk, I have exclaimed, in despair—' Is it even so?'   Yet, for the most part resigned, I was occupied by reflection—on those ideas you, my beloved, planted in my mind—and meditated on our nature, our source, and our destination.   To-day, melancholy would invade me, and I thought the peace I enjoyed was transient.   Then that letter came to place its seal on my prognostications.*   Yet it was not the

---

* Mrs. Shelley here alludes to a letter from Sir Timothy to Lord Byron (who had written to him on the subject), in which the baronet undertook to support his infant grandson, if the mother would part with him.—ED.

refusal, or the insult heaped upon me, that stung me to tears. It was their bitter words about our boy. Why, I live only to keep him from their hands. How dared they dream that I held him not far more precious than all, save the hope of again seeing you, my lost one. But for his smiles, where should I now be?

"Stars, that shine unclouded, ye cannot tell me what will be! Yet can I tell *you* a part. I may have misgivings, weaknesses, and momentary lapses into unworthy despondency; but—save in devotion towards my boy—fortune has emptied her quiver, and to all her future shafts I oppose courage, hopelessness of aught on this side, with a firm trust in what is beyond the grave.

" Visit me in my dreams to-night, my beloved Shelley! kind, living, excellent as thou wert! and the event of this day shall be forgotten.

" *March* 19*th*.—As I have until now recurred to this book, to discharge into it the overflowings of a mind too full of the bitterest waters of life, so will I to-night, that I am calm, put down some of my milder reveries; that, when I turn it once, I may not only find a record of the most painful thoughts that ever filled a human heart even to distraction.

" I am beginning seriously to educate myself; and in another place I have marked the scope of this somewhat tardy education, intellectually considered. In a moral point of view, this education is of some years' standing, and it only now takes the form of seeking its food in books. I have long accustomed myself to the study of my own heart, and have sought and found in its recesses that which cannot embody itself in words —hardly in feelings. I have found strength in the conception of its faculties—much native force in the understanding of them —and what appears to me not a contemptible penetration in the subtle divisions of good and evil. But I have found less strength of self-support, of resistance to what is vulgarly called temptation; yet I think, also, that I have found true humility (for surely no one can be less presumptuous than I), an ardent love for the immutable laws of right, much native goodness of emotion, and purity of thought.

" Enough, if every day I gain a profounder knowledge of my defects, and a more certain method of turning them to a good direction.

" Study has become to me more necessary than the air I breathe. In the questioning and searching turn it gives to my thoughts, I find some relief to wild reverie ; in the self-satisfaction I feel in commanding myself, I find present solace ; in the hope that thence arises, that I may become more worthy of my Shelley, I find a consolation that even makes me less wretched in my most wretched moments.

" *March* 30*th.*—I have now finished part of the *Odyssey*. I mark this. I cannot write. Day after day I suffer the most tremendous agitation. I cannot write, or read, or think. Whether it be the anxiety for letters that shakes a frame not so strong as hitherto—whether it be my annoyances here—whether it be my regrets, my sorrow, and despair, or all these—I know not ; but I am a wreck.

" *May* 31*st.*—The lanes are filled with fire-flies ; they dart between the trunks of the trees, and people the land with earth-stars. I walked among them to-night, and descended towards the sea. I passed by the ruined church, and stood on the platform that overlooks the beach. The black rocks were stretched out among the blue waters, which dashed with no impetuous motion against them. The dark boats, with their white sails, glided gently over its surface, and the star-enlightened promontories closed in the bay ; below, amid the crags, I heard the monotonous, but harmonious, voices of the fishermen.

" How beautiful these shores, and this sea ! Such is the scene—such the waves within which my beloved vanished from mortality !

" The time is drawing near when I must quit this country. It is true that, in the situation I now am, Italy is but the corpse of the enchantress that she was. Besides, if I had stayed here, the state of things would have been different. The idea of our child's advantage alone enables me to keep fixed in my resolution to return to England. It is best for him—and I go.

"Four years ago, we lost our darling William; four years ago, in excessive agony, I called for death to free me from all I felt that I should suffer here. I continue to live, and *thou* art gone. I leave Italy, and the few that still remain to me. That I regret less; for our intercourse is [so] much checkered with all of dross that this earth so delights to blend with kindness and sympathy, that I long for solitude, with the exercise of such affections as still remain to me. Away, I shall be conscious that these friends love me, and none can then gainsay the pure attachment which chiefly clings to them, because they knew and loved you—because I knew them when with you—and I cannot think of them without feeling your spirit beside me.

"I cannot grieve for you, beloved Shelley! I grieve for thy friends—for the world—for thy child—most for myself, enthroned in thy love, growing wiser and better beneath thy gentle influence, taught by you the highest philosophy—your pupil, friend, lover, wife, mother of your children! The glory of the dream is gone. I am a cloud from which the light of sunset has passed. Give me patience in the present struggle. *Meum cordium cor !* Good-night!

> 'I would give
> All that I am to be as thou now art;
> But I am chain'd to time, and cannot thence depart.'"

INDEX.

Ass, Adventure with, 37.
Atheist, Shelley as an, 42.
Atheism, The Necessity of, 82. What it did for Shelley, 86. What it did for Hogg, 89.

Babies, Shelley's notion about, 70.
Browne, Felicia Dorothea, Shelley corresponds with, 6.
Byron, Lord, Shelley reads his "English Bards and Scotch Reviewers," 94. Intimacy with Jane Clairmont, 206. Result of intimacy, 206. What he did, 206. Influence of Shelley, 213. Trelawny's first meeting with, 216. Conversation with Trelawny, 217. Personal appearance, 218. Firing at a mark, 219. Conversation with Shelley, 219. Praises Swift, 220. "Don Juan," 221. Warned against Shelley, 221. "If we puffed the Snake," 221. Real opinion of Shelley, 222. Remark to Trelawny, 223. What he called Shelley, 223. Contrasted with Shelley, 225. Determines to have a yacht, 241. Daily routine, 243. Working on his fears, 249. Treatment of Leigh Hunt, 250. Reception of Mrs. Hunt, 250. Row with soldiers, 252. At the grave of Williams, 260. "Don't repeat this with me," 261. Ill with swimming, 262. At the grave of Shelley, 263. Wants Shelley's skull, 263. A close, calculating fellow, 268. Shabbiness to Mrs. Shelley, 268. Debts, 269.

Clairmont Jane, her independent life, 191. Christens herself "Claire," 191. Injudicious influence on Mary Godwin, 193. Godwin talks to her, 194. Elopes with Shelley and Mary Godwin, 194. Refuses to return with her mother, 195. Returns with the fugitives, 206. Meets Lord Byron at Sicheron, 206. What she had wished to become, 206. Gives birth to Byron's Allegra, 206. What Byron did for her, 206.
Curran, John Philpot, pays no attention to Godwin's letter of introduction, 131. Shelley fails to see him, 132.

Elephantiasis, Shelley's dread of, 168.

"Gebir," Shelley's admiration for, 64. What befel his copy, 64.
Godwin, Mary Wollstonecraft, considered a child, 191. Character of, 192. Acquaintance with Shelley, 193. Shelley falls in love with her, 193. Unhappy at home, 193. Mrs. Godwin's remark to, 193. Reads by her mother's grave, 194. Her father talks with her, 194. Elopes with Shelley and Jane Clairmont, 194. Displeasure of her father, 195. Harriet Shelley's opinion of, 199. Receives a letter from her father, 205. Married to Shelley, 205. Birth of her first child, 206. Introduced to Trelawny, 216. Threatens Shelley with a party, 224. Williams intercedes with her, 225. "Don't tell Mary," 227. Looking for Shelley with Trelawny, 230. "What a wild goose you are, Percy," 232. Account of Byron's row, 253. "Is there no hope?" 258. Byron's shabbiness to, 268. Extracts from Journal, 269.
Godwin, William, Shelley introduces himself to, 130. Gives Shelley a letter of introduction to Curran, 131. Advice to Shelley, 131. Hogg's acquaintance with, 172. Hogg invited to dine with him, 172. Personal appearance, 173. Inquiries about Shelley's absence, 173. Hogg's reply, 173. Goes to dinner with Hogg, 173. Dietetics, 174. Goes to sleep, 174. Anxious about Shelley, 174. Discourses about Homer, 174. Questions Hogg about Shelley, 175.

Sans-Souci Series.

CRITICAL NOTICES.

From the New York World.

"Indeed the only fault that can be found with the initial volume of the Sans-Souci Series is that it is *too good*—that there are too many plums in the pudding."

From the Boston Post.

"The public can now look forward to the extension of a work *every bit as unique and interesting as the Bric-a-Brac Series*, and in some respects it promises to prove its superior."

From the New York Evening Post.

"A volume which is full of interest from its first page to its last one. . . . A delightful book which every lover of good biography will read with interest."

From the Worcester Spy.

"The book is full of characteristic and amusing anecdotes, and is as attractive in its tasteful exterior and elegant typography as in the literary and historical interest of its contents."

From the Philadelphia Press.

"Here, in 320 pages 12mo, is as much reading matter, and for $1.50, as is to be found in an average octavo volume."

From the Christian at Work.

"In this department of editorial work Mr. Stoddard is perhaps unequaled; certainly unexcelled. The binding is a marvel of beauty. The Sans-Souci Series cannot fail to attract the intelligent reader."

From the Philadelphia Inquirer.

"We have a book in reading which the art of skipping is never called into requisition, a book bright with interest from beginning to end, to be read again and again and enjoyed always."

From the St. Louis Republican.

"One can hardly afford in the great pressure of reading matter to lay down one of these books until it is finished lest something less worthy should intrude between its pages and contaminate it."

From the New York Times.

"It was a happy idea which led the publishers to prepare the Bric-a-Brac, and now this Series, for public acceptance, and they were extremely fortunate in obtaining Mr. Stoddard's assistance in the undertaking. He is an able and compact editor."

From the Congregationalist.

"We can honestly recommend the book as a good one to buy—or borrow."

BRIC-A-BRAC SERIES.

Opinions of the Press Regarding the Series.

" Edited finely, and in appearance simply elegant."—*New Haven Journal and Courier.*

" There is something entirely original and fresh about the contents of these pretty volumes that makes them particularly attractive. The delicate morsels of literature are so well served as to be easily digested, and at the same time so agreeable in taste as not to be readily forgotten."—*N. Y. Daily World.*

" The *Bric-à-Brac* is the most attractive and entertaining series of books that has been projected for many years. No happier thought ever came from the brain of a publisher than that which culminated in presenting these compilations to the world. *Multum in parvo* is here carried to its fullest stage of development, and with a result that has brought forth general commendation."—*Boston Saturday Evening Gazette.*

" The purpose of this series is as unique as its execution is successful. The plan is to gather from all biographical sources recently issued all the most interesting reminiscences of celebrated men, and to present them in compact form. A more delightfully piquant series could not well be prepared, and the artistic beauty of literary and mechanical finish in which it is presented throws about it charms rare and racy."—*Troy Times.*

" Richard Henry Stoddard has performed a real service to literature in his ingenious compilation of the '*Bric-à-Brac Series.*' * * * These books are printed neatly, with attractive bindings, and are sold for $1.50. We have had no books from the press for some time so well worth the money. They introduce us to famous authors, and tell us in an hour as much good as the average mind cares to know."—*N. Y. Herald.*

" There has never been a work of the sort conceived with a better comprehension of the needs and taste of the vast numbers of all sorts of readers, for whom it is designed. * * * One can take up any of the volumes and read hour after hour without fatigue, or the slightest relaxation of interest; while another, who has but time to give to a page or two, will surely find a dainty intellectual lunch prepared for him."—*Buffalo Commercial Advertiser.*

" We have found infinite delight within these silver-drab covers, as delicate in color as are the rare personal *morceaux* which they contain in quality. * * * * * * Mr. Stoddard is making a very popular series, and we can cordially mention it as one of the best in the whole range of light, healthfully-stimulating literature."—*Rochester Democrat and Chronicle.*

" These volumes contain about the most charming collection of literary gossip of its kind that can be found."—*N. Y. Commercial Advertiser.*

" Each succeeding issue of this *Bric-à-Brac Series* demonstrates afresh Mr. Stoddard's fitness for the work of conducting it, and gives new proofs of his sagacity and discrimination. By its intrinsic value, its unique design, and its exquisite mechanical execution, the series appeals strongly to all lovers of the biographic and autobiographic in literature."—*Boston Journal.*

Each one vol., square 12mo, cloth, $1 50. Any or all sent, postpaid, on receipt of price by the publishers,

SCRIBNER, ARMSTRONG & CO.,

743 and 745 Broadway, New York.